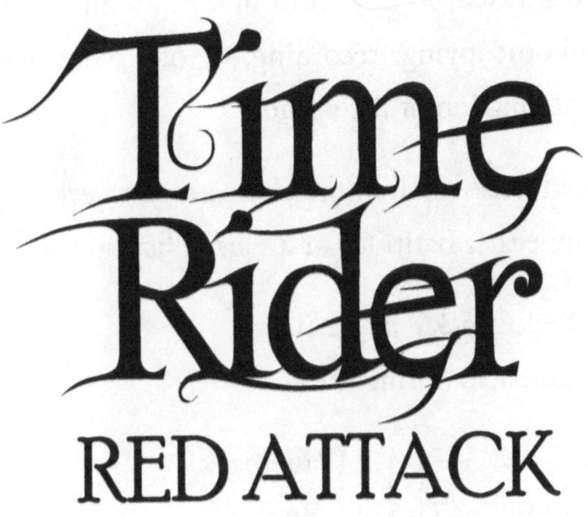

Time Rider

RED ATTACK

JACK KING

Time Rider - Red Attack / Jack King
1st Edition Paperback: Spring 2016

ISBN 13: 978-0-9973471-4-2 (Paperback)
ISBN 13: 978-0-9973471-5-9 (eBook)

Editor: Amy Nedrow
Interior Design: Susan Veach
Cover Design: Richard Turylo

Other books by Jack King:
Time Rider - Wildertrek
Game for the Middle Kingdom

Readers may contact Jack King at:
www.Jack-King.com
authorjackking@gmail.com
@authorjackking (Twitter)

Printed in the United States of America
Published by Author (PBA)

Dedication

For those who bravely fought
in our second war of independence . . .

Acknowledgements

To my high school teacher Mr. Wood
who taught that history and adventure travel together...

This novel is a work of fiction. Names, characters, places, and events either are products of the author's imagination or are used fictitiously. Any resemblance to actual incidents, locales, or people, living or dead, is totally coincidental.

CONTENTS

Chapter 1
CROSSE ME IN, COACH

TJ Cockrell and Samantha Robertson sat in the heavy wooden patio chairs, cooling down under the protective shading of the massive awning. The wind was blowing harder now. It came in sharp sudden spurts, gusting through the open deck area into the covered space beyond. The spring breeze as it swirled about them felt good on their hot, sticky, sweat-soaked bodies.

They had rushed to get there, but now neither one was in a hurry to begin the task ahead.

Samantha's mom had picked them up after practice and dropped them off at TJ's house where they were supposed to be studying together. They had mid-semester English, Math, Science, and American History tests scheduled for tomorrow, in that order.

"Mom! I don't have time take a shower. Just come and get me twenty minutes from when you usually do. I'll be waiting at the field gate with Tege," Sam had argued with her mother that morning. "You don't understand. We need to get to his house quick and start hitting the books."

"But honey, you'll be all stinky and gross." Her mom had winkled her nose. "Young men like girls who smell flowery and feminine, like a lady should."

Sam had rolled her eyes up at that, and insisted her mother come earlier that day.

TJ never showered at the athletic locker room anyway, preferring to wait until he got home to the comfort and privacy of his own bathroom. He liked to take long lukewarm showers, thinking over happenings of the day, plotting his evening, fantasizing about what, when, and where his next adventure might be. In fact, TJ was imagining that right now, picturing himself traveling alongside the intrepid Jim Bridger; speaking French, Spanish, plus several native Indian languages, meeting famous figures from the western pioneer days, and traveling on dangerous quests for furs and fortune. He had decided that being a mountain man was an exciting life.

Another one of his fantasies was being an officer in the Tennessee militia commanded by the fierce and fearless Andrew Jackson during the Creek Indian War. Davy Crockett, he remembered from his history, had fought under Major General Jackson in that War.

A little over a year ago, he had gone back in time to 1802 frontier Tennessee. While trapped in the past, he had several thrilling adventures, spoke to the teenaged David Crockett, met some cool people including one very special girl, but also met some very bad individuals intent on killing him and taking the lives of those around him. His experiences had grown him up in a hurry, so to speak, and helped him later survive a pair of home invaders upon his return to the present.

TJ and Samantha sat facing one another. Well, at least their bodies faced each other. Samantha had her head turned toward the nearby pool, watching the white-tipped ripples rolling across the aqua-blue wind-caressed surface. The reflection of the late afternoon sun upon this perpetual motion sparkled like hundreds of diamonds. The sight was mesmerizing and relaxing at the same time. She felt herself getting sleepy, but she knew she mustn't fall asleep or their study plans would be messed up.

She'd put on her wind breaker over her uniform after practice and the fabric was stuck across her shoulders and back of her neck from the residue sweat.

"Ahhhh, come on, girl." Samantha stirred in her chair, pulling the wind breaker loose from her sticky body and shaking her head a couple of times. If she became too drowsy, Tege would make her a disgusting cup of coffee to wake up, and she hated the taste of coffee. The smell of it was almost enjoyable, but it tasted terrible to her. When she tagged along with friends to Starbucks, she always got a smoothie or a tea drink of some kind while they gossiped and sipped strong latte beverages.

For his part, TJ had his head tilted back on the chair, resting on the topmost horizontal bar as he was daydreaming, his eyes closed to block out the still bright late afternoon sunlight filtering through the awning. He held his tall glass of iced tea balanced on his stretched out left knee, letting the coldness sink into his aching joint. He had a lingering headache from an on-the-field collision with a defensive player as well as a throbbing knee from another smash-up, courtesy of a fellow Middie teammate.

Some teammate! TJ thought. The first incident had been an accident; the defensive player had turned the wrong way and they'd smashed noggins together. The second incident had been—well, it had been intentional, he knew for sure. Wincing, he shifted his weight in the chair to get more comfortable against the thick horizontal slats of the unpadded seat.

A sliding glass door opened behind them, and a warm voice called out: "Y'all doin' all right, children? Either one o' you want a refill on your teas?" Dora, an older lady who did housekeeping three times a week for the Cockrell family, stepped out onto the patio. She peered over at the two teenagers with a kindly expression on her age-lined face.

"I'm good," said TJ, his head balanced on the rung and his eyes closed.

"Hmm, I guess I'm okay, too," replied Sam, eyeing her more than half-full glass. "But thank you so much for asking, Mrs. Hicks," she added. She liked Dora. Although the woman's husband, Charley, had died three years ago, everyone called her Mrs. and she continued to wear her wedding ring.

"All right, sweeties. Just call out if you want anything more now."

Dora went back inside to finish up her cleaning chores and the lazy, late afternoon quiet reinvaded the patio. A small shadow streaked across the thin awning fabric as a crow flew overhead, cawing in annoyance at something. Then more silence.

Sam glanced over at TJ. He had his head leaning backwards. His mouth was wide open now. He wasn't sleeping or snoring yet, but she thought he looked funny, nonetheless. She placed the cold glass against her cheek, grateful for the icy feel, and studied his slump figure some more.

In her mind, TJ was very handsome. He had curly, light brown hair she thought was cute, and brown 'puppy-dog' eyes she thought were adorable. He was above average height. TJ had a slim but taut physique that was surprising strong and agile. She knew he'd taken training in martial arts for years and that he was a black belt in something. She herself had taken several courses in practical self-defense for women and was pretty good at it. She was quick and feisty. However, she never could remember whether TJ's belt was in Karate or Judo or Kung Pao—*no, that's an Asian dish, silly*—or Tai something. Whatever. That wasn't important to her, and the fact didn't impress her one bit. All she cared about was TJ being the special kind of person he was toward her.

She smiled and recalled how they'd first met in the

spring drama production at high school over a year ago. She had invited herself to lunch with him, and he had accepted her offer.

Tege was so different in many ways, all good, from other boys she had ever known or heard about. Some girls, a few promiscuous, had begun dating much earlier than she; TJ was her first real boyfriend. They were careful not to go further than kissing, hugging, hand-holding, and the like. TJ was cool with that, even though he had mentioned the word 'love' to her.

But she knew about a lot of the behavior of most boys in school and church from gossip, from her friends' descriptions, from ex-girlfriends' catty comments, from general reputation, and from casual acquaintance. Unlike them, TJ was a true gentleman, and not just in the old-fashioned way either. He cared about her views, her thoughts, her emotions, her intelligence, and her happiness. What she said and what she felt were very important to him.

She lifted her damp, long, , reddish-auburn locks out of her face and curled the other side behind her ear. She'd undone the tight ponytail half an hour ago and shaken her mane of hair free, once the sweat had begun drying. Thinking about the hours of hard studying ahead, she exhaled, a trace of worry etched upon her pretty face. TJ was a solid, around student, she knew, but Math and American History were not her strong points.

The resting form beside her spoke. "So, how was your practice today?" TJ asked Samantha, breaking the stillness. He turned in the chair again, trying to find a comfortable compromise between his bony bottom and the unforgiving slats. His eyes were open, staring at the canopy above as he kept his head and neck tilted back, trying to ease his pounding headache.

"Fine. Well, except for that cow Betsy Hammon. She kept harping at the new girl, Janie Perkins, the entire practice. She just wouldn't shut up. *Every* time coach put Janie in during scrimmage, she had to say something negative." Sam frowned. "I don't like her attitude. Neither does anyone else on the team.

"Oh! Plus, she criticized Janie nonstop during drills. Real sneaky about it, too. She'd wait until she got close enough to Janie, and then she'd say it, you know, just loud enough so coach wouldn't hear her."

"Yeah, sounds like something she'd do," replied TJ, who'd heard Sam's complaints about Betsy before.

"I like Janie. So do most of the other players. She works her butt off in practice. She's not very talented, but she tries hard. Pretty decent at passing. She's just not coordinated when it comes to . . . you know, catching the ball, and stuff. But she's getting better. And she's a sweet girl."

They lapsed into silence for several more minutes, listening to the sporadic blowing of the wind and the occasional sound of a car passing by in the street. Just being lazy now, they both knew they were postponing the ordeal to come.

Sam let out a sigh of relief that a hard day of school and practice was over. She twisted in her own chair to get some feeling back in her right leg.

"How was your afternoon, Tege?" she resumed the conversation.

Without bringing his head level to see her, still gazing at the awning, he mumbled, "Just peachy keen. Yepper depper. It was spectacular in every way."

"You poor baby."

He was silent for a bit. The knee was hurting worse. He didn't feel like giving a long explanation.

There wasn't a lot to tell, anyway. But her asking got him brooding about his recent situation. TJ scowled at the awning.

He'd been having problems of his own during the boys' lacrosse practices. Lacrosse being a new sport that year at Highland Hill High School, nobody was expert in it yet, even the upper classmen. Except, of course, Coach Loggins. Or the new kid, WP. Wayne Loggins had been brought in from Brentwood High, a ranked state team, to build and train a lacrosse team from scratch and make it competitive. Fast.

TJ's difficulties centered on the new boy, Wilson Presley; the other so-called expert. Teammates nicknamed him 'Pelvis' Presley because he was quite dexterous in his lateral moves, often leaving opposing players twisting or falling in his wake.

Yeah, the dude is shifty, TJ had to admit. *Too shifty, in more ways than one.*

Wilson's family had moved from Pennsylvania before start of term to the Knoxville area. He had played up, and even started most games last year as an eighth grader for the Haverford School club team, a real powerhouse, TJ had heard. He was arrogant, quick, and good. Worst of all, he faced off against TJ during scrimmages.

Hey, I can handle tough competition, TJ encouraged himself. What he couldn't deal with was the illegal contact. He'd found out early on Wilson was a dirty player in addition to being skilled. In TJ's opinion, the boy didn't need to do the other garbage to beat his man. He did it, TJ was convinced, because he enjoyed hurting and humiliating people. Part of his skill was cleverly inflicting injuries to other players, both on his own team as well as on opposition.

That's how TJ got his banged-up knee. Courtesy of a swift side kick from Wilson in passing close by. Coach didn't see it happen during a fierce group battle for the small rubber lacrosse ball that had been jarred loose from a defender's racket onto the ground.

"You did that on purpose," he accused the boy, rubbing his knee.

Wilson just laughed, and said under his breath,

"Prove it, you punk," before racing off to rejoin the continuing play.

TJ stared daggers at the back of the departing player, before he, too, ran to catch up. Even then his knee was stiffening up, but he made himself play without a limp, knowing coach would take him out if he thought he was hurt.

What Wilson hadn't found out yet was that TJ was a bit of an expert in martial arts. He knew all about sidekicks and roundhouses. As busy as he had been with academics, lacrosse, theater, Sam, friends, and his new church, Tege had resumed his Tae Kwon Do training in earnest over the past year. He had just earned his second degree black belt in TKD. Having beaten one of the more obnoxious bullies at Highland Hill School last year in eighth grade, TJ assumed he was through with bully issues once and for all.

He was wrong.

He decided, after this last practice, that Wilson constituted a whole new category of bullying: The sneaky underhanded type of bully who, publicly at least, is considered a pretty good dude by most people. Only his victims recognize him for what he is.

A deceitful little—TJ didn't finish his thought. He didn't have to; whether he thought it or not, the dude was one of them.

"I told you I got kicked in the side of the knee by Wilson, right?" he responded to Samantha.

"Yeah, you did. Is it feeling any better?"

"Not really. That was a crummy thing to do. I have a headache, too, I didn't mention; it's even worse than the knee."

"I'm sorry, sugums," she pushed out her bottom lip in a pitiful but oh-so-cute pout, as she always did when she was trying to show sympathy.

TJ shrugged. "It's okay. I'm man enough to take it."

"I *know* you are," she teased, leaning toward him with her hair hanging down over her face in a most provocative manner.

He looked over at her, grinning in spite of himself, and admiring her beautiful long locks and sparkly eyes. That's one of the many things he liked about her; she has so much personality! "Well, a few more minutes of loafing; then we've got to start studying. Okay?"

"Okay," she said, though without much enthusiasm.

TJ nodded back.

"Okay, snookums," she added, mischievously.

"I told you I don't like that name," he grimaced, good-naturedly.

"That's why I said it," she winkling her nose at him and brushing her hair back in an alluring manner.

"Okie-dokie." He was smart enough not to challenge her. Her cuteness defeated him every time.

TJ stretched his arms out and sat straight up in his chair, twisting his torso left and right to work the kinks out of his back. Swishing his glass around to break up the ice cubes stuck together in the bottom, he took several big gulps of the cold sweet tea. Then he drained the last of the liquid, and let a large cube slide into his mouth to chew on.

Except for his seeming inability to catch Wilson at his shenanigans, Coach Loggins was a great coach, in TJ's view. He knew a lot about the game, studied players as much as he studied plays, and tailored his motivational techniques according to the personality, skills, and makeup of the individual. Because no one on the team was a snitch, and because Wilson was careful not to perform his underhanded tricks on the upperclassmen whose pride wouldn't allow them to let Wilson go unchallenged, Loggins had no reason to know what Wilson was up to unless he saw him doing it. Wilson always waited until a crowd was around him to nail his intended target, a freshman or sophomore. Lately, too often that target was TJ, who was getting more and more praise from coach as he learned the game.

In fact, he remembered that right before the 'incident' Coach Loggins had complimented him in front of his teammates during a timeout for his overall play on the previous scoring drive.

"That's what set him off. Pure jealousy," he mumbled.

"What'd you say, Tege?"

"Oh, nothing, just talking to myself."

She raised her eyebrows and clucked her tongue. "I'm dating a loony."

"Of course," he grinned. "Loons have more fun."

Coach Hanover, Ms. June Hanover, was the girls' lacrosse coach. Both Sam and TJ considered her a competent coach, though she was still young, just out of college. But the girls on her team knew she had been a full scholarship player on a strong Division II college back east, plus she had been an overachiever on competitive club teams throughout junior high and high school.

The girls had started the routine of calling out, "Crosse me in, coach," whenever they wanted to get put into the game, meaning 'Stick me in'. Since three of the girls were dating boys on the male team at the beginning of the season, the guys picked up the habit, except they were much more vocal and creative in asking Coach Loggins when they wanted to go in.

"Oh come on, coach. Please crosse me in. I can handle that guy. Come *on*."

"Coach Loggins, I promise I won't double-crosse you if you crosse me in. You know you can count on me."

"Crosse my heart, coach, hope to die. I'll shut that dude down. Guaranteed. It's in the bank."

TJ never used the phrase. He didn't have to. He found coach turning to him, more and more, much to the chagrin of a certain character named Pelvis.

Tege exhaled sharply. He slapped his hands on his

thighs and forced himself up. "We've got to get started, Sam. We have a couple hours at most until Dad gets home, and you know he going to kill another hour of study time with him making his fancy spaghetti dinner and having a sit-down meal at the formal dining table. We'll have, maybe, an hour and a half to two hours, tops, after that, until you have to go home. Girlfriend, there's a ton of notes, review material, and test questions we've got to cover in not much time."

"I know," she grimaced. "Let's *do* it."

"Are you drowsy? I can make us a big pot of coffee," he asked, grinning yet again. She hated coffee. "Seriously, though, I can make you some hot tea. It's got as much caffeine as good ol' java."

"Honestly, I don't need anything else to drink, Tege. I'm full. I drank a big bottle of SoBe while waiting for you. I threw the empty away before you even got there. And now I have this iced tea, of which I haven't even finished half of it. You make the coffee. I'll just smell it while it's brewing."

He laughed and reached for her hand. "All right. Let's go in."

They left the relaxing cool sanctuary, hand-in-hand, ready to do battle with the books.

TJ turned and took one last lingering look at the shaded patio and the sparkling pool beyond, before stepping inside.

Chapter 2
A DISAPPEARING ACT

"So you two decided you had enough of cat-napping," said Dora. Hearing the heavy glass door open and click shut, she turned and saw the pair traipsing through the game room that adjoined the patio and opened into the small dining nook off the big kitchen where she was cleaning up.

"I wasn't sleeping," answered TJ.

"Is that so? You sure gave a good impression of it, young man." She beamed at them. "You kiddos want me to fix you something to eat before I go? A little snack, perhaps?"

"I'm not hungry right now, Mrs. Hicks." Sam shook her head, politely.

"Well, I'm starving," said TJ, unwilling to pass up a chance at food. Besides, Dora was a great cook, as he well knew.

"How about I make you a PBJ sandwich, hon? Or I can do a BLT right quick."

"Yummm, a BLT. That'll hit the spot. Thank you,

Dora. Oh, and would you mind, making a small pot of coffee while you're at it?" He smiled big at her and then gave her his patented forlorn puppy dog expression.

She laughed. "Of course, I'll be happy to, sweetie. I'll have a cup myself, too, if you don't mind." Her eyes crinkled with pleasure. The old lady delighted in taking care of the Cockrell household and fixing after school eats for TJ when she had time. She had five grandkids; the oldest was two years younger than TJ. She doted on all of them and considered TJ almost part of her family now.

"Hey, do you want use the big table in the formal dining room or use the breakfast room table here to do our studying?" TJ looked at Sam.

She thought for a second. "Oh, let's do it in the dining room. There's a lot more space to spread out, and we have a lot of stuff."

She raised her eyebrows, a smug appearance on her face. "I printed out every single question at the end of every single chapter for both English and History. I also *handwrote*—thank you very much, Samantha, he said to her—the answer below each question using my notes from the review sessions. It took me a long time," she sniffed.

"Yeah, well, thank you very much, girlfriend of mine. I'm super impressed."

She put a hand on hip and fake-glared at him, thinking he was making fun. "Listen, just because you get better grades than me . . ."

"No, really, I mean it. I'm impressed. You always wait until the last moment to start studying. To do all that work in preparation for some serious cramming. I think that's awesome." TJ nodded his head several times in an exaggerated fashion.

Sam walked over and shoved his shoulder. "You're such a tease." She giggled. "Tege the tease."

He gave her his forlorn look, too, which made her laugh even more. It was an old joke between them. TJ was unable to say anything mean, rude, or teasing to a girl. He was known around the school, by his buddies as well as Sam's best female friends, as a boy you could confide in, knowing he would keep your words in confidence and always offer back encouraging advice.

It was a positive trait he'd developed over time, by having been the recipient himself of such empathetic listening and counseling from his beloved little sister, Natalie, but also in part because of the character-building experiences he'd gone through during his first great adventure into the past. Natalie now lived in Atlanta with their mother. TJ's mom and dad had gotten divorced over a year and a half ago.

As they talked, Dora bustled around in the kitchen. Soon the sound of bacon sizzling in the pan was heard, followed by the metallic thump of fresh toast popping up. The tantalizing aroma of coffee brewing mixed with the mouthwatering bacon scent invaded the little breakfast nook, and Samantha found herself wandering into the large kitchen area to better smell the coffee. She wished the dark thick beverage tasted half as good as it smelled.

R-i-n-g, r-i-n-g.

Sam hurried to pick up the wall phone to answer the call. "Oh, hi, Professor Cockrell."

"Hi, Samantha. I take it TJ is right there?" he said.

"Yes, sir. Just a moment." She handed the phone to TJ, who had followed her into the kitchen. The delicious odors were making his stomach growl with renewed hunger.

"It's your father. He wants to talk to you."

"Hey, dad."

"Tege, I hope you're not gorging yourself on so-called snacking. I know how Dora loves to baby you. She'll fix a full-blown meal if you let her. Don't ruin your appetite, young man! Remember, I'm planning on cooking a sumptuous spaghetti dinner for the three of us when I get home. That means eating at the formal dining table, a nice sit-down meal with the good silverware—no wet bar, no couch, no watching TV, no laptops, no patio. Agreed?"

"Yes, sir. I agree." He thought about all of the junk they'd just dumped on the big table in preparation for their study fest. They'd have to transfer everything to the small table, fast, as soon as they heard the back garage door slammed shut and the alarm beep indicating the professor was home.

"Good. I'll be home as quick as I can. I love you, son."

"I love you, too, dad."

TJ hung up the wall phone. He turned back to Sam and smiled. She had witnessed the touching display of father and son saying they loved one another, and it never failed to move her. Tege was nonchalant yet sincere about both the act itself and the words. So many boys she knew couldn't say that to their steady girlfriends, let alone to their dads and moms. *It was a cool thing*, she often thought.

She knew TJ and his father went to a big church; that Tege was active in the youth group and the professor participated in a men's group. It was one of the things she admired about TJ. He had become active in the church about six months ago after they had already been dating several months.

He was committed to his new religious beliefs but without being overly religious. He was just a good person, in her mind. He had a good heart, and he treated other people with dignity and kindness, even if they didn't always deserve it.

Tege took a seat. Dora was just putting a plate of the hot BLT sandwich and cold pickles on the little breakfast table, along with a large glass of milk with ice cubes in it, just the way he liked it. He motioned for both of them to join him. Sam sat across from him. Dora poured herself a full cup of coffee, added a bit of milk and one half spoon of sugar. She gave a sigh of contentment and sat down next to TJ, the chair creaking as her bulk hit the seat.

She glanced at both of them with a kind expression. "Looks like you two have a bunch of studying to do." She nodded. "My two oldest grandsons, Johnny and Michael, have got to hit the books tonight, too. One's in seventh grade and the other is in sixth grade. They do seem to load the kids up today. I don't remember it's being that bad when I was in school. Course, that was so long ago, and so much has happened, you know, in science, and inventions, and computers, and whatnot. It makes me dizzy, thinking about all the new technology and things you youngsters have to know about these days."

She paused and took a deep sip of the still steaming coffee. The few drops of milk she'd added hadn't reduced the hotness of the liquid one iota; it merely lightened the color to a dark rich brown. For TJ, though, she'd filled his cup with two-thirds coffee and one-third milk, with a little bit of half-and-half creamer added at the end plus a cinnamon sprinkle on top.

After a few swallows, TJ set his mug down. He had a serious air when he turned to Dora. "Tell me. What did the doctor say about your tests?" She'd gone in for a biopsy of suspicious dark spots on her skin.

"Oh, yes, I meant to ask you, too. Is everything all right, Mrs. Hicks?" Sam's eyebrows furrowed together in concern.

The older lady thanked them for asking. "Well, it's not cancerous, thank the Lord. I've got to go back next week to have them lance the four spots off me. Not looking forward to that, I can tell you, but that's better than what it might have been."

Just then, TJ's iPhone reverberated with its familiar William Tell Overture, the sound muffled inside the pocket of his athletic shorts. It was the standard ring that he'd never bothered to change to a cooler tune.

He pulled the phone out to answer. "Hello?"

It was Jason Williams. TJ's dad had been dating Jason's mom, Helen, for eleven months, and the family had switched from downtown First Baptist to the big nondenominational church where the two Cockrells went, the Northmark Bible Fellowship.

"Hey, dude, what's up?"

"Just hanging with Sam and getting ready to cram for mid-terms. What are you doing?"

"Setting up the band and sound equipment with Ben, Fred, and the other guys for the regular youth service Sunday. We're also practicing our songs for the big shindig. Don't forget we'll have the 'Youth on Fire' concert Saturday spring break weekend."

"Oh, yeah. At church, right? Thanks for reminding me. What time?"

"It'll start at six thirty. But you and Sam will need to be there twenty or thirty minutes early to get a good seat. The place will be packed."

"Remember we'll be gone on spring break. If we make good time coming back we should be able to make it, though. By the way, how come you're not studying tonight?"

"Man, I'm acing all my classes." He laughed. "No, seriously, they let everyone use the time to study for tests in all of my classes today but one. I also skipped lunch to study. So I'm prepared."

"*You* skipped a meal?" TJ asked incredulously. In addition to being a fantastic drummer as a young teenager, Jason had a reputation as a big eater. He was a wiry boy, but he could wolf down as much food as a huge offensive lineman on the school's football team.

"Sure, I had a big breakfast at McDonalds and then Ben picked up a pizza on the way to church, so I got my carbs in, dude." He paused. "I guess you know your dad is taking Mom out to Le Parigo Saturday night the week after spring break."

"Yeah, he mentioned it."

"You think he might be popping the question?"

"Can you keep a secret?"

"To the death, man."

"He showed me the engagement diamond ring. It's *gigantic*."

"Dude, I don't know if I can stomach you as a brother-in-law. That's messed up. You're bad enough as a hanger-on to somebody cool like me."

"Yeah, right. In your dreams. You're lucky I let you tag along, little bro."

Jason laughed again. "Don't say that out loud. I can't have people thinking I'm related to urban white trash."

"That's me, all the way. Uber trashy! Hey, keep it quiet about you-know-what."

"You got it. Later."

"Yup."

Mrs. Hicks finished her coffee and stood up to leave, as TJ laid his cell phone on the table. "Well, sugar, I've got to get going. Nice to see you again, hon," she beamed over at Samantha. "You two don't stay up too late studying now. I always heard for every hour of sleep you miss, you wind up forgetting an hour of what you studied. So it don't make no sense to burn the midnight oil, children."

Sam smiled at the older lady. "We'll be sure to get plenty of sleep tonight, Mrs. Hicks. I'm very glad you got a good report from the doctor."

"Thank you, hon. You're a sweetie."

"Bye TJ." She picked up her huge purse from the end of the little table and made her way to the front door.

"Bye. See you next Monday."

Sitting across from Sam, TJ resumed his attack on the no-longer-hot BLT sandwich. He gobbled it down anyway, taking gulps of coffee in between frenzied bites while Samantha watched him eating.

"You're such a little hoglet," she said, gazing at him with feigned disgust, as he shoveled food into his mouth. Tege finished eating and the two of them went into the formal dining room to study. They started with Math, her least favorite subject. They spent about forty minutes on that before tackling Science, her second favorite subject. They were about half way through their study of the English exam advance questions and textbook review when Sam leaned back, stretched her hands up and let out a big yawn.

"Sorry. I need to stay awake." She forced her eyes wide open, and gave herself light slaps on either side of her face. "Hey, did you say the bathroom down the hall was out of order?"

"Yup, the plumber's coming tomorrow. It's got major problems. Dad says we may have to replace the toilet."

"Yuck. Should I use the upstairs one on left or the right, then? The left one, correct?"

"Right," mumbled TJ, his mouth crammed with a big bite of sandwich.

Sam shook her head, still not clear on which one to use. She took his reply to mean she should go to the master bathroom in his dad's bedroom down the second floor hall to the right instead of the smaller bathroom on the opposite end of the hallway that was shared by TJ and his sister when she lived there.

She raced up the stairs and down the long hallway.

All that liquid was hitting her. She slowed as she entered the huge bedroom. It was still feminine and fancy and formal—just the way it had been when Mrs. Cockrell lived there. TJ's dad had never bothered to change the décor after their divorce; he was too busy and didn't care about issues of appearance and fashion. It was her first glimpse at the big bedroom and Sam liked its ambience very much. Even in a hurry to use the restroom, she just had to walk around a bit and admire the bed covers and furnishings and color of the walls and accessories. In a wing by the bay window on the left, she saw a tidy, compact office setting. She noticed, too, a little plain green book lying on top of the small sturdy desk by itself.

Instantly, both her eyes and her mind were drawn to it.

What it was about the tiny green book that attracted her, she couldn't say. But from the moment she spied it, she forgot about her urgent need and even about the bedroom decorations that had been so appealing.

Is it a diary? It sure looks like one, she thought. The more Sam stared at the book, the more it compelled her to pick it up. She knew she shouldn't snoop like that, and she felt a mild twinge of guilt. Yet an inexplicable, albeit overwhelming, curiosity now burned within.

"This is crazy. I shouldn't be sneaking around other people's private things," she mumbled.

The allure of the little green object, whatever it was, was very strong. Sam hesitated in her internal debate, and then took three doubtful steps forward. Very nervous now, she hovered over the book, still struggling within. She shot a furtive glance to make sure TJ wasn't standing by the doorway, watching her. *Of course, he isn't there! How silly of me.*

Finally, she made up her mind. She took a deep breath and reached for the book.

I'll just take one quick peek, see what's inside, and put it back down, she justified her action.

As her fingers touched the green book, from the point of first contact, a tingling sensation flowed from her hand throughout her whole body, like a soft electrical shock.

"Oh!" Sam cried out, shaking her hand to free it from the overpowering connection of the book. "Get . . . get away from me!" She tried to let go of it. But however hard she tried Sam couldn't put it down or shake it loose.

"What's going on? Stop it!" she redoubled her frantic efforts to cast away the little green tome.

She stared at the book in utter amazement and confusion. The green cover, which had been blank, was now filled with moving, ever-changing, frightening scenes: Burning buildings off in the distance; people jammed together with carts and wagons filled with possessions; streets and roads flooded with fleeing crowds; and the faraway glint of bayonets and rifles and marching soldiers all in red on a dusky late afternoon. Where, Samantha didn't recognize the place, nor have any idea what it all meant.

Sam was scared out of her mind.

Suddenly, it was if she were in a trance and falling asleep at the same time. Sam's mind clouded in a dream-like misty state. As if from a great distance, she saw her own hand—she had no control over it—turn the page on the once blank cover.

Against her will, she opened the book up. She felt herself going deeper, deeper into the fog, her body tumbling to an unseen ground. She wanted to scream, yell for help, but nothing came out of her mouth.

Samantha awoke out of the mist, with a start.

Chapter 3
PANIC IN WASHINGTON

Disoriented, her mind spinning, it took several long moments before Samantha could gather her wits and begin processing the unexpected vision before her. Her pretty eyes were wide with alarm as she stared at the confusing sights.

What? How did—?

She found herself standing in the middle of an unknown street in the middle of an unknown city. The air was filled with din and dust kicked up by panicked hordes of people rushing past. They all appeared to be fleeing. From what, she was almost scared to ask. But the maddening crowds seemed to her to be afraid of some approaching doom.

The scene before her was total chaos. The more she saw, the more anxious she became. Groaning under her breath, wringing her hands, Samantha twisted around, searching in all directions for anything that looked familiar. "What's happened to me? Where *am* I? Who are all these *people*?"

There was nothing recognizable. Nothing made sense. No street signs. No billboards. No landmarks. No policemen she could talk to. No familiar buildings. Well, except for the one structure on her right that she *thought* she'd seen before. Maybe in a picture somewhere? She shook her head, but couldn't recall.

Worse still, all the people she could see were uniformly dressed in historical costume, like some bizarre neighborhood masquerade party. The buildings looked quaint, too. Like some sort of European town from a couple of hundred years ago.

A person slammed into her body from behind, almost knocking her down. "Hey, watch where you're going."

"Pardon, miss, but the soldiers be almost here. Run girl! Run for your life." A heavyset man stumbled past, calling out over his shoulder as he went. From his receding profile, Samantha could make out a jowly chin and long curling sideburns that became salt-and-pepper toward the end. Strangely enough, even in her own trepidation, she still noticed what he was wearing: An old fashioned dark-gray tailcoat and high-waisted trousers that seemed more colonial than modern. The poor man had a look on his face like a frightened animal running from an approaching predator.

Soldiers? What the heck is he talking about? The man's terror was contagious. She had no inkling of the danger he spoke of, and no clue where she was or how she got there.

Holding back tears, she fought against the shock and unreason that threatened to suffocate her.

"This is just crazy! How can I be here . . . this, this isn't *possible*," she whimpered. "One second I'm in the big bedroom at TJ's and next I'm in some weird town with people dressed up, like in a play or at Halloween party for adults."

But that couldn't be because she also saw children and teenagers mixed in among the many grownups in the fleeing crowds. Everyone was wearing strange clothes.

"Boom!"

"Boom! Boom!"

Off in the distance, she heard a faint yet unmistakable rumble of deep blasts. Confused by the sounds, she listened carefully. The noise was a continuous barrage but wasn't a set pattern. Sam screwed up her face trying hard to remember.

I know I've heard this before. What is it? Almost like explosions they were. The ground seemed to shake.

She racked her brain. Then it hit her!

"*Gone with the Wind!* Why, why it sounds just like the cannons in *Gone with the Wind.*"

Samantha swallowed. Cannons mean armies. Armies mean fighting. Fighting means war. Her mind went into hyper-drive with the crush of scary images and notions now racing through.

Abruptly, a few individuals thundered past her on horses, galloping down the street to make their escape. Samantha jumped out of her skin as they went by, torn from her thoughts. She glared at the departing figures, half angry, half baffled, putting one hand over her racing heart and the other up to her throat.

Horses? Horses! Where are the cars in this place?

On either side, ornately-designed carriages and raw-hewed buckboard wagons alike whipped around her, their drivers flailing whips to spur their horses faster; each carriage or wagon filled to capacity with persons and possessions. It was obvious the stately carriages were for the wealthy and the plain wagons for the poor, she thought. She shook her head in disbelief and amazement. These were vehicles of transportation she'd seen only in movies or history books or when doing homework research on the Web. Interspersed among the horses and buggies, dozens of bodies strode by, their hands clutching valuables and their backs burdened down with snapbacks stuffed with heirlooms.

Suddenly, a voice cried out from above the mad scramble of the ground level.

Looking up, she saw a girl, her face white with fear staring out of a second story window of a building across the street.

"Sir, can you please help me?" she pleaded with a passing older man, but he shook his head, grunted no, and kept walking.

"Ma'am?" she called out to a lady carrying a toddler in one arm and meager possessions in the other. The woman scowled at her with agitated eyes and rushed on.

Signing in frustration, Samantha put her hands on her hips and glanced up. The sky, dotted with a few clouds and the moon beginning to show on the horizon, was darkening quickly. Wherever she was, it was approaching evening time. It was also muggy and quite warm for the time of year, she thought, *much warmer than good old Knoxville*. For the first time, Sam noticed she was sweating again.

"Gosh, I'm getting hot. This is awful," she complained, reaching around to wipe a bead of perspiration trickling down the nape of her neck. Her searching fingers touched ruffles. Samantha jerked her hand away in surprise.

"What . . . what the heck do I have on?" She glanced down and found she was wearing some type of old fashioned high-necked dress—"This is tacky looking. Ugh! What happened to my Highland Hill team jersey and my shorts?" Not that Sam cared one bit, but the bodice was buttoned in front and the pleated skirt had a gathered back. The sleeves were full at the shoulders with flared cuffs over the wrists and hands. On her feet, her expensive Nike lacrosse shoes with variegated sole and medium cleats were gone, too, replaced by lady's leather shoes with one and half inch heel and tapered toe.

The shock of seeing her beloved lacrosse uniform

gone, mysteriously replaced by such hideous clothing was too much. Her wind breaker she didn't care about but her jersey was important to her. To make matters worse, she felt something atop her hair which wasn't there before! Reaching up, she pulled down what looked like a maid's hat off her head.

At that, Sam screamed. Bloody murder. *Enough is enough!* No one scurrying about her even noticed, but she was furious. "Look, *you*, whatever you are, I want my own things back!

"Now!" she hissed, snapping her fingers. "Right now!" she stomped her feet for added measure.

But it did no good. Yelling at an unknown *something* relieved a bit of her tension, but it returned none of her clothes to her.

"This is terrible. It just . . . sucks."

Sam took a deep breath. She turned to the left and the right, determined to make someone stop running long enough to tell her where she was.

"'Cuse me. Excuse me!" Jamming her hat back on her head, she clutched at a passing girl who looked to be a little older than she was.

This time the person halted, although the girl's face was white with panic.

"Can you tell me," Sam said, grasping the girl's sleeve with one hand while waving her other hand at the buildings around them, "what is this place?"

"W-what do you mean, miss?" the girl shook

her head, confused by Sam's question. All the time, the poor girl kept tugging at her sleeve and glancing at the far opposite end of the street, where the menace was approaching and streams of people, horses, and wagons continued to flee in their direction.

"I *mean* . . . where exactly *am* I?" Samantha asked, impatiently. She gripped the other person's garment even tighter.

The girl stared at Sam like she was touched in the head. "Why tis the city o' Washington." When Samantha shook her head at her answer, the girl added, pointing, "That's the President's Mansion over yonder. We locals call it the White House."

"*White* House, did you say?" Samantha screwed up her face.

"The. White. House. You sure about that?" Sam turned and gawked at a handsome building on the other side of the street. It was situated several hundred feet off the thoroughfare and fronted by a large lawn, well-kept but with patches of dirt mixed among sections of green grass. Yes, she had noticed the structure before. So there was something familiar about it after all. Staring intently, Sam recognized the facade of the structure.

"But, but it's only partially built. What happened to the rest of it? Has it been destroyed?"

"No, miss, tis all that's there." The girl's voice was frantic. "Please let me go. Please, miss. The British soldiers are coming."

"What do you mean, the British soldiers are coming? That doesn't make any sense. We're not at war with England. My dad was over there on business the summer before last. I was in middle school. Our family got to stay with him in London for a whole week."

"Are you British?" For a moment, the girl's eyes opened even wider.

"Of course not!" Sam huffed. "Do I sound British to you? I'm American."

"Aye?" The girl looked doubtful. "Well, ma'am, the redcoats I'm told are only a few miles outside the city."

Sam's eyebrows knitted together. What the girl was saying was gibberish, but her terror was real enough. Sam took sudden pity at her genuine fright. "What's your name?"

"'Tis Molly, miss."

"I'm Samantha, Molly. Nice to meet you." The girl looked down at her sleeve still in Sam's grasp.

"Oh, yeah, you can go now." Sam released her grip. "Stay safe. And Molly. Thank you for the, uh, the information." *Although it's all nonsense*, she thought to herself.

Molly nodded, giving Samantha a weak smile before adding, "But you can't stay here, miss. 'Tis not safe. The soldiers, they'll . . . they'll take advantage of a lady's virtue. Savages and brutes, they are."

"You go. I'll be fine." Samantha glared at the distant end of the street. She had no logical reason to think she would be okay and yet she had an inexplicable peace about the strange situation she found herself in. Plus she'd always been fearless.

"Wait! Tell me. The President and his family and all the staff people, are they still alive?" she called out after the retreating girl mentioning the President's last name. "Although I suppose the Secret Service and military will keep them safe," she added, to herself.

The girl halted for just a moment, and replied, "Tis President *Madison*, miss. I don't know of—whatever you said. Tis very strange." Molly looked at Samantha with intense sympathy, as if she now knew for certain Sam was mad. Then she turned and hurried away, shaking her head.

Sam stood watching the girl fade into the crowd. She looked over at the uncompleted White House, thinking, and then made up her mind.

"Hey, I don't understand any of this. How I got transported from Knoxville to Washington D.C. is just bizarre. Crazy. Like science fiction. And all these weirdoes in costume, what's up with that?" she clucked her tongue.

"But I know Dad will take care of the rest of the family in a real emergency. Plus, I don't see form of transportation that could get me back home anytime soon, anyway.

So . . . if my country's now at war, if the U.S. is in deep trouble, the least I can do as a junior citizen is help out."

Samantha started across the avenue and then stopped suddenly, slapping her forehead. "Wait a sec. Before I touched that stupid book, I was on my way to the bathroom. I had to go. Really bad, too. And now. I *don't?*" Of the bizarre happenings she'd experienced in the past several minutes, that fact was perhaps the strangest phenomenon of all. "What on earth could have done that to me?"

Shaking her head in further disbelief, she screwed up her face and decided to take action. Fighting her way through the passing throngs of people and carts and animals, she made it to the other side and marched over the long green lawn toward the beckoning front entrance.

As she walked, she kept hearing a slight clanking sound inside the folds of her dress. It puzzled Sam.

She stopped for a second and began feeling around the waist area. She discovered there were pockets sewn into the sides of the garment. She could feel hard circular things beneath the fabric. Digging her hand in, she pulled out several coins and studied them front and back.

She remembered. *I had fourteen dollars in my shorts' left pocket at practice.* She stuck her hand in again, fishing out the rest of the money. Yes, it was fourteen dollars. In old-time gold and silver coins.

Chapter 4
INSIDE THE PRESIDENT'S HOME

When she reached the glass-paneled front door surrounded by two imposing Greek columns on either side, to her surprise she found it unlocked and ajar.

"Hello?" she yelled through the crack. A vertical slat of dim yellowish lighting seeped through the opening into the late afternoon gloom.

"Hello? Is anybody there?"

Frightened but determined, Sam took a deep breath and pushed the heavy door wider still. "I'm, I'm coming in now. Don't shoot me," she added. She heard faint footsteps and soft voices beyond. Gathering her courage, Sam shoved against the door hard and walked in.

Before her, she saw a large entry room filled with elegant furniture and lavish accessories. Candle-holders were lit and mounted around the four walls.

"So *that* explains the yellowish light," she whispered.

Throughout, fine paintings adorned the walls and luxurious red velvet curtains hung from each of the towering ceiling-to-floor windows. Overall, the massive room was very impressive indeed, just as she had imagined the White House would be.

"Yessum, miss. Did you comes to help us?" At the other end of the room, walking toward her, Sam spied an elderly black man of most dignified bearing, starchily dressed in what she assumed was a butler's type uniform. He was followed by two black youths in similar clothing.

"Oh, hi. I'm Samantha Robertson. Ah, yes. I heard the capital is under attack. And I came. Just, you know, just to offer any assistance I can. To President—I mean, to the President."

She added, "Madison, I mean, President Madison," recalling what the girl in the street had told her. The whole episode was all very confusing to Sam.

"All right. You comes this way, please do, miss. The Lady Madison and the rest o' the folk be in the formal dining room. The state room, we calls it." The older black gentleman was very prim and proper, she thought.

"Yessum, we gots to hurry," he said more to himself than to her. "Dem devil Redcoats be here most any minute now."

He led them from the spacious room through a smaller adjoining room and out into another big area where an exceeding long dinner table had been set, Sam noticed, with fine china and silver flatware and a meal for what looked like dozens of expected guests.

As they entered the room, an attractive woman

dressed in a white taffeta gown with puffed sleeves, ruffled neckline, and waist belted by a pale rose satin sash, turned to view them. She had a determined expression on her otherwise elegant countenance.

Wow! That must be Dolly Madison. The First Lady Dolly Madison. She was tall—*just about my height,* Sam observed—and had jet black hair arranged in tendrils framing her profile with the back pulled up into a tight chignon. She was surrounded by several men, some more servants, and two workers Sam spotted who seemed intent on removing a huge painting off the opposite wall.

Sam glanced at the painting but then took a second look.

Why it's the portrait of George Washington, the one Mr. Smith said was the most famous of all his pictures. Mr. Smith was her history teacher at Highland Hill High School.

Her eyes narrowed in slow disbelief as she continued staring. There was something about this painting. She had studied art history in school and had seen a lot of classic works displayed in the Knoxville, New York City and London museums. Most were copies, but the colors of this piece seemed vibrant and new and fresh. *Too fresh. It looks like an original.* Unwanted terrifying thoughts came to her and her face blanched. *Oh my gosh. If that's the original, then what year is this? Have I gone back in time? What's happening to me?*

Dolly Madison saw Sam's countenance grow pale and assumed she was fearful of the approaching British troops. As was her habit when attending to guests and others, Mrs. Madison's generous blue eyes missed nothing, even among the most crowded of gatherings.

"Dear child, please don't let yourself be frightened. These fine gentlemen, I'm sure, will see that no harm befalls the good ladies of this house." She motioned at the small crowd of men around her.

"Who send you to help us?" Dolly looked at Sam with expectation. Just then, one of the men exclaimed at the two attempting to free the gigantic portrait from the wall.

"Oh, never mind that now," she waved her hand indicating the answer was of little importance to the situation at hand. "Whoever sent you, we're most grateful, and certainly can use all the hands we may get." Dolly smiled at Sam, turning her attention back to the tricky matter of the portrait.

"Madam, I'm afraid they may damage the canvas if they persist in tearing away the wooden frame in such manner," said the man who had exclaimed in concern. He leaned forward for a closer inspection.

"See here on this one spot, there's already the faintest of scratches on the painted surface."

"So, my good sir, how do you propose we proceed? French John, I must tell you that under no circumstances do I wish this precious symbol of our country's beginning, this wonderful masterpiece, to fall into the hands of the British. We must hurry, no matter what course of action we choose."

"Let it to me," French John replied, with a resolute visage. "Jennings, go fetch me a good cutting knife off the table."

When the young servant returned with a sturdy looking blade, Sam and the others watched as French John meticulously, slowly, cut away the heavy canvas from its wooden imprisonment. Finally, the thick fabric was loose from the frame.

Sam cranked her neck to see the famous portrait up close as French John and Jennings handed it over carefully to two waiting men for safekeeping. *What kind of material is that painted upon?* She wondered. Unexpectedly, an image of the little green book flitted across her mind and the thought, *English twill fabric made of linen*, popped into her brain, unannounced and unwanted.

It freaked her out. She flinched as the image flashed within her brain. And once again, the ever observant Dolly noticed.

She walked over to pat Sam on her shoulder. "I know, my dear, I know. It's hard to think of leaving our home and spiriting away precious possessions and invaluable artifacts that rightfully should remain here, safe and secure for future generations to admire." Dolly wiped a lonely tear streaming down her lovely cheek.

"No. Stop, Mister Barker! You must not roll it up! It might crack the paint."

The two men looked at him.

"Sorry, but it's a delicate thing, gentlemen. Please, I urge you—and you, Mister DePeyster—by all means, lay it flat with its back against the bed of your wagon. Naturally, you know to use a tarp or some such material to protect it from the weather as well as hide it from enemy eyes."

"We'll take good care of it," said Barker, unoffended by French John's scolding. Instead, he nodded agreeably at the man. Turning to Mrs. Madison, he added, "Don't worry, Molly. It's safe with us."

"I know it will be, Jacob." She gave him a radiant smile. "Thank you for your judicious arrival and able assistance. The President will be very grateful." She reached out and squeezed his forearm since his hand was already holding the painting. Samantha didn't know it yet, but Jacob Barker was a close friend of the Madisons, and like Dolly, a member of the Quaker religion.

Dolly and the rest watched as DePeyster and Barker each grasped the ends of the canvas. They carried it through the house and out the front door to a waiting wagon, which was being held safe from the fleeing throngs by Barker's personal aide.

"Well," Dolly clapped her hands, "that's done now." A worried expression crossed her brow. "But where, oh where, are my darling husband and his dear friends. They should have been here hours ago. I pray God for his safety, wherever he may be."

Looking around, she found the head butler and his two helpers and motioned to them. "Would you please gather some refreshments and take it to our brave troops. Sukey tells me remnants of soldiers are beginning to gather outside the mansion. The poor dears are exhausted beyond belief.

"Margaret, would you help also?" she called to a servant girl, trembling and frightened out of her wits in the corner of the big room. "And could you assist them, too? I'm sorry, child, I didn't get your name." Dolly turned to Sam, standing nearby.

"Samantha. Samantha Robertson, Mrs. Madison." Not knowing what else to do or what the proper etiquette was, Sam curtsied and smiled back. Suddenly, she felt shy and awkward in the presence of such a distinguished lady from the past.

"What a good girl you are. A brave one, too. We're very glad to have your help." Dolly reached out and stroked Sam's hair once, almost like a mother would. She beamed encouragingly at Sam. For a second her own courage faltered and then sighed. "While there's still time for such niceties, I must complete the letter to my sweet sister Lucy before I go."

"Yes, Ma'am," said Sam. She watched the First Lady turn and walk toward the furthest door. Before

Dolly could make her exit, however, one of the remaining men in the formal dining room stopped her. He wore an expression of deep concern.

Sam didn't mean to listen in, but the man's voice was loud and insistent.

"Molly, I must insist that you leave this instant. The fact of the matter is you should have left hours ago. You're tempting fate. We—"

"Darling Charles, I do appreciate your concern," she interrupted him. Her voice grew glum. "Pray, let me first finish writing my sister, collect what valuables I may on the way out, and we'll be off."

Samantha felt a tug on her sleeve.

"They need our help outside, miss." The other girl stood waiting, her face tense and eyes wide. A little impatient, Sam thought, but mostly scared. She felt a tiny surge of sympathy. *I bet she's close to my age.*

"Yes, I'm coming," Sam answered. "My name is Samantha, but you can call me Sam. You're Margaret, right?"

"Aye."

"Listen, I'm a little afraid, too. There's a lot I don't understand yet about what's going on in my life right now. Somehow, deep down inside, though I can't explain it I have the strangest feeling things will work out just fine." Sam gave Margaret a wry grin.

"Trust me on this. Stick with me, and I'll make sure you're safe, okay?"

"Whatever you say, miss," replied Margaret doubtfully.

Sam repeated, "Again, my name is Samantha. It's okay to call me that."

"Yes, Samantha," Margaret nodded, and they left the room to help the other servants bring out food and drink to the clusters of tired, defeated soldiers gathering outside their President's home.

Chapter 5
IN SEARCH OF SAM

TJ finished his last bite of sandwich and took two huge swallows to drain the last of his coffee, leaving a trace of the dark brown grounds in the bottom of his cup. In the absence of Dora and Samantha who disapproved such feats, he leaned back and belched several times, each one louder than the last. It was a gift he had, the ability to do explosive burbs in succession, the occurrence of which never failed to amuse his teammates and other guy friends.

Funny how girls can't appreciate my comic abilities, he mused. Like his dad, he loved watching old reruns of the Three Stooges, Marx Brothers, Abbott and Costello, Laurel and Hardy on the TCM channel. Pure genius, he thought, and the more the slapstick, bathroom and dining room humor, the better.

"Well, I'd better get started," he said to himself, standing and pushing away his chair. "No telling how long Sam's going to be. Girls," he snorted with fake derision.

He collected the plates and mugs off the little

dinette, soaped and rinsed them with hot water, and placed them in the dishwasher before moving to the big table.

TJ pulled the big history tome from the stack of textbooks and opened it to the semester's first chapter. Rifling through, chapter by chapter, he took his tablet and began making notes of topics and questions he knew would be featured on the upcoming test. After fifteen minutes of this, he began to wonder about Sam. Unlike most girls, she was quick about her business and seldom took longer than six or seven minutes in the restroom, max.

Was something wrong? From the time he finished his meal, cleaned up the kitchen, to now, it was more than twenty minutes, he guessed.

Shaking his head, TJ got up and jogged up the stairs, turning right at the hallway and down toward his father's bedroom.

As soon as he saw the little green book next to Sam's collapsed body on the floor, he knew. The book had slipped out of her hands, landing face down with a corner of it trapped beneath her splayed right elbow. Its center pages were bent against the hard wood flooring. Its front and back covers were now blank.

His heart froze. It was hard to breathe.

"Oh no. No, Sam, no. You couldn't have." He clutched his chest and stumbled over to the edge of the big bed, plopping down with a glazed look on his face. His dad must have left the book out in plain view, he surmised. Otherwise, Sam wouldn't have seen it. Wouldn't have been captivated by its pull.

Groaning, TJ covered his face with his hands. Impulsively, he started to reach out to shake her shoulder but then he pulled his hand back. It was no use. She was out *there*. Nothing he could do *here* would wake her up.

I've got to think! Where could she be? What time period? What year . . . month . . . day? What predicament did the green book put her in?

No matter how much he forced it, his brain was moving slow, refusing to cooperate.

"Dad, you screwed up again!"

Yet another unintentional, but crucial mistake on his father's part. Professor Cockrell had forgotten to lock the book up in the little office desk in the bay corner a year earlier, leading to TJ's first unforeseen and danger-filled frontier adventure.

Now Samantha was trapped, as he had been. Somewhere in the past. Like *Jumanji* the unpredictable magic board game from the movie, he knew the little green book could not be controlled. You could only react to the situations the book placed you in. You played the game by its unwritten rules, never knowing what those were for any given adventure.

Just the fact the book had accepted Samantha as a participant was a shock.

TJ gulped hard. A very scary idea just crossed his mind. *What if the little green book only works for one person at a time?* That would mean Samantha would be on her own, as he was for his first adventure. He couldn't go to her or help her out in any way.

"I've *got* to be able to reach her. I've just *got* to!" said TJ desperately.

The one thing that gave him hope was the book somehow protected the participant from serious injury or death, and always returned the player to the present.

"At least I know Sam is safe, no matter what." But where she was, was anybody's guess.

"Okay. All right. As soon as I touch it, I'll know whether or not it works for more than one person per adventure. Either I get in. Or I don't. I know in a few more seconds.

"Meanwhile, try to think where Sam may be. It's all about history. Use logic to deduce the answer." He breathed in deeply, his brows furrowed together.

"The last time? Well, the last time, I was studying about frontier Tennessee, and bingo, that's where I landed. Now we're studying the War of 1812. That means there's a good chance Sam was sent back to that time period."

The more he thought about it, the more he became convinced. "That's the logical choice. I *have* to assume the book will place me there, as well. I *have* to believe I'll find her once I'm in."

TJ gritted his teeth with determination. Standing up, he straightened his shoulders and marched over to the little green book.

"Hey, I've done this before. I just have to trust my instincts."

He reached out for the book. "Here goes nothing."

Instantly, the energy of the little green book fastened onto his fingers then the rest of his body like a magnet attracts iron. The cover changed before his eyes into a kaleidoscope of sandy beaches, inland bays, wet marsh lands, dazzling sunlight upon incoming aqua-blue ocean waves, a very old Spanish-like city, a primitive fortress with black cannons being moved into place, bands of Indian braves, and soldiers marching, marching in bright red uniforms.

"I have no idea what I'm looking at," he mumbled.

As he did at the beginning of his frontier adventure, TJ felt himself falling into a dreamy haze, a foggy mist. Falling down, down, down.

But this time, he wasn't afraid.

When he awoke out of his haze, TJ found himself in the middle of a forest of tall pines. He clucked his tongue.

"Woods again. Always the woods. Why can't I be sent to a breath-taking mountain setting or luscious tropical paradise, either one filled with gorgeous females all in love with me?"

However, wherever he was, it must be semi-tropical, given the temperature and trees, he thought.

He turned around in a full circle to better gauge his surroundings. He looked up. Through a few holes in the tree canopy above, he could discern small patches of overcast blue sky tinged with a sprinkling of rain clouds. It was hot and muggy, and sweat was already reforming on his brow.

"Well, the good news is it's not freezing, like last time."

Wherever he was, it seemed to him to be late afternoon, judging by the lengthening shadows scattered on the ground.

TJ stiffened. "Uh oh, I've got company," he whispered.

Some fifty yards from his position, just coming into view was a squadron of soldiers, marching single file around a heavy thicket patch off in the distance. As the rest of the unit made its way past the heavy undergrowth, they were visible through the gaps between the towering trees. If he could see them, they could see him. Worse still, they were headed in his general direction. They were all dressed in the unmistakable red uniforms which TJ recognized from his history classes as the British redcoat of two hundred years ago.

They're going to the fort or settlement or whatever it is that's behind me. About a hundred yards away in a clearing, TJ had seen the outline of rough-hewed walls, built of long heavy logs stacked on top of the other. The section of wall visible through the trees, he noticed, had a row of waist-high square openings. Noses of black cannons peered out of the yawning spaces.

"Halt! Who goes there?" A burly soldier with sergeant stripes bore down on TJ before he could even make up his mind to hide or come forward. Too late, he'd been spotted.

Quickly the group of soldiers caught up with their leader and surrounded TJ. The beefy sergeant strode forward and planted himself in front of TJ, his thick nose and bad breath not ten inches from TJ's surprised face. The strong reek of rum made TJ's eyes water.

The man looked TJ up and down, sneering at his rough servant's garments which had patches here and there. TJ followed the man's eyes down and took the opportunity to see what he was now wearing.

At least, the green book knows what it's doing with the costume changes. He knew if he'd been found in an American soldier's uniform or even a rich person's attire, things would go much the worse for him.

"What's your name, bumpkin?"

TJ thought fast. In his last adventure, he'd had to create a make believe past for himself to avoid ticklish questions about his real life. *He thinks I'm some kind of manservant, so I'll play along.*

"My name is Thomas. Thomas Jackson." The soldier's belligerent stare unsettled him. "Sir," he added, to placate the man. "My, uh, my old master left me stranded here."

"So he left the trash behind and went on his merry way, did he, now? What's the matter with you, boy? Lazy?

Good for nothing? You a thief? Stupid? Disobedient? All of the above?" The sergeant fixed Thomas with a penetrating look.

"What was your master doing in these parts anyway? What was his business here?"

Not knowing where on earth he was at the moment, Thomas improvised. "He was from . . . he was from . . ."

All the soldiers drew in a little closer, hanging on his answer.

"Well? Are you plain stupid, boy? Speak up! Cat got your tongue?"

He looked beyond Thomas at the surrounding circle of men, and guffawed loudly. "Aye, like most of the rabble in this pestilence-ridden country he can't understand the King's English. The quicker we teach you arrogant rebels some manners, the better it'll be for all concerned."

The redcoats all sniggered.

"I'm not a rebel, I'm an American!" retorted Thomas, hotly.

The sergeant struck Thomas a glancing blow with his open palm, staggering the boy.

"I'll thank you to keep a civil tongue in your head when speaking to me, you filth. Now answer me and tell me quick! What was your master doing here?"

"He was from . . . from New Orleans. A trader." Thomas rubbed his burning cheek. "He came here to trade. But he wasn't happy with the arrangement once he got here. So he went back.

"He left me behind. Why, you might ask? Well, because . . . because he didn't like me. It's that simple. Nothing against my work or my attitude. Or my intelligence either." He squinted, still with a touch of defiance.

"Huh. *New Orleans*, you say? Very interesting, that."

"Flat out, Master Cockrell just didn't like me," Thomas repeated, determined to make his story stick. "He's a strange man, very hard to please, changes his mind at the drop of a hat." His description was the exact opposite of his own patient, thoughtful father, whose name he picked.

"Well, boy, I don't much like you or your tune either, and shan't leave you here to cause mischief." The sergeant glanced over the circle.

"Kingsley! Patterson!" he barked.

Immediately, two soldiers stepped forward.

"You'll confine the prisoner to quarters. Hold this Yankee brat under watch for further questioning. New Orleans?" he said again.

"Notify both Colonel Nicolls and Captain Woodbine of the situation."

The soldiers saluted the sergeant. Each took a position with Thomas in the middle. The taller one had flaming red hair and a lanky jaw with mutton-chop sideburns. He nodded at Thomas and said under his breath, "Now mind yourself, laddie, and there'll be no more trouble." His expression was serious but not unkind. The other man had a disinterested, half-drunk look, but his features were hard and cruel. *This one can be dangerous. Watch out!*

Thomas had no choice but to go with them.

He figured his face had a bruise from the sharp slap, but that was the least of his concerns. He still didn't know where he was. More importantly, he didn't know where Sam was, either.

It wasn't a very promising start. *Little green book, I hope you know what you're doing*, he thought glumly.

Chapter 6
BALTIMORE BOUND

Sam followed Margaret to the kitchen where the head butler, Edward, and his two helpers were gathering up bread, cheese, apples, grapes, pears, and random items from the pantry supplies, as well as some remnants of food including scraps of meat left over from the formal dinner preparation. These they piled willy-nilly into baskets, buckets, large pots, whatever they could find on hand, to take to the exhausted bands of soldiers gathering outside the President's House.

There was a sense of panic about the workers, as if they couldn't wait to finish this last chore and rush out of the mansion into the oblivion of the coming night.

Seeing the two girls enter, the head butler spun around. "Girl, here!" Edward snapped, handing Sam one laden basket and one filled pot to carry out. Sam balanced the iron-cast pot against her hip with her free hand.

"And you." He shoved into Margaret's trembling hands a large metal baking sheet plied with a small mountain of foodstuffs.

Edward waved the girls toward the front door beyond the kitchen entryway. As soon as this remaining duty was done, he himself intended to flee and seek safety elsewhere. Only his honor as a valued butler, as a recent freedman, and his steadfast loyalty to the President and Mrs. Madison kept him at the task at hand while danger was fast approaching. He knew enemy cannon shot and errant musket balls were no respecter of persons.

He turned back to the business at hand, briskly selecting and putting items in whatever containers he could find. He snapped his fingers at one of his helpers, Peter, to come take away the two big wooden buckets at his feet, both filled to the brim, and follow the girls out the door. The fellow ran past them with his burden, bumping Sam's elbow on the way around her, so eager was he to be done and be gone.

"Scared to death, aren't they," Sam scowled at the youth's back.

"We're all scared, Ma'am. The British are coming." Margaret was weeping now as she stumbled forward with her load.

"I told you to call me Samantha," chided Sam. "And another thing. Everyone here keeps going on about the British. The British this, the British that. They're coming. They're almost here. So . . . what about the British?"

Sam took two huge steps to get ahead of her and then turned facing Margaret, stopping her in her tracks. "What year is this anyway?"

"What year? You ask what year it is, miss?" she frowned in confusion at the question. "Samantha," she added, remembering to call Sam that. "Why, it's 1814."

"18—," Sam gulped. She felt the blood draining from her face. "I was afraid of that. Okay. Okay." She was breathing deep to keep her head from spinning. "That makes sense. That was Dolly Madison I just met. *The* Dolly Madison.

"And this is the War of 1812," she said to herself. "And we've been studying the War of 1812 in history.

"And the month?"

"Tis August, miss."

"August. Right." She glanced over at Margaret's perplexed face. "Of course it is."

Shaking her head, she felt the blood returning. Under her breath, soft enough that the other girl couldn't hear everything, Sam said, "Well, it is what it is. I don't know how in the world I got here . . . except for that stupid little green book. But I'm here now. Obviously. This basket is heavy. It's real. I'm struggling to hold this pot against my side. It's real, too.

"Whatever has happened to me, this is no simple dream. I'm *here*."

Margaret watched Sam mumbling to herself with growing concern. Her new companion must be a bit touched in the head, she decided. She made a mental note to take necessary precautions being around Samantha.

At that moment, Sam looked at Margaret and saw

her continued expression. She grinned in spite of herself. "Don't worry, girlfriend. I'm not crazy. Really, I'm not. I, aaahhh, I fell down. Hit my head. Yeah, that's right. I fell down, and I'm just now getting my senses back," she lied.

"Okay, miss," Margaret nodded, still with a look of worry on her simple face.

The two girls mended their way with their burdens through the mansion to the front entrance. Outside they saw clusters of soldiers, some lying down, some sitting, some wandering about, others standing still as if waiting for something to happen.

Sam approached the nearest group. She set the laden pot down and held out the basket for the men to take what they wanted. One large pudgy soldier began grabbing massive handfuls until Samantha looked crossly at him and snapped, "Hey, save some for the others." Sam was never afraid to speak her mind.

Standing behind her, Margaret gawked at Sam's audacity.

The man glared at her. In the early evening heat, he had streaks of sweat still streaming down his fat face. The collar and armpits of his soiled uniform were wet with dark stains. He stared to reply, but then thought better of it and tossed one hand's contents back into the basket.

"Och, Mason. Mind yer manners. Tis being polite to the young lady you ought be," said the next man in line, a tall, lanky but rather handsome soldier who couldn't have been more than a few years older than Sam. He had a thick brogue. "Jest 'cause the lass got sass, as we say back in dear sweet Ireland of me childhood, tis no cause to be uncivil."

"Lady!" The heavier man snorted, turning and eyeing Samantha up and down. "Why, I've seen more ladyship in a muddy pigpen, I have."

The taller thinner soldier scowled and took a menacing step toward Mason, causing him to shut up and stumble backwards with his cache of grub. The soldier continued to stare at Mason's departing figure. He watched him disappear behind another group of men huddled around the two food buckets of Peter some fifteen yards away. He shook his head with disbelief as he saw Mason shove his way between waiting soldiers and reach with his free hand for yet more food, despite the disapproving looks and comments of his comrades.

"Tis sorry I am, miss, but Mason's always been a bit o' the hog," the young man smiled at Sam, taking only one item, a delicious red apple, out of the basket. "Here, let me help you." He reached down and lifted the heavy pot off the ground and began going from one soldier to another until the pot was empty. He then took the cooking sheet from Margaret and did the same, bringing it back to her when all the items were gone. He nodded and winked at the girls and pocketed his apple for a later snack.

"Aren't you hungry" asked Sam. "One apple is not much to eat."

"I'm a feared I won't be here long enough to eat proper, anyways," he grinned ruefully. "I'm told me regiment is off to Baltimore as soon as we catch our breath."

Margaret was both shy and scared, but her desire to know details of the recent fight overcame her hesitancy. "What happened in the battle, sir? I was told we lost badly," her eyes looked like those of a frightened doe, he thought.

"Aye, they spanked us good, they did. I'm new to the army, I am, but I swear it don't take a genius to know what went wrong. Green troops," he lowered his voice so the two officers standing nearby couldn't hear. "Weak commanders. Poor positioning."

He sighed. "All we can do now is hope and pray to make a stand in Baltimore. As sure as me name is Andrew McCready, that twill be their next stop, I'm a guessing."

"Ah," exclaimed Margaret. "I have relatives in Baltimore. A married auntie and an old maid auntie live there, and some second and third cousins, too." Her voice shook. "I plan on leaving. Tonight. Before they get here," her eyes looked fearfully in the direction of the assumed approaching British troops. "But with all the riff raff and so many people fleeing, both the good and the bad, tis not safe for a single woman to be traveling alone.

"Not all men out and about tonight are gentlemen. Like you," she added, blushing.

"McCready!"

Andrew craned his neck. It was his commanding officer, 1st Lieutenant Butler. "Right, I've got to be a goin'," he tipped his military Shako cap to the girls. "Thankee for the pleasure o' meetin' the both o' you. And the fine apple, miss. I'm sure I'll enjoy it soon.

"Oh, and I'll do me best to let you what's what before I leave." He gave them a big wink before turning on his heel.

They watched him striding away. The summer heat of the day was winding down to warm petulant breezes that tickled Sam's face and blew strands of hairs over her eyes and nose. The earlier clamor of the rushing crowd had quieted as the majority of escapees had already made their exit from the city. There was a long moment of silence. Then Sam cleared her throat. The image of the little green book had floated across her mind and somehow she knew what she was supposed to do.

"Say, uh, listen, Margaret. I'll be more than happy to go with you to Baltimore. Two are safer than one, you know. Plus, I can be pretty darn fierce if threatened. I've had serious training in self-defense including some martial—" Sam caught herself. This was 1814. Martial arts, kick-boxing, judo . . . all that would be unknown to people in Margaret's time. "I mean, let's just say, girlfriend, that I know how to defend myself if I'm attacked."

Margaret nodded, frowning slightly, trying to make sense of Samantha's speech.

"Yes, miss, somehow I think you would be

formidable as a foe." She half-smiled, indicating Sam's offer was appreciated and accepted.

"I need to get my things from my room before we start, miss." Margaret pointed up the street in the direction most people were escaping. "And how about your things, miss?"

Sam raised her eyebrows and shook her head. "Nada."

"Na . . . na-da?"

Sam laughed at herself. She had to be more careful with letting 21st century slang slip out in her conversation. "Forget it. Wrong word."

Margaret eyebrow furrowed together in further confusion.

"I have nothing to get," Sam explained.

"Nothing? You have no other clothes or possessions, miss?" Now Margaret was greatly concerned about her companion. It was rare she met girls poorer than she. Her face filled with instant compassion. "We can share," she nodded.

Sam smiled big. "Well, thank you, Margaret. That's very generous of you." Sam looked down at the cooking sheet, pot, and basket lying on the grassy lawn next to their feet. "I suppose we should take these back inside before we go, don't you think?"

"I suppose, yes, miss."

They picked the utensils up and walked to the front door.

"No need to put them back where Edward got them from. The British are going to steal or burn or ruin everything anyway."

"How do you know for sure what they'll do, miss?" Margaret wondered. She gave a nervous glance at the shadowed outline of Sam's face. Such odd or unusual things her new companion kept saying, she thought.

"Hmmm. Just guessing?" Sam responded. "Seems like something they would do. Don't you think?"

"Yes, ma'am."

"You mean, yes, Samantha." Sam smiled at her. "Come on, girlfriend. No more calling me miss or ma'am. Agreed?"

"Yes, miss. I mean . . . yes, Samantha."

"That's better."

Before they left the lawn and stepped out onto the street on the way to Margaret's little rent-room, Andrew caught up with them.

"We'll be a leavin' in thirty minutes with orders to march tonight to Baltimore. So, if you two lassies want to travel along with me unit, I'll be makin' sure no one bothers you."

Sam looked over at Margaret. "It's fine with me. Safer that way."

Margaret agreed.

"We're going to Margaret's place to collect her belongings. We'll meet you back here in fifteen minutes and wait for your army unit—what do you call it?"

"It's called a platoon, miss."

"Yeah, your platoon. We'll meet you back here and then we'll be ready to mosey."

"Mosey?"

"Yeah, mosey. You know."

She drew a blank look from both of them. "It means, ahhh . . . it means ready to travel.

"Oh, mosey. Right. I'll try to remember that one, lassie." He gave the girls a semi-formal bow, taking his long cap off with a fine flourish, and headed back to Butler and the other soldiers.

"Means ready to travel," she repeated and sighed. "Yes, it does." She'd done it again. Sam made a mental note to herself: *I've got to stop using modern words. It's confusing the heck out of them.*

As they restarted up the street, no longer crowded with the panicked hordes—most people having already made their escape from the city—Sam become lost in a swirl of glum thoughts, striding beside the quiet Margaret.

Now that she was over the initial shock of discovering she was back in time to 1814, and now that she was no longer busy with an immediate task, her mind was racing.

Sam knew she was far braver than most girls. Resilient and resourceful, too. But not knowing the answer to her problem was almost more than she could bear. She wished she could make her mind focus on something else besides her present dilemma.

Sam had a bad habit of grinding her back molars when she was agitated. To her surprise, she found herself grinding away, as they walked. She clamped her mouth shut with a scowl, hoping Margaret hadn't noticed.

Would she ever get back to her time again? And if so, how? When? Where?

Chapter 7
PRISONER IN PARADISE

Patterson and Kingsley marched Thomas in double-time, winding through the thick pines toward the crude fort off in the distance. The rest of the soldiers followed at a normal pace.

As they got closer to the fort, Thomas thought he saw spots of silvery blue and the occasional flash of the late afternoon sun upon what he assumed was the surface of water in the woods beyond.

Upon reaching the front stockade gate, which was wide open, the mean-looking soldier shoved Thomas in the back with the stock end of his musket, causing Thomas to pitch forward a bit. The man scowled at him and spat brown juice on the back of his feet while his companion kept a neutral look on his face. The two escorted Thomas through the large center yard toward a long connected row of log cabin quarters built against the opposite wall. Out of the corner of his eye, Thomas noticed construction of various other rooms and buildings on either side.

The two soldiers led him to the centermost

building in the back. As they got near, the shorter stockier soldier grabbed Thomas by his elbow, yanking him off his feet to an abrupt stop.

"Halt, you scum!"

The taller soldier winced. "There's no need for all that," he mumbled under his breath. He glanced over at the other and jerked his head toward door, "Edward, why don't you announce the prisoner. I'll stay here to, ah, guard our very, very dangerous man here."

Edward growled his displeasure at losing yet another opportunity to harass Thomas. He glared at both his comrade and the boy for a second before marching forward and knocking on the door, then stepping back and standing at rigid attention as he waited for an answer.

A young officer with curly brown hair flowing over his ears and over his stiff uniform collar opened the heavy wooden door. He was working on growing a beard, perhaps to hide his youth, but the result was not at all encouraging. The sideburns were thinly populated below the top of his protruding ears. Worse, the patches of facial growth around his mouth and chin were so light as to resemble baby hair. More comical, in Thomas' estimation, was that the hair on his face turned reddish the further it traveled down his elongated profile, giving him a bit of a monkeyish look.

"Yes?"

"A prisoner for Colonel Nicolls and Captain Woodbine to interrogate. Sir." The stocky solider saluted briskly. "We found him in the nearby woods, suspicious-like, with no good answers why he's here and what he's up to. Sir."

"Just a moment, Corporal." The young officer disappeared back into the building and Thomas heard voices speaking inside.

The young officer reappeared at the door, motioning Corporal Kingsley to bring the prisoner inside.

"Yes sir." Kingsley saluted, did an about face, and resumed his position on the other side of Thomas. The two soldiers strode forward with Thomas in the middle, delivering him to the door. Kingsley again took the opportunity to slam the stock of his musket against Thomas' shoulder blades, shoving the boy inside.

Thomas stumbled into the room, but caught himself. He took two more steps before halting at attention, face rigid, only his eyes moving, slowly scanning the quarters from side to side. There were quite a lot of people in the room. What he saw surprised him.

Across from Thomas at a cluttered worktable sat two officers. The one on the right was an imposing figure of man, his bright red officer's uniform topped by a stern countenance. His eyes were deep and piercing. He had heavy eyebrows, a high broad forehead, with wavy black hair, combed back, that was beginning to gray at the temples. His massive handle bar mustache rested on top of an even more massive beard that billowed down several inches around his jaws and chin. There were strands of curled wavelets protruding at the bottom of the beard on both sides.

Thomas got a chill up his spine. *Yikes. Dude is not someone to mess around with.*

Surrounding the table were three scary looking Indians and a handful of junior officers.

The big man stood up, his eyes fixed on Thomas's flushed face.

"Boy, what do you have to say for yourself, hey?" he snapped. "This military post and its immediate surroundings are restricted areas. I command here by authorization of the King of England, by the grace of God, and we are welcomed, personally, by the Spanish governor of Pensacola, Manrique himself. Our operations here are top secret."

He leaned forward on the desk, jutting his spectacular beard and riveting eyes closer to Thomas. "Well? What of it? Who are you and why's your business here?"

Thomas gulped. The big man was way intimidating.

"My name is Thomas Jackson, sir. I was left here by a trader. A mean—"

"A trader? From where?" The officer was abrupt and more than a little impatient.

"New Orleans, sir. He's a mean man. A little—"

"Trader of what, young pup?"

"He meant to . . ." Thomas had to think hard and

fast, "I think he wanted to do some business with the Spanish, but changed his mind because of the hostilities. The fighting, sir. He never confided in me, of course, but that's what I think. I believe he chickened out and turned back."

"Hostilities, you call it?" The big officer growled, raising an eyebrow.

"Yes sir." Thomas prayed none of them noticed the little beads of sweat beginning to form above his lip and on the sides of his face. Whenever he got stressed out, this same thing happened.

"All I know is the man was a little crazy, as I was going to say. I never knew what it was that displeased him so, but he ditched me."

"Ditched you? You mean left you here? How was he traveling? All a foot, or on horseback?"

"He came by ship and marooned me on land. Sir."

"That makes no sense. You're either lying or a fool. The Atlantic is a good fifteen miles south of here. Much of that land is near-impossible to travel a foot and difficult by horse. It's all marshland and swamp. And an ocean vessel couldn't go up the river waters."

Thomas thought fast. "Well, Master Cockrell didn't exactly put me down here. It was several miles further up the coast." He added, "Where the land's drier. Less marshy. Sir." Thomas could tell he didn't believe his story. He did some quick calculating.

"It was mid-morning, I guess, when he forced

me ashore. With no water or rations of any kind. After stopping at a creek to satisfy my thirst, I started walking north, keeping the river in my view. I walked five or six hours through the brush and the trees and the thickets before your people found me. I also took a quick nap at noon."

The big man scowled at him, as if trying to read his mind.

"I don't believe you. Firstly, you've given us no good reason why he would desert you. Secondly, your clothes are too fresh looking. A man slogging through this muck of a forest would be drenched in sweat, several times over, covered in filth. This God awful heat and humidity that only the bugs and the snakes and the varmints seem to love," he muttered under his breath.

"Thirdly, you're obviously an American working for a presumed American. Fourthly, Great Britain is at war with America, and none of you are to be trusted."

The officer stared at Thomas, while silence filled the room. The faces of the others were grim and not at all encouraging. The Indians in particular frightened him.

"I say you're a spy. Deliberately put here to gather information and report back to your superiors, whoever and wherever they are, on our operations. Your ruse of a man-servant is a flimsy cover-up."

Thomas gulped. He trusted the power of the little green book would continue to protect him now, as it had before.

"Colonel Nicolls, if I may be so bold as to make some inquiries of our, ah, guest. If you would permit me?"

His companion seated at the table, silent to this point, spoke up.

"Yes, of course, Captain, indeed." Sitting down now and leaning back in his squeaky chair, Nicolls waved for the other officer to proceed.

"You tell us, young man, that your Master was from New Orleans, and we have no tangible reason to disbelieve you on that point. What do you know about the city itself? How long have you been living there?"

Steady. Just stay steady. Gotta be crafty, Tege, old man. Thomas knew he couldn't divulge real information on troops, fortifications, battle plans, of which he remembered several important facts from his study that semester as well as his recent cramming for the history test. The Battle of New Orleans, the resultant American victory, and reasons why they won had been designated extra bonus topics for the exam.

His mind buzzed. "Actually, sir . . . I was born in Charleston and became his servant when his ship arrived there in late spring."

"When was that?"

"Late May, I believe." He hoped his calculation was correct on how long such trips ought to take.

"You're not sure?"

"Yes, sir, I'm positive it was late May. We made a stopover in Spanish Cuba before reaching New Orleans.

Master Cockrell had the idea of running goods to Pensacola for trading. But, as I said, he chickened out at the last moment and turned around without porting."

"What kind of goods?"

"Cotton and whiskey and some hand goods. Sir."

The Captain raised an eye and sneered. "I wouldn't think the fine people of Pensacola would have much use for cotton imported from New Orleans." He coughed. "After all, Florida borders an American *slave* state. The Spanish inhabitants also have a much more refined taste than rot-gut whiskey. I've heard rumors that Georgia makes whiskey, too. Appalling stuff, but passable for these swine Americans, I suppose."

He looked at the boy keenly. "Also, there were two notable storms that occurred in the timeframe you claim. One in the Carolinas and another in the Caribbean, as I recall. Both within your ports of travel. What, between dodging British ships patrolling the Atlantic coastline and dodging the summer hurricanes, two-three months is not much time to go from New Orleans . . . to Charleston . . . to Cuba . . . back to New Orleans . . . to Pensacola.

"Now, is it?" His voice was smooth as silk but deadly. "How did you really get here, boy, and who were your accomplices? Are they still in the area?"

Thomas remained silent. He couldn't think of a suitable yarn to answer the Captain's suspicions.

It was the bad cop, good cop. And just like the

movies, it was the good cop who'd nailed him. Thomas was sweating profusely, numb in his fear.

"Lieutenant Smith, take this boy under guard until we make a decision about him. Naturally, you may feed him and give him water to drink, if thirsty, but watch him."

Colonel Nicolls spoke up. "Thank you, Captain Woodbine." He focused his intense visage upon Thomas.

"Do not try to escape, in the meantime. You see Coowah Yeehaw and Seti Nokosi standing here?" He pointed to the two largest, most fierce looking Indians, who had been watching everything with impassive faces. "Their names mean Big Wolf and Charging Bear. They're Seminole warriors. Hardened in battle. They have a great distrust—one might say a reasonable hatred—of you Americans. They know all of this land. Every creek, every marsh, every swamp, every tree, for many miles around. If you try to escape, they will catch you."

He bent his huge torso forward at Thomas to emphasize his point.

"And once they catch you . . . they will cut off your nuts and scalp you and drag you back here, dead or alive. If you're still alive, we'll finish the job by hanging you as a spy.

"Do you understand me, boy?"

Thomas' voice was a whisper, "Yes. Yes, sir." He knew the power of the little green book, but still, the images conjured up in his brain by the Colonel's threat were frightening, nonetheless.

The Colonel dismissed Thomas with curt wave of

the hand and returned to his business at hand. Lieutenant Smith marched him to the door. Looking out, Smith saw both Patterson and Kingsley loitering in the yard. It was obvious they were both hoping to find out what happened.

It was lucky for Thomas the young Lieutenant didn't particularly like Kingsley. He motioned instead to Patterson, who hurried forward.

"Take charge of the prisoner. Give him food and water. Watch him, but no need to shackle him." Smith glanced over his shoulder toward the open door, and then looked back to Patterson. The Lieutenant shivered at the very thought of the two savages. *Poor lad.* "The Colonel says he will sic Big Wolf and Charging Bear on him, with no mercy given, if the boy even tries to escape. The Colonel and Captain will decide later what to do with him. But for now, just stay with him, Corporal."

"Yes, sir."

Smith turned to go inside.

Kingsley rushed over to Patterson, angry, his voice a harsh whisper so Lieutenant Smith couldn't hear. "Why the devil did he give him to you? I'd make 'im sing. And quick!"

"He's already talked, Ben." Patterson gazed down at his beefy comrade. "You know you just want to torment the lad."

Ignoring Kingsley's bluster, he looked at Thomas and elbowed him. "Come on, boy, let's get some food in you."

Leaving Kingsley cursing under his breath, Patterson led Thomas to the right, toward the last building in the long row. "When did you last eat a meal?" he asked.

Thomas couldn't tell the man it was an hour ago of *their* time that he had been sitting down in a comfortable air-conditioned kitchen nook . . . eating his favorite sandwich with his girlfriend getting ready to study about the war he was now involved in. It was bizarre. Surreal.

Yet that's how the little green book operated.

He lied. "I got a moldy crust of bread and even moldier cheese at five bells this morning. I'm starving, Corporal."

The soldier smiled kindly. "You can call me Henry, lad."

They reached the last building. Henry paused for a moment before he opened the door for Thomas. "Are you really a spy?"

"No," Thomas truthfully answered. "I'm a victim of circumstance. Trapped in a situation beyond my control. I have more questions than answers myself."

Henry looked down at him for several seconds. "You know, lad, I think I believe you. I'm pretty good at reading people and you don't have the feel of a deceiver about you."

At least, not in the way you think, thought Thomas.

Henry pushed open the thick wooden door and led the boy in.

Chapter 8
TAMING THE SHREW

"Not to complain, Andrew, but how much longer until we get there?"

They had been walking for over two hours now. Both of Sam's big toes were getting rubbed raw on the outer side by the constant friction of the poorly fitting leather slippers. She had flat soles, too. Another problem, since the shoes offered zero arch support.

In short, her feet were killing her. She did her best to keep her stride constant without hobbling, but it was getting harder by the mile.

"Ah, we be makin' real good time, miss. Another four hours or so. A little less, maybe." Andrew smiled encouragingly at the two girls. "'Tis about forty miles. A baby march."

Margaret, as usual, didn't say a word of complaint. For someone so timid, she was resilient, Samantha was learning.

Sam blew a raspberry at the unwelcome news and kept slogging forward. She hoped her feet would hold out. As far as she could see, this so called main highway between Washington D.C. and Baltimore was nothing more than a winding country lane; plenty of ruts, holes, overhanging limbs, dead branches here and there on the road, stones and uneven ground the entire way. She'd already tripped a couple of times over things she couldn't see in time in the darkness.

Weary, they traipsed alongside the talkative Andrew and his platoon for what seemed almost the entire night. Meanwhile, a number of other platoons and miscellaneous groups of soldiers had caught up with Andrew's unit, stretching the columns of soldiers out over three hundred yards.

Fortunately, Andrew made it a point to keep his line steady with the girls so he could converse and visit with them along the way.

The men marched fast, propelled faster, Samantha suspected, by the threat of the British troops behind them in Washington.

The troops talked little and spat much tobacco. Except for Andrew's company, it was an exhausting, gloomy, and smelly affair. Sam winkled her nose. Every once in a while, the wind would change directions, blow from the south, whipping the unpleasant body odors toward her.

Andrew had kept cleaner and taken better care of himself, it seemed to her. He didn't smell bad at all; unlike his comrades, she supposed he took the opportunity to take a dip when his unit had crossed rivers and streams. Most of the other soldiers, especially the older ones, all stank of sweat, dirt, urine, cheap alcohol, tobacco, and general foul breath.

The trip took over six hours, having begun around seven that night. It was the wee hours of the morning when Margaret knocked on the door of her second cousin's door on the row of shanties off Aliceanna Street in downtown Baltimore within hearing distance of the sea gulls and waves and winds of the nearby ocean.

Margaret knocked again, but there was no sound except for dogs barking off in the distance.

"Here, let me try it." Sam pounded the door. Loud. Hard.

She was sweaty. She was tired. Her feet hurt. She was thirsty. She needed a long drink and an even longer sleep. Athlete that Sam was, little mousey Margaret had matched her step for step. *I guess they really were in better shape back then. I mean, back now.* Sam thought, ruefully.

She started to pound the door again, when an irritant voice called out. She heard shuffling steps inside.

"Who is it? What do you want? Land sakes, it's after midnight. You trying to wake the dead?"

The inside latch was loosened. The heavy door cracked open, revealing a sullen middle-aged woman standing with her thinning brown hair mixed with gray strands splayed in all directions poking out from her nightcap. Her face was sour-looking.

"Here! Here! What's all this to do. A hammering on good folk's doors in the middle o' the night."

"Cousin Angela, it's your cousin Margaret from south way."

"Margaret?" The woman growled. "Margaret who?"

"Margaret Petty Beechum, if you please. Your second cousin once removed."

The woman stared for several seconds, working the ancestral logistics out in her mind. Finally, she opened the door. "And who is this?"

"Samantha—"

"Samantha Robertson, ma'am," interrupted Sam. "We, uh, we worked together at the White House."

"The what?"

"I mean, the President's Home."

The woman looked down the road they had come, in the direction of Washington, her eyes filled with apprehension. "They say the British will be coming."

"Yes, they will," said Sam.

A man's head appeared behind her shoulder. His face was grizzled, lined with ravages of old age and drink and his face was covered with a long white beard down to his chest where it flopped out over a big puffy beer belly.

"Who's this?" he demanded in a guttural bark.

The woman turned her head and glared at the man. "Just me relatives, Hamilton. Just me family. Go back to bed. Don't need yer loud voice a addin' to the general commotion."

The man stared at the two girls. He grumbled a bit, and then shuffled off into the darkness of the room.

"So, I've got a couple of refugees at my doorstep." She had her hands on hips and an unwelcome expression. "In the middle o' the night. Fleeing from the British and a wantin' me to take you in, hey? A wantin' handouts and free room and board, no less."

"Actually, I have some money on me, ma'am. I can pay you what it is worth." Sam replied, to Margaret's amazement. "Right now, my feet hurt real bad. We both could sure use a drink of water and some sleep."

Hesitating, the woman gave Sam a shrewd look before relenting and opening the door all the way. She brought them a bucket of water with a dipper, out of which the girls drank to their heart's content. Sam also splashed some water on her dirty face and neck, rubbing as much of the grime off as she could, while the woman snorted at her vanity.

The girls were then led to a cramped untidy back room filled with casks, barrels, and pails of all sizes in various stages of construction. In the yellowish haze cast by the candle held by the woman, Sam saw two long connecting work shelves on the adjoining back and side walls. On each shelf were planes, drawknives, a broadax and other tools used in the making of the barrels.

"What does he do here? What's all this?" Sam asked curiously.

"He's a cooper," answered Margaret.

"A cooper?"

Margaret nodded, "Yes, he builds barrels and casks for people. He also repairs broken barrels and such."

"Interesting," said Sam, but she didn't think so. She walked around the debris to the right-hand shelf and handled a drawknife.

The woman left and returned shortly with a couple of threadbare blankets and shabby pillows. Handing these to Margaret, she left for good, taking the single candle with her. The darkness was suffocating to Sam.

"What do these pillows have in them?" She asked, patting the pillow between her hands.

"Corn husks."

"Boy, this life gets better and better. Curse you, little green book," she mumbled softly.

With no light to guide them, the girls had to feel and push things out of the way, and stack the foremost casks and barrels on top of those behind to make enough room for their pitiful pallets.

Definitely not twenty-first century living, thought Sam. But she was so exhausted she fell asleep seconds after her head hit the dusty pillow.

"How much for us to stay here?" Sam asked the woman the next morning.

"How long do you figure on being here?"

"I don't know. I guess until the British leave the area," Sam said. She thought fast. She had fourteen dollars, but no idea how long she would be trapped in this time and no hope of earning more money in the interim.

"I'll give you a dollar every other day, hard cash, for the both of us," Samantha said.

"Let me see it." The woman was not convinced.

Sam fished in her dress pocket and pulled out a silver dollar.

Without a word, the woman yanked it out of her fingers, leaving Sam a bit stunned.

"Well now. Well, missy. That may do for your room . . . but what about your meals," the lady countered, the silver coin clutched in her greedy paw. "Hungry mouths cost a fortune and we ain't rich."

Angela Sampson, for that was her married name, was a washer woman. Monday through Saturday she took in soiled garments from wealthy Baltimore residents and washed and folded the clothes for pick-up. Sam had noticed racks of hanging clothes in the main room when they first entered the house, but paid no mind to them at the time.

It was made clear she and Margaret would have to earn their meals. Soon, she came to hate the feel and smell of laundry. Except for periods when the volume of clothes slacked off, it was back-breaking labor, dawn to dusk. Drawing buckets of water from the communal well at the back of the building complex. Heating the water to a boil over the smoky old cookstove. Hand washing and scrubbing each new batch of clothes with the crude soap. Hanging the clothes out to dry on the handmade racks and strung clotheslines in the main entry room. Then taking the clothes down and folding them, while working on other batches in various stages of completion.

For nearly three weeks, she toiled alongside Margaret. Every night it was the same.

"Margaret, how can we slave away like this? Working our fingers to the bone every day, fourteen hours most days. And for what? Thin gruel? Crusts of bread? Gummy biscuits my grandmother would laugh at? Half-cooked bacon and pig parts? Dried up cornbread?"

"But miss. We should be thankful we have a roof over our heads and food and drink. Tis good food, too, I think. What would we have done if the British had captured us?"

"Better red than dead," Sam laughed bitterly. "They couldn't be any worse than this hellish existence."

"Miss!" said Margaret, shocked.

"Forget it. Forget I said anything." But long after she lay her weary body down for the night on the dusty floor beside Margaret's pallet in the grubby work room, her tormented mind continued to spin. Samantha was by nature a cheerful confident girl. But now as each dreary day ended with no hope in sight, she fought depression.

When will this nightmare end? When will I get back to the future? How can I get back to the future?

Hot tears trickled down the sides of her upturned face as she twisted and turned to get more comfortable on the lumpy pillow. *I miss you so much, Mom and Dad. Tege, I miss you; I love you. My teammates, my school, my house, my friends. My life! I want it all back!*

Thankfully, their drudgery was relieved somewhat. Andrew came to visit them two or three times a week, often during lunch or sometimes in the late afternoon. From him, they learned the whole city was becoming a virtual fortress.

This day, he came at noon break, carrying a laden basket with him.

"Beautiful damsels in distress, your stalwart hero in shining armor has arrived!" he said with a grin. "Let's see what we have here. Well, well, well. I brought some good cheese." He lifted it out of the basket to his nose and smelled. "Why, here's a fresh loaf of bread baked just this morning. And look here! A magnificent bottle o' wine. There's more than enough for everyone," he winked at Angela, who showed signs of displeasure at the stoppage of work.

"Oh, and I've got some urgent news, I have," he added, more somberly.

Angela ceased her nagging and grew quiet to listen.

In the few brief moments of silence, they could hear noises from the back room where Angela's old husband, Hamilton or Ham for short, was busy working on the barrels and stumping about.

Angela called him Master Sampson, whenever she was put out with him, for it was little enough he was master of.

For her part, Sam avoided contact with Ham as much as she could. If his wife was not present, the old man's eyes followed Samantha wherever he was in the same room. It gave her the creeps.

In between healthy bites of the cheese and bread, Andrew spoke again. "Aye, the diligent folk of the city have been busy bees, they have. No takin' them by surprise. No sir. Already, they've got breastworks a goin' up on Hampstead Hill and all around on the east side. When the British land, they'll have to pass that way to get to the heart of the city. We plan on givin' them a stout surprise." Andrew's visage was both stern and courageous.

"So it's true. They're finally coming." Angela's face blanched.

"Aye, Madam. Lookouts have been a followin' the British fleet for the past two days. They've been a sendin' regular reports by messengers on horseback to General Smith and the Committee of Vigilance and Safety. The British have already passed by Annapolis and are sailing up the Patapsco, heading toward us as we speak."

"Oh, saints above! What are we a goin' to do?"

"We'll fight them, Madam. And we'll win!" Andrew's eyes were alight with the excitement of impending battle.

Angela plopped hard on a nearby stool, her face

graying with fright. For the first time, she consented to join them for the meal, although the girls and Andrew had offered to share their food every time he brought over good things to eat.

That afternoon, after Andrew's visit, Angela gave the girls time off. "What use is it to wash and clean, if the British burn everything to the ground?" she lamented.

Also for the first time, she became kinder to Sam and Margaret, fearing this night would be her last on earth.

That evening, Sam offered to fix up Angela's hair, an gesture that surprised and delighted the older woman. Only the wealthy could afford to have their hair done.

There was a single mirror in the entire house. It was a large ornate object that rested on the fireplace mantel in the large room. Sam had Angela sit down on the stool facing the mirror. She took the candleholder and placed it on another stool beside her, where the light from the three candles shone around Angela's head.

Samantha had trained as a hair stylist the summer before. She considered herself to be darn good at it, too, having practiced on almost all of her friends, and friends of friends, with excellent results. She removed Angela's work bonnet, and combed out her hair to the ends before beginning.

The big scissors were not the best, but Sam trimmed away loose ends. She raised the back into a stylish length above the collar and layered the sides and bangs into a soft body. The cut, of course, was modern, and except for Angela would be unknown for another hundred and fifty years.

The impact upon Angela when Sam was finished was astounding. For the first time, her hair, although dirty and unwashed and graying here and there, beautifully shaped her heavy cheeked face and offset her stubby chin. She looked and felt like a different person.

"Why . . . why . . . it's lovely, miss. It's . . . it's—"The woman got teary-eyed. Words escaped her. She kept angling her face this way and that in the mirror, getting different perspectives of the cut, but no matter how she turned her head, she loved the result.

Suddenly, she turned and grabbed Samantha in a tight loving hug, tears streaming down her face.

"Thank you, miss," was all she could say, over and over, her fears forgotten for the moment.

But the British were still coming.

Chapter 9
THE BATTLE JOINED

In the wee hours before sunrise, in the dark rolling bay waters and mist well beyond range of the small cannons of Fort McHenry, American spies scattered along the shore line could discern the ghostly outlines of British warships massed within the harbor. They could see countless dozens of small boats being lowered into the pitching waves from the sides of the ships. Each boat teemed with many soldiers and one or two officers.

The news was soon relayed to Major General Smith who was in charge of the overall land defense of Baltimore. He and his officers decided on taking the offensive to the British army. An attack force was assembled under the command of Brigadier General Stricker.

Napoleon had been defeated in Europe. Now Great Britain was turning loose her most war-hardened veterans upon the recalcitrant Americans who must be taught a hard lesson. A lasting lesson. Britain was master of the world again, and if fate smiled upon her, she would soon regain control of her wayward former colonies.

Fresh from the destruction of Washington, D.C., Baltimore was their next chosen victim.

Upon hearing the gossip the British had landed that morning, eager for battle, Andrew had harassed his unit commander until he was released from the platoon and allowed to join a volunteer rifle company as part of the troops handpicked to slow the British advance and buy city defenders more time for setting their defense. The men were in high spirits as they marched out to meet the British.

"So where are you from, Samuel?" Andrew asked the man next to him.

"Tis a little spot called Brookeville southwest of Baltimore. Practically everyone is a Quaker." He looked at Andrew. "Rumor has it that the President took refuge at the old Bentley place when the British burned the capital down."

"I heard that one, too," said Andrew. He clinched his jaw. "I pray we get to fight. I'm ashamed for the way we ran at Bladensburg and most eager to make amends, even at the cost of me life."

"They say the British General Ross is a brave but arrogant son of a bitch. He'll fight. He believes any one of his damn redcoats is the equal of any three Americans. You'll get your wish. There'll be a battle . . . sometime today.

"I hate the British," Samuel added bitterly. "They killed my favorite uncle and one of my grandfathers during the late War for Independence."

Late that morning, the American General Stricker deployed his troops halfway between the city's fortifications at Hampstead Hill and North Point where the British troops had landed and massed at the end of the peninsula.

As the men slowed to a halt, Andrew noticed boggy patches off in the distance on both sides of their location. Running through the swamp-filled woods were fast flowing creeks, on the left and the right. Their steep banks were heavy with impenetrable thickets, beyond which lay large sections of marshy turf, all forming a natural defense and making the dryer middle ground where they'd stopped an idea place to deploy.

Andrew watched the soldiers and horses pulling the battery of six 4-pounder field guns in position across along the front line.

Andrew breathed easier.

So Stricker knew what he was about, then. It would be much more difficult for the British to slog through that nasty terrain to out-flank the Americans as they had done at Bladensburg.

An hour later, two local farmers, their faces and hands burned tan by the blistering summer sun, approached the General and talked in low-pitched but angry voices.

The British had halted at a neighboring farm to let their men take a meal, they said. Worse still, marauding bands of sailors had been sent out to plunder other farms, including theirs.

Stricker listened intently, asking few questions. He decided then and there to force the issue. Better to draw the British into battle on his terms than wait for a possible surprise night attack by the blasted redcoats.

"Major Heath," he barked to one of the junior officers standing nearby.

"Yes sir, General."

"Select two hundred and fifty men for immediate action. Take one of the cannons with horse. Choose some fellows known to be excellent marksmen. Your objective is to seek the enemy, engage pickets and outlying troops, bait them into battle, and then lead them to our main force, here."

"Yes sir."

"Stand and fight as long as you can without sustaining heavy casualties. But remember. Your primary goal is to provoke them into following you. That means an orderly and controlled retreat back to our position, as best you can."

The news of the planned sortie spread through the troops.

Overhearing it, Andrew rushed up to Heath. "Major, I'm an outstanding shot, I am. I want to fight, sooner rather than later."

"What's your name, soldier?"

"Corporal McCready, sir. Andrew McCready. I can hit a deer at a hundred and fifty yards and a fast moving fox, turkey or squirrel at fifty, sir."

Major Heath frowned. "Deer and varmint don't shoot back, soldier. Have you done any real fighting?"

"Yes sir. I shot four British at Bladensburg. Two were killed."

"How do you know that?"

"I hit one in the head and the other dead-center in the heart. Sir."

He looked at the eager face in front of him. "Okay, soldier. I'll put you in the sniper squad. I'll see what you can do when the heat's on. Aim at the most senior officers you see once the action starts."

"Thankee, sir. You won't be disappointed."

Heath's troops moved out, his snipers and advance guard in front. Fifteen minutes later, they met British pickets.

"Riflemen, conceal yourselves among the trees. Those who can, climb up your tree for greater visibility. Target any officers you see, from sergeant rank and up. Now go!"

Crouching low, Andrew ran forward with the others, racing in between tree trunks to hide himself behind a massive gnarled oak. Unfortunately, the tree's lower limbs were too high for him to grab ahold of to climb up. He dropped to the ground instead, lying flat with his musket's tip poking through the leaves and grass and aimed at the approaching clusters of British soldiers.

Suddenly, a cacophony of shots broke out on his

left and right, puffs of gray musket smoke streaming into the warm September day.

Cries and shouts and curses filled the air on both sides.

Andrew saw a lieutenant rushing forward, the top of his dinner bib still tucked inside his high collar. He was yelling commands at the men milling around him in confusion.

Andrew took careful sight and squeezed the trigger.

"One down, and more to go," he whispered, his face aglow with excitement.

His musket ball stuck the young officer in his chest, knocking him backwards to the ground. Another volley of shots rang out, most from the Americans, but a few retorts from the scrambling redcoats.

"Bejesus, I don't believe it."

Just then Andrew saw a General—a real British General!—on a great white horse and riding into the midst of the British troops with his mounted escort. His handsome face was stern yet flushed with purpose. Many of the British soldiers turned toward him as he rode in. They recognized him at once. Some shouted hurrahs, energized by his presence. Their leader was with them.

Andrew hurried to reload his gun, hoping to be the one who got him.

He heard two shots from up in a tree. The General swayed in the saddle, blood staining the front of his thick breast coat. He groaned once, called out for help, and sagged heavily, his body toppling over to be caught by a passing soldier before it hit the ground.

Enraged at their loss, the British attacked now with renewed ferocity. A volley of enemy musket fire peppered the limbs above and trunks below. Two young American snipers fell from their tree limbs, killed by the return fire.

Andrew jumped up from his hiding place to join the hasty retreat back to Heath's main force. Another soldier to his right was struck down by a hail of bullets as he fled. The fellow cried out once and tumbled forward.

Andrew couldn't stop to help him. He just kept sprinting, dodging this way and that through the jumble of trees, musket balls zinging past him. Some came close. Most shots missed him by several feet. But one grazed his trousers near the hip bone, tearing a gash in the cloth and burning a red line across his skin.

He ran until he was out of range of their guns.

They were in for it now, he knew. The British would be coming for vengeance as well as conquest!

It was mid-afternoon now. The troops had been arrayed for over an hour in the field. A few men's nerves were such that they soiled themselves in their uniforms waiting for battle. Others were sweating profusely. Still others were clammy cold, shivering even in the soft autumn sun.

Andrew knelt, watching, determined, on the front line of the American formation, his rifle braced across his knee, cocked and ready to aim, as the red-coated British troops advanced in the distance. A heady combination of edginess, energy, and euphoria was building inside him. Only battle would provide release.

The Americans' six cannons had been loaded with pieces of broken locks, nails, horseshoes, and scrap metal, a deadly mishmash designed to tear chunks of flesh out of a man's body.

"Steady, men. Steady," said Sergeant Major O'Hanley. His fat bearded face was streaming sweat despite the cool fall breeze, which was blowing harder as the day progressed.

"Wait 'til you can see the whites of their God-forsaken eyes, lads. Then let all hell break loose upon the devils."

There was a slight wail as the wind picked up and a strong gust rattled the leaves in the tops of the nearby trees. A few birds sang out. Men's bodies twitched with apprehension and anticipation, waiting. More silence.

Suddenly, a few muskets blasted and then the entire front line of soldiers, kneeling, and the second line of troops, standing behind them, emptied their barrels into the approaching red columns sixty yards away. The cannons roared from the back and there was a whistle overhead as twisted metal parts hurled toward the British lines.

And the British ranks returned fire.

Acrid smoke from more than a hundred firing muskets boiled into the swirling wind, overhead. Curses and yells filled the air. Here and there men crumpled to the ground, some staring now with unseeing eyes, others screaming out in intense agony. The anguished howls of pain and suffering of fallen comrades affected those still fighting, assaulting their senses and their nerves.

Och, tis like I'm in the very portals of hell, itself. Steeling himself against the surrounding madness, Andrew kept reloading and firing, reloading and firing until his arms and shoulders ached, making damn sure whoever he aimed at went down.

All at once, the soldier to the left of Andrew cried out. His body jerked backwards as from an invisible force, legs shuddering and blood spewing into the air and onto the ground from a gaping wound in his throat.

Andrew took one look at the poor fellow and paled. It was frightening to see a man die in agony right next to you.

Andrew swallowed hard to calm himself. He gritted his teeth, clinched his eyes shut once, and forced himself back to business.

"Sorry, Benjamin. Tis sorry I am," he said, shaking his head.

There was nothing he could do for the man. His moans soon ceased, relieving Andrew of the burden of hearing him.

He resumed shooting with a vengeance, a fierce resolution upon his handsome countenance.

The intense fighting and shooting continued for

several hours. The two lines did not meet in hand-to-hand combat, but stood firing into each other's ranks, around trees or over open ground.

Without warning, there came a loud commotion from the right side of the American line. Soldiers were beginning to break out of formation and fall back.

The loud voice of Sergeant O'Hanley and some officers could be heard over the din.

"The sneaky bastards have managed to outflank our side, lads. Look sharp now!" O'Hanley's burly figure hustled into view. He waved the men back.

"Retreat, men, but retreat in good order. Keep pouring lead into 'em. Stay steady, lads. We don't want a rout! Keep calm. And keep together."

Andrew drew back with the rest of them. But every dozen yards or so, he'd stop, reload, aim and shoot another Brit down for his fallen comrade Benjamin.

Dusk had begun to fall. Under cover of darkness, General Stricker gathered and withdrew his troops to the main defensive position at Hampstead Hill.

The British didn't pursue them that night.

Chapter 10
RESIDENT SLAVE

"Will they be back soon, do you think, Henry?" Thomas whispered the question to Patterson.

Patterson leaned in close to answer him so the other soldiers couldn't hear him. "They've gone to recruit more braves and talk up the Colonel's plan. They'll be gone two or three days, lad."

Thomas wiped the sweat out of his eyes and rested a few minutes on the handle side of the big ax he'd been wielding. He glanced around to make sure their conversation was not being watched by the leaders of the chopping crew. Patterson seemed unconcerned for himself, but Thomas could get in trouble.

Trouble meant pain.

He'd already earned a few lashes for not working fast enough. He quickly learned to hustle and keep up the pretense of diligence.

Only Patterson was kind to him.

The next morning after his capture, a mere hour after dawn, Thomas had been awakened. Lieutenant

Smith had marched him in front of the officers' quarters with Kingsley and Patterson as guards on either side.

Lieutenant Smith was young, haughty, and disdainful of all Americans. His blond curly locks and sideburns jutted out of his Shako cap which was set at a rakish angle on his head. He would have been handsome except for the pockmarks left on his forehead and cheeks by some dreadful childhood disease.

There was a sneer on his lanky face as he barked his command.

"Will the prisoner step forward?"

Thomas nodded and took one stride. Kingsley took the opportunity to push him in the small of his back, causing him to lose his balance.

Lieutenant Smith either didn't notice or didn't care about the shove.

"The prisoner has been charged with high crime of spying, as our court of inquiry has determined. However, our commander has decided to extend leniency and *not* hang the prisoner. Instead, the prisoner will be sentenced as a common laborer doing whatever is demanded of him by work details, officers of any rank, and other tasks assigned to him."

He looked sternly at the boy. "And if the prisoner fails to do what is asked of him, quickly and precisely, the prisoner can expect harsh corporal punishment for any slovenly work or insolent behavior.

"The prisoner must *not* attempt to escape. Any

attempt will result in capture, torture, and death by hanging, as described in lurid detail by our commander. Does the prisoner understand these terms and conditions of his sentence?"

Thomas gulped. "Yes, sir," he said in a subdued voice.

"That is all. Corporals, do your duty."

They set him to doing the most menial tasks and grueling work; chopping trees, cutting logs, carrying the lumber to the builders, hauling water from the river for the cook and the men to use, digging trenches, playing gofer for the carpenter and his two apprentices, waiting hand and foot on any British officer passing by who wanted something done right then.

In particular, he hated daily latrine duty which included shoveling dirt on top of the open waste in the communal ditch located a hundred yards in the forest downwind from the fort.

The noncom soldiers delighted to take a crap when Thomas was in the middle of this lovely chore, selecting an area he had just covered for their personal business so he would have to do it all over again. "Hey, you! You scum! You missed a spot."

It was beyond humiliating; something he couldn't imagine doing in his past-present world.

One day, two soldiers squatting ten yards apart guffawed at the boy and took turns cracking bad jokes.

"Bloody hell, I can't tell if it's the shit or it's the boy that smells so bad, mate."

The men roared at their own humor.

"These Americans stink worse than the redskins we got hanging around here." The other lowered his voice so that the handful of Indians and the one British officer standing within their line of sight couldn't overhear.

"I say these ex-colonials are not much better than savages and swine themselves, hey, Mason."

"Johnson, you got that right. Cowards and weaklings, the whole lot of 'em—" He strained, getting red in the face. He grunted once and then grimaced with relief as a large stool plopped out. "Whew! Well, they can't fight worth a damn, that's for sure."

"They couldn't even protect their own President and his capital."

The man smirked at the boy, daring him to say something. Thomas remained silent and kept digging clumps of dirt out of the hard grassy turf and shoveling it onto the smelly pit at the opposite end, far away from the two snickering soldiers.

So Thomas was forced to be a slave laborer as well as a prisoner at the fort.

Construction was going on inside the fortress itself and outside, in the land between the fort and the river. Within the fort, more living quarters and supply rooms were being built. Beyond the fort, Thomas helped a crew set up a huge octagon-shaped armory building where an ever expanding cache of magazines and munitions was kept. Circling this weapons depot, the workers set in the ground rings of palisades surrounded by moats as defensive deterrents. An earthen water battery was constructed overlooking the nearby river banks.

Thomas observed that they already had enough weapons and ammunition to field an army four times the size of their current force. "What are they planning on doing?" he asked himself. He'd learned most of the important facts and events of the War of 1812, but this was an episode his history class hadn't covered.

As a twenty-first century American teenager accustomed to constitutional guaranteed liberties and the ease of modern conveniences, both Thomas' body and spirit were brutalized being a slave worker with zero freedom.

Except for the senior officers, who ignored him, the rest of the British with the exception of Henry jeered and insulted him continually. His back, sides, arms, and shoulders ached from all the hard labor. He was tired and discouraged. For the first time, he began to doubt. *Little green book, are you really in charge of my circumstances this adventure?*

But most of all, he was deathly afraid of Charging Bear and Big Wolf.

The fear of them was always on his mind, even though he knew the little green book had kept him safe on his previous trip into the past. But the hulking, sullen presence of the two savages nevertheless made him fantasize just how painful it would feel having his privates cut off and his scalp removed while he was still alive. A hanging was child's play compared to those perceived agonies.

Although Charging Bear and Big Wolf were often gone from the fort, there were constant bands of rough-looking Indians about, both Creek and Seminole braves. The Creeks had lost the battle of Horseshoe Bend where hundreds of warriors had been killed by the combined American, Choctaw and Cherokee forces. Since then, remnants had continued to wander south into Spanish Florida to avoid their enemies but hoping for ultimate revenge.

Most unusual, he thought, Thomas began seeing more, and more, black men arriving at the fort, too. A few had women and children with them. The majority of the men were single. They often came in the middle of the night—alone, or in pairs or small groups.

They had to be escaped slaves, he reasoned. Florida was part of the Deep South.

The ex-slaves' makeshift village outside the compound was growing bigger, week by week. None of the blacks were being forced or even asked to work, he noticed. They were left alone except when there was a meeting. Every once in a while their leaders would meet with the British commanders. It seemed to him they were making future plans together.

He asked Henry about this one day.

Since Patterson felt the idea of Thomas being a spy was far-fetched, he had no problem telling the boy a few general facts. Nothing would come of it, he was sure. He was convinced the boy was harmless; just a poor unfortunate victim in the wrong place at the wrong time in front of the wrong people, he considered.

"Well, boy, Colonel Nicolls is a visionary, he is," Patterson answered. "He hopes to gather an army of the mistreated, the malcontents, and the natural foes of the United States. His goal is to form an army of them, under British leadership of course, to rise up against the Americans. There are hundreds of thousands of slaves in your southland he hopes will revolt. There are also a considerable number of Indian tribes who consider the white man to be their mortal enemy."

"But you're white."

"I'm British, boy. And we're fighting a common opponent: The Americans."

Kingsley passed by right then. "Hey you!" He glared at Patterson without speaking to him. His venom was all for Thomas.

"What the hell are you doing loitering about, you filth? You're a prisoner under condemnation as a spy. Get your lazy arse busy. Or I'll have to report you to the Lieutenant and make sure he dishes out some more punishment. As a sweet reminder, boy. I'll make you wish you'd never been born."

Kingsley stared Patterson down, daring him to take

up for the boy. When Patterson didn't react, he turned back to Thomas, his bloodshot eyes boring holes into the boy. After several seconds, Kingsley stalked away but slammed his meaty shoulder into Thomas as he passed, knocking him hard to the ground.

All the soldiers were bad, but Kingsley was pure evil, in Thomas' opinion. He despised him.

Day after day, for nigh three wretched weeks, Thomas toiled away, becoming more despondent about his own plight and about ever finding Sam. The only good result he could see was his body was getting more muscled and toned with the demanding labor.

Each week seemed like a year to him. At night amidst the dropping temperatures made more uncomfortable by the high humidity and whipping breezes, he shivered under his threadbare covers. He lay in misery on the hard pallet, twisting and turning for hours on the uneven ground. His sleeping spot had been placed by the front gate just inside the walls, so contemptuous were the British that he would try to flee.

Kingsley wished Thomas would escape, so that he could enjoy the torture and hanging soon to follow. The soldier was disappointed morning after morning seeing the boy standing at the end of the chow line for his meager breakfast ration of thin gruel and occasional overcooked fatback from some wild pig the soldiers had killed.

Thomas began having constant thoughts during the day and dreams at night about his dad and sister and missing his old life and friends. The same thing had happened during his first adventure, of course, but this time it was different. It was far worse. He was not in command of the situation in any way that he could see, and he was no longer sure the little green book was in control of his destiny, either.

The uncertainty was mental agony, tougher by far than the physical hardship of the labor.

"Samantha, wherever you are, I just hope you're safe and unharmed." Every night, when alone under his covers, he whispered a prayer for Sam and his family.

Chapter 11
ASSAULT UPON FORT BOWYER

One morning shortly after breakfast, Lieutenant Smith came to talk to Thomas. He personally didn't see the sense of it, but then, orders were orders. His duty was to obey whether he agreed with orders or not.

"Colonel Nicolls is taking part in a coordinated attack upon an American fort. It's on Spanish soil now wrongfully claimed by your government. You will get more details once aboard ship. For reasons of his own, Colonel Nicolls has decided to take you along as his, let's say, man-servant for the expedition. However, during this venture you will still be considered a prisoner of the British Empire condemned under threat of death."

Smith stopped to let his words sink in.

"There will be a large contingent of Indians as part of the military force. Charging Bear and Big Wolf will be leading the native band. So there is no hope of escape for you, lad. None, whatsoever. Unless, of course, you prefer, shall we call it, the *alternative* route to obtaining *ultimate freedom* from this life." Smith grinned evilly. He paused again to savor the effect of his last words on the boy's face. As expected, Thomas grew glum at the news.

"Your party will be traveling on foot following along the Apalachicola River to the mouth of the Gulf. There your party will be picked up by warships of His Majesty's Royal Navy." Smith's chest swelled with noticeable pride at the mention of the British Navy. It was conceded by virtually every civilized nation that Great Britain was the greatest naval power in the world.

"That is all. The expedition will depart in one hour." He turned to go, but then remembered one last stinger.

"Oh, and by the way, boy, en route to the coast, you will be guarded by two Indian braves. Specially assigned for your duty. Cold-blooded they are. Take great delight in relieving captives of certain portions of their anatomy. Quite good at it, too, I'm told," Lieutenant Smith sneered at Thomas and spun on his heel to leave.

The next hour Thomas's brain filled with nightmarish thoughts, each one scarier than the previous. He tried to control his mind, but he was panicked.

He now had no confidence in the little green book. His goose was cooked. He felt forsaken, without hope, without family, friends or his girl, in a cruel time two hundred years past.

"Lad, I just heard the camp gossip." Patterson came up to Thomas' side and leaned over, whispering. "It could be worse, you know. You could be left here for Kingsley and the others to torment you." Patterson nodded.

"At least with Colonel Nicolls, you'll be safe. He knows what he's about and I doubt he'd put you into the thick of the battle anyway. You're not a soldier trained to fight."

He nudged Thomas' elbow. "Just relax. Think of it as a vacation from nasty latrine duty and all the rest of the unpleasantries."

Thomas breathed out, heavily. "Thanks, Henry, for the encouragement. I'll do my best to not freak out."

"Freak out? I'm not familiar with that saying, lad." Patterson shook his head with a bewildered grin. "Is that an American figure of speech?"

I can't use modern slang, Thomas reminded himself. "Oh, never mind, Henry. It just means, I'll try not to worry too much."

"Right. Fine. Well . . . good luck, lad." Patterson gave him a cheerful wink and strode off for his day's duties.

That day, he marched with the rest of the expedition with the two Indian guards by his side. Even when he had the call of nature, they followed him to his spot and watched as he did his business. It was humiliating and unsettling at the same time. He couldn't help having crazy thoughts about them slicing off his thing as he peed in front of them.

Finally, by late afternoon they arrived at the shore a mile north of the marshy mouth of the river as it dumped into the Gulf. He could see four large ships of war anchored two hundred yards off in the water, pitching gently in the calm waves. Soon a flotilla of rowboats came to pick them up.

Thomas was put in the same boat as Colonel Nicolls and his entourage. His two guards were no longer with him; they rode in another boat filled with Indians.

Thank goodness. They were scary.

The salty breeze and fading sunlight felt wonderful on his face and neck as the sailors rowed the short distance through the placid, bluish green ocean.

Once board their ship, which Thomas learned was the HMS Hermes, the flagship of the small fleet, Colonel Nicolls beckoned him over. Thomas noticed his cheeks and forehead looked flush and the Colonel seemed sluggish in his movements and speech. Thomas wondered if he was sick or something.

"Remember at all times, boy, that you are still a condemned war criminal accused of spying against his Majesty. This expedition is merely a reprieve from your sentence of forced labor at Fort Prospect Bluff," Nicolls growled in his deep voice. "In the interim, you will act as my man-servant. You will be available at my call anytime night or day. If you do not perform to my expectations," he hesitated for effect, "you could get lashes." He gave Thomas a grim look.

"Yes, sir," Thomas said meekly. The man was frightening enough, what with his long heavy beard, piercing eyes, and commanding presence.

"Your first assignment is to see the steward of this ship, bring me a hot toddy of brandy with molasses added, come find me in my quarters, and tell me what you know about the Americans' defenses of Mobile Bay."

"Yes, sir," gulped Thomas, not knowing what in the world he could tell the man that would be truthful or satisfy him. All he knew about Mobile was three facts: It's a present day city in the state of Alabama; it was an important port city during the Civil War; and that it's located near the Gulf Coast. Being from Tennessee, he never had much interest or need to learn about Alabama.

Little green book, if you're still there, help me!

Thomas found the ship's steward and got the toddy mixed. The man was an older seaman. He had pure white sideburns and bushy hair around his sides and back of his head. But the top of his pate was shiny bald. He was garrulous and friendly to Thomas. The fact that Thomas was a condemned spy didn't seem to bother him in the least.

"Aye, I was born in Lancaster. A beautiful old city by the sea coast. Haven't been back, though, since I left me home as a young lad. About your age, matter o' fact."

He handed a huge shot glass, filled to the top, to Thomas with a big grin. "Governor, this'll put the color back in the Colonel's face or I'm a two-faced monkey.

"Ahhh, tis good to be sailing again. On the move. By the way, me name's Jim. You're Thomas, I'm told."

"Yes sir."

"Oh, no formality with me, young mate. So, you're a hardened criminal are you?" he said with a chuckle.

"Not really, sir. I mean, Jim. I was wrongly accused."

"Aren't we all, lad? Aren't we all, every mother's son of us!"

The steward directed Thomas to the officer's quarters located in the aft section. There were two identical rooms, the man explained. Captain Percy had the one room. Colonel Nicolls, as the visiting officer, would be given the other.

To Jim, used to sleeping in a sagging hammock along with other junior officers who had their own hanging beds in the fore section, the officer's quarters seemed luxurious. For his group, every night brought constant swinging as the hammocks rolled side to side with each pitch of the waves.

When Thomas knocked on the door, he heard Colonel Nicolls call out from the opposite room. "In here, boy."

Oops, wrong room.

Opening the other door, Thomas saw that the tiny room had a narrow bunk built into the wall, and a little table with two chairs set in the middle of the room. The Colonel was sitting at the table.

Thomas thought the Hermes was very, very small compared to modern vessels. *This thing is half the size of the swimming pool on the Royal Caribbean.*

"Come inside, boy," Nicolls barked. Thomas

stepped in and handed the Colonel the toddy. Nicolls took two small sips, savoring the mellowness of the brandy and molasses mixed together.

He still didn't look well to Thomas.

Nicolls took more a few more nips, swishing the fiery blend against his tongue before slowly swallowing.

Finally, he looked up.

"Well, lad, I think you know why I brought you on this trip, hey." He eyed Thomas with stern expression. "Now down to business! My supposition is that you've traveled as a seaman or crewmen on vessels belonging to privateers plying their illegal trade all up and down the coast. These are individuals working insidiously against the interests of Great Britain, Young though you may be, I suspect you know much more than you let on."

He stared at Thomas. "What do you about know about the American defenses of the Bay of Mobile?"

At that moment a wholly unexpected, previously unknown, but situation-saving fact flashed into Thomas' brain. *Fort Bowyer*.

It was all Thomas needed to improvise.

"Fort Bowyer, sir," he answered.

Nicolls leaned forward. "Yes?"

"It's, uh, it's . . . well, it's heavily fortified, sir."

He nodded. "The American troops are stronger than you think."

He didn't know this to be true, but it sounded good. And besides, it might give the British second thoughts about their planned attack.

"Heavily protected, you say?" The Colonel was very interested now. "How so?"

"I don't know all the details, sir. But I've just heard from numerous sources that the Americans have been very busy strengthening their position there."

He was silent, hoping that his gambit was paying off. After all, Nicolls has already tried and condemned him as a spy. Why not act the part now, he reasoned.

The Colonel leaned back in his chair, a look of concentration on his face. He stared at the wall above the boy's head for several long seconds.

"Good. Very good. That's useful information. If you continue to give me details like this, I may be willing to commute your sentence somewhat, boy."

He waved Thomas away. "That's all for now. You may go."

As he walked out and shut the door to the room, Thomas broke into a huge smile. A sailor hurrying by saw his grin and wandered what he was up to.

"Yea. So, little green book, you're still with me after all," he said. More than anything else that had happened yet on this adventure, the sudden insertion of the thought, *Fort Bowyer*, gave him hope. If the green book was still working, that meant it was still in control.

For the first time, Thomas breathed easier.

That night, the ships sailed due west. They followed the shore line on the starboard side. Thomas could make out the shadowy silhouette of land in the darkness. Well before dawn, they reached their destination and anchored off the coast. The soldiers and sailors were all hands on deck.

Nicolls motioned, snapping his fingers and growling at the boy standing nearby.

"Here, sir." Thomas hurried over. He was groggy with sleep, hungry, thirsty, had to pee in the worst way, and was chilled with the pre-dawn winds blowing off the sea.

He followed the Colonel into his boat along with the other men; his legs were stiff from the cold and shivering a bit as he clambered down. The last two men into their boat carefully lowered a 5½-inch howitzer hauled from ropes off the side of the Hermes. Their little boat bobbed in the waves and the wooden bottom creaked and moaned under the combined weight of its occupants as it moved.

Within minutes a large fleet of rowboats floated in the bay. Soon all were headed for land.

During that night, Thomas had overhead sailors talking as he'd lain down to sleep on the crowded deck. Several dozens of British Royal Marines had made their own pallets all across the deck so that there was barely room to move, bow to stern.

"I'll be glad when we get all these bastards off our ships," said one sailor, cursing under his breath. "I heard there're hundred and thirty Marines, about a hundred Spanish, and nearly six hundred of the Indian buggers."

"Well, at least we're not carrying those savages on

board the Hermes. Some of those redskin devils I saw crawling over the sides of the Sophie and Carron are enough to give you the shivers. That big chief, the one they Charging Bear. He sets my teeth on edge just to look at him. God help whoever he gets ahold of. There won't be enough body parts left to take prisoner once he's through cutting and hacking."

"Aye, mate. Our own Marines are bad enough. Arrogant lads, every blasted one of them."

Once the entire force was safety landed on the shore, Nicolls gathered all the men about him and gave instructions. The Indians stood outside the circle scarcely paying attention; their methods of fighting were their own.

"Where we're standing is about eight or nine miles to the east of the American fort. We'll march in and attack first by land. If we're successful, there'll be no naval bombardment necessary. While we may not have the element of surprise, we do considerably outnumber the enemy. Hence, I expect and demand the utmost dedication of purpose and courage in battle.

"Commanders, organize into your groups and head out."

Nicolls, however, stood rooted at his spot while the men about him gathered into squadrons and units.

"Boy! Prisoner!" he yelled out.

Thomas rushed up to him.

"I'd hoped to recuperate with a good night's rest. But most unfortunately, it seems . . . it seems that I'm still incapacitated." He caught his breath. "Unable to continue on this expedition." He leaned forward, putting his hands on his knees.

"In regards to you, your choices are thusly. You can come back to the ship with me. Or you can stay with the expedition under the watch of Big Wolf and Charging Bear. I leave it to you to decide, boy."

Thomas made his choice quickly. Staying with the attack force, there was a chance, however slim, of getting away. On the boat out on the sea, there was no hope of escape.

"I'll stay," he said.

Nicolls nodded and called out for the two Indians. They looked even more frightening close up. Hulking shadows in the pre-dawn light.

Nicolls went back to the Hermes. Thomas was forced into a trot to keep up with Charging Bear and Big Wolf. Their long-limbed effortless strides equaled one and a half of his normal steps, so he had to jog the entire nine miles. Past the beach, into the tall forests, through constant brush, wet marshy ground, heavy ground cover, and maddening thickets that entangled his feet and scratched his legs and arms.

Gosh, I thought I was in good shape before. Lacrosse, doing wind sprints for coach, even running a 10K, is child's play compared to this, Thomas thought as he wheezed and fought for breath, fighting his way through undergrowth and dodging in between trees. The two Indians seemed unaffected. He suspected they could travel all day at the same pace without tiring.

All too soon the expedition reached the outskirts of the fort and the soldiers and Indians began to assemble into battle lines.

There was no time even for Thomas to catch his wind. His heart rate was still racing from the exertion of the nine mile run when the commands was given.

"Charge!"

"Ataque!"

The Indians said nothing. Each group of natives moved silently, sleekly, forward by tribe.

Thomas stayed with the Seminoles, in between Charging Bear and Big Wolf. He had no choice. They ran half speed. He sprinted to keep pace.

The ground leading up to the landward side of the fort offered little cover. The land was flat. No trees. No brush. No gullies or hills.

It was a killing field.

Two hundred yards. One hundred and fifty yards. One hundred yards and closing fast.

The American battery opened fire with deadly intent. Seventy yards out and their troops began a barrage of rifle fire with withering impact.

Up and down their ranks, the Indians yelled their blood-curdling war cry. They quickened their pace the closer they got. But already, one in ten was down. More were falling.

Beside him, Big Wolf's head exploded, covering Thomas in a gory spray of skull fragments, gray brain chunks, scalp hair, and skin. A cannonball had hit him in the very center of his forehead.

Seeing this, Charging Bear screamed his hatred of the white Americans and ran full tilt now, leaving Thomas behind.

Thomas slowed, running just fast enough to keep from being trampled by those behind him. Instinctively, he began angling toward his left, glancing over his shoulder for oncoming Indians. He dodged between the hordes of maddened braves. He collided with one man, knocking him down while he lost his balance. But he kept on weaving among the rushing figures until the mass of bodies thinned out. Finally, he was alone on the edge of battle, watching the lurid scene before him, of figures stopped in their tracks by some blow, others falling down with mortal wound, a few pitching forward to the ground in fear.

War is ugly. War is brutal.

Suddenly, unexpectedly, Thomas felt dizzy.

This can't be happening, can it? A familiar haze surrounded his senses and filled his mind. The battlefield began disappearing before him in a white mist.

"No, not again! Green book, not *now*!"

Too late.

He felt his body falling down, down, down.

Chapter 12
THE FLAG IS STILL THERE

That morning, a relentless booming noise began. It shook the walls of the old place. All around the room, Sam could see little puffs of dust being stirred up by the jarring.

Soon she was sneezing so much she scarcely could catch her breath. Finally, she got her sniffles under control.

The pounding sounds puzzled Samantha greatly.

Arching her back to relieve muscles stiff from over an hour of leaning over the wash, she stopped working, taking the opportunity to wipe away the beads of sweat dripping down her bangs and forehead onto her nose and cheeks. The sweat was caked with dirt from the fresh clouds of dust.

Ewww, that's disgusting.

She looked over at her companion.

"What's that sound?"

Margaret knew, but she was too frightened to answer Sam. Instead, the girl wrung her hands and dabbed at her eyes filled with tears of terror.

When the unknown disturbance began, the two girls were busy hand-washing garments, as usual, pulling and scrubbing from their mounds of dirty clothes piled beside their big buckets of soapy hot water.

Sam listened more intently now, her curiosity piqued. Each boom was too dull, its duration too short, and the overall pattern far too regular to be thunder, she decided.

She racked her brain.

"It's cannons, isn't it!" she called out, remembering it was the same sounds she'd heard when she first appeared in the capital city.

"That's what it is. The British are bombarding us. They're . . . they're shooting at Fort McHenry, aren't they?" she said, recalling her history classes of the school semester. She was rather proud she remembered *something* from all her studying for the upcoming test.

Just then Angela came into the room with Ham padding behind her.

"We're in for it now, girls. Ohhh, may the Good Lord above spare us. If they break through, there's no telling what they'll do."

Angela shook her head in dismay. "Why, the whole city's a hotbed of privateers, all a looting and attacking British ships the past two years. They call us damned pirates anyway. They plan to burn the city down to the ground and rape all the women and children."

"I don't think they'll get through our defenses,

Angela. In fact, I'm sure of it," said Sam in a matter-of-fact tone.

"And how do you know, girl?" Angela turned toward Sam with a whitened face, agitated, hands on her ample hips. "How would you know anything? What? Because that handsome chuck-about, Andrew, has been filling your ears with all his brave talk?"

Of course they couldn't know what she knew—their events and outcomes had already been cast in history long ago. She understood nothing yet about the little green book and how it worked. But somehow, deep in her being, she just knew that history would not and could not be altered.

Ham had started his staring routine, oblivious to his wife's presence. Angela was so flustered about the British bombardment, she didn't notice or care.

The old coot kept feasting his eyes.

Geez, I've got to get out of here before I lose my temper and slap him a good one.

"Well. If we're going to be overrun by British soldiers anyway, there's no sense in Margaret and I continuing to wash these clothes, is there? After all," Samantha gave Angela a cool look, "our houses might be burned to the ground and all of us fleeing for our lives by nightfall.

"What's say, Margaret? Want to join me for a nice walk outside? I'd like to see all the action. If redcoats are coming, it's better to be outside where we can run away than stay here. Cooped up. Trapped in the house. Waiting for them to bang the door down."

Margaret let out a strangled cry and gave Sam a most pitiful look.

"It's okay, sweetie. Come on. Go with me. I'll keep you safe. I've been dying to see something besides these four walls for the past several weeks and now's my chance."

"Why, you ungrateful little—"

"Stop right there, Mrs. Sampson," Samantha cut her off. When badly treated, Sam took abuse just so long before she fought back. Angela was a hard taskmaster, never satisfied, always complaining. That night Sam had cut her hair had only brought the girls a short reprieve from her sharp words.

"I've paid you for every week. In cash. Plus I've worked my fingers to the bone in forced labor to make up for the rest of whatever it is you say I owe."

She folded her arms and stared Angela down.

"We'll make a deal. If the British don't overrun and torch everything around us and I'm still in town, I'll eat my words. I'll come back and continue to pay you and work for you. But on *this* day, a day you feel might be our last I'll not be stuck here like a trapped animal."

She started at once for the door, turning to face the other girl before walking out. "I'm leaving, Margaret. Are you coming with me or not?"

Margaret glanced at her second cousin, once

removed, whose countenance still showed shock from Sam's saucy attitude. "I . . . I don't know . . ."

"It's now or never, girlfriend. Better coming with me than bending over a wash bucket for the next eight hours. I've got money. We can eat. It might be a nice day outside. We won't know if we stay inside, will we?" she smiled at Margaret.

"Oh, alright. I'll come," she scurried over to Sam's side like a scared rabbit.

Samantha grinned at the two adults standing there with their mouths open.

"Don't wait up now. We may out be out late with boyfriends. And if the British come knocking, tell them we think they've got silly accents and really bad teeth and stupid humor. Oh, and their breath stinks, too."

The girls went out and the door slammed shut.

Sam was disappointed. It wasn't a beautiful day; it was rainy-misty, but mainly foggy. The morning sun tried to peak out of overcast skies above with a few rays sneaking through in between the slight bursts of showers. But the sea winds were fresh and invigorating.

Doesn't matter. Time to party and cut loose.

The British weren't going to win, so why not have some fun. She giggled to herself.

Samantha walked a few yards down the street, and then stopped. She sniffed the air and looked up at the gray sky and stretched her arms out. It felt so good to get out of that dump, she thought. Margaret halted beside her but didn't do any of those things.

"Okay, girl. Which way to Hamp Hill? Or whatever Andrew called it?" she said without glancing at Margaret. "I want to go where the action is."

"He said it was Hampstead Hill. But I don't rightly know where, miss. I've been to the city the one time before and that was to visit Angela when I was a child."

"Hey, you!" Sam called out to a dapper looking middle-aged gentleman passing by. "Yes, you. Can you tell us how to get to Hampstead Hill?"

The man assumed they had to be servant girls by their clothes and the damp splotches all over the front of their blouses and dresses. Yet he was courteous nonetheless.

"Washer women, I presume? And why, pray tell, would the two of you desire to *head* toward danger as opposed to away from it?" His words were plain-spoken but he smiled kindly at them.

"We have a friend who's a soldier. His name is Andrew. We have the day off and we thought we'd go watch our boys beat the British," said Sam.

"In that case, the Reverend Percival Bartholomew Langley at your service, young ladies," he bowed with a flourish and beamed at them. "Patriots, I see. Two pretty patriots at that, but of course the beauty inside is always more important than the beauty outside, isn't it?

"Patriotism. Quite an admirable trait. By all

means, let me change my course and lead you to your destination. After all, bravery is not found alone in the male of our species, is it?"

This guy's a real talker, thought Sam. "Sure, we'd be grateful if you could show us the way."

He led them in the opposite direction for several blocks before turning on a major street heading east. His stride was slow but purposeful. He whistled tunes as he walked; a few melodies of which Samantha recognized as old-time boring hymns they sung now and then in her modern day Methodist church.

They passed by a man sitting with his back against the building wall. His head was down and he appeared to be talking to himself. He wore a threadbare dirty overcoat that had many tears here and there and patches on the bigger rips. Sam suspected he was the equivalent of an 1814 homeless person; a street beggar.

Seeing him, the Reverend halted and fished in his trousers for some coins.

"Here you go, Angus. This time make sure you spend it on bread and not the devil's liquor. Children, allow me to introduce you. This is Robert Angus Smith, a brave veteran of the late War of Independence. He has fallen into hard times in the passing years, but we do what we can to help lift him up, body and soul.

"Angus, the widow woman Mrs. Anderson says to tell you to come by her abode after church next Sunday and she will feed you a nourishing meal."

"Ah, wuzzat? Whud ye say, Reverend?" Angus was busy patting and feeling the outside of his old coat, trying to find the pocket opening to put his new money in.

"I said, my dear Angus, that the widow Mrs. Anderson told me to tell you to come by her place next Sunday and she'll have a nice dinner prepared."

"Dat's good. Dat's good. Sweet old lady. Yessir."

He looked up. "Say, uh, where, where ye be a goin', Reverend?" His speech and eyes were already blurred and it wasn't ten o'clock in the morning.

"I'm escorting these two young ladies to the front lines. They desire to see our lads whip the British good and proper, they do."

"I fought in the big war. Fought real good, too. I know sumthin' 'bout soldiering. Say, I'm a, I'm a gonna come wid ye, Reverend. Jest, jest wait a minute. Wait fo' me."

The man rolled forward onto his hands and knees from a sitting position where he had been slouching against the brick wall. He tried to lift an unsteady leg to put one foot on the ground, but his foot slid. He tried again. The third time, he succeeded. Next, he put his hand on his knee to help straighten and raise his body up. But his hand slipped, bumping his red nose on the side of his kneeling leg.

He smiled a toothless grin. "'Tis hard, so early in the mornin', Reverend."

The girls stood watching. Sam was amused. The reverend waited patiently.

Finally, the man made it up, although his legs were shaky. He reached out and put a hand on Reverend Langley's shoulder to steady himself.

"Gimme a moment and I'll be ready to go." He gave another toothless beam at the girls as Langley held his elbow to help get him moving forward.

They started down the avenue together.

Now that Samantha was out of the gloomy confines of the house, away from Angela's sharp tongue, the rest of Baltimore looked quaint to her in morning mist. Picturesque. Almost charming viewed from the outside. They passed building after building. She tried to imagine being on a vacation by herself in the past-present year of 2013, visiting an old sea resort on the east coast. The illusion helped Sam forget for a moment she was in the year 1814. It made the cloudy morning seem a little fresher and more hopeful.

After walking several miles, winding through the Baltimore streets and leaving the city proper behind, they could see ahead of them a huge semicircle of men. Most were standing, alert. A few were sitting. Fewer still were lying on the ground, sleeping or relaxing. All, however, had rifles and other weapons with them. The tops of the sandy brown earthen bulwarks beyond peered over the heads of the soldiers. There appeared to be thousands of men to Sam. The mass of bodies continued into the distance in either direction.

If the British hoped to invade by land, they would be hard put, indeed, to defeat such a large and entrenched army, Sam thought.

They approached within fifty yards of the outermost groups of soldiers, and Samantha changed her mind.

"Reverend Langley," she said sweetly, "I really appreciate you bringing us all the way out here. But we'll never find Andrew in this crowd. Plus we can't see the fighting anyway with all the bodies blocking the view. Why don't we go back to the city, instead? If you have time to join us for lunch, I'll treat everyone. I have some money. You're invited as well, Angus.

"After lunch, I'd like to go where I can see Fort McHenry instead."

Langley bowed and sighed exaggeratedly.

"Ah, the whims of the female race, Angus. Changeable as the wind itself! Of course, one would be wise not to repeat those words to Mrs. Langley, the missus. Best not to stir up the nest, as they say.

"Yes, yes, our best is never quite good enough," he laughed and winked at the girls. "To wit, another adventure awaits us. Come, young ladies. You, too, Angus. I know an unpretentious inn by the bay that serves passable fare. But more importantly, it offers an excellent view of the harbor including our stalwart fortress. Keep your fortune to yourself, young miss. This day, I'll buy substance enough for everyone present."

With that, he turned jauntily around. They began to retrace their steps back into the city.

The return walk was both breezy and rainy. Even Langley grew silent in the face of the wind-blown sporadic sprinkles. The two girls had no coats or slickers of any kind and so they were damp head to toe by the time they reached the inn.

"Ah, here we go, young ladies." The reverend held the big oak door open wide for the girls and smiled as Angus shuffled inside.

Reverend Langley brightened at the sight. Though it wasn't cold outside, the owner, Edgar Bluetooth, had lit up the two large stone fireplaces to warm up guests from the off again, on again showers of the day. There was one placed at either end. The heavy logs were blazing and cracking in each, spreading heat and a pleasant yellowish light around the great room.

Nice! Just the thing to break this chill. Sam was so glad to get inside out of the weather where it was cozy and dry.

The establishment set on a busy street facing the harbor, just as the reverend had said. Called the Pacing Pony, it offered sleeping rooms to passing travelers on the second story. Sam thought it quaint with its own musty charm. The morning crowd had thinned out, leaving a few men, eating and drinking alone or in company, scattered among the old oak dining tables that were scarred and scratched with age and use.

Half of the patrons lounged back in their chairs, relaxing and smoking their pipes after their meals. Curling strands of thick smoke rose into the ceiling rafters, filling the room with a menagerie of pungent odors, some quite pleasant and some quite offensive to the uninitiated nose of Samantha.

"Master Bluetooth! So thoughtful of you to light the fireplaces on such a damp windy day. The ladies and I thank you, sir." Langley gave his usual bow which Edgar ignored.

I guess everyone else thinks he's as big a blowhard as I do, thought Sam, watching the slight grimace on Bluetooth's face.

"Yes, yes, this way, girls."

The reverend led them to a table nearest the opposite fireplace, taking care to sit at the chair closest to the comforting heat of the roaring blaze.

After the pitiful meals and gloominess of Angela's place, Sam viewed the inn as a major improvement. Although she had not been starving at Angela's, the impromptu meals brought to them by Andrew had made a huge difference. The inn's fare looked tempting when it was set on the table.

"This looks good, reverend. Thank you."

"Yes, thank you, kind sir."

Angus said nothing; his mouth already so full he couldn't speak even if he wanted.

"You ladies are most welcome. And Angus, remember," the reverend gave him a disapproving glance, "we must pray before eating, giving thanks to the Lord above for our bounty here." He waited for Angus to chew and swallow his big bite.

"Let us say grace."

Everyone bowed their heads except for Langley and Angus, who kept staring with longing at the food on his plate. Knowing his friend so well, the reverend clucked his tongue. He reached over, placing his hand on Angus's head and forcing it down. He then bowed his own head.

"Oh, Lord, we thank you for the feast you have made possible. We thank you for your love and for taking care of our earthy needs. I pray your blessing and strength upon our brave lads in their battle for virtue and country. Above all, Heavenly Father, we thank you for the gift of your precious Son, Jesus, and the price He paid on Calvary for our sins and shortcomings. This we pray in the name of Jesus. Amen!"

Wow. Long grace. Samantha was ready to dig into the inn's fare with a hunger that surprised her.

It was bland but filling: Ham slices, cold potatoes, kidney beans, fresh corn, bread baked that morning, now cold but still chewy, and stout mugs of ale for all.

She belched after the meal and reddened, popping

her hand over her mouth. "Oh, excuse me. Where are my manners?"

She was embarrassed, but the others seemed to pay it no mind, as if girls and women burping and belching at their repast was a common thing.

Once the meal was over, the others stood up, ready to go.

"Well, I've overspent my morning a wee bit. I must get back to the parsonage and begin working on my sermon for Sunday. You, ah, you young ladies are most cordially welcome to attend our services at First Congregational Methodist Church on Waverly Street in downtown. Ten o'clock sharp." Langley waited, hopeful.

Sam spoke up. "I think I'll stay here, at least for tonight. You said this place has bedrooms to rent. Right, reverend? I appreciate the offer to visit your church. But I'm not sure where I'll be. Margaret, how about you?"

She pulled on a fallen lock of hair. "I'm going to go back to Angela's. I've got no place to go to." She seemed afraid of hurting Sam's feelings. "I'm so sorry, miss."

Sam nodded. "Fine. Sure. Do what you gotta do, girl."

The reverend bowed once again before leaving. "It was a pleasure meeting you and being of some service, young lady. I pray God's richest blessings upon you. Come, Angus. Time to depart. You, miss, may walk with us as far as it serves your purpose. You know your way around the city, do you?"

"Pretty good, sir. Thank you, but I'm sure I'll find my way." Margaret still looked like a frightened rabbit.

Finally, after a few more goodbyes, they left. Sam walked over to Bluetooth and inquired about a room.

"It's a dollar a night and that includes dinner and breakfast," he said, eyeing her washer woman uniform with a disbelieving scowl. "Payable in advance."

"Yes, I've got the money," Sam said, not bothering to hide her annoyance at the man's lack of respect. She dug in her skirt pocket and pulled out a silver dollar coin.

He looked at the money in her hand with an equal mixture of surprise and scorn. She could tell he thought she'd earned it as a woman of ill repute. He leered at her and yelled up the stairs. "Hump! Hump, come down here. Right now. We've got another, ah, another *honored guest* for the night," he said, forcing himself to give Sam a crooked smile.

Presently, a man came rushing, almost monkey-style, down the stairs. His legs and upper body was deformed and he indeed had a noticeable lump just below his neck, causing a large budge in the back of his shirt. His speech was a bit slurred, as well. Samantha had to listen closely to understand what he was saying.

"Let mees takth yourth things to yourth roomsy," he said, looking around for her luggage.

"I don't have anything to carry. Sir," Sam added, very respectfully. "It's just me."

She had a cousin that had Down syndrome and also had a friend whose little brother was mentally challenged. Samantha always treated them with the utmost kindness and courtesy.

"Show her to her room, Hump," growled Bluetooth.

Hump nodded at his boss and waved a hand for Sam to follow him. She noticed he had bent fingers. "Disth way, missy. I takth youth there."

When they got to her room at the end of the hall, right side, Sam reached in her pocket again. She seized several coins, pulling them out into the palm of her hand to find a quarter to give to Hump.

"This is for you, Hump. You don't have to give this to Bluetooth. I'm giving it to you to keep. It belongs to you," she repeated herself to make sure he got the message.

Hump stared at the coin for several seconds, making Sam think he didn't comprehend. But finally, he broke into a jagged tooth smile as big and happy as could be.

"Mees keeps sith. Yess, Hump keeps sith." He nodded vigorously and continued nodding his head at her as he backed away from the door.

"You're welcome, Hump. Thank you very much for taking me to my room. Bye, bye now." She waved at him.

Hump smiled even bigger and turned to go down the hall.

"He's a real sweetheart. I hope old Bluetooth doesn't treat him too badly." The thought made Sam angry for a minute. She hated intolerance and meanness in people. She despised bullies of all stripes and sizes.

It was now mid-afternoon. Sam had nothing to do but wait for nighttime to fall asleep. Walking around the edge of the bed to the wall—"At least, it's got a window."—she peeked out.

"Whoa! The room's nothing to write home about. But the view . . . the view is just spectacular."

Before her delighted eyes was a panoramic scene of much of the bay, including the awesome sight of Fort McHenry on its little peninsula jutting into the harbor. Even in the broad daylight, she could see the dark bursts of smoke appearing and disappearing like a patchwork from the continuing bombardment by the British fleet offshore.

The constant thunder of the cannons had already become a background noise in her brain. She didn't even notice the booming anymore, her ears were so accustomed to the sound.

She lay on the bed in the stuffy little room. Without her willful permission, her mind began questioning the futility of getting back to the past-present. Back to her real home with family and friends. Back to the twenty-first century.

"I can't think about it. I'll go crazy if I dwell on the future." But no matter how much Sam tried to block out such unwelcome and unhappy thoughts, her brain continued to pump out a maddening queue of 'What If's' and 'How Come's' and 'What To Do's' into her conscious being. Sam was normally quite optimistic. Alone, in her room, the unending stream of questions all without satisfactory answers got to her.

She began crying, erupting into uncontrollable sobbing. She cried so hard, she got a tremendous headache and her eyes throbbed with swollenness. Finally, Sam had no more tears left to shed.

It was no use. She had no one to talk to. Nowhere to go for relief. No plan of attack. No solution to the problem.

"I've got no way out of this mess. I've just got to roll with the punches . . . until somehow . . . some way . . . . I can find an answer that will take me back home."

Right then, the image of the little green book floated across her mind. It puzzled her and made her mad at the same time. *It was all that stupid book's fault!* Yet once her flash of temper had flared and gone, the picture of the little green book gave her unexpected hope and comfort. Why, she didn't know.

Exercise had always helped her in the past when she became discouraged or frustrated. So despite her pounding head, Samantha got down on the floor and began doing repeated stretching, yoga, leg lifts, girl pushups, and tummy crunches. After that, she did hard aerobics and jogging in place.

Sam's head throbbed with renewed pain but she ignored it. She pushed herself until she was past fatigue.

Dusk was approaching and the shadows began lengthening in the little room. Throwing her exhausted form onto the bed, Sam took the cool soft pillow and rested it upon her forehead. It helped ease the pain of the headache some.

She fell, exhausted, into the deepest sleep. Without dreams, without wakening. She slept until just before sunrise.

She awoke refreshed. Renewed. All negative thoughts of defeat and failure were gone. Sam sat up in bed and stretched prodigiously, then remembered.

Instantly, she hopped up and dashed to the window. "Yes! Yes! It *is* still there!"

Her eyes were riveted upon Fort McHenry. A huge American flag waved, undaunted, in the early morning mist. The sea winds whipped its end to and fro with vigor. Red cannon fire and black smoke burst toward it and all around it.

Yet the flag of young America—*her* America in the future—was still flying high, proud, and glorious!

The flag was still there. In that moment, Sam was the proudest she'd ever been to be an American citizen. Land of the free and home of the brave!

Chapter 13
PIRATE RULES

When Thomas awoke from the mist this time, he didn't have to look far to hazard a guess about his newfound situation. Right in front of him stood a group of pirates arguing among themselves, swearing, and pointing out to sea.

"Curse the Americans! I've got no place on this blasted excuse o' an island to hide me spoils what I got from the last raid." He jerked his thumb at the ocean beyond. "Got to keep it out of their greedy hands. Besides which, I can't be a leavin' the missus and the brat right now. Arghhh, she's a saucy young wrench. Hot blooded woman she is. Had the cheek to tell me—tell me, the great Adolphe Toussaint!—that she'd find herself a better man if I left them again."

"Maybe they're only interested in hunting down *his* treasure and capturing *him*. Maybe they'll leave the rest o' us be," said another brigand, lowering his voice conspiratorially. He jerked his head in the same direction. "Not all o' us work for *him*."

"Yes and maybe cows can fly, too. I tell you the Americans will take everything back they can find, whether it's part of the brothers' loot or ours."

Thomas glanced down. Yep. He had pirate clothes on, too. Being a smart history student, he connected the dots. *War of 1812. Buccaneers. Has to be Jean Lafitte's gang.*

Gazing into the distance, he saw, like two heavyweight boxers, a row of pirate ships in the bay facing off against vessels-of-war flying the American colors. He began counting. There were nine, no, make that ten, pirate ships all in a line. Versus a fleet of four . . . five . . . make that six U.S. warships.

The American ships were firing. Heavily, too, it seemed, from the constant spurts of fire and smoke coming from their cannons. The pirate ships were offering no resistance that he could see, except for blocking the attackers' path ashore.

Other than the one-sided battle going on in the waters and the constant yammering of the nearby arguing men, the scene before him was almost idyllic. A perfectly calm and peaceful day, Thomas thought. The late morning sun was shining in a glorious blue sky. The wind was blowing crisp and clean, but not too hard. The melodic sound of the waves breaking on the near shores was soothing.

As Thomas continued watching this breathtaking scene, he spotted boats being lowered from the sides of the pirate vessels, each boat crammed with little figures of men, hurrying into place. Suddenly, on several of the pirate vessels orangey yellow flames shot up, licking the bottom of the sails and roaring across the dry pitted timber of the deck.

The resulting smokescreen and the distraction of prize vessels ablaze hid the hasty retreat of the rowboats from the prying eyes of the attackers. Lafitte's pirate crews were craftily making their successful escape out of the very jaws of defeat. They were determined not to fire upon the Americans but equally determined to make their getaway.

The first of the escapee boats from the pirate ships hit the shore just as the Americans began aiming cannon shots at the village compound itself. Thomas heard the ominous sound of the heavy cast balls as they whistled overhead and everyone ducked or dropped to the ground.

He turned to see where the cannon blasts were landing. One struck a wall of a spacious mansion on a lush hilltop. From it, a solitary figure soon rushed forth heading for the beach. The men from the boats leaped out to see their captain Jean Lafitte coming toward them in great haste.

"Ahoy, men. Make haste. We must away to Grand Isle. There are boats and small vessels aplenty on the other side of Grande Terre. More than enough for all of us. Take whatever possessions you can carry on your person."

He stroked his goateed chin, pondering. "Once the Americans leave their destruction, mes l'amis, we'll return and set up camp again. However, sooner or later," he sighed, "I'll have to go to New Orleans to plead in person with General Jackson. I would rather have the Americans win this war than the British. I want my brother Pierre freed. And I will have to fight in court, I'm sure, to get our lawful assets returned to us."

Without knowing why at first, Thomas felt compelled to join the growing mass of escapees from the pirate ships. Then the image of the little green book floated across his mind.

Okay, book. I'm with you. Part of the unfolding plan, one step at a time.

As he hoped, his presence wasn't questioned. Every man was concerned with his own welfare. Thomas quietly blended in with the group of pirates leaving the second wave of boats, trailing behind Lafitte and his entourage. Watching the pirate and his leaders swagger forward, he had to admit: Jean Lafitte looked every bit the swashbuckling, debonair ladies' man history had portrayed him as, even in the face of disaster.

Lafitte and his men hurried forward. Thomas had to walk fast to keep up with them. As the band entered the village, Thomas heard shouting and alarmed voices all around him. The attack of the American warships and the unexpected abandonment of his pirate ships by Lafitte had caused a panic among the other residents.

One or two cannon balls struck close enough to maim some unlucky souls, but now the Americans had stopped their barrage.

Soon blazes began leaping up here and there. Glancing about, Thomas saw a few pirates were busy torching buildings that looked like warehouses. The black smoke rose and mingled with the brisk winds, turning what had been clear crisp air into a gray sooty haze blanketing the entire island.

It seemed like an omen of impending doom.

The enemy cannon balls had caused enough damage, he thought, but some pirates were determined to deny the Americans any chance of apprehending their possessions, munitions and the like.

Thomas lingered in the background watching, while most of the men raced to their hiding places for loot they could carry away on their persons. Some had wives and girlfriends and children of all ages to say quick goodbyes. There was much emotion and weeping on the part of the families. More than a few pirates had several lady lovers on their string. These departures were messy, loud, and confrontational. Some fights broke out among the contesting women, with hair-pulling, eye-gouging, hard slaps to the face, punching, kneeing, and the like.

One nasty catfight erupted close by Thomas. He stood rooted, fascinated and unable either to take his eyes off the scary scene or to walk away.

He was stunned by the viciousness of it. A few of the pirates stopped for a few seconds to watch with looks of detached amusement.

Gosh, such things must be commonplace, Thomas thought.

"You, you disgusting little *bitch*! I tell you Pierre

belongs . . . ughhh . . . belongs to *me!*" A young brunette grabbed the top of another woman's scalp. She yanked the flaming red locks as hard as she could and began swinging her opponent around, the better to rip hair out from the roots.

"Why you stupid, ugly Cajun slut. He told me he loved me best, said he was giving me *all* the jewels." The redhead clutched the wrist of the brunette as they swung, digging her green-painted nails deep into the skin and drawing blood. With her other hand, she scratched at the other's face trying to reach her eyeballs. Meanwhile, a third woman, an older, voluptuous lady with flowing jet-black hair and dark skin was clawing and kicking at both the other girls as they pivoted in a group circle.

To say the least, Thomas was shocked and unnerved. Unlike the petty play-fighting he sometimes saw among rival girls at school, these women seemed to hate one another. They wanted to kill. It was a good thing none of them had pistols or swords or knives, he observed. Otherwise, there would be one or two dead bodies after the fray.

Thomas pulled himself away from the sight and hurried to join a cluster of pirates leaving for the opposite end of the island. He was glad to be going with the rest of the men.

"The women are worse than the guys," he said, shaking his head.

"Ha! Like black widow spiders, every one of them. Doesn't do to turn your back."

Thomas had been overheard.

"Or to let the spiders gather together in one place," cracked the pirate, a dark-headed debonair-looking man. His bright yellow silk shirt was wide open, showcasing a lean muscular chest with thick black hair curling out. His fine mustache and goatee were each curled at the ends. He took a big stride toward Thomas to join up with him.

"Ahhh, but you've got it right, young mate. It's always the female o' the species that's more deadly."

He winked and added he'd had four pretty women fighting over who was his true love and therefore got to keep most of his loot and belongings still left on the island.

"What these girls don't know is I got me at least ten other women strewn all over New Orleans and the Caribbean. Even one in Mexico. All waiting for me to hit their port. All thinking they're the one.

"Angel's my name," he grinned rakishly, extending his free arm to shake hands. Angel had a huge bundle of loot tied up in a blanket under his other arm.

"Hi. I'm Thomas."

"A bit young you are. But no younger, I deem, that I was when I began my career as a noble privateer." He grinned again. "What ship were you on?"

Just then the name *Queen of India* sailed into his mind, followed by the image of the little green book.

"I was on the Queen of India," Thomas said, without hesitation.

"Ahhh, yes. The Queen. Sunk by a British fleet off the coast of Jamaica two weeks ago. I'd heard all hands were lost when it exploded. But you'd know that. They say the ship was carrying a large load of munitions for Barataria as part of its cargo when it was attacked."

Angel turned his head and looked at the boy as they walked with the others. "So how did you manage your, uh, escape when all others perished?"

Thomas had always been good at acting. Now his creative juices flowed. He thought fast. "Well. I was in the crow's nest when the Queen blew, you see. I had lookout duty that morning. The explosion caused a huge crack in the main mast just above the deck line. The top half, as neatly as you please, toppled and sagged into the water as the crack deepened. I was dangling just three feet above the water when I jumped in. I used a piece of timber from the wreck to swim to shore without the British seeing me. I looked around for live crewmates in the water," he hesitated at this point, giving Angel an appropriate expression of deepest compassion, "but all I saw were dead bodies. Over the next week or so, I made my way back until here I am."

Angel gaped at him.

"I wasn't injured at all. Not even a scratch. I was high enough when the explosion happened that all of the flying debris and soaring flames missed me."

At that, Angel's mouth was open wide.

"Boy, I've seen some strange things in battle and heard many hard-to-believe tales. Anyone who can cheat death like that is one lucky man."

He shook his head in astonishment.

"If we get into a scrape, I think I want to stay by your side. You're a good luck fortune."

Thomas smiled slightly, making Angel even surer of his assumption.

It took them over twenty minutes to reach the other side of the island. Every person except for Thomas had sacks, boxes, chests, buckets, or pillow cases stuffed with their ill-gotten treasures and other valuables, making their jaunt slower than it might have been. A motley collection of smaller sailboats, rowboats, large canoes, and paddle flatboats waited for the fleeing pirates in the shallow inland bay.

By chance, Angel and Thomas managed to board the same vessel as Lafitte and his brother. It was the largest of the rowboats, able to carry up to twelve passengers. Jean greeted Angel cordially. Angel was one of his more enterprising and loyal followers.

"Captain, you remember the Queen of India that sunk off Jamaica?"

"Of course. I lost a small fortune as well as much needed munitions and all the crew on board. It was a bitter blow to both my pride and my pocket."

"Thomas here was with the ship that day. He alone of all the men escaped with his life."

"Is that so?" Lafitte raised an eyebrow. "I hadn't realized anyone survived the awful explosion."

Thomas repeated his made-up story to the Lafitte brothers and the others. By their expressions, he could tell they all believed his tale without question.

"Hmmm. Well done. Well done indeed. You sound like a resourceful lad to me, Thomas. Methinks I should take you on as part of my lead ship's crew."

Thomas blushed at the undeserved complement, but managed to mumble, "Thank you very much, sir. Really, it was sheer blind luck. I don't merit any praise."

"My, my. Manners and humility, too." Lafitte twirled the end of his waxed mustache and contemplated the boy for a moment. "The rest of you swabs could do with such an example."

With that, Jean turned his attention to the matters at hand. The past including the Queen was gone forever. He had the present and future to deal with, and the unwanted American invasion of his home base was a major setback.

Although Lafitte planned to return to Barataria, he knew he soon would be visiting the ribald mistress of the Mississippi, the city of New Orleans.

Thomas watched the shore disappearing as the rowers in his boat strained against the swirling currents. His thoughts mirrored the pirate's. *Yeah. Next stop. Battle of New Orleans.*

Chapter 14
MADAME BIJOUX INSTRUCTS

Samantha stood looking out the window for a long time, enthralled by the glorious sight of the unconquered Fort McHenry outthrust on the tip of the peninsular a mere half a mile away.

A typical teenager, Sam never gave much thought to patriotism and citizenship. But at that moment, she was the proudest she'd ever been to be an American. For a brief interval, the dry dead stories from her history textbook became alive to her.

Finally, she turned from the wonderful scene and stared, uncertain, at the modest room with the cheap bedstead and the rough knit blanket covering it.

What to do next? Where to go?

After the inspiration of the battle won, the heavy feeling of depression began returning. She was still in a real quandary. Nothing had changed about her situation. Doubt and despair flooded her being, replacing the brief high she'd experienced.

She fought hard against the tears. Instead, Sam got

angry. Madder than she'd ever been in her entire life. Her lips pursed together in a tight line of fierce determination.

She wasn't a quitter and a whiner and she wasn't going to start now!

"No! I *won't* let this situation get me down. Impossible as it may seem, I *won't* be defeated. I don't know how or where. But some way I will figure out a way to get back to my own world and my own time."

She took one step toward the bed when it hit.

Her mind numbed into a haze, a swirling mist. Almost as if she'd been given a heavy dose of anesthesia as a white fog leaked into her brain removing everything else in sight.

"What is going on?"

Eerie it was. Then she remembered the first time it had happened.

"No! I can't be doing this again. I—" But the shabby room with all its meager contents was disappearing fast. Her body was already falling. Falling. Falling down to unseen ground.

She awoke. The first thing she heard was the sound of musical instruments playing a melody sad yet sweet, violent but haunting. Sam recognized the unique tones of violins. There were other instruments, too. And voices singing: wild, young, and free. Sam could hear the rhythmic pounding of footsteps madly dancing even before her vision adjusted to the strange new sights.

It was nighttime. She turned slowly, all the way

around. There were huge tree trunks right behind her, perhaps fifteen yards away, and in the darkness, she saw the cascading of treetops fading into the skyline in all directions. A heavy solid object was right in front of her, but past its end and beyond it, there seemed to be part of natural clearing filled with the people and activity. If she listened very hard, she could make out the background sounds of crickets and owls and other birds and forest critters over the raucous music and singing.

Wherever she was, it was colder than Baltimore. That meant she was either farther north this time or it was much later in the year. Instinctively, she glanced down. "Oh, brother. Now I've got different clothing on, and more layers of it, too. Nothing stays the same, does it on this…this *adventure*," Sam whispered to herself.

Samantha reached out and touched the big object in front of her. It was wooden. As her eyes adjusted to the darkness, she found she was standing in the shadows on the other side of a large horse-drawn cart with four ornate walls and a curved roof with a little smokestack sticking out. From movies she'd seen, she guessed.

Why it must be a gypsy wagon.

The shadows under the big cart and beyond its end flickered and flashed.

What's causing that?

When she stepped around the wagon and peered out of the darkness she saw the rest of the camp. There was a crackling campfire with a roaring blaze in the middle of the clearing which accounted for the strange flickering. Around the outer edge of the hollow was a large circle of wagons, each with a team of still tethered horses. She counted nine of the big carts. Sitting around the fire on felled logs or on the ground were a dozen or more men and older boys looking on, listening and clapping with enthusiasm. Many others, old people, young children, and women, some with babies, stood behind those seated. The men, who had been drinking heavily Sam suspected by the many jugs she saw next to them, called out repeated encouragements. A few drunkenly attempted the words to the wild song.

"The love witch, the love witch, she is cold and wicked inside."
"Young men everywhere, I tell you beware, run from her and hide."
"She'll break your heart, poison your mind, and rot your very soul."
"Until she makes you a love-crazed zombie, under her evil control."
"Emeralla is her cursed name, stealing men for the devil is her game."
"Run, run away, as fast as you may, Emeralla is seeking fresh prey."
"The night is still young but Emeralla is old, as old as the stars above."
"She won't rest until she's got you caught in her foul web of love."

Four gypsies stood well off to one side. They were all playing instruments, tapping their feet to the rhythms they produced. Having taken a music course last semester, Samantha recognized two violins, a pan flute, and a mandolin.

Between the musicians and the seated observers were three exotic beautiful young women dressed in gaudy colored tight skirts and revealing blouses, vivid scarfs about their necks, dancing with abandon yet somehow in concert . . . swaying, twirling, prancing, and stepping gracefully as a unit while they sang the song.

Two girls shook and struck bright green-painted tambourines as they moved. The third dancer clicked castanets in perfect time.

The scene was lively and carefree. The tempo continued faster and faster until the dancers became a blur of motion and the music became frenzied.

Still the pace quickened.

Suddenly, the instruments exploded in a virtual chaos. The dancers spun, twisted, weaved in unison and then threw their bodies forward to the ground in a collective bow, their lungs heaving for breath, their bodies tingling with a final jolt of adrenalin from their furious movements.

Wow! Kinda like rumba, belly dancing and ballet all rolled into one. These girls are way limber, thought Sam, a bit envious.

The moment the music and dancers stopped, Sam's

presence became noticed. First one face and another, then more, until finally, all turned and stared with curiosity at Sam, who looked back at them, her body frozen and her eyes wide with alarm. The entire camp saw her now; it was no use hiding. She took a huge breath and stepped out of the half shadows into the full light.

A handsome older woman dressed in lavish colorful gypsy attire stood up and majestically strode toward her. To Sam, she appeared to be a well-preserved sixty. Her carriage was ramrod straight and she moved with catlike grace. She had a commanding visage, intense presence, with dark penetrating eyes and thick wild black hair that carried beginning traces of gray around her temples.

Gosh, whoever or whatever she is, she must be an important person, thought Sam, because she noticed even the hard-bitten gypsy men bowed their heads and stood up or swiveled their knees inward to let her pass by, out of respect for her position.

Gathering her courage, Sam stuck out her hand to shake and said, "Hi, I'm S—"

"Yes, yes, I know. You're Syeira. A messenger from my second cousin Emerentia arrived several days ago. He told me she said you might be coming to join us from our other tribe."

"I'm—what? No, I'm not. I mean I'm…I'm," Sam faltered, not quite sure how to respond.

That stupid green book is putting me in awkward situations! She fumed, and not for the last time.

Her brain whirled. Sam decided on the spot to play along until she knew what she was up against, gambling the real Syeira wouldn't show up. If she did, Sam would be in a real jam. However, at that moment, the image of the little green book and the phrase: *She's not coming*, floated unbidden into her mind, interjected from an outside source.

Oh great! The book, again?

Involuntarily, almost imperceptible, Sam shook her head at the strange occurrence but had to recover because the woman was watching her closely.

"All right then. Okay. Yes, I'm Syeira. I'm your girl and I've come to join your…tribe."

The woman viewed Sam's odd response with some suspicion. She stared deep into Sam's eyes as if she could read her mind, and she looked Sam over, head to toe, and walked around her, as if evaluating what kind of person Emerentia had sent her. Finally satisfied, she said, "My name is Madame Bijoux. Emerentia may not have told you, but I have been the leader of our clan since the passing of my husband seven years ago. You will stay with Cezelia, I think. She will show you what to do."

The corners of the Madame's mouth tightened. "You will learn quickly that those who do not work, who do not obey, do not eat." Under her breath to herself, she mumbled, "Emerentia has always been too soft, too lenient on her tribe's young girls.

"Come! Now!" she said imperiously, clapping her hands twice.

Sam (now called Syeira) startled at the command. Gathering her courage, she followed Madame Bijoux through the crowd of bodies still mingling around the campfire. People turned to stare at her as she passed; one of the men and an older boy made catcalls, which she ignored. Madame Bijoux took her to another wagon on the far side. It was painted brilliant orange but the roof, door, window shutters, and wheel spokes were a garish red. Each wagon likewise was painted in lurid shades, but each was different from its mates. All the harnessed horses were stout of size, and black or deep chestnut in color. All the people were dressed in clothes that were flamboyant hues. In the flickering duel between the night shadows and the crackling fire, the overall effect of the circus colors swirling in and out her line of vision, she had to admit, was a little spooky.

Syeira thought of werewolf and other fright movies she'd seen as a kid that always had a band or two of gypsies as part of their scary plots.

They soon reached the other wagon. The Madame leaned over the driver's railing and rapped hard three times on the heavy wooden door.

"Just a moment. I'm coming, I'm coming," an irritated voice called from inside. The door swung open and Syeira saw standing there a petite raven-haired girl a little older than she with very pretty eyes, gazing down at the two of them with a sulky expression.

"Cezelia, this is Syeira, of whom I spoke to you this morning. She will be sharing your wagon with you, your grandmother, and little sister."

"Wouldn't it be—"

"Enough! We've already discussed this. No more argument. Yes, it will be crowded with the four of you, but you can manage it. I have no other place to put her. All the other wagons have grown men or older boys and I want no trouble with her being here."

Cezelia gave Syeira a cold, calculating stare up and down, her lips turned in a petulant frown. "Oh, she'll be trouble all right, as comely as she is. I can already tell. That old wolf Armand, for one, will be on her quicker than the devil on a lost soul."

"No, he won't! I warned him earlier if there was any bad behavior on his part, he would have to leave the tribe. And if you play the slut and tempt any of the men," the Madame turned and stared daggers at Syeira, "I will lash you within an inch of your life, myself. You'll wish you'd never been born."

Cezelia got a satisfied smirk on her face. "Madame means it, too. She has a twenty-foot rawhide whip that's she an expert in using on people and animals…who deserve it."

"For your information, I already have a boyfriend and I'm committed to him for the present," retorted Syeira with some heat, glaring from one to the other. "Also, I was raised to be a good girl with high moral standards."

Madame Bijoux raised her heavy eyebrows in mild surprise.

"Oh? I heard tell you were a bastard child raised by a drunk of an uncle and a senile grandmother," the Madame replied skeptically. "You should know, right from the start, I won't tolerate anyone who lies to me. Or steals from the tribe. Or causes fights or dissention among our people. Of course, doing these things to outsiders is a different matter; we must do what we must do to survive and keep the tribe together."

"You're wrong about me. I'm honest as the day is long, I'm still a virgin, by the way," (Cezelia snorted out loud at this.), "and I don't fool around or lead boys on, either."

"Well…," the Madame looked at Syeira's earnest expression. "Perhaps I've judged you prematurely. I shall see."

She snapped her fingers at Cezelia. "You, girl, will be responsible for training her in the way. I want no problems or petty games from you, either. I can already see you are jealous of her. Behave yourself, and treat Syeira as a sister."

Cezelia nodded obediently. But her eyes said she didn't like it one bit. After the Madame had gotten out of range of her voice, she commanded Syeira, "Wait here!" She disappeared inside the wagon. Syeira could hear her knocking about. Presently, Cezelia came out. She was clutching a portable-folding table in one arm and balancing what looked like Tarot cards, a crystal ball, and what Syeira assumed were other Fortune-telling items against her body with her other arm.

Syeira shivered at the sight. She wanted nothing to do with such things. Now she knew what the Madame meant by the 'way'.

Cezelia set up the table beside the wagon facing the firelight. She placed the items on the tabletop and motioned to Syeira. Despite what the Madame had instructed, she didn't bother to mask her strong disapproval of the other and indifferently asked, "So, girl, do you have the gift? Or not?"

Syeira regarded the objects laying there with faint disgust. She knew she should put on a better front, but just couldn't bring herself to act excited about the topic at hand.

"Not," she replied, staring at the deck of Tarot cards.

Cezelia noticed this, and gave a wicked grin. "So, girl, you're worthless to the tribe except for what you can sell your body for, is that it?"

"I already told you and the Madame. I'm a virgin. For real. I don't give my body away or sell it, either," Syeira met her spiteful look with defiance. "Look, Cezelia," she folded her arms, "I'm not your enemy. Or competitor. No matter what you think. We're on the same side, aren't we? I assure you I have zero interest in any man or boy in this camp, just in case you're sweet on someone. If we can't be friends, at least we can work together while I'm here. For the benefit of the tribe, of course."

She held Cezelia's angry eyes with her own. "Do we have a deal?" She stuck out her hand to shake.

Cezelia ignored the hand but nodded with a scowl after many seconds had passed. Clearly, she was not used to any other girl in the camp speaking to her in the bold, candid way Syeira did.

"Fine then. Let's get on with this, shall we?" smiled Syeira brightly.

They spent the better part of two hours going over the tricks of the trade before calling it a night. Syeira listened and feigned interest this time, knowing Cezelia would report back to the Madame on her progress. The next morning after breakfast, the Madame took Syeira aside for a walk through the woods.

"Cezelia informs me you don't have the gift and you seem ill at ease in doing Fortune telling."

Syeira started to explain, but the Madame waved her down. "It's okay. You can ply the customer with a few simple questions—if you know the right questions to ask—and fake your answers to fit their life history. Most of it is educated guesses and telling the customer what they want to hear."

She gave Syeira an appraising glance. "As pretty as you are, the men will be paying more attention to your looks anyway, the young women will tend to identify with you, and the middle-aged women will be remembering how beautiful they were at your age. No one will be listening very hard to your words. Just play along with their natural fears, inhibitions, dreams, desires, lost loved ones, past romance, and the like."

The Madame stooped for a minute to pick some wild mushrooms she saw along the path amidst the forest ground cover. She put them in a little sack she had tied to her dress belt. "These make for a good gumbo sauce," she said, before continuing.

"For example, if they seem to be the fearful type, you tell them of impending doom based on what they fear the most. If a family member or beloved relative has died, you tell them the spirit of the person is in the room at that moment, and you make up words of what the spirit is saying, using their own life history. If they've been unfortunate in love or lost a lover to another, you tell them new love is on the horizon and create an imaginary person that's better than the one they lost. If they wish wealth or fame or success in a business plan or some venture, you tell their deepest desires are about to come true, and replay their own dreams back to them in an altered but improved setting. Always get the customer's money before you give their fortune. You can make nice with them and ask your questions first, if you're more comfortable doing that, but you must take payment before you tell them what they want to hear. Also, be sure to tell them that if they don't give you all the money or if they mock or laugh or get angry at you, a most horrible evil—a double curse—will befall them.

"Do you follow what I'm saying, Syeira?"

"Yes, Madame, I understand." Syeira kept a straight face, but hoped in her heart she wouldn't have to do any such performances. *Little green book, please get me out of this mess, the sooner the better!*

"Good. And now we go back to camp."

Later that night after supper, Syeira stood by herself in the outer group of people watching the night's entertainment. More music and dancing. The Madame was occupied on the far side talking with a middle-aged man Syeira assumed to be another clan leader, based on the serious conversation they seemed to be having. Suddenly, she was bumped from behind and a man's hand reached around to grab her breast as she tumbled forward.

"Sorry about that, my chickie." There was a coarse laugh. "Didn't see you standing there."

She regained her balance at once and angrily spun around to see a man with a light pink-colored puffy silk shirt unbuttoned almost to his navel exposing a thick hairy chest. Both his scalp hair and beard were thick, black, and curly, too. She'd seen him around the camp and ignored his constant searching eyes. He looked greasy and gross.

"Why did you do that? Don't you ever touch me again."

The man laughed even harder and leered at Syeira.

It was obvious he thought he could do whatever he wanted. He was enjoying the sport immensely.

"I said get away from me, you…you pervert!" *Unbelievable! What a contemptible jerk.* She was furious and disgusted at the same time.

In response, he raised his hands, hovering his meaty palms inches from her chest. "Just trying to keep you from falling down, my little salope."

He raised his right eyebrow and gave a sick grin he thought irresistibly suave. "You're a feisty one. I like that. I think it's time we got better acquainted. Close up and personal and in private, if you take my—"

The words choked in his mouth. Syeira stepped forward, ramming her right palm into his nose then slamming her knee as hard as she could between his legs as he reeled back from the hit to the face, splaying his thighs and exposing his groin for her attack.

"Ughhhhh," the man groaned. He violently cursed. Blood trickled from his busted nose onto his mustache and beard. His swarthy face purpled. His knees buckled and he collapsed, clutching his privates in agony.

People around the campfire stared at the figure of the man, now rolling and moaning on the hard earth, his hands wrapped between his legs.

"You stupid fool. I knew you'd cause trouble sooner or later! I knew it the minute you stepped into this camp." Cezelia had rushed over, hands on hip, after witnessing the tail-end of the episode. "That was Armand you just attacked! He's one of our leaders."

"Well, he shouldn't have tried to grope me, then! A girl's got a right to defend herself," said Syeira hotly.

"What is this, then? What has happened here?" Of the corner of her eye, the Madame had seen Armand fall to the ground and come to investigate.

Before Syeira could answer, Cezelia chimed in with her version: Armand was simply trying to be friendly and the little tramp viciously kneed him. But others close by had seen everything from start to finish, enough to give the Madame the truth of the matter. Several people had been asked by the Madame in confidence to keep an eye on Syeira and they all knew Armand's reputation. So when he snuck up behind the girl, they watched it unfold.

The Madame was true to her word. She banished Armand from the tribe that very night. Although he raged and swore eternal revenge, Armand was forced to leave. Adding insult to injury, his second cousin and papa, who shared the same wagon, refused to go with him. The wagon stayed behind with them. His papa had always been close friends with Danior, the Madame's deceased husband and he would remain loyal to the Madame, he said. Besides, he'd never approved of his son's wild wanton ways.

From that moment on, Syeira sensed Cezelia's attitude toward her, at least outwardly, seemed to change for the better. The following day all the horses were harnessed up and the caravan of wagons creaked and jolted as they left the uneven root-filled forest ground and spilled out onto a winding, weed-infested, narrow country road heading south.

"Where are we going now," asked Syeira.

"New Orleans," answered Cezelia. The tribe has many relatives and friends in that city."

"Oh," Syeira replied, wondering what strange new adventure the green book had in store for her next.

Chapter 15
THE TWO JAILBIRDS

"It's so beautiful with the sunlight on it," she said to herself.

As the caravan rattled ever closer to the city, Syeira could see the silvery shine of the sun's rays upon the smooth-rolling expanse of the mighty Mississippi off in the distance. The gypsy band stopped more often now to take advantage of gullible travelers heading north, many who wished to have their futures told. Being smart, perceptive, and friendly, Syeira became skilled in asking the customers leading questions about their lives, hopes, and fears, the answers of which Cezelia cunningly interwove into her predictions. However, she refused to perform the actual deed of fortune-telling herself.

Besides, Cezelia wants to be the star of the show, anyway, which was more than fine with her, Syeira shrugged. She knew Cezelia believed she had the gift of foretelling, although to her, it seemed all a fraud. However, between her talent as the sidekick and Cezelia's acting ability, the two made a good team despite her unease about anything dealing with the occult.

Jack King

As the gypsy tribe entered the outskirts of New Orleans, it was late afternoon. Syeira sensed an atmosphere of fear and intrigue among the local populace. The tribe's business had begun to fall off. People ignored the caravan, the deeper they traveled into the city. From her history class, she remembered there were spies everywhere during this time from every major European power, passing information and misinformation either to the Americans and their allies or to the British and their allies.

Everyone knew the British troops were coming. And soon.

Battle was in the wind. The French Creoles, Haitian refugees, free blacks, mulattos, privateers, Americans, Spaniards, and other Europeans all jostled for security and advantage amidst the growing tensions. Mutual suspicions and accusations—false or otherwise— were rampant. No one trusted anyone much except close family and friends, and even then kept an open eye out. As a consequence, the clan was not welcomed with the usual open arms as on its previous trips to the city.

Gosh, everyone distrusts and dislikes the gypsies, observed Syeira, watching first a Spaniard then a European then an Irishman then an American from South Carolina curse at Cezelia for politely offering to tell their fortunes and offering gypsy items for sale. All of them stalked away, holding their wallets or pouches tight, fearful of pickpockets while their attention was diverted.

"Oh, go on. Keep your filthy money, you fat

monkey, you borey corey, you," Cezelia muttered under her breath at the last one. "I hope your ugly mother sits on a snake."

She scowled at the man's heavy backside as he pushed his way through the crowd. "Merde! The Madame will not be happy with us!" She looked glumly at her partner. The afternoon had been pretty much a waste: One slim wallet with little money in it snatched by her while Syeira had the customer busy answering questions, only two fortunetellings, and no trinkets sold, to show for their efforts.

This casual thieving and pickpocketing of outsiders by the clan was something else that made Syeira very uncomfortable. She refused to steal from customers despite the Madame's dire threats and Cezelia's lazy attempts to teach her the basics. She glanced away whenever she spied Cezelia or anyone else doing it.

Her forced involvement, even indirectly, weighed upon her conscience. "I hate what these people do to make a living. Just hate it," she whispered under her breath. Cezelia had gone to the wagon for a minute or two. Fifteen feet away, another pair of camp workers was playing a wealthy older Southern woman for a sucker. Syeira watched with unfeigned disgust. She couldn't wait to leave the gypsies the first chance she got.

Her opportunity would soon come, but not in the way she imagined.

The convoy trundled along toward its final

destination, nearing the French Quarters. Some members of the clan called out here and there to individuals they recognized along the bustling streets and sidewalks, ignoring the fact that most of the responses were muted or indifferent. The gypsies didn't care. There may be war in the air and other people may be afraid, but it had nothing to do with the tribe. They were a proud, happy, and free-spirited group, undaunted by the problems and pressures of the outsiders' world.

"Hey, Cezelia. What's going on up there?" She jerked her chin toward the far end of the street. There seemed to be a disturbance brewing. Peering over the heads of the jostling throng in front of them, they saw a small band of angry men beyond, milling about, some armed with weapons. Suddenly, several of the men—the leaders, Syeira supposed—started yelling and gesturing at the approaching gypsy caravan.

The group of men bulled their way through the press to get to the lead wagon. Two of the men wore constable uniforms, badges and side pistols, and strutted forward importantly. Three other men walked close behind them, pointing, cursing, and glaring at the gypsies. One held a hunting rifle dangling toward the ground, but his countenance was fierce. A sixth man trailed behind the rest. His expression was a bit sheepish yet determined.

Syeira recognized him at once. It was her attacker, Armand!

As the cluster of men shoved their way through,

still others began following them, curious what was going on.

Upon reaching the tribe, they halted. The man with the hunting rifle leveled it in the direction of the assembled clan and glared at them before speaking. "As we done told you, these gypsy skunks…these dirty thieves…robbed me, my brother, and our cousin two days ago as we were traveling north, minding our own business, visiting the old folk's place forty miles outside the city. We'd gotten a late start and had stopped to make camp before pushing on the next morning. We didn't notice anything missing until we got to Pap's house and searched our saddle bags. These vermin crept up in the dead of night and stole our wallets and money pouches off our persons as we lay sleeping in our camp—mind you, between us we had close to fifty-two dollars in paper money and silver and gold coins. Every bit of it gone."

The man paused and cleared his throat. "That's a hell of a lot of money these days, boys. And I know it was them because their damn wagon ruts and horse tracks are the only marks we saw on the ground hurrying back to the city after we done discovered we was robbed. The *only* marks we saw, mind you," he said again for emphasis.

"This gypsy fellow here backs up our accusation." He jerked his head toward Armand, lingering behind him.

The head constable, a barrel-chested man with a trimmed beard and finely made broad-brimmed hat slanted on his imposing head, fixed the gathered tribe elders with a stern look. "Well, what do you all got to say about that? You, sir, speak up!" he addressed the tallest and most commanding of the gypsy men, thinking he had to be the main leader.

The Madame took a regal step forward. She drew herself up to her full height, rearranging the puffy sleeves over her plump arms, and gave the two constables a withering look. Syeira had to admit that if nothing else, the lady had style and forcefulness.

"I'm in charge of the clan, and I assure you we had nothing to do with it. We're just honest folk minding our own business and helping some needy souls here and there who desire our, uh, special expertise in matters of foretelling and life guidance."

"She lying, constables!" A coarse voice came from the back.

Armand pushed his way to the front and halted, sneering, insolent, a few feet from the Madame, one hand on hip and the other pointing almost touching the tip of her nose. "I know her and her people. The sly old witch is lying! It's their nature to rob unsuspecting travelers. I'm telling you they stole from these men."

Revenge will be so sweet, he thought.

The Madame slapped his hand away. "You! You are a lazy…good for nothing…two-timing…tchew!" She spit the words into his face. Her wrath was intense, forcing the big man to take a half-step back.

"I say piss on you! You couldn't keep your bibitte in your pants, so we threw you out of camp. Always bothering every woman and girl in sight, you were. You never once did a full day's work. Worthless you are! Always complaining, always blaming others, always accusing, always stirring up strife."

The Madame fixed him with her evil eye and said with a voice of utter contempt. "If it wasn't for your father who I esteem we would have kicked you out long ago."

His swarthy face flushed. The battle was joined.

He glanced at the two constables. "Believe me, good sirs. If you will search each person and all the wagons, I'm sure you will not only find the missing money but other stolen items, as well. They were coming into the city to fence their goods for food and supplies for the winter. There's an old Cajun coot named Octave who they use for that purpose. He runs a pawnshop. His fat wife keeps a brothel on the second floor. Near the French Quarters. The tribe has other people they can use, too, to get rid of things in a hurry with no questions asked."

The head constable glanced at the other. Their eyes met. Of course, they knew where Octave's Pawn Emporium was because they both frequented it as upstairs customers.

The man with the rifle growled. "I say we search the whole darn camp beginning with this here hag and her wagon."

His companions all nodded strong agreement,

egging the constables to take prompt action. A number of men in the listening throng yelled out their support.

Instantly, the Madame's face became an inscrutable mask, her mind calculating the odds. Her leaders murmured among themselves, uneasy. They faced three men with guns, two of them the law. She knew the gypsies were not popular. They were often scorned or feared by outsiders. There was no telling how many men in the crowd would join in the hunt, once started, becoming a rummaging mob.

Armand was right, of course. They did steal from outsiders, whenever the opportunity presented itself. Just as long as they could do it without violence to themselves or their victims. The tribe after all was peaceable. There was just one gun in the entire camp, although every grown man and every older boy carried a long-bladed knife in the pants pocket or tugged inside the belt. The pillagers would find a great deal of loot, not all of it stolen. But she had no means of proving even the lawful items belonged to her people either. A mob action would wipe them out.

The Madame stretched her hands with the palms out toward the constables in the universal sign for a halt. The crowd quieted for a few seconds, waiting to see what she was up to.

The new girl was expendable. She was near worthless as a producer, anyway, and she had been the cause of the rift with Armand in the first place. And Cezelia, her wagon-mate, wasn't much better. She had become a nuisance with her petty jealousies and constant complaining.

The coldblooded decision was made on the spot.

"I never saw any of the money myself. But I know who took it from these poor men. That's right. We do know who the guilty ones are. I didn't tell you at first… because…because, well, we try to protect our own. From outsiders. But…now that I understand a most grave injustice has been done. Naturally, amends must be made. The thieves brought forth."

She drew a deep breath, as if it was a most difficult and mortifying experience she was going through. "The tribe elders informed me after it happened. I think one of the two guilty persons spent most or all of the ill-gotten money for a new horse with a peddler passing by. Anyway, she has a new beast alongside her other animal. You may take the horse as payment along with the culprits."

It was all a lie, but for the good of the tribe, a few must be sacrificed. It was always so. She turned and looked at her leaders, nodding imperceptibly. They understood her plan without speaking.

Two of the older boys had done the thieving. They were chosen for their special abilities. Both were exceeding quick, quiet, and agile, able to move through night shadows without making a sound or waking those in a sound sleep. They were the best pickpockets in the camp.

There was one new girl in camp. One new horse.

And it was harnessed to the wagon belonging to the other girl, Cezelia, and her family. The horse had been bought two months ago, replacing an old mare that had broken her leg and had to be put down. The payment for the purchase had come out of the tribe's general fund, for a generous portion of all stolen monies and all fortune-telling was set aside for the communal purse.

"Bring me the traitors to our honor, traitors to the dignity of our tribe! Fetch the females named Syeira and Cezelia. Also, the new horse." She clapped her hands sharply, and three leaders departed to do her bidding.

The Madame eyed Armand shrewdly. He knew the ways of the clan. He knew they would never part willingly with their ill-gotten gains. The surrender of the two girls into custody, especially Syeira, was to placate his wounded male ego. The concession of the animal was to placate the three victims. A good horse was worth fifty or sixty dollars—more than enough to cover their loss.

Syeira and Cezelia were bought forward, protesting and struggling to break free, but to no avail. There were no eye-witnesses, and one party's word against the other. The Madame thought this was an acceptable loss given the alternative. Each constable grabbed ahold of a girl by the arm, and the three men took possession of their new mare, stroking her flanks, looking at her hooves and teeth, and agreeing they'd gotten a fair exchange for their troubles.

From within the gypsy gathering, Cezelia's grandmother and little sister held hands and observed the episode in shocked silence. Both were dry-eyed, though. Neither hysterics nor pleading would change the verdict. They knew better. The Madame's word was law.

Bartered justice, New Orleans style, had been served.

Armand stood watching the two girls and the horse being taken away. He turned to face the Madame, with a self-satisfied grimace. She returned his stare, boring into his imprudent eyes with her most evil look. The foolish man had brought this upon himself. She murmured a horrible curse, her lips barely moving. He shivered as though a chill wind had blown against his bare flesh. Then it was gone.

He was an outcast now. All of the gypsies gazed at him without pity. He was subhuman, a pitiful worthless creature. No other tribe would accept him into its fellowship. The curse would come upon him without warning and he would get his recompense for his disloyalty. A moment of blind fear seized Armand by the throat and he couldn't breathe. Panicking, the big man spun hard on his heel and ran after the departing constables, disappearing into the crowd.

The girls were taken to a medium-sized colonial residence flanked by quaint looking buildings on either side and up and down the street in the oldest part of the French Quarter. This entire section had been untouched by the great fire of 1794, and this particular home had been converted to contain inmates upstairs, with an office and living quarters for the head constable and his family downstairs. The building was a pastel-colored stucco two-story with a flat Spanish-style tiled roof. The intricate ironwork on the upper balcony was matched by heavy decorative bars fastened against the windows to prevent any escape from that avenue.

The girls' pockets, purses, shoes, caps, and outsides of their clothing around their midriffs were searched or patted for any hidden weapons or objects that could be used as a means of getaway. Two of the five jail cells were allocated for female prisoners. They were pushed into one of the the rooms and the metal-barred door was slammed shut and locked.

Okay, green book. This keeps getting better and better. I hope you know what you're doing. Syeira looked around the cell, biting her lower lip, hands on hips and shaking her head.

"Great. Wonderful. Just what I wanted for Christmas. It is getting close to Christmas, right? A little cozy jail-time with my new BFF's," she said sarcastically. "That stands for best female friends, by the way," she glanced at Cezelia and the other occupant, who eyed the newcomers with bleary disinterest from the upper bunk bed.

Cezelia snapped at her. "I don't know what you mean. You blabber on about nonsense half the time. What is this Christmas you prate on about? Huh? I know many outsiders, people in New Orleans, observe a day called Fat Tuesday, but that's next month, early January, I think. We have nothing to do with it."

"You don't know…about Christmas?" Genuine shock registered on Syeira's face.

Cezelia slumped down on the lower bunk, her elbows resting on her knees and her head cupped in her palms. "All I know is you cost me my freedom and my horse. You've been nothing but trouble ever since you came into my life. I wish you'd shut up, you ti pitin!"

"Did you just call me a bad name?" Syeira glared at her, her temper rising. Normally she kept cool, calm and collected, no matter the circumstances. But after all she had gone through in this weird adventure, she was in no mood to put up with more stuff. Not from Cezelia.

"Don't do that! Not a bright idea."

"Oh, you think you're some kind of tough girl because of what you did to Armand?"

"That's right. Don't push me. You have no clue what I can do."

The two stared daggers at each other until Cezelia caved in first. "Fine, then. I'll ask you *pretty please*, miss priss, if you would not talk to me any more tonight."

The constables had crammed three women in each of the two allotted female rooms, although there were just two bunks and one chamber pot per cell. It was all Syeira could do not to gag at the awful stench. Thankfully, the chamber pots were taken out and emptied every morning by the constable's helper when the prisoners' meager breakfasts were brought in.

Three prostitutes were in the adjoining cell; one

girl was younger than Syeira. Her face was caked with garish makeup. Her eyes were lined, over bright, and flitting from side to side and all around like some small frightened animal on the constant lookout for predatory carnivores. She looked years older. It didn't help that the remaining three cells on the other side of the prostitutes' room were packed with men, most of them inebriated. One was in for petty theft. Another for assault with a knife. The remainder was carousers. Those not passed out were loud, foulmouthed, and obnoxious, badgering the prostitutes for sexual peeks and dirty talk.

"Oh come on, darlin'! You've got a nice figure, you do. Not a bad face, either. Wouldn't kick you out o' me hay loft or me bed either. How's about a quick look, hey? Just lift up the skirt a little bit or open your blouse a little. Show off your goodies for me and the boys, here." There was much hooting and clapping.

Finally, Syeira had enough.

"Just shut up down there! And leave those poor women alone. I…mean…stop it! NOW! Your guys are nothing but stupid jerks. No one can get any sleep with your constant yakking. And you're not a bit funny."

There was dead silence from the men for half a minute. But then they started up again with great glee and included Syeira, who they couldn't see very well through the layers of intervening bars, in their abuse and insults.

Lizzie, the other occupant in Syeira and Cezelia's room, was there on charges of vagrancy, public drunkenness, and disorderly conduct. Sadly, it was a too frequent occurrence with her, spending most of her meager earnings as a baker's assistant on drink trying to forget the departed unfaithful Frank and her miscarried baby of past spring. Syeira heard her pitiful story the next morning before Lizzie was released.

It was getting cold in the cell with the night temperature. "Hey. Hey, you there! Don't ignore me, I'm talking to you. Say, can I at least get a blanket and pillow since both of the bunks are taken?" Syeira had to put up a royal fuss with the night watchman, but she was beginning to shiver and wouldn't take no for an answer.

The heavyset man scowled at her imprudence, but he shuffled into the outer room anyway and brought her a threadbare dingy blanket but no extra pillow. "This is all we got, gal, so settle down."

Holding her nose, she picked up the full chamber pot, careful not to tip it, and placed it in the far corner across the room before making a poor pallet for herself in the horizontal space between the end of the bunk bed and the jail bars. Syeira lay awake long into night after the men quieted down, her mind fixing first on one hopeless plan of escape then another.

Please, green book, you've got to get me out of this mess. And quickly.

The next day brought the sobering news of the defeat of the assembled American flotilla at Lake Borgne by an armed fleet of British sailors and Royal Marines.

Throughout the morning hours and well past lunch, acquaintances and well-wishers of the two constables trickled in to talk about the battle and speculate what the British might do next. If anything, they agreed, the battle had perhaps delayed the British approach and demonstrated the city would be not be an easy conquest. In the afternoon, the lead constable and a friend came upstairs to check on the prisoners, four of whom were to be released at nightfall.

"Aye, that little ruckus gave the bloody British a taste of American resolve, it did," boasted the day watchman.

"Yes and no," replied the lead constable. "We lost control o' the lake, we did. And rumor has it they've got twenty-five thousand men headed our way." He frowned. "The cream o' the crop, as it were. Hardened professional soldiers. They whipped Napoleon's grand army."

The friend shook his head in response. "I doubt General Jackson will be able to muster much more than three or four thousand lads to meet 'em when they come."

The three men stood talking with booming voices not four feet from Syeira's cell. She overheard everything. Suddenly a desperate idea formulated in her brain. If she could just convince them she had valuable information for General Jackson, almost like she was a spy for the Americans, perhaps she could barter for her freedom!

From her last minute cramming for the history test which was to be on the War of 1812 and its causes, she retained two promising facts. One was the British had a total of eleven thousand troops for the Battle of New Orleans, far less than what the American feared. The other was the three British commanders had disagreed over the assault strategy. An image of the little green book floated across her mind along with the words *Thornton flank attack*, and *main attack two columns*. They meant nothing to her but she realized they might be important, too, in addition to what she remembered from her studies.

"I know some things that General Jackson would be very interested to learn," she called out, grabbing a bar with each hand and pressing her face against the railing space in between. She repeated her bold statement, louder this time and with more confidence.

"What's that you say, missy?" The lead constable turned to face her. "You? A gypsy vagabond? Why would you know anything worthwhile? And where would you pick up this incredible information, a mere slip of a girl?"

Her mind spun. She improvised. "I'm not really a gypsy. You see, I just joined the caravan to make it safely into the city. I know things from…from confidential sources, let's say. Top secret. I was going to tell the General or one of his staff myself once I got here.

"And I didn't steal the money either. That was two older boys who did it. The Madame blamed us because, well, she was upset with Cezelia," she nodded over her shoulder at the other girl, "and me."

"And why was that?"

"Our fortune-telling business had fallen off. We weren't bringing in enough money to suit her. Just before that, the gypsy man who followed you tried to molest me and got kicked out of camp. He had it in for the tribe—especially me. So when you confronted the Madame, she was already mad at me. She figured if I hadn't been in camp, none of this would have happened. She was glad to sacrifice both of us," Syeira said.

"That's your story, huh?"

"Yeah, that's it. You can look me in the eyes and tell I'm speaking the truth about the robbery. The two of us didn't do it."

"What do you want me to do about it?"

"Send a messenger to the general. Someone you trust and who's reliable. Give General Jackson my vital information. All of it. In exchange, release me. Drop the charges. Those three victims got reimbursed for their losses. Besides, you have the wrong people locked up.

"Let me go. Her, too. That's the deal."

The head constable scratched the fine beard on his chin, thinking. It was true the men had gotten overcompensated for their stolen money; something that rarely happened in his line of work. The girl was honest, too. He could see that for himself. He had no doubt now the clan head had not been truthful about who the real thieves were.

Finally, he spoke. "Jessie?"

"Yessir."

"Go fetch me some paper and my favorite pen off my desk. Bring an envelope, too. Missy, you, uh, you write everything down. Seal your note in the envelope, proper like. I'll take it down to the line myself and make sure the general's aide hands it to him. I'll explain your circumstances. If the general decides you should be freed after reading what you've got to say, well and good. If he thinks you're a fraud or what you've said is garbage, you'll stay where you are. The earthworks are only four miles south of the city, up around the Rodriguez Canal. I should be back in two-three hours."

The paper was gotten. Syeira jotted down the four points, rechecking what she wrote, and folding the paper to fit within the proffered envelope.

Three hours later, the lead constable returned. He had an inquisitive yet friendlier expression on his broad face. "It's a puzzlement how a young thing like you could possibly know what you know…but the general was right pleased to have your details on the British strength and plans. Quite pleased, indeed.

"Jessie!"

The day watchman hurried over from his ramshackle desk beside the door. "Yes, constable?"

"Ladies," he took a mock bow, "I'm a man of my word. Jessie, let 'em go. Let 'em both go."

Chapter 16
O'GRADY'S NEW MAN

Jean Lafitte made his way with a few of his lieutenants from Grand Isle to a friend's house, and later, on to New Orleans in secret. Meanwhile, several of his men, Thomas with them, snuck back to their island stronghold in the middle of the night a week after the Americans' attack, but the invading force had already gone. Thomas noticed the largest of the burned warehouses still had a heap of smoldering ashes in the center of its charred ruins and the bitter smell of smoke still lingered in the air. Understandably, Lafitte was incensed by what he regarded as wholesale unwarranted pillage of Barataria. How dare the Americans steal away the pirates' treasures, itself mostly stolen property! Lafitte had offered his services in good faith to the American side, all the while stringing along the British hopes, in a dangerous game of cat and mouse. Despite the setback, he remained determined to offer his assistance to General Jackson in exchange for pardons and other considerations.

A fair trade for both parties, he thought. He had

flints and munitions and cannons and men who knew the backwaters and swamps in and around the city of Orleans better than anyone.

A few pirates had attempted to clean up the mess left by their own preemptive burning and the invaders' rummaging, but most men were so disheartened from the loss of their goods that morale was very low. Angel's abode was undamaged and further, he had managed to hide most of his jewels and coins inside the old wood burning store, covering up the items with a layer of old ashes and fresh pieces of wood. Having no place to sleep, Thomas accepted Angel's hospitality to stay with him, his little son Auguste nicknamed Auggie, and his lively black-haired young mistress Annika.

Of course Thomas knew the final outcome. But it was fun to play dumb and act fearful regarding the impending battle and the apparent long odds of an American victory.

"So what do you think our chances are of beating the British?" he asked Angel one morning as they sat around the little wooden table in the gray-walled shanty waiting for Annika to serve a hearty breakfast of scrambled eggs spiced with Cajun seasoning, slices of ham, strong black chicory coffee, and the remainder of the last night's creole style cornbread muffins, a little stale now but still tasty in Thomas's hungry opinion.

"They say Jackson is a fine general. A tough man. Good at motivating his troops. It all depends on how much time he can buy before the British invade. How well he sets up his line of defense. How many men he can gather to his cause and if he can arm those men."

He smiled at Thomas. "That's where Lafitte has something of great value to offer, I think. The Americans are low on ammunition. They don't have enough qualified sailors to man the ships they have. They don't understand how to use the local terrain to their advantage. We have all those things they need."

Thomas listened, leaning forward, his elbows propped on the tabletop and his face cupped by his hands. He maintained a rather convincing intent expression, he thought. He nodded in agreement with Angel's words. "Yes, I can see that. I believe we would be big help to General Jackson. If *only* the Captain can persuade him to accept our offer of service."

"We shall see. Nothing has been set up yet." Angel eyed the boy's face. He supposed Thomas could be trusted. But then again, Lafitte's plans were secret, and spies were everywhere these days.

Annika set the table with food and drink. She placed Auggie next to her on a chair piled with two big cushions enabling him to sit with his arms at table height. The little boy didn't like the feel of the soft small curds of the scrambled eggs in his mouth, spitting out half again as much as he swallowed; a fact which kept Annika busy and irritable.

"You stop that, Auguste. Right now. Or I will spank

you good!" She thrust her hand under his chin to catch the last spit-out, and forced it back into his protesting mouth until all of it was back inside. She glared at him until he chewed it and she saw his tiny Adam's apple move up and down in obedience.

Thomas watched in amused silence at he ate, wondering if he was that difficult, too, at the same age.

After finishing the meal, he and Angel stepped out into the bright sunlight to view the makings of the day. The petulant clouds of yesterday afternoon had melted away in the night, leaving a brilliant beautiful morning with mild winds and subdued waves far out to sea. They talked at length of many things until Angel was called in to a pirate council meeting.

Thomas waved at Angel as he hurried away. The beach was deserted now. All of the men were at the meeting or else busy with other things. The women were tending to their household chores. The children were off playing games in the thickets and woods beyond the village. There were two young boys a hundred yards further down the beach trying their luck seine-fishing in the mild surf. Faraway, on the blue-streaked ocean horizon, he could make out a ship's billowing white sails. A pair of seagulls passed overhead, fussing loudly.

He kicked the soft caramel sand beneath his feet a few times and signed, thinking about Sam and his dad and when he might see them again.

Then it hit. The fog. The all too familiar sleep-like

trance. He was falling, falling, falling. Everything around him disappearing in the swirling mist as his mind and body succumbed to the unrelenting force.

He awoke to find himself standing in a deserted alleyway wedged between the colorful walls of two multistory structures.

Ah yes. The little green book. Yet again.

Jaw clinched, more in resignation than determination, Thomas stepped out into a quiet thoroughfare at the open end of the narrow alley. By the position of the sun overhead, he could tell it was about mid-morning. The street was empty except for a scattering of people, most walking rapidly. In a hurry, he supposed, to reach their respective destinations. The morning rush was over. Curious, he glanced up at the brightly painted walls beside him and at those across the lane. He noticed their ornate railings and unique architecture. All the houses and shops and offices looked much the same on the outside.

Why I recognize this place. This has to be…the Big Easy. It's gotta be.

He'd been to the modern day city twice as a kid with his parents on vacation. It was one of his dad's all-time favorite places to visit in the states. Obviously, the Spanish facade of the French Quarters hadn't changed much in two hundred years.

Thomas discovered he'd guessed right. A large sign visible two stores down boasted of the finest haberdashery in the whole city of New Orleans. Squaring his shoulders and raising his chin up, Thomas strode forward in the direction of downtown. Southward. Ready to handle the next segment of the adventure as it came.

The further he went, the more he heard folk around him speaking a peculiar dialect. He could make out just a few words here and there. He assumed they must be talking in French or a Creole version.

"Bonjou," a very pretty light-skinned girl said to him and smiled as they walked past each other.

Distracted by her friendliness yet pleased, he called out over his shoulder, turning his head to see her fully, "Well, hello to you, too."

He bumped shoulders with the next person coming past, a plump arrogant man dressed in a business suit. The man scowled and snapped at him as he rushed on, "Excusez-moi." But it was obvious the person felt Thomas was at fault.

"Sorry, sir." Thomas was embarrassed. The pretty girl had seen his clumsiness. She giggled and waved and then blew him a kiss. Now his face was beet red.

He smiled anyway and waved back. Shaking his head, he resumed his course. Five blocks later, the small crowd of passersby had thinned considerably. There were a few people left on the street. Thomas slowed down, waiting for another mental suggestion from the green book, not quite sure what his final destination should be. Suddenly, two rough-looking men emerged out of the shadow of a tavern bar. They headed in his direction.

Thomas halted, unsure whether to keep walking as though he hadn't seen them. Or stop and face them. He knew from his past adventure and what his dad had said that he couldn't be seriously injured while under the power of the little green book. Yet he still wondered. He was glad he knew martial arts, in any case.

He decided to stop. He pivoted, keeping his knees and arms bent as he did so, his hands up in front his face and straight, his body turned to the side, feet wide apart, and his balance almost casually shifted to his right leg.

His unexpected change in stance and strange defensive posture confused the two men, but only for a moment or two. After all, he was a mere boy; they were men, two of them, both armed and deadly. Thomas had left all of his pocket change in his gym bag at his home back in the future. But what about the little sack filled with a few gold and silver coins. *Angel!* The young pirate had taken a liking to him and had gifted it to him that morning in a fit of generosity. "It's not good to have nothing, lad," he'd said.

Thomas had the money pouch slung around his neck, visible. It was that the men were after, he knew.

They glanced up and down the street and spotting no one to interfere, they closed the distance between them and the boy. One pulled a long knife from beneath his trouser belt, as he came. The second man patted a handle of a blade protruding from his pants top and grinned at Thomas. His message was clear. If one knife didn't get the job done, the other one would. A gun was not needed. It made noise and brought unwanted attention. A knife was much better.

They took a position on either side of him, blocking any retreat up or down the street. Hulking. Menacing. Reeking of sweat and filth. Rotten breath. Smelling of cheap tobacco and even cheaper liquor.

"Your pouch, boy. Hand it over."

"I don't know, Maurice. This one acts like trouble. I don't like the looks of him either. Weaselly. Stupid. Ugly. Bah! I think we should do him for acting like he was gonna stand up to us. I feel like slitting a throat this morning. It'll make my day, hey?"

He laughed maniacally and his partner sniggered. Suddenly the crazy one lunged, the tip of his knife aimed at the middle of the boy's stomach.

Thomas was ready. Stepping aside in a lightning move, he grabbed the man's knife hand by the wrist as it slashed by, seizing the front of the man's shirt with his other hand and falling backwards. As he fell, he jammed his feet hard into the man's torso and flipped him over, keeping his grip firm on his opponent's wrist as he tumbled forward head over heels.

The man's arm twisted as he landed on his neck and the knife dropped to the ground. Thomas leaped up and kicked the knife away, out of reach. He had no need for knives.

The second man stood rooted, his mouth open

in total surprise at the scene. His face darkened with a mix of shock and fury and he reached for his own knife. But before he could even pull it out, Thomas spun 180º and slammed his foot into the man's jaw with a perfect roundhouse kick, knocking him down.

The two fallen men stared at Thomas unbelieving, and then jumped up and ran for it in the other direction, leaving their knives where they lay. They wanted nothing more to do with their would-be victim.

Thomas watched them go. Suddenly, he felt a little faint, even weak. Though it was nearing winter, he was sweating. He drew a deep breath and exhaled very slowly. Heart still racing. Mouth dry. Sparring with his Tai kwon do partners, even competing in the martial arts tournaments, was nothing like this—this was real, life and death, street fighting.

A booming voice called out behind him. He spun around to see a burly figure approaching, but this one appeared friendly. The man wore what looked like a uniform and had a badge fastened above his left shirt pocket.

"Why, you handled those scumbags right proper, you did. And you're…you're just a boy." He looked with keen interest at Thomas.

"Aye, a bit of stout fisticuffs that was. Never seen anything quite like it, to tell the truth. Odd style o' fighting, but very effective, it seems. I caught the end of it as I was coming out of the jail house there." He jerked his head over his shoulder in its direction.

"I've been trying to catch those two rotten eggs for months now, but they've got too many hidey holes and too many friends among the worse elements of the city. They disappear after every killing and every robbery like the rats they are."

He nodded his head affably and stuck out his meaty hand. "Och, lad. My name is Patrick O'Grady. I'm the head constable for the downtown district o' the city. I run the local jail here."

Thomas shook hands. "Hi, my name's Thomas. Thomas Jackson."

"Pleased to make your acquaintance, young Thomas." O'Grady looped his thumbs under his belt and examined the boy in front of him. "You know, I could always use more prime help. From what I've seen, you're right handy. If you're looking for work, I'm losing Jessie, my day watchman. You just keep a lookout on the prisoners in the cells. Bring 'em food and take out the toilet pans. Clean the front office and downstairs now and then. Doesn't pay much. But you get two free squares a day, a free cot in the cell room to sleep, and the satisfaction o' seeing riffraff put away."

Thomas knew when the little green book was leading the way. "Why, yes. Yes, sir, I could use a job, steady meals, and place to stay."

"You're hired then." The constable slapped him on the back. "Follow me, youngster. You'll start today which is December 16."

"Huh? It's the middle of December?"

"What's that you say, Thomas? Lose track o' time, did you?"

"Oh, not really. Never mind, sir. Mumbling to myself." It had been the middle of September when he was with the pirates. He knew then the green book had moved him forward into time three months.

The battle for New Orleans was nearing. Events were drawing to their conclusion, both for history and for him and Sam, unless he very much mistaken.

Thomas followed the constable the few blocks back to the jail house. It was there he learned that Sam had been a prisoner, briefly, but had been released the day before. Apparently, she'd made quite a good impression on the constable, unlike the typical women of the night and female derelicts who frequented the jail cells. From the tale O'Grady told him, backed by the night watchman's later rendition, it had to be her he was sure. The description of the girl and the information she knew matched Sam's features and facts about the British troops they had studied together for the history test in the future. He noticed she was using a different name in her adventure, just as he was.

So Sam's in the city now, too. And disguised as a gypsy, no less! Well, that's no worse than me being a pirate, I guess.

Thomas chuckled. He determined to keep a sharp lookout, but had faith the little green book would eventually, sooner rather than later, bring them together of its own accord.

Chapter 17
ARTISTE OF EXAGGERATION

Syeira and Cezelia walked out of the stuffy jailhouse into the chilled evening air. It was already mid-December. The wind was blowing from the nearby ocean in sharp sporadic gusts that whipped against the girls' bodies causing them to shiver. The temperature, Syeira gauged, was in the high forties. *And it's dropping fast.* Their clothing was too lightweight for them to stay outdoors for the night, plus it wasn't safe to do so in any case, Syeira knew. The city had too many criminals and scoundrels loose in the darkness and alleys.

They needed a place to stay, but Cezelia was no longer her responsibility.

"Do you have someplace to go? Someone you know in the city?" Syeira asked the other girl, who stood shaking a bit from the fierceness of the breezes and looking both defiant and forlorn.

"No! Wait, yes. I know someone. Maybe. A third cousin who used to have a shop in the south of the city." She glared at Syeira. "But you can't come with me!"

Syeira just laughed.

"Pleasant to the very end, I see. As much as I appreciate your *overwhelming* generosity and concern for a sister jailbird—especially since I just got *your* butt out of the clink, thanks for nothing—I wouldn't be interested anyway. I have my own plans."

Syeira eyed Cezelia coldly. "Well, so long. It's been real. Don't let me stop you." She put her hands in her pockets and continued to gaze at the girl until she reddened in the face and stalked away in the opposite direction.

"You be sure to write me every chance you get, now," Syeira sang out, watching Cezelia scanning the street side to side, already fearful of each new darkened alleyway and shadowy figure.

Syeira frowned at the back of the retreating girl, now a block away. Shaking her head, she pulled in a deep breath and let it out slowly. The wind was picking up. She glanced up and down the street. There appeared to be an inn of some kind at the other end.

Thank goodness, I still have the means to pay them. No thanks to you, girlie.

As Syeira should have expected, Madame Bijoux had been tipped off by the jealous spying Cezelia. She'd discovered the new girl had money of her own when Syeira bumped against the edge of the little table inside the wagon one morning with Cezelia staring at her. The coins inside Syeira's pocket made a tell-tale metallic clanking sound. Naturally, the ever greedy Madame had demanded all of

Syeira's cash later that day as a condition of her staying with the tribe. With Cezelia standing nearby, observing, arms folded and a satisfied smirk on her face, Syeira had emptied out both her pockets. But the little green book had floated an image of coins and shoes in her mind the very first night there, giving Syeira the idea. As Cezelia and her mother lay sleeping beside her on the hard wooden wagon floor, she'd slipped as many coins as was comfortable flat inside each shoe before firmly reinserting each foot. Thereafter, she'd been careful to keep her shoes on at all times, even when sleeping, a curious habit that mystified the ever watchful Cezelia.

The coins in the bottom of her shoes had escaped the constables' attention, as well. Unless the prisoner was a wealthy individual with connections or a man both big and dangerous looking, the lawmen confiscated any valuables they found off the more hapless prisoners and divided the loot.

She looked one last time at the pitiful form of Cezelia. Syeira turned and walked in the opposite direction. The building she'd noticed was an inn after all. Not too seedy. Not luxurious either. She stopped. Looking to see if anyone was watching, she took one shoe off, removing two silver dollars and replacing her shoe before going inside.

"Sir, I need a room for one night," she told the bored desk clerk behind the counter. Glancing about she saw a number of suspicious characters. She added in an extra loud voice, "I have a pistol concealed inside my dress," she raised one eyebrow, "and I know how to use it, too."

At that, several of the men raised their heads from their newspapers or stopped their conversations, staring at the outspoken pretty girl by the hotel desk. The clerk jerked his fat cigar out of his mouth and stared at her.

Just a precaution, Syeira assuaged herself. She hated lying but the lobby was filled with hard-bitten men. She didn't know yet the little green book protected those whom it sent back into the past from real harm.

"You want it for the whole night?" he asked, looking her up and down with a jaded eye.

"Of course for the whole night! What do you think I am?" she snapped at him.

"Oh. My pardon, *duchess*. There'll be a dollar fifty. In advance. If you want breakfast, that'll be fifty cents extra." He squinted at her, still suspicious.

"Here's two dollars." She slapped the coins on the desk.

"Room two upstairs. *Miss*," he said mockingly, sliding the key across the desk along with a half dollar in change.

Real gen-u-ine customer service. "Thank you, sir."

The next morning she arose and paid for a decent enough breakfast in the crowded dining wing off the lobby. Her cash was almost gone. Enough for three or four more nights at the hotel including meals.

Syeira sat after the meal, thinking. "What can I do

that's honest clean work to earn money?" she said softly, drumming her fingers on the dining table as she pondered the question.

In her mind's eye, the green book re-appeared… followed by an image of herself standing and sketching a caricature of a seated person. "Why, of course," she said, slapping her thigh in excitement. At school she was famous for her near lifelike drawings of people where she added comical exaggerations of prominent facial features. She knew she was a talented artist.

"Where can I buy art supplies," Syeira asked the morning clerk at the desk. "You know…color paints, brushes, canvass paper, stuff to paint pictures and stuff."

The shriveled little man behind the counter scratched the back of his graying head and screwed up his face. "Well. You might try Pierre's one block down and three blocks over. He does store signs and such. Might have some extra supplies he could sell you. Maybe."

"Guzman, you mangy old cur. Didn't I ask you to have my darn sheets washed yesterday? Especially since Chicken Maria kept me company the night before?" A heavy bearded customer had shoved in beside her at the desk, demanding the clerk's attention. He turned and winked at Syeira. "Maria…Chicken Maria…she's a big woman of strong appetites," he chuckled and nodded knowingly to Syeira. "Makes a mess of the bed sheets, though. Every darn time."

Syeira moved away from the man, glaring at him

but talking to the beleaguered clerk, "Mister, that's just gross. *Not* something I need to hear. And thank you for the directions, sir."

Head up, shoulders back, and the lines of her mouth tight with disgust, she marched out of the hotel with the handful of men still lingering in the lobby ogling her as she passed them by.

Out in the street, Syeira followed the simple directions to Pierre's place. The shop itself was a small nondescript building but it had a large gaudy sign hung across the outside above the door. Inside, there were containers of paint in all different colors neatly stacked against one wall. An assortment of heavy paintbrushes, cleaning rags, paint trays, canvas sheets of all sizes, and several cans of turpentine, lay grouped in the middle of the room. Facing the other wall was an ancient wooden counter that showed numerous knife scars and carvings against its dark grainy surface. It looked like it had once belonged in a bawdy barroom. Behind it on a lone barstool perched Pierre, who looked up as Syeira entered.

The proprietor turned out to be a talkative sad-eyed Frenchman. "You say you draw? Ah, that's good. And what do you draw, my jeune Madame? Portraits of people? Animals? Nature? The creations of man? Much better to show the creations of God, no? I myself sketch cats and dogs of all kinds for amusement when I'm not painting signs. On the whole, I find they have much more interesting personalities and a higher level of intelligence than most people I've had the misfortune to meet."

"Oh, well, I do portraits and such. But with exaggerations of people's facial features."

"Je vois. I will be happy to sell you some basic supplies. In fact, I have an extra easel and drawing sheets. Also an unused wooden palette on which the paint pigments is not dried out." He turned toward her. "Do you do watercolors, too?"

"Ah, yes. I do both."

"I will give you one of my watercolors, too. Ceramic."

"Thank you very much. That's nice of you."

Pierre kept talking. He'd come from France. She soon learned that he'd lost an older brother, plus a much beloved uncle, plus his troubled first marriage all because of the Napoleonic Wars. She noticed the three fingers were missing on his left hand. He told her he'd lost them as a sailor during the naval Battle of Trafalgar.

"I'm so sorry to hear all that. Really. You poor, poor man," she cooed encouragingly, not knowing what else to say. "Say, your English is pretty good."

"Oui. My new wife is English. And learning other languages comes easy to me. Like painting. I also know some German and Dutch."

The normally cheerless Pierre brightened having a captive listener who was female, pretty, and young. He told her his second wife was much younger than he, too.

With Pierre rambling on and reluctant to let her

leave, it took much longer than expected to buy her supplies and make her goodbye. But once done, Syeira decided to walk the downtown area to find the most expensive looking hotel and set up her easel close to its front entrance. Along the way, she also spotted a clothing store and nipped in to purchase a fur-lined lady's jacket against the growing cold. The proprietor also sold her a rickety high-backed chair, paint faded and water stained but still usable, for her customers to sit on while she worked on their portraits.

It felt good to be in control. Even for such a little thing. To do something besides fretting about the situation. So far, the little green book or whatever it was, was in charge.

Syeira took a position on the cobbled sidewalk near the grand entry of the elegant Hotel Maison de Ville. The doorman and management had no problem with a pretty young female artist working outside their building. The doorman smiled encouragement, and the assistant manager, a young dandy in his mid-twenties, often stepped outside to chat with her when things got slow.

It was now late morning. That afternoon and the next day she did a total of nine portraits. She got a dollar for each one, except for the last three drawings. Three men who looked like her idea of swashbuckling pirates sauntered out of the hotel just before dusk, saw her, and headed her way. The first two paid her three dollars each. Not to be outdone, the last and most important man—it was obvious by the way the others deferred to him—

gave her a whole ten dollars, a most courteous bow, and a gentleman's kiss on her hand. Syeira blushed furiously. Even in the approaching darkness, she knew it must be noticeable, which made her all the more embarrassed. Naturally, the man studied her face. He smiled knowingly. He was very handsome and dashing.

"Captain Jean Lafitte at your service, Madame." The pirate bowed again.

"Oh my." Syeira giggled, then held her hand up to her mouth and giggled again. Not knowing what else to say, she mumbled, "So very glad to meet you. And your men," she nodded to the others. "Thanks for letting me draw you. It was a real honor. Sir." She blushed some more. "I, ah, I hope it meets your approval. I did exaggerate your chin and forehead a little bit there."

"Quite the contrary. Excellent likeness. You are as talented as you are beautiful, my dear girl. Will you be here tomorrow and the next day and the day after, perhaps?"

"Why, yes. I plan on making this my permanent spot. Next to a luxury hotel, you see. You know what they *say*. Location, location, location." She waved her hands, a bit nervous. "It's the foundation of good marketing," she laughed, her voice higher than usual.

"Well. In that case, I'll have more of my men stop by for you to do their portraits then?" He grinned with a rakish smile and nodded once before turning to leave with his men.

"Wow. Just…wow." She said after they left.

Chapter 18
TOGETHER AGAIN

Guillaume had been brought in that morning under heavy guard to the jailhouse. Old Gully had been up to his usual tricks. Meaning he got roaring drunk. Insulted whatever females were present—whether ladies or otherwise. Smashed chairs and bottles over every man within reach who dared to disagree with his crazy slurred pronouncements. And made himself a royal nuisance to the string of woe-be-gone drinking establishments he chose to frequent for the night. Even his accompanying shipmates knew to leave him be when he got so plastered.

Thomas perked up right away when he saw his stumbling figure held upright by the two guards, each taking a shoulder to help carry his dead weight. Gully was a long-time member of Lafitte's band; a valued seaman when sober. That meant the captain must be in town, too!

Later, at the end of his shift, after Gully had spent almost the entire day sleeping off his drunk and had regained his wits, Thomas approached the cell, calling his name. Old Gully rose up, swinging his legs over the side of the cot into a sitting position.

"Argh, who be asking?" he mumbled, holding his head between his hands.

"It's me. Thomas. I, ah, I stayed with Angel and his lady when everyone returned to the island." When Gully didn't reply at first, he added, "I was on the Queen of India. Remember? It exploded and sank."

"Attendez un peu." Gully rubbed his forehead with his left hand, eyes squinting, staring at Thomas' face. "Seems like…ah, yes. I know you now. Tommy boy, you be."

"That's right. That's right, I'm Thomas." He looked at the pirate. "Gully, is the captain in New Orleans? Is Lafitte in town? Where's he and the rest of the men staying, do you know?"

"The captain and the other leaders are living high on the hog at the Maison. The rest o' us swabs be fending for ourselves. Some got wenches they be staying with." He looked around ruefully. "And then there's old Gully here—pomee!—enjoying the free food and grand comfort of these here rich quarters." He cackled at his own joke. "Mal pris, boy, mal pris."

"Thanks, Gully, for the information."

"If you see Angel and the rest, tell 'em I'll be out two mornings from now. Three days rotting in jail. 'Cause I'm not willing to pay the blasted fine." He cursed and scratched his ragged beard, thinking. "The captain was supposed to meet with General Jackson today, I heard."

"Really? That's good news, isn't it?" Thomas

leaned in closer, his hands on the bars. "Well, you take care, Gully. I'll see you around, okay?" He looked at the derelict man with a certain fondness. Gully was, after all, part of the crew.

"Thanks again, man." Thomas waved goodbye to him and hurried out the door through the outer office and into the street, excited to see his pirate friends again.

Minutes later, he turned onto Toulouse Street. Five blocks from the Hotel Maison de Ville, Thomas recognized her figure. There was Samantha—his Sam!—standing on the cobbled sidewalk with what looked to be a palette in one hand and a paintbrush in the other. There was an easel set up in front of her. And she seemed to be…painting…of all things. Doing one of her famous portraits, he supposed.

Now that's just crazy! He grinned in anticipation. *Oh, boy is she going to be surprised. Little green book, I knew you'd come through for me.*

A slender man—almost dainty—stood posing several feet from her, his body stock-still and his head upturned to best catch his profile in the intermittent sunlight, waiting for his picture to be done. In between the man and Sam, pulled off to the side, was a solitary chair, ignored by both.

The day had dawned overcast and gloomy, with the sun breaking through with occasional brilliant shafts only to be diminished or hidden behind the shifting cloud masses.

Thomas quickened his steps, hoping her concentration on the task at hand would allow him to walk up unnoticed behind and tap her on the shoulder. *I'm so mean!* He chuckled.

Sure enough, she was leaning close to the canvas, her head swiveling from her work to the man's face and back again, engrossed in putting the finishing touches on his portrait. TJ snuck behind her, waiting until her brush was in mid-air so he wouldn't mess up the picture. He tapped her shoulder twice before she turned to see who it was.

"TJ! You're here!" she shrieked in delight, nearly dropping her brush and palette in her shock. She set her instruments down beside the canvas and wrapped her arms around him in a hug so tight he couldn't breathe.

He hugged her back and gave her a long hard full-on kiss. They clung to each other and kissed some more for a full minute. Finally, they both come up for air.

"So." He drew a deep breath and exhaled dramatically. "What's up, girlfriend?"

"You…you big sneak, you…but I'm so glad to see you." She sighed, too. "It's been so lonely. So hard." Sudden tears leaked out of the corners of her eyes. She hugged him fiercely one more time and kissed him again.

"Oh, TJ! TJ, I'm so happy you're here with me. You have no idea. How much I've wanted to see you." Samantha released him, a humungous smile plastered across her pretty mouth. The petulant breeze, hinting of afternoon showers to come, was stronger now, tossing her bangs and the long ends of her hair. In response, she lifted her beautiful reddish-auburn locks out of her face and tucked behind her ear in an unconscious seductive manner, just like she always did.

It felt so good to see her, to be with her. TJ stared at her loveliness. Every part of him was exploding in happiness. *Thank you, little green book!*

"You can't imagine what I'm been going through. Or can you?" She narrowed her eyes at him with a trace of accusation. "You've done this before, haven't you? Tell the truth. Haven't you?"

They both heard repeated coughs, soft at first then louder. Sam's customer was becoming impatient.

"Oh, excuse me, sir. So very sorry for the delay. This is a long-lost friend of mine, you might say." She hurried over to the canvas and picked up the paintbrush and palette and began painting with renewed speed. She beamed at the man. "I'll have this finished in just a minute. Just a few added touches here and there." Her smile lingered as she worked.

"There. How does that look?" she glanced at her customer before turning and winking at TJ.

The man, dressed in finest European clothes of woolen tan suit, beige cotton-spun shirt and coffee-colored hat, was a dandy, and Sam had captured the essence of his appearance in a full length drawing. The man had agreed to pay two-fifty for a head-to-toe portrait. He stood admiring his likeness and particularly his face for some time, stroking his dark goatee and muttering words like "Hmmmm," and "<u>Très bien</u>," and "Amusing. Quite." Once satisfied, he turned and bowed to Sam. He took money out of his inside coat pocket, counted the payment, and handed to her.

Sam tore off the canvas sheet at the top edge with precision and rolled it up for the man to carry. He gave her a foppish grin and bowed yet again. "Madame, I have many friends in this city. I will tell them of you. Au revoir." He spun around and headed for the entrance of the Hotel de Ville, where Sam supposed he was staying.

After the man was gone, Sam took TJ's hand in hers and looked into his calm brown eyes. "Tege, this whole…whatever I've been experiencing…has been insane. I would have thought it was all a dream. But I keep waking up. To another day. And then yet another day. My senses tell me it's reality, too." Her earnest voice carried a hint of desperation, of unknown fear.

"I can feel…touch…taste…see…smell…talk…hear…move around. Objects are solid. People are real beings. Not figments of my imagination or shadows from a dream. What is all this?" She probed his face, eagerly.

"You've been through this experience before. You *know*. Tell me, TJ. Tell me everything. Everything that's happened to you! The whole outrageous unbelievable tale from beginning to end. What's going on here? How did I—how did we—end up here? More importantly, how do we get back? To our future selves?"

"I'll tell you everything. But first, you tell me your story. I came back into the past to find you, Sam. With the help of the little green book, I found you, didn't I? Although you don't know it—yet—neither you nor I need rescuing. At least not in the sense you think. We're safe. And we *will* get back to the future. Trust me. So, you tell me yours, first, girlfriend."

"TJ, how can you be so flippant? We're two hundred years in the past. None of the people we know and love will be born for many generations. We're lost." Her lips trembled. "I miss my family. I miss my other friends. I miss my life."

TJ took her into his arms again and held her, nestling her chin on his shoulder and the top of her head against his cheek. Their bodies swayed together, side to side in slow motion, as he shushed her anxieties. "We'll get back, Sam. We will, sweetness. Promise. I'll let you in on the big secret. But I want to hear your side before I do that. Okay?"

"Okay, snuggle-bunny. Sugums. *Snookums.*"

"Hey, not that!" said TJ with fake exasperation.

Sam laughed in spite of herself.

"If the hotel, there," he jerked his head toward the deVille, "has a fine dining establishment, let's find an empty table in a deserted corner, get something to eat, and catch up. That could take a while." He leaned closer in. "We might as well be comfortable. Right?" He glanced up at the troubled sky. "It looks like it might rain, too. Wanna go inside?"

"Sure."

Having already nipped into the hotel twice before to buy a quick meal while she was plying her craft, Sam knew it had an eating place that was quite nice for that section of the city. Many wealthy businessman and travelers stayed there. She dried her tears and calmed her fears. TJ gathered up her stuff. Together they strolled into the hotel. Once settled into a quiet cozy nook within, they ordered a breakfast. Sam began to tell TJ everything that had befallen her since she touched the little green book: The burning of Washington, the flag still flying high over Ft. McHenry, the gypsy band; and now New Orleans.

"Say, I found out Captain Lafitte and his leaders are staying right here. At this very hotel," TJ winked after Sam had completed her tale. "That's why I headed this way, you know. Needless to say, I was surprised to see you skulking around. Like the big mischief-maker you are." He reached out and nudged her elbow resting on the table. "But all the while I trusted the little green book to put us together. Sooner or later." He shrugged. "I wasn't worried at all." He leaned back in his chair.

"That's old news, boy toy. I already knew Lafitte was here." She grinned like a cat about to swallow a canary. "You see, I did portraits of Lafitte and a couple of his men."

"Really? Hmmm. That's cool. Way cool, my beautiful artiste. Well anyway, I hope to bump into him or Angel or some of the others while we're here."

"Angel?"

"Yeah. He's one of the pirates. We became buddies. Sort of. I stayed with him and his girlfriend and their little boy for a short time back at the island." TJ proceeded to tell Sam of all his adventures on the quest to find her. Then he told her of his first trip into past where he landed in 1802 frontier Tennessee and faced Indians, bandits, ruffians, wild animals, and assorted bullies and dangers along the way.

Sam hung on TJ's every word, her expression alternating between awe and frank disbelief. Toward the end, she felt she was maybe—just maybe—beginning to understand the power of the little green book.

"Amazing. Flat out…amazing. Scary, though." Sam shook her pretty head. "You couldn't be harmed. You wouldn't be remembered. You didn't control when you returned." Her eyes were big as saucers, thinking about the implications of what she'd heard. "The book itself brought you back to the future. But when *it* was ready, not before."

She gave him a flummoxed smile, worry lines etched across her forehead. "Let's hope the book doesn't change the rules of the game, Tege."

"It won't." He told her of the history of the book as he knew it including his father's past experiences.

"Well, that's a relief. It seems it always works and always brings you back."

They finished their meal and stories. They sat, lingering, each lost in his or her own thoughts for the moment. The rain that had been threatening all morning long started in earnest. They listened to the drumming of the hard showers upon the walls and windows of the building. The sound was soothing and made them both sleepy after the good meal. Just then a band of pirates appeared in the elegant foyer adjacent to the dining room. They had come in from the outside.

Angel was among them.

TJ saw him and called out his name.

Angel halted, staring through the entry way between the two rooms in their direction. His face brightened when he recognized Thomas. He hurried over with a huge smile to their table.

"How goes it, my young cockatoo?" he exclaimed, slapping TJ on his shoulder. "I thought I should never see you again, my friend." TJ stood up to shake his hand.

"Pray tell, who is this charming lady?" He clicked his boot heels together and gave Samantha a slight bow, a twinkle in his dark watchful gaze.

"Angel, this is Samantha. She's my steady girl. She came to the city to be with me."

"Enchanté, I'm sure." Angel looked at Sam

appreciatively. "Forgive me, Thomas, for I doubted your good taste, earlier, but now I see I was mistaken."

TJ grinned. "Yeah, I got real lucky with Samantha. Dating up, as they say. She's above me in looks, intelligence, and class. Especially class."

Sam rolled her eyes and giggled a little.

"Tell me, Angel. How did Lafitte's meeting go with General Jackson? Good, I hope."

"You heard about that, eh?" Angel was taken aback. He stroked his mustache before answering. "It was secret. Only we leaders were supposed to know the details. However, the captain did convince the General of our loyalty and value to the American cause. We'll provide arms, men, knowledge. We'll fight. In return, the General will see to it complete pardons are granted for all privateers for our past, ahhh, indiscretions, shall we say. Everyone under Lafitte."

TJ knew that, of course, from his history classes, but he acted surprised.

"That's wonderful news, Angel. The best. For the whole gang, me included. So what's next on the agenda."

"We will not fight except in direct defense of the city. The General, however, is more ambitious and determined to challenge or stop the British if he can before they reach New Orleans. I suspect there will be at least one mêlée before the big battle."

"You may be right, Angel," said TJ, again playing along. He knew in advance Angel's supposition was true, knew the name of the very skirmish. He held out his hand and they shook once more. "Leave word for me at the front desk when the captain is ready to assemble the men together for the main event. I'll come, ready to fight."

"Tege!" Sam gasped. "You can't do—"

TJ waved her down. "It's okay, Samantha. I know what I'm doing; I *won't* get hurt. Remember," He raised his eyebrows significantly, "what we just talked about."

"Oh. Okay." She still seemed flustered at the thought.

"See you around, Angel." He waved at the pirate, and Angel waved in return.

TJ and Sam spent the next week seeing each other for breakfast at the deVille every day. Sam was earning enough from her portraits to switch hotels. They spent evenings together, walking the French Quarters, having dinner at a different place every night. They talked about their past present…their families, friends, the meaning of all their adventures in the present past…and when they might return to the future.

TJ felt the climax of their mutual time-travel-history adventure was fast approaching.

On the 24th from mid-day on, the constable, TJ, and the eavesdropping prisoners heard the good news repeated from a continuous stream of giddy visitors to the jail house. General Jackson had led a daring night raid, they all said with great excitement, on General Keane's unsuspecting troops near the Villere and LaCoste plantations. Although the fighting, they'd heard, had degenerated into hand-to-hand combat fighting in the smoky darkness, it had caught the British unawares and stopped their immediate advance toward the city.

Already, the men exclaimed, General Jackson was intensifying efforts to build up fortifications and earthworks around the south and east of the city

Yeah, the real battle is fast approaching. TJ looked up from his little desk at the latest group of eager intruders and rubbed his chin. *And guess what else, yahoos. We win this next one. Big time.*

Chapter 19
GENERAL CARROLL COMMANDS

Vern Cockrell pulled into the garage at seven fifty-seven that evening. The professor sat in the switched off car for several minutes, mentally reviewing the end of the day, his brow furrowed in mild frustration. He sucked in a deep breath and let it out slow. He hated discord, unnecessary stress. He avoided arguments whenever possible. His ex-wife, TJ's mother, had loved verbal sparring and quarreling, it seemed to him. It was the main thing he didn't miss from their failed relationship after the ugly divorce.

The professor felt drained. He was over an hour later than usual arriving home, but it couldn't be helped. Two graduate assistants had gotten into a heated dispute over research responsibilities. It was a needless turf battle with each, frankly, infringing upon and stealing credit for a portion of the other's work. He'd played intermediary, settling them down and defining, once again, exactly who did what. On top of that, one of his doctoral candidates, well known for her indecisiveness and quirkiness, was still struggling with her thesis and he'd had to help redirect her choice of topic. For the fourth time. Very smart candidate but total lack of focus.

Well, the kids should be inside busy studying now.

He sighed. Vern shook his head to clear away the lingering thoughts and grabbed the briefcase off the passenger seat. Once inside the house, he walked down the back hallway, passing by the large office-den and a bathroom, to get to the kitchen area with its adjoining breakfast nook.

There was no one there. "Tege? Sam?" Hearing nothing, he marched over to the entryway to the formal dining room and stuck his head in. They weren't there, either.

Vern stood, puzzled. "Maybe they decided at the last minute to go to Samantha's home to study." Although TJ did say the plan was to get together and study here.

"Hmmm."

Naturally, he'd check the upstairs rooms first before calling the Robertson's. No need to seem anxious over what was almost certain a simple case of teenage fickleness. He strode into the large living room, crossing the thick plush carpet with faster steps now, and began climbing the stairs two at a time.

"TJ!" He said the name much louder, hoping to hear a response. There was silence. He turned toward TJ's room, leaning in at the door, but it was empty. He then spun around and walked down the hall to the master bedroom—his bedroom. What he saw inside made his blood run *cold*.

The two bodies were lying face down on the floor; one figure slumped partially over the other. The bottom half of both torsos extended beyond the wood floor onto the thick carpet. The top of their heads was three feet or more behind the barrel-back chair and the small desk. He could see several center pages of the little green book had been bent back by the force of hitting the hardwood floor as it landed the first time. It now lay with its cover down, six inches past TJ's outstretched fingers.

Vern gulped.

"Oh, no. *No!* This can't have happened. Not again." The professor blanched. He grasped his chest as though in pain. Stumbling into the room, he reached the end of the bed and collapsed into a sitting position—frightened, but already calculating, thinking hard—elbows on knees, palms cupping his shocked visage, staring in frank disbelief at the crumpled bodies and crinkled little green book on the floor in front of him.

"Vern! You fool! You've done it again." He growled.

"This time, you left it on top of the desk in plain sight. Remember?" He smacked himself on the sides of his face with his open hands in irritation. It was a little over a year ago he'd gotten careless once before. He'd left the small desk unlocked, allowing TJ to find the green book. His son had picked it up and been thrust back in time to frontier Tennessee days for a wild adventure.

He inhaled in frustration for the second time that evening, filling his lungs to maximum capacity and holding it, holding it, lost in concentration, before exhaling raggedly. He winced at his scary conclusion. "I never thought it was possible until now." He stroked his chin, his eyes frowning. "One user at a time, I always assumed, based on my own experiences and those of Professors Manchester and McCarty. But it's plain to see that they've *both* gone into the past."

It was the only scenario that made sense. "TJ would never seek another adventure without getting my permission first." Unless, of course, the boy felt it was an emergency, that he had no choice but to do so.

He envisioned the whole scene in his mind. "Samantha must have come up here for something. Of course, she was drawn to the book. It's like a…like a human magnet; one can't help being attracted to it." He saw Sam seeing it on top of the little desk and picking it up out of curiosity. He saw her body fall to the floor. He saw TJ coming upstairs a little later to check on her. When Tege spied the book on the floor, naturally the boy knew what had happened and went after his girlfriend.

Until now, the professor hadn't known for certain. Would the power of the book work for more than one individual, concurrently? It must have! He just hoped TJ and Sam had landed in the same time period and same place. But then he'd never had the opportunity or need to prove that particular hypothesis with a partner. And the previous owners of the little green book never had that experience either.

Would the awesome power behind the little green book work for three people as well as two or one? He was about to find out! He had to find out. He'd often fantasized about taking a time-travel trip together with his son. Although he knew the book protected the recipient from real physical harm, he still felt anxious this time.

Without further hesitation, Vern Cockrell stepped around the bodies, stooped down, and scooped the green book up as it lay just past TJ's limp outstretched hand. An instant shock, much like electricity but softer and gentler, flowed from the little book through his hands into his body. He took a huge step back to distance his lanky frame from landing on top of TJ and Sam. Ignoring the strange but familiar sensation, in the few seconds he had remaining before the little green book took control of his being, Vern smoothed out its bent pages in the middle—*my old friend!*—closing the book up and flipping it over to study the front. *The pictures always provide a clue where it will land me.* Already its cover was flowing with spirited images of men in buckskins and uniforms and sleek horses standing under massive stately oak trees in front of a most picturesque and placid plantation home. Soon other visions appeared, in sequence, melting away the original plantation setting.

As the swirling mist closed in, the professor shouted toward the disappearing bedroom wall in front of the vanishing work desk, "Hang on, kids. I'm coming. I'll find you!"

A dreamlike trance overcame him. He yielded to the smoky-white aura that filled his mind and surrounded his being. He felt his body falling, falling to an unknown place.

When the swirls of fog faded away and his consciousness returned, Vern discovered he was a lone observer behind a large cluster of men, all facing forward with their backs to him. No one saw him materialize. The posture of every man in group was casual yet confident. Most were standing, but not at attention. Some leaned languidly against the nearest tree. A few were mounted, their horses gazing at the closest clumps of tasty grass within their reach. And a small handful at the very front sat cross-legged on the turf, or else reclined back with their elbows propped against the soft ground. Every man was listening intently to a youthful but enthusiastic army officer addressing them from the topmost step of the front veranda of an elegant plantation house.

Vern looked down to see what he was wearing. As a noted professor of nineteenth century American history, he recognized the uniform of a militiaman. One of the states. Southern, of course. He guessed circa 1815 or thereabouts; early century, for sure. The plantation was the scene from the first picture that appeared on the book cover. His left hand held the butt of a Kentucky long rifle braced over his left shoulder. There was a smallish leather pouch slung over the opposite shoulder. The bag nestled against his upper abdomen. He was certain it contained flints, rifle balls, and gunpowder. He could feel the weight of a heavy knapsack strapped across his back and chest.

Being a veteran of past adventures via the little green book, the incredible change in circumstances and clothes didn't faze him. One bit.

So he was in the army now. Who's army, he was about to find out!

Vern reached out and tapped the person closest to him on the shoulder. The man turned half around, eyeing the new arrival with interest. "Say, ah, I just got here. From Knoxville."

"Knoxville, hey? That's a far piece east o' here. My wife's got some cousins from that neck o' the woods."

"I'm," Vern glanced at his sleeve, "I'm a corporal. Cockrell's my name. First name's Vernon, but most people call me Vern." He nodded friendly like at the man.

"Howdy, there, stranger." The man spat a stream of dark brown chaw juice on the ground then wiped his mouth. "I'm Peter Mulcahy from Murfreesboro, a little one-horse place not too far from here. I'm known as Pete. Or Mule, short for Mulcahy. Take your pick.

"Knoxville, uh?"

They shook hands.

"That's a right far piece, ain't it?" he repeated. "You come all that way on foot, did ya?"

"Last part of it I did. My horse got lame about fifteen miles back, you see. Had to make one stop after that. Just arrived a minute ago, matter of fact. What's going on?" Like TJ, the professor had become an expert on fibbing to cover his real story when on an adventure.

"Major-General Carroll is talking to the men right now. Getting 'em fired up. We'll pull out at daybreak tomorrow heading for New Orleans." He nodded with vigor and spat some more juice. "I'm right eager to whip some British butts."

"Me, too," smiled Vern. *General Carroll. He commanded the center of Jackson's main line at the battle where the heaviest of the fighting took place.* "I'll wager we beat them bad." He winked at Mule.

"Ya, boy!"

The man gave Vern a hearty slap on the shoulder and motioned him forward, making room for Vern to join him with his row of comrades. Together, they listened to the end of the major-general's fiery speech.

"The British shall not prevail in the coming clash. They shall not win and they shall not capture the city of New Orleans, that glorious queen of the Mississippi, that jewel of the delta. Gentlemen, true Tennesseans all, we shall proceed with all haste to the aid of General Jackson and our fellow countrymen."

He paused for emphasis, his steely gaze looking out over the assembled troops. "Let us serve with highest honor! Let us fight with the greatest valor! The redcoat

British would reverse the course of history and return us again to bondage under their thumb. Let it not be so! In the morning, we sail forward to battle and ultimate victory!"

The men whooped and hollered, many throwing their hats high into the air and several firing their pistols or rifles overhead. One rider was bucked off his horse when the animal shied from all the sudden noise and loud gunplay, but he soon remounted, ready to go.

The professor ate supper that night with Mule, his friends, and other soldiers around a blazing campfire in a hayfield that now lay harvested, shorn of its crops and laid bare to the earth waiting for the next planting season. Adjacent to the small hayfield on either side were large tobacco fields extending to horizons of woods to the left and right so far away the trees looked tiny. The plantation had begun experimenting with cotton as an alternative cash crop the year before. The cotton field stretched back of the mansion beyond the vegetable garden, wedged between the tobacco acres.

In the near distance, the professor could see two other campfires with militiamen gathered around them, talking, laughing, playing cards, smoking, eating, resting, or sleeping. The mood everywhere was high-spirited and boastful. The British devils were already defeated in their minds!

At daybreak, the men marched or rode their horses north of the young city of Nashville to board a makeshift convoy of waiting boats on the Cumberland River shore.

"Just a few days and we'll be there, Vern, my man," said Mule. "Just a hop, skip, and a jump."

The trip, however, wasn't fast. Steamboats were a new technology. Only a few existed. None were yet available for such a large party, in any case. From the Cumberland, the boats had to be rowed to the far end of the Ohio River and then tread their way down the broad sluggish expanse of the great Mississippi.

The second day of the journey a wicked rainstorm blew in, drenching men on the open decks and slowing the progress of the caravan of boats even more. Mule scrutinized the boiling black clouds with a practiced eye. "It looks like this here's gonna last through the rest o' the day and into the night, boys. Better hunker down."

"Darn this weather," groused Catfish Murphy, tugging his heavy army coat tighter around his body and crouching with his back to the howling wind and rain. He got his nickname because he dearly loved the muddy but distinctive taste of fresh catfish. Another reason for his moniker was the man wore a long thin mustache with a stringy soul batch beneath his bottom lip that altogether resembled the whiskers on his favorite fish. "Never been there, but I hear they got some fine women specimens down that way. French. Spanish. Cajun. Creole. You name it."

"You're always thinking about that, Cat," grinned Big Bert, a mountain of a man from Memphis, who'd earned his living as a saloon bouncer and also as heavy-handed enforcer for a rich landlord before signing up for the military to fight Indians.

"I can think about 'em wet or dry, hot or cold, day or night," he retorted, his lanky face locked into a scowl at the unending pounding of the cold deluge.

"With your ugly mug, the only way you'll get close to a pretty lady is paying double," cracked Tom Jenson.

"Shut your face," retorted Cat.

Tom just hooted. Cat was as skinny as a scarecrow. He had about as much strength as one, too. No one feared his surly outbursts. Tom knew he could tie him up in a knot with one hand behind his back.

The two men bantered back and forth, as much to pass the dreary time as to argue.

Ignoring the verbal sparring around him, Vern sheltered his eyes with from the driving rain with both his hands and stared straight ahead, trying to gauge the distance to the far off horizon of the gray churning waters. If the storm persisted, the flotilla of boats would make for the most likely looking bit of shore where they might dock, tie down for the night, and maybe find some wooded shelter to be able to cook a hot meal.

The going was slow and monotonous. Petty fights broke out from sheer boredom or frustration and officers had their hands full keeping peace.

It was late December when they arrived at the loading docks beside New Orleans. Vern exhaled with relief as they pulled up beside the wooden wharf.

Just put me inside the city, free to search for them, little green book.

He hoped to cross paths with TJ or Samantha there, but it was not to be. That day or the next or the many days following. The professor knew enough to play by the rules.

I mustn't grow impatient.

The professor decided he would stay with the militia. For now. When the green book provided a change, only then could he make a different play. No army desertion for him. He'd learned from experience to trust the little green book. He saw the current move, the current circumstance, whereas the book managed all the steps through the end-game.

Of course, he still didn't understand how or why it worked. But he had faith the little green book would somehow make things right before the grand finish. It always had, before. He believed it. Simply because it was the truth.

Major-General Carroll marched his men to where the bulk of Jackson's troops were busy turning the Rodriguez Canal south of the city into a heavily fortified line of earthworks against the expected British assault. Carroll had arrived none too soon. The British sent out probing columns of soldiers the next day. After the British ceased their exploratory thrusts, the Americans, some of Carroll's militia including Vern, began constructing artillery batteries to protect the bulwarks.

It was back-breaking work, several days of it, but the professor knew it was critical to their ultimate success.

"My whole body aches, Mule," said Vern the morning after the last of the eight batteries had been brought in. Everything was installed up and down the length of Line Jackson. He arched his back and twisted his torso and shoulders left and right several times to loosen his stiff frame. "I'm not used to doing hard labor like this."

"Hard? You call this hard? This here's child's play, Vern. You're too soft." Mule jerked his head at the professor, calling to another soldier. "Jimmy, the man thinks this is rough. He doesn't know *rough*, does he?"

"Aye, fighting the Red Sticks…now that was some tough slogging, that. So was beating off starvation as a young sprout in Ireland. Day after day with a stomach so empty you could near see me spine from the front side. Me and my brothers. Taking beatings from our good for nothing drunken father. Watching me saintly mother slowly weaken and die for lack of proper food. Then seeing me oldest brother die of scurvy in front of me on the voyage here to America. *Those* were rough times."

"Didn't know your story, Jimmy, me lad. Sorry. Right sorry I am to hear all that." Mule was somber. "But things are better now, hey?"

Jimmy said nothing, staring out past them.

Vern coughed, unsure what to say.

They looked down below at the passing noise.

Except for the rampart laborers still working like Mr. Cockrell, Jimmy and Mule, the rest of General Jackson's troops were conducting a dress parade or watching it; a bit too confident of their position, it seemed to the professor.

Just then, everyone heard a chorus of ominous booming off in the distance. The crescendo increased until it sounded like continuous thunder. Soon the frightening whistle of cannon balls hurling through the sky reached their ears, sending most of the men scrambling for cover. One projectile struck the land between the soldiers' campsites and the freshly built artillery line. It blasted a huge crater in the ground showering fragments of sod and grass hundreds of feet upwards. Most of the shots, the Americans could tell, seemed to fall clear of their artillery batteries, slamming into the earthworks or short of the line altogether.

Some of the gunners hastened to man their posts and return fire as best they could.

The exchange of artillery fire continued for three hours, with the more numerous British guns finding a few targets. Several American guns were knocked out.

"Sad news," gulped Mule, joining Vern around a campfire that evening, sitting beside him. "I heard Dan Cheatham's dead. A shell struck the front end of their cannon. Busted it all up to kingdom come. One of the fragments hit him in the neck. Near took his head off."

Mule's eyes got moist and his voice choked. "Got to know him pretty well…yessir, pretty dad gum well the last three weeks or so. Decent lad. Kentucky militia, he was. Couple other gunners were hurt bad, too.

"Say, Smith told me your artillery unit got hit, too. Says he was standing sixty or seventy yards away and saw the debris from the blast cover you up like a cloud. Why weren't you injured? That makes no sense whatsoever. A near direct hit like that and all that shrapnel striking around you."

Vern knew why, of course, but he couldn't tell his friend the real reason. "Just lucky, I guess."

Mule stared at Vern, unconvinced. "Must have a bloody guardian angel somewhere then." He stared morosely into the fire, watching the interplay of changing colors and sparks ascending into the night air. "Well, anyway—" He slapped his knees with his hands before rousing himself to stand up to fetch a tin of coffee. "Hard to lose good people like Dan. But glad that skirmish is over now, friend."

"Yeah. Me, too, Mule. Me, too."

The professor just remembered. Today was New Year's Day, 1815. The big battle was fast approaching.

Chapter 20
BEHIND THE JACKSON LINE

TJ corralled Chief Constable O'Grady the next morning as soon as he saw him enter the room. "Sir, I'd like to start working half days, if you don't mind."

O'Grady folded his muscular arms over his beefy chest. "Huh? What for, lad? Not unhappy, are you? You're doing a fair enough job for us." He frowned a bit.

"Oh, *no*, sir, everything here is fine. I'm happy with the work. You're a great boss." TJ hesitated. "It's just that I, ah…well, you see, sir, I want to be in the front line with Captain Lafitte and the rest of his men. I'm very anxious to know what they're planning and how I can help. Once the actual fighting starts, of course, I'll need to take the whole day off. Or days, if need be. However long it lasts. Until the battle is over." He looked expectantly at the constable.

"So you want to fight the redcoats, do you?" The big man stroked his cropped beard, considering the slight boy standing before him.

"Yes, please sir."

"A mite young, aren't you, lad, to be so eager for death? The front line will be the most dangerous place to be, you know."

"I'm not afraid." He knew—although O'Grady didn't—that the little green book would keep him safe, no matter what. "You've seen me fight before. Believe me, in some ways I'm much, much older than I appear to be." *Yeah, two hundred years in the future, older.* "I'm determined." He gave O'Grady a dogged look. "I know I can fight as well as a grown man, if it comes to that."

I can't really hurt anyone just like they can't hurt me.

The constable laughed. "Aye, that much I can see. A real banty rooster, eh? Mature beyond your years." His manner became more solemn. "Hoo dawgie, I expect all of us will be in the fighting, one way or another, before this is all done."

TJ waited.

The constable signed. "Fine, then, lad. Better to be brave than a coward, I always say. Life's too short to be hanging your tail between your legs. Face what comes with head high and stout heart. I expect you want to start it today, do you?"

"Yes, sir. After lunch. And I promise I'll work extra hard on the hours I put in."

"I know you will, boy."

"If you don't mind, after today I want to work afternoons. That way, I can walk to the front in the morning and see what's going on. If I don't make back for the afternoon…well, you'll know by that the fighting's started."

O'Grady bit his bottom lip, frowning some more. He didn't like the uncertainty. But he had no one else dependable he could rely on for the daytime position, even for a tentative half day's labor. The lad had proven to be his best worker, even better than the old night watchman, who'd been employed there for many years.

"All right," he growled, irritated. "Fair enough. Mind, though, you best be checking in every day unless the bloody British are driving hard steel at your throat, boy." He glared at TJ.

"Will do. You've got it, sir. Work or fighting it is, one or the other." Tege gave the big man such a confident yet sloppy grin that constable softened despite himself.

So after a half day of work at the jailhouse, TJ had a quick lunch with Sam at the hotel before asking directions at the front desk and heading out to the front line south of the city. Before leaving, he had to reassure Sam again that nothing bad could happen to him under the power of the little green book. She still seemed a little doubtful.

The walk from the city to the Jackson Line was several miles. By good fortune, a young soldier was heading to the front and he offered to let TJ double up on his horse for the rest of the trip.

Once there, TJ thanked the soldier and slipped off his horse. He wandered through throngs of bivouacked troops, stopping to ask which way to the artillery line and earthworks. He hoped he was heading in the right direction.

Near the front, he chanced upon a group of his old pirate comrades. They were all huddled around a large crackling fire, staying warm, jesting and laughing. Fat Duck had just told a ribald joke about a one-armed whore he knew from Jamaica. The man was pear-shaped, bulging around his waist but tapering off around his chest and butt, with slender legs for such a rotund body elsewhere. His weird stuttering laugh did sound a lot like a quacking duck to TJ.

The privateers were a motley bunch. Their varied and often strange appearances, range of nationalities, bravery governed by mutual greed, and fierce independence tempered by the code of pirate loyalty, made them a unique fighting force within General Jackson's amalgamation of troops and allies.

TJ stood behind them, waiting until the guffawing died down before revealing his presence.

As soon as he stepped into the fire light, several men called out happy welcome. More than one reached out and pounded him on the back, glad to see the boy again.

"Petiot! You made it!"

"Thomas, you found us after all," said Angel, shaking his hand.

"About time, you sluggard."

"If you'd stayed away much longer, you'd miss all the fun."

TJ acknowledged the greetings, a huge grin plastered on his face. It was good to see his old companions again. "Where's the captain and the others?" he asked.

Angel jerked his head over his shoulder. "We have the next four camps right in front of you. Everything else behind and on either side belongs to other troops. The general's quarters are a short ways beyond our last campsite. Lafitte and his brother are meeting with Jackson and his officers as we speak. They think the British are waiting for the rest of the army to arrive before attacking us, so they're using the time to plan their strategy of defense."

TJ nodded. He knew this already of course because of his history lessons. The main engagement was now a week away. Even though he was pre-aware of the outcome and the larger details of the fight, he still shivered with anticipation. This battle would keep America independent from Great Britain. Without a victory here, the young United States would be surrounded and strangled by Britain's complete control of the Mississippi basin and the Great Lakes, a scenario that would essentially doom the nation into servitude if not outright reformulation into British colonies.

All around him, salutations done, the pirates resumed their discussions, boastings and joshing, leaving TJ to sink into his own deep thoughts.

The Battle of New Orleans would prove to be vital

to the future of the United States. To his personal future, as well as countless generations of people not yet born.

As TJ pondered these things, his chest swelled with sudden pride at being an American. *The most unique nation in the history of the world.* With a unique destiny to play in forging true freedom for untold hundreds of millions of humans, who, apart from the existence of America, would never know personal liberties or the chance to pursue individual happiness. Angel caught the earnest expression on TJ's face and asked, "You seem befuddled, my friend. Perhaps the cares of the day are upon you. A little tired, maybe? Have you eaten?"

TJ shook his head, snapping out of his contemplative mood. "Oh, no, I'm not too tired. And yes, I could use some food.

"Sorry, Angel. I was just…thinking. About some things."

"Did you work it all out in your mind," the pirate smiled. "Come. Pierre just made a cauldron of his famous gumbo. Most of us have already eaten. But the pot's been left on the edge of the fire. Half full. Still hot.

"It's very tasty, I assure you."

"It sounds wonderful. I'm getting hungry, just hearing about it."

Angel stepped over to the tent he shared with Clovis and Rene. He disappeared inside and came back with a bowl and spoon. "Here. You may use mine. The pot's on the other side of the campfire."

"Thank you." TJ went around the blazing fire to the other side and dipped the large wooden bowl into the middle of the still steaming cauldron. He spent the next ten minutes spooning the thick brown stew-like food into his mouth and savoring each bite. Boy, Angel was right! The dish was spicy and delicious. Whatever the meat was, it was tender, succulent, and sinfully good. He refilled the bowl twice and kept eating until his stomach was full as a tick.

I can't pig out like that again. But it was worth it this one time! He grinned to himself and let out a big belch.

"Better?" asked Angel, as he returned the bowl and spoon.

"Oh, yeah. *Much* better. Thanks for the meal."

Fat Duck moved over to make room for him to join the men around the fire. "Have a squat, Petiot." He patted the ground next to him.

Someone pulled out a dilapidated deck of cards. "Who wants to play? Gaston? Duck? Angel?"

"Aye, for me. You in, Thomas?" asked Angel with a wave. "Got any of my money left on you, matey?"

"A bit. But not enough to hang with you card sharks." He laughed, followed moments later by a tremendous yawn he had to gulp hard to suppress. He roused his head and stretched his arms to the sky. "Man, all that good food has made me sleepy. I better take a walk or something to wake up." Curious, he looked in the direction of the General's encampment. "You know, I think I'd like to see the headquarters."

"Well, just make sure you don't get commandeered into repairing busted artillery bulwarks with the other poor devils. Hard dirty work, that," advised Fat Duck, thinking how much he'd hate doing manual labor with his soft muscles and love of ease.

"Hey, I'll be very careful and stay away from anyone I see with a shovel or pick in their hand." TJ grinned as he stood up. He turned and strolled out of the pirates' camp toward General Jackson's site.

He spotted a few other pirates he knew as he crossed through the next four campgrounds. He called out their names and waved as he passed by. The men beckoned to him to stop and visit, but he said he wanted to see the front first; he would come back later. He kept walking. Now there was a slight hill cresting in front of him. As soon as he topped the small rise, there before him on the other side laid a big meeting pavilion with an American flag atop its peak undulating in the soft evening wind. The large structure was surrounded by a horseshoe cluster of smaller burnt-gray tents on its other three sides.

"So this is headquarters." He glanced about with great interest. There were officers and soldiers coming and going, a beehive of activity.

Looking past the headquarters, he could make out a tiny curving line of ramparts and artillery guns off in the distance, many rows of campsites beyond the General's bivouac.

And that's the famous Jackson Line.

There was a young soldier standing at attention outside the more spacious of the tents in the headquarters area. An American flag was fastened to its top, too. TJ noticed its flaps were open. As he walked a couple of paces to the left, TJ found he could peer into the tent's interior. There was a dark-gray haired man sitting inside at a portable desk with his back to the opening. The man's frame, TJ observed, seemed long and lanky. His tousle of thick wavy hair piled high above his crown and flowed down the nape of his dark blue dress uniform's collar. Bullion and gold trimmed epaulets adorned each of the shoulders. TJ watched him, fascinated. After a bit, the man stretched and leaned forward in his chair, propping his right elbow on the tabletop and resting his chin within his cupped hand.

"General Andrew Jackson," whispered TJ, an expression of admiration upon his face. He knew from his study of history that Jackson would go on to become one of the country's most forceful Presidents, the first man of the people, so to speak.

He stood, idol-worshipping, for several minutes more, before turning to see what else he might spy. He called out to a passing officer. "Sir, do you expect any more cannon fire from the British, or do you think they're done shooting at us?"

"What's that? No, the redcoats are through for now, I reckon. I don't expect any more cannon fire until the big one starts." The man, a Colonel, stopped and spun around to face his questioner. He looked TJ up and down, apprising him. "So you're one of those scalawag pirates, are you? Why, you're just a pup. A bit young to be on the battle field, aren't you, boy?" He frowned and shook his head. "You vermin haven't been much use to us, so far, except taking up space and food. I hope your lot knows how to fight when it comes to it."

TJ returned the man's stare. He knew Lafitte's men would anchor the center of the Jackson Line with great bravery during the British assault. They may be crude, unorthodox, and disrespectful of military and other authority outside that of the pirate code, but they were fierce fighters when necessary.

"You're wrong, sir. Our men will acquit themselves as bravely as any men under your command. That, I can promise you."

"Oho! You can promise me, you say, you little braggart, do you?" The officer spat on the ground with disdain. "I don't know why the General even bothered to deal with your kind of people. You'll like as not cut our own throats instead of the British when the fighting starts." The man snorted and stalked away.

"You'll see. You and others like you will wind up eating your words before it's all done," TJ called after the man's departing figure. He watched the man's haughty strut until he turned the corner and disappeared behind a row of tents.

TJ was more determined than ever to go to the

front. *That officer got me mad. The idiot! Lafitte's pirates are brave. I'm brave, too.*

Now that the shelling had stopped, it should be a peaceful stroll. He stepped around the semicircle of headquarter tents and picked his way, still angry, through the rows of campsites and among the figures of soldiers that were huddled around fires or busy doing evening chores. The jaunt took longer than he thought and his irritation vanished as he hurried on. In the darkness, he'd misjudged the number of bivouacs between the General's quarters and the artillery line. There were still perhaps a thousand men crowded into the remaining land. Walking up the middle of General Jackson's encamped soldiers made him realize just how many troops were in the American army for the Battle of New Orleans. And it made his head spin when he considered that some of the biggest Civil War battles involved a hundred and fifty thousand or more men between the two armies North and South.

TJ had reached the next to last queue of campsites when a wonderful familiar voice shouted, "Tege! My boy! TJ! Over here!"

He froze in his tracks, pure shock on his face. He turned to face the speaker. "Dad? Dad! You're here, too?"

Father and son rushed to each other, hugging, pounding one other on the back, beaming so big their grins resembled the ear-to-ear smiles painted on a clown's face. A few nearby spectators chuckled, watching the happy reunion.

"Wow! Just wow! Dad, I can't believe it. It's so good to see you."

"I'm glad I found you, Tege. It's taken some time. I knew the little green book would lead me to you. Sooner or later. Have you seen Samantha? Do you know where she is?"

"Yes, she's here! In New Orleans. Staying at the Hotel de Ville and doing portraits of people outside. Can you believe it? I have lunch with her every day."

"So that's all of us, then. The three of us together." Vern laughed, relieved to have located both of them in the same area. "You must tell me everything…all your adventures since you arrived. Let me guess the beginning. Sam saw the book left out—my mistake, sorry—and she got curious and picked it up."

"Yes, that's right."

"And then you went after her."

"Right again."

"The book does exert an overwhelming attraction. It's hard to resist. I expect Samantha was terrified at first. Oh, well. What's done is done. She's resilient; a resourceful girl. So far, none of our excursions into the past have been bad, have they, son?"

"No. I became more grownup and confident after my frontier adventure."

"We'll just trust some good comes out of this jaunt, as well." The professor smiled. He looked down at his uniform. "As you can see, the little green book made me part of the militia. Tennessee, to be specific. Under the command of Major General Carroll. I don't have a lot of freedom to come and go as I please. Yet. You?"

"I'm part of Captain Lafitte's outfit. We're a loose bunch and until the fighting starts, I'm at liberty to go where I want, when I want, do what I wish."

"Nice. Let's, uh, let's find a campfire that's not so crowded and tell each other our stories. That one over there," Vern pointed to the light of a fire one camp over on the left where one man sat warming his hands and feet, one stretched on the ground close in so his whole body could catch the warmth, and one stood heating his backside against the flickering flames.

They walked over, sat down on the side opposite the other men and began to talk in low voices of their respective adventures. TJ told his dad about his capture and treatment by Colonel Nicolls' troops in Florida, the failed assault upon Ft. Bowyer, joining Jean Lafitte's men on the island, arriving in New Orleans alone, finding Sam, and then reconnecting with his pirate friends. They were part of the American force confronting the British. Vern recounted his much shorter tale of becoming a member of the Tennessee militia, the slow cumbersome travel down the Mississippi to the city, until now.

"And what of Samantha's escapades?" asked Vern, curious.

"Why don't I let you ask her yourself when you meet her? There's nothing going on here right now, and we both know the big attack won't happen for another week. With all the inactivity, you're bound to get some time off from your unit. You know, a military pass they call it, right? You can come with me to the city and we can both see her."

"Sounds like a fine plan, son. Your camp is less than half a mile away. Come check on me every day after breakfast, if you're free, to see what my status is for the day. Or I can fetch you if I get a pass first." The professor breathed a huge sigh of relief. He'd found both the kids and their respective situations were much better than he had feared.

Yes, the little green book has a way of making things work out for the best, Vern thought, with great contentment.

He and TJ lounged back unto the softness of the grass, a couple of feet apart. Each propped up on an elbow resting on their side so they could face each other as they spoke of many things. Father and son had formed a unique bond, a secret pact, born of their heretofore separate but somehow similar travels into the long ago years of history past. TJ picked at blades of grass, by turns listening and speaking and silence. They talked long into the night, sharing thoughts and feelings about this latest adventure. They both agreed it was unexpected but really cool that the little green book involved all of them in the grand scheme.

A year ago, with the professor's reluctant blessing, TJ had taken Natalie, his little sister, into their confidence and told her all about the book and his first trip into a wild frontier past. Now with Sam, there were four total people in the whole world who knew of the existence of the wonderful yet unpredictable time-travel powers of the little green book.

Tege couldn't wait to see the surprise on Sam's face when she saw his dad there, too.

Chapter 21
THE THREE PROVOCATEURS

TJ visited his dad the next morning after a quick breakfast of leftover gumbo and delicious campfire biscuits made by Angel. Much to his delight, he discovered Mr. Cockrell, along with three other soldiers, had been given the whole day off as a reward for their hard work on constructing the earthworks for the artillery line. The five of them walked the several miles to the outskirts of the city, enjoying the clean fresh air and bright sun in a cloudless azure sky. The weather was fair and a little warmer than the previous four days, with just a few sharp breezes now and then to remind them it was winter.

Entering the city, they split up; one man on his own, two soldiers staying together to find the nearest tavern for an all-day drinking binge with perhaps a lady or two in tow, and Tege and his dad heading for the Hotel deVille.

Outside the hotel's entrance, TJ glanced at his dad. "She generally doesn't get up too early. She likes to take a long breakfast, too, to help kill the time. Let's check the dining room first."

They walked into the seating area and, sure enough, spied her in a far back spot away from the morning crowd filling the tables closest to the door and the middle of the large room.

Sam was busy reading an English version newspaper as they approached. Her head was turned to her left, concentrating on the paper spread out on the table there. Her plate of mostly untouched food sat in front of her. She didn't see them coming.

"Good morning, Sam," said TJ, brightly.

"Oh, Tege!" She jerked up and put her hand to her chest. "Don't scare me like—" Her eyes widened when she saw them both. "Mr. Cockrell?" She moved her hand to her mouth, which was hanging wide open in shock. "My…my goodness. You're here, *too*." Recovering from her surprise, Sam's pretty face broke into the widest smile. She jumped up to give TJ and his dad big hugs.

"You jerk, you," shoving TJ in his shoulder after her hug. But she was laughing as she did it. She swept her lovely auburn hair out of her eyes to look at them both.

"Remember when I told you there was much more to the little green book than my frontier adventure last year. Well, my dad's just the person to give you a detailed account." TJ took the chair across from Sam and Vern sat next to him. Vern motioned to a passing waiter and ordered coffee for him and Tege.

"Are you going to eat all of that?" TJ pointed at the mess of uneaten eggs and three pieces of bacon strips left on her plate. "I'm still hungry even though I ate earlier."

"Just because I take my sweet time in eating doesn't mean I won't eat it," huffed Sam jokingly. "Unlike some people I know who wolf food down like a dog without even tasting it. You can have one of my pieces of bacon. Maybe." She winkled her nose at him. "I guess."

"Sir, hold up please," the professor snapped his fingers at the back of the departing server. He looked at TJ. "What do you want? Eggs? More bacon?"

"Scrambled eggs and side of bacon for me."

"Waiter, can you bring two orders of scrambled eggs and bacon to go with that coffee? Thank you very much."

While the morning crowd in the dining room emptied around them, they sat and ate and Vern told Samantha the history, as he knew it, of the little green book. Wide-eyed with anticipation, she learned how Professor Edward Manchester, distinguished historian of 18th century European politics, had many years ago given the book in his old age to Professor McCarty, well known scholar of 19th century world history, who in the twilight of his career had, in turn, bequeathed the little green book to Vernon Cockrell, eminent professor of 19th century American history and author of two highly acclaimed, best-selling Civil War battle novels. Each man had used the book—or more accurately, the book had chosen *them*—for time-travel trips into the past wherein the professors had gained firsthand knowledge of famous persons and events, and also witnessed lifestyles of common folk of the era.

Professor Cockrell told her of his previous two forays into the past. The first time at the bloody Battle of Shiloh in Tennessee, and the second at the monumental Battle of Gettysburg in Pennsylvania. He'd discovered both of them 'gone' and the little green book on the floor when he got home that evening, he said. So naturally he picked up the book, too, to search for them in the past.

He repeated what he'd already told TJ; that of his own brief and boring adventures since landing as a member of the Tennessee militia.

She discovered anew that TJ's temporary acquisition of the book had been, in pure human terms, a random chance, a mere mistake. But neither the professor nor Tege knew for certain whether the little green book had *meant* to be discovered by him. Just like they didn't know if it was *intended* to be picked up by Sam. All they knew for sure was that once thrust back into the past, the recipient—or the participant, in the words of Mr. Cockrell—would be kept safe and brought back into the present when the little book's purpose was completed.

How and when the little green book operated remained a complete mystery. It was its own master. But the answer to *why* it did what it did lay, perhaps, in how the player was enriched, becoming in the process a better person or better professional. TJ thought *he'd* become more mature, more confident, more appreciative of life from his first great adventure. But he'd already shared that observation with Sam over the course of several of their dinner dates in the city.

"Before you ask, I'm afraid I don't know who had the book before Professor Manchester. If Professor McCarty knew, he didn't confide in me and I never thought to ask him." Vern looked into Samantha's eyes, waiting for her barrage of questions. None, however, were directed at him. Instead, she turned to TJ.

"How long were you gone, Tege? In real time, I mean. Approximately when did you leave the present? Your house, that is. What time was it then, about? And what time was it when you returned back to the present. To your house."

TJ knew her personality and facial expressions as well as anyone. Sam didn't easily become rattled or anxious. Whenever her brows were knit together like that, though, it indicated something was troubling her.

"It was a little after six, may five or six minutes after. And it was about seven thirty-nine when I returned. So I was gone an hour and a half of our time."

Samantha bit her lip, worried now. "You told me you were gone into the past for a total of four days and three nights." They could almost see her mind calculating.

TJ shook his head. "Sam, I don't believe there's any correlation between the length of time spent in the past and the amount of time that takes within the present. Trust me on this. Dad was in the past almost as long as I was on each of his two trips but his lapse was only a few minutes away."

He turned to his father. "Didn't you once tell me Mom was out shopping that first time but she could have returned home at any moment, and you couldn't be gone for long without her knowing? That was on the Shiloh trip."

"Yes, and on the Gettysburg outing, she'd just dialed her sister from the kitchen phone when I went up to the bedroom and locked the door. She'd yak for at least thirty minutes, sometimes an hour or more, when the two of them talked. But again, she could have cut the conversation short, and so I had no guarantee of much time then either, did I?" The professor explained.

"You see, Sam," TJ took a thoughtful breath, "I think, somehow, the little green book takes into account the unique circumstances of each adventure—going and coming. Don't ask me how it does it. I just have a strong feeling that it does.

"I'm real comfortable with that assumption." He smiled and winked.

The professor chimed in. "My instinct tells me Tege is right about this. I don't think you need to worry about any of us being gone days on end and being declared missing persons before we make it back."

"W-e-l-l…if you say so," but she was not totally convinced.

Right then, they all heard a loud commotion and angry shouting voices coming from the adjoining lobby beyond. Whoever the people were, the group seemed to be heading toward the dining area, judging by the approaching sounds of the scuffling. Suddenly a group of people spilled through the entrance into the room. They saw five men, and one young woman being forced along by an older man who had tight hold of her arm.

"You mal hombre, you filthy American swine, you! Stay away from my little sister or the next time I catch you I will do more than beat your ugly face," screamed one man who appeared to be in his late twenties or early thirties to TJ. Beside him another was hollering Spanish obscenities at the American.

The second shouter must be related to the first, perhaps a brother or cousin, TJ thought. They looked alike. A middle-aged man, French by his accent and a hotel employee by his uniform, stood between the two enraged men and the object of their wrath, who indeed wore a bloodied face.

The older man now began yelling at the young woman, partly in Spanish and partly in broken English. The only words TJ understood were *little tramp* and *disgrace to the family honor*. The girl struggled to break free but the man's grip was too strong. Her expression was that of a trapped animal. Defensive, frightened, yet still defiant.

"Gentlemen. Gentlemen! Calm yourself. Tempers, please." Beseeching, the middle-aged hotel worker stretched out his thick arms as a last resort, planting a ham-like hand against the chest of each of the two angry men, holding them at bay. He seemed exhausted as well as exasperated. It had already been a very trying morning before this row…what with the drunken party last night in rooms thirteen and fourteen that carried into the wee hours…the bellman spilling down the stairs and damaging the expensive luggage of one of their best returning customers, a rich plantation owner from Cuba…and the dangerous grease fire that scared the kitchen staff and ruined the breakfast of a large group of traveling businessmen.

Ignoring his hands on their chests, the two younger men kept trying to get at the beaten man.

"If you must fight, take your fighting outside." Now the hotel manager grabbed the men by the front of their shirts holding them tight. "I won't have you attacking one of our guests inside our hotel no matter how justified you think your action is. Keep it up and I'll have no choice but to fetch the constable."

The man holding the girl stiffened. "The fat constable! I know him well. That piece of mierda! He wrongly jailed me three years ago for something I didn't do, just because I'm Spanish blood. Someone else in the neighborhood was the guilty party; a thieving convict from Cuba. It was common knowledge around town. But no! The constable was too stupid to do real police work and instead falsely accused and arrested me at my own home. Him and his sidekick."

The older man grew beet red and spat on the floor.

"Lazy ignorant Americano like the rest! Uncivilized. They all are. No breeding. No culture. Not like my beautiful homeland of Spain. They're American trash. Like this animal here who claims he loves my daughter and wants to marry her, but all he will do is corrupt her. Over my dead body, he will. Bah!"

The older man grew beet red and spat on the floor. Scowling, he jerked his head around, taking in the rest of the dining hall. He noticed TJ and the rest for the first time and grew more sullen, if possible.

"Si. And just like that stupid Americano boy over there. He *works* for the fat constable. My sons have seen him going in and coming out of the building." Further enraged, he strode over to TJ's table still dragging his poor daughter along. His two sons followed him, leaving the erstwhile boyfriend and hotel worker alone for the moment by the entryway.

"I am Antonio Garcia Iglesias, descendant of a titled bloodline," the Spanish father said, jutting his chin up. "I am the third generation to live in this city. My grandfather settled here in his youth when everything in this region was under glorious Spanish rule. My great, great uncle was of nobility with wealth and access to the royal court back in Spain. I dislike and distrust the British for their arrogance and ruthlessness. However, at least they are cultured as are all pure Spaniards and the continental French."

He sneered. "But I despise Americanos. You're a vulgar pretentious race. Even those with money are barbarians. Money can't change the beast nature of a man. I say you're a pig, boy. What do you say to that?

"And who are these worthless people with you?" He fastened his black eyes upon TJ, Sam, and the professor, and loosened his grip on his daughter's arm. Free now, she pulled away and rushed to the side of her lover. One brother cried out and ran back to confront the American again. One brother stayed with his father staring down TJ and his dad.

TJ stood up, heaving a sigh. *Here we go again.*

He moved to a spot between the tables that gave him more space to maneuver, keeping his vision focused on both the Spanish father and his son. Mr. Cockrell started to rise, but Samantha checked him. "Let me. I've had a lot of self-defense training. Not as much as Tege of course, but I can hold my own, I think. Plus, I know a few dirty tricks that females can use against guys when they have to."

"I can't let you face a grown man," Vern protested, pushing away his chair to stand. "Besides, none of us can really hurt someone—or be hurt—under the power of the little green book."

She gave him a pert smile. "No worries then. You can sit back and relax and watch the Bobbsey Twins in action." She took several steps to come beside TJ. Both of them squared off in their respective combat postures.

The older man and his son gaped at them in amazement and broke out laughing.

"Si, si! This is how stupid the boy is. He actually

thinks he and the girl can take us. Like all Americanos, they're all bluster and no brains. You, there," the father growled at Vern. "At least you're a grown man. Are you going to sit there and let children fight your battle?"

"You may be surprised at what my son can do. I know I am. Often. But he's in no real danger." Vern placidly gazed at the older man.

"So we have an Americano adult who's a coward and his two young idiots," the son hooted.

"You take the old guy and I'll handle the other one," TJ said out of the side of his mouth.

"Right."

At that, the two Spaniards laughed louder than ever. They glanced once in the direction of the door to make sure the third man had everything under control there. He was still arguing with the hotel worker, his sister and her boyfriend, but nobody had left the room.

The son darted at TJ, swinging his right fist straight for the boy's nose. Tege pivoted his body sideways, smoothly deflecting the man's swing with his left guard. He tagged the Spaniard as his body passed by with a hard right, palm flat, just behind the ear at the base of the skull. The man pitched headlong, staggered, and fell to his knees, dazed and confused. But he recovered and jumped up, shaking his head.

If I was back in my own time without the little green book, that dude would be out cold for five minutes, at least. Fight over.

But here, he knew he couldn't hurt someone; nor they, him.

Watching his son's futile attempt, the father yelled his surprise. He lumbered forward, hands out, aiming to tie the girl up using his strong arms. His own daughter, who was about the same size as Sam, he'd held easy with one firm hand. Yet Sam stepped forward, slapped his outstretched arms aside, twisted and kicked him hard in his privates, dropping him to the floor in momentary agony.

Normally such a blow would incapacitate a male opponent, but Samantha watched the older man get up, clutching his crotch and backing away from her in disbelief.

Now TJ and Sam were back-to-back, each facing their own opponent. Tege turned and winked at Sam and whispered so only she could hear, "Jump right at the last second." Somehow she knew what he meant.

Now the son and the father were beyond rage and thinking, how could two children defeat them? Two big adults in the prime of Spanish manhood? They rushed pell-mell at the same moment in a blind fury. In the blink of an eye, at the last possible second, TJ leaped left and Sam leaped right, and the two men collided head-on like two maddened animals in the ring during a bullfight in Barcelona. What the teenagers couldn't do to them because of the mutual protection of the little green book, the men could do to themselves. Both were knocked out cold.

Vern got up from his spectator's seat. "Well. So much for Spanish nobility and dignity," he quipped, regarding the crumpled figures on the floor. "Shall we go?"

TJ and Sam nodded. The three left the man and his son lying there to dream, perhaps, of past Spanish glories and a world where all gold flowed to Madrid and the Spanish navy still ruled the civilized oceans. They stopped at the entrance to the dining hall when Sam said, "Wait a sec."

She turned to face the remaining belligerent son and the bloodied boyfriend who was now holding the sister around her waist. "Do you love this woman?" she asked the American. Startled at the question, he didn't hesitate for a moment but looked the brother in the eye and said with a firm voice, "I do love Juanita. And what's more, I want to marry her."

"You slime—"

"Shut it," said TJ. When the man took a step toward him, Tege replied, "I'm sure you saw a bit of what we did to your father and brother. If not, take a gander over there," jerking his head at the unmoving forms on the floor beside their old table.

The man stopped, glaring daggers at both TJ and Sam, but not daring to continue his advance.

"What do you do for a living? I mean, what kind of work do you do?" Sam asked the boyfriend.

"I'm a baker by trade. I was taught everything I know by Dowell McLavish, one of the best chefs in the city.

I just opened my own shop, too. It's small. But business is growing," he glanced over at the brother, lifting his head proudly as he spoke. His right eye was partially closed. His lip and nose were still bleeding. The right side of his face was purpling from the beating. "I rent a room in the hotel. They give me a discount because I sell them baked goods cheap. You probably ate something of mine at your breakfast." He pulled Juanita closer to him. "Staying here allows me to meet and tell other patrons about my shop." He looked down at the girl with his one good eye. "She came here to see me, that is true, but just to eat breakfast with me before I opened my shop for lunch customers. She was *not* coming up to my room, no matter what *they* think," he said. "We were to meet in the lobby first and then proceed to the dining hall. I respect her more than I have any other woman I've ever known. I'm crazy about her. I want to make her my wife."

Sam queried Juanita, "Sounds peachy keen, so far. Tell me the truth. Does he treat you well? Like a lady?"

It was her turn to be taken aback. This younger American girl was so forward, so bold, so forceful. She seemed mature well beyond her years.

"Well, yes. He does…he is always gentle with me. Always listens to what I have to say, what I think about things. Very thoughtful. Very kind. Much more so than any of the *Spanish* boys I know." She gave her brother a fierce look. "Besides. I deeply love him, too."

"I guess that answers that, doesn't it?" Sam gave

the brother an incredulous look. She put her hands on her hips. "And you call us stupid. Let's review, shall we? Number one, he's good to her. Number two, he loves her. Number three, he has a job…has his own business, for Pete's sake. Number four, he respects her and wants to marry her, not bed her like a one night's stand. Number five, she loves him. Sounds like a pretty decent catch to me.

"So what's your problem?" Sam reached out and shoved the brother's shoulder. He started to react but then saw TJ tensing up and backed off. "Get with the program. You tell your father and brother that TJ and I come around here. A lot. Tell him that we'll be watching. You give this man any more hassle you'll have us to deal with. We'll know, too. We have ways of finding out."

Now it was TJ's turn. "What you've just committed is assault on a hotel customer without just cause. Also, your father and brother tried to attack a *defenseless*—" (Vern chuckled at this.) —"boy and a girl for no reason than we're Americans and I work for the constable. This hotel employee is a witness and will confirm everything. I can have all three of you arrested today. This afternoon, in fact. You're right. I do work at the jail. And, uh, guess what, hombre? I'll be starting my shift in an hour or so." TJ clucked his tongue and nodded.

"Keep it up, and all of you could wind up in the slammer…for a nice long free vacation."

With that, the three of them strolled out of the

dining room, all feeling they'd just done their good deed for the day.

"Despite the unpleasantness of these particular cultural specimens, at least we can say the Spanish influence has given us much of the unique architecture of the French Quarters today…or two hundred years hence," mused the professor.

"Ah yes. Let us not forget the *noble* touch," laughed TJ. They walked out onto the sidewalk. "You know, until just now I didn't think about the fact there could be people living here who want the British to win."

"Yes, that's true, especially of persons—or their parents or grandparents—who settled here from Spain. If the British win, which we know of course they won't, they intend to give control of the entire territory back to the Spanish crown to administer on Britain's behalf."

"No wonder they hate Americans so much," said Sam. "I feel sorry for that girl and her boyfriend, though. He seems nice and you can tell they're both in love. I hope it works out somehow."

"We're on it, remember?" grinned TJ.

Chapter 22
STRANGER IN THE CAMP

TJ went to the jailhouse to work his afternoon shift, while Sam and Mr. Cockrell spent the day walking through the French quarters and seeing much of the rest of the city. The weather was nice and Sam felt the walkabout was refreshing, particularly after all the commotion at the hotel dining room.

"Gosh, it's not very big, is it?" exclaimed Samantha, as they sat down to the outdoor patio of a quaint little eatery to enjoy a late lunch that afternoon. Sam had visited the city with her parents twice before, once when she was in grade school, and again last spring, so she had an idea of the size of the bustling metropolis of her future time.

"No, it's not. I think the population is less than twenty thousand. Maybe closer to fifteen thousand."

Sam processed that fact.

They sat and munched on their French croissant sandwiches, watching the street and sidewalk traffic pass by. Sam could tell that the New Orleans of January 1815 had a very diverse and eclectic collection of city dwellers: Cuban, Jamaican, other Caribbean islander, French, black, creole, American, Spanish, European, unknown origin, and other English. She supposed many of the blacks she saw were even now, or had once been, slaves, and the thought made her uncomfortable. She hated the idea of slavery in any form. It was the one thing about the history of America she wished she could go back to the nation's beginning and eliminate slavery overnight with a magic wand. Owning people like animals or livestock was…well, it was a horrible thing. She frowned.

They finished their meal and the professor escorted Sam to the hotel and through the lobby. He wanted to make sure the hostile Spaniards had left the premises and that Samantha was safe. They said their goodbyes and Vern left to cover the several miles to the militia camp near the front line. Darkness was approaching and he didn't like the idea of getting lost along the way.

The next morning, TJ had a quick breakfast with Sam then hurried over to the camp to see his dad.

"I'm afraid you made that walk for nothing, Tege. It doesn't look like I or anyone else will be getting leave. Even the top brass sense the British could strike any day now." He lowered his voice. "Of course, we both know what day and when they will attack, don't we," he winked. "You should know that, you've been studying the War of 1812 in your history class this semester."

"Yeah. Today's the fourth, so it's four more days including today, and a night," said TJ, counting off in his mind. "The morning of the eighth. Crack of dawn, to be precise."

"That's right."

"I'm going to stay in town the next three days. Keep an eye on Samantha. I'll come back to the pirates' camp late afternoon the seventh, ready for the battle."

"Okay, son."

"I'll see you then."

TJ stopped by his old camp to chat with Angel and the others before heading out. Once back in New Orleans, he took all of his meals with Sam. In the mornings, he stood close by trying to stay warm and watching her do portraits of passing customers. In the afternoons, he went to work at the jailhouse. They both had to bundle up with an extra layer of clothing against the sudden gusts of wind outside. Although the temperature stayed a bit warmer than before, it was still chilly standing around, doing nothing much except painting or looking on.

They didn't see any more of the forbidden American boyfriend or his lover, Juanita, or of her father or brothers inside or outside the hotel. In between portrait customers, they stomped their feet and rubbed or folded their arms together for warmth against the sharp breezes.

"Now that I think about it, I do remember seeing him once, Tege. There was one morning, I couldn't sleep and I come down to breakfast early that day. The place was crowded, but I do recall him sitting at a table by himself among the crowd."

Samantha sighed. "I sure hope he's okay. And I hope she doesn't get too much more grief from her family. He did seem like a nice person."

"Yeah, he did," agreed TJ.

"He's handsome, she's pretty." She winkled her nose like she did sometimes when she was contemplating. "They looked good together, don't you think?"

"Sure. Well, maybe not so much. He had a black eye, bruised face, and broken nose." TJ grinned. "Always seeing the superficial rather than the substance." That would get a rise out of her! In reality, outside of his little sister, Sam was the most grounded, level-headed girl he knew and always considered inner character before outer appearance.

She narrowed her pretty eyes and gave him a mock scowl. "Now you know that's not true, TJ Cockrell. Otherwise, I'd be dating Jake Hemsley instead of you!"

Tege clammed up. Jake was a new kid who'd won the starting quarterback position over Brad Simmons, the former starter whose dad was the assistant head coach. Jake was handsome as could be but also full of himself and a real rake with the girls.

They ate dinner together at the de Ville and afterwards TJ went back to the jail for the night. It was boring spending the mornings just watching her paint, and they'd already seen what there was to see in the city. *Being back in time is not always the great adventure*, he mused before sliding into the rickety cot under the threadbare covers, and blowing out the candle on the little stand.

"Just one more day before the big fight, though!" he said, a drowsy grin on his face.

"I've decided I'm coming to the front with you," Sam informed him the next morning over breakfast.

"Wait…what? No way," exclaimed TJ. "It's not safe—"

"I thought you and your dad said none of us can get hurt while we're here."

"Yes, but…" he had to think fast, she had a most determined look on her face, "but other people, the people who belong here, can get hurt. Some of them may die. Close to you. You'll see them drawing their last breath in agony. Some may be horribly wounded, blood and guts everywhere—a gruesome sight a nice girl shouldn't have to witness. For sure there'll be mass gore in the front ranks of the British soldiers. Both of us already know that.

"No, Samantha. It's a bad idea." He shook his head. "I don't buy off on that."

"*You* don't buy off—hey, since when do you tell *me* what to do?"

"I'm your loving boyfriend who wants to take care of and protect you, remember?"

Sam huffed. She started to say more, but thought better of it. She knew arguing wouldn't change TJ's mind. Besides, she already was forming a secret plan in her mind.

"Fine. You go on. I'll just stay here and keep doing my safe little portraits of the respectable, law abiding, harmless citizens among the passing crowd."

She had him there. More than once as she waited on the sidewalk for another willing customer, she'd been approached by bleary-eyed drunks, smelly beggars, and taunting lechers young and old. She'd learned fast how to deflect unwanted advances and comments, before TJ showed up on the scene.

"Well. Okay, then." TJ was taken aback. It wasn't like Sam to give up a good disagreement, and more so, if she felt she was right. "I guess that settles that." He looked at her one eye raised, wondering what she was up to.

"You sure you're cool with me going by myself?" He asked in a doubtful tone.

"Yeah, I'm cool." She smiled enigmatically.

He had things to do before he left for the front lines. He didn't have time to spend guessing what her game was. TJ's mind was already filling with imaginations of the approaching battle now. He nodded approval of Sam's apparent capitulation, and picked his fork back up to finish the meal. He still had to swing by the jailhouse to tell O'Grady he wouldn't be in that afternoon. Since of course he couldn't know in advance the attack would happen tomorrow at dawn, he'd have to make up a plausible story but he could handle it.

After all, I'm a pretty good actor!

Ten minutes later, Samantha watched TJ excuse

himself and walk out the dining room. She sat tapping her hand on the table until she made up her mind for good. In strolling around the city with Mr. Cockrell that day, they'd noticed and stepped inside several interesting stores. One of the shops they visited was four blocks down and two blocks over. The proprietors, two middle-aged men with graying unkempt hair, dealt in colorful clothing that was favored by pirates, gypsies, seamen and the like, judging by the type of customers coming into and out of the ramshackle store.

"Well, well, well. Smarty pants TJ, Mr. Captain Lafitte, and the rest of you scurvy mateys, you may be getting an unannounced reinforcement come night fall," she grinned to herself.

Meanwhile, Tege made up a suitable tale about how the pirate chief believed the enemy would attack if not tomorrow then the next day for sure, and he wanted all his men in camp ready for action. The burly constable stroked his chin beard as he listened, but let TJ go. He had a rather envious look on his heavy face as if he wished he too was going to battle rather than babysitting a jailhouse full of drunks, petty thieves, and vagabonds.

"Shoot a few redcoats for me, then, boy." O'Grady reached out his huge hand to shake. "Come back in one piece if you can and try not to get yourself killed."

"I'll do my best, sir," TJ replied, knowing full well he may not deliver on the first request and was guaranteed the second by the little green book.

TJ arrived in camp right after the pirates' noon meal was finished. "Where's Angel?" he asked the men still sitting around the campfire smoking their pipes or cigars. Their mood was much more serious than usual, he noted. Normally Lafitte's entire crew was filled with gaiety and swagger at all times. They were braver than most among Jackson's troops and also more boastful, but all of them sensed battle was nearing. If not tomorrow, then the next day; if not then, why the day after that. They knew their side was outnumbered. Rumors still flew about the size of the British forces. And these were the cream of His Majesty's Army; hardened veterans of the Napoleonic Wars.

"Where did Angel go?" repeated TJ.

"He's gone to the front lines to have a look about," answered Fat Duck, turning a bleary eye toward the boy. He'd been drinking that morning. Everyone acknowledged Duck was a steady hand in a jam but unlike the other pirates, he needed liquor courage to boost his resolve.

"Thanks," Tege nodded and headed off.

The disposition at the front was even solemner. TJ saw General Jackson in the near distance riding his favorite white, Sam Patch, along the curving line of artillery placements, inspecting the readiness of the troops and batteries, and encouraging the men as he passed by. Tege couldn't find Angel. He called out his name several times and looked in every direction, searching among the clumped masses of soldiers, but to no avail. He spotted his dad standing beside an artillery station. It was positioned almost straight ahead less than ninety yards away. Vern was deep in conversation with two other soldiers.

TJ headed toward him, though still keeping an eye out for Angel as he passed the crowds in between.

"Hey, dad. What's going on?" He said as he approached him.

Mr. Cockrell turned toward his son and smiled. "Tege! You made it."

The other two men gaped at TJ. "So your boy's a pirate? One of Lafitte's gang, is he?" The older of the two soldiers' face turned into a slight scowl. Apparently Lafitte didn't have the greatest esteem among many of Jackson's troops.

"Why yes. Yes, he is," Vern replied to the man without missing a beat. "His mother and I divorced a while back and I lost track of him until a couple of days ago. Discovered he was part of Captain Lafitte's crew," Vern fibbed. *I'm becoming expert at this. Something that should hold me in good stead as a professional historian*, he chucked inwardly.

"My boy's a stout one, too, or so I've been told. Brave and courageous in battle both on sea and on land. Already quite the ladies' man, as young as he is." *The tall tales just keep coming!* Mr. Cockrell grinned, watching his son's face redden with brief embarrassment.

"Enough, dad. E-nough. Please," TJ laughed. He jerked his head over his shoulder, indicating he wanted to talk in privacy away from the listening ears of the present company.

"Excuse us, gentlemen," said Vern.

They walked several yards and stopped behind a group of soldiers.

"What's up?" asked Mr. Cockrell.

"You go first."

"Well, let's see, Tege. Hmmm. General Jackson is making yet another inspection of his defense. You may have seen him horseback as you were walking up. Our breastwork is constructed using a liberal amount of good thick Louisiana swamp mud. I should know! I helped to build my own little section of it, and dirty miserable work it was. But the rampart's fourteen to twenty feet thick throughout its length and should give our soldiers ample protection from the British shells." The professor stroked his chin. "Of course, as part of a cannon crew, I'll be expected to stay with my artillery unit unless the British break through our front line. Which, of course, we both know they won't.

"Your turn now."

"Okay. As you might have suspected, Sam wanted to come with me to the front. But I think I argued her out of it."

"Uh, huh," said the professor, unconvinced.

"And we didn't see any more of that pleasant Spanish family or the boyfriend either, so no problems there."

"That's good."

"I'd like to be with you when the fighting starts, dad. So I'll just spend the night in your camp and let the guys know where I'll be if they want me."

"I agree, son. I'd like you with me as well."

TJ clucked his tongue. "Gosh. Half the day's already gone. It'll be a short night, too, because we'll be getting up long before dawn. I may want to turn in right after supper."

"Tell you what, we'll both hit the hay soon. Why don't you go notify Lafitte—or whoever you need to—and come right back here."

With that, Tege said goodbye to his dad for now. He returned to the privateers' site to tell them of his plan. Angel had made it back, and TJ spend some time listening to Angel, Fat Duck, and Mario argue who were the deadliest snipers among Lafitte's band. The three all agreed Simon was indeed the best overall long shooter, but Angel and Duck thought Clovis was second best, while Mario argued for Rene. And nobody agreed on who was the third or fourth best.

In the end, as with many disagreements, they put their money where their mouth was, and decided to make heavy bets on each of their chosen number two, three and four candidates. The other pirates placed bets, too, on their favorites, adding three more shooters to the list of performers. It meant that the bettors had to watch their own plus the other candidates and someone had to keep track of how many British soldiers each shot down. Since

Pierre was the only man who hadn't put his money down and was acknowledged to be among the most honest of them, he was tasked with keeping a total count for each of the shooters.

Only pirates would make a game of killing in the face of danger, thought TJ. *That's either very sick. Or very fearless.* He couldn't make up his mind.

"You do not wish to bet, Thomas?" said Angel, an inquisitive grin playing upon his handsome face. "You might get lucky, make some real money off the redcoats' sorrows."

"Thanks, but I'll pass," replied TJ. "Anyway, I have a strong feeling that all of you may be good shots when the battle comes."

"So you tell fortunes, now, my young friend?"

"Perhaps," answered TJ. "Listen, I need to be getting back. I told you I met my father here. He's a soldier in the Tennessee militia. He and my mother divorced some time ago."

"At least you know who your father is," frowned Angel. "I never met mine. Well, take care, my good friend. When the fighting starts, keep your wits about you and keep your head down." He reached out and playfully shook TJ's shoulder. "I hope to see you again, all in one piece. After we win, of course."

"Same to you. However, I have a feeling I'll come out of it safe and sound, without a scratch."

"Still the fortune teller, eh?"

"Sure. See you, Angel."

Early evening, as the last of the ebbing rays of the winter sun vanished below the horizon and the thin crescent of a new moon began its ascent within the evening sky, an unknown individual, sparse of build and words but garbed as a pirate, appeared at the privateers' camps, going from site to site making mumbled low-voiced inquiries about their young comrade who was named Thomas. It wasn't until the secretive stranger found the camp where Angel and the rest of his colleagues sat making merry and guffawing about Fat Duck's failed mid-afternoon reunion in the city with his former love Belladonna that the mysterious person found an answer.

Rising from his comfortable place by the campfire, Angel addressed the stranger. "Looking for Thomas? Must be very urgent to seek out someone out of such a large encampment of soldiers. There are several thousand here. Not an old enemy of his come to do him in, are you? That would be an unnecessary undertaking, perhaps, since he—and all of us—will soon be facing the threat of death in battle," Angel joked.

The individual kept his features hidden inside a hood pulled forward as far as it would go. Angel could make out the tip of a smallish nose, a faint mustache above the upper lip, and a dark bandanna—he couldn't tell its color—wrapped around the forehead. The person's body was turned to avoid the light of the campfire upon his face. His voice sounded a bit odd, like the person was straining to make it deeper or as if he was trying to camouflage his speech.

"Thomas is my half-brother," the stranger replied.

"His half-brother?" Angel mused. "He never mentioned a half-brother to me."

The person was silent for a minute as if thinking.

"Yes?" said Angel, growing impatient.

Finally the stranger answered. "My mother was Father's second wife. After their divorce, Thomas went to live with his real mother. I stayed with Father until I was twelve when I…when I left home to become an apprentice bricklayer in another city." Another pause. "But I gave that up because the master was cruel and also he cheated me of wages. So I went to sea instead working on a ship that carried goods and passengers between Jamaica and New Orleans. I returned home just this month to find father gone. Some neighbors told me he'd joined the militia to fight the British. I also got a letter from Thomas' mother telling me he'd become a pirate with your Captain Lafitte. The rumor was that Lafitte was fighting the British, too. So I came back to the city, hoping to find both my half-brother and my father."

"What's your name, stranger? So you're a seaman? What was the name of your captain or your vessel? Are you Thomas' older or younger halfling?"

Another pause.

Angel frowned at the continued delay.

"I'm called Sam. I'm Thomas' younger. And you wouldn't know either my captain or his ship. He's…he's

British. Lives in Jamaica. I quit because it became too risky sailing with an Englishman when my country's at war with Britain."

A long tale but somehow that made it seem more plausible to Angel. He drew a calculated breath. This time he more carefully examined the individual standing in front of him, who was angled to keep his face in the shadows and the firelight upon his back. The person was almost the same height as Thomas, he judged. The jacket and hood hid the person's physique. He could weigh the same, or perhaps ten to twenty pounds less than Thomas. It was hard to tell. However, after further thought it seemed logical to Angel the person's story could be true. He decided to tell him where his half-brother might be found.

"Walk straight ahead this way"—he pointed—"until you see the artillery along the front line. Your brother should be with your father, and if so, they will be together at one of the gun placements. I'm thinking it will be the first set of cannons you see."

"Thank you, sir," the person mumbled in a low voice.

"Good luck, halfling of Thomas. Or so you say." Angel bowed.

And so it was, not ten minutes later that the mysterious stranger found his prey, based on the pirate's instructions.

TJ felt a tap-tap-tap on his left shoulder. He

turned. There was Samantha pulling the hood off her head and grinning at him like a Cheshire cat. She wore a dark green bandanna around her forehead with her hair hidden tucked inside, and had a black mustache inked in above her lips.

Tege looked up to the sky, and shook his head at the sight. He then grabbed the hair on the sides of his head. "What am I going to do with you!" He groaned— only half faking—and held out his hands as if to ask why. "Sam! Doggone it. I asked you not to come. This is no place for a girl. This is war! Seeing men die is not pretty. Plus, even if you can't be physically hurt, you can still be harassed. I bet there aren't any females in this whole army camp. Not all of these soldiers here are *gentlemen*. You… you…" he couldn't finish his thought, he was so flustered.

Mr. Cockrell, watching TJ's reaction, chuckled. He shook hands with Samantha. "I was expecting you to show up, young lady. Sometime this evening."

"You were expecting her?" sputtered TJ.

"Well. I can't say I knew with 100% certainty. But I anticipated her ignoring your silly orders and coming along directly." Vern looked at his son. He reached out and grasped TJ's shoulder, shaking it playfully. "Lighten up. After all, this is a member of the female species we're talking about, Tege. They do unexpected things and they do what they want when they want. The quicker you learn that one fact, the better you'll get along with the opposite sex as life goes on, my boy."

"Since I've been here, I've had to deal with several jerks who couldn't keep their hands or filthy talk to themselves. You know this because we already talked about it. Please! I think I can take care of myself."

She gave TJ a reproving glare, but then softened and smiled. "Look, I appreciate you being protective of me. And caring and all that. It's one of the many things I like about you." She laughed. "Your friend Angel was a little suspicious. You'd have been real proud of me, Tege, of the tall tale I told him to find out where you were. It was almost as good a yarn as you can do."

"Yeah, well…" He looked grumpy. "You're here now, so I guess we'll have to make the best of it, won't we."

He said under his breath so she wouldn't hear, "Since you're such a good actress, why don't you act like you're not here."

Chapter 23
BATTLE FOR THE AGES

Samantha hadn't eaten since lunch, so Mr. Cockrell led her over to the artillery quarters campfire for some grub. Being exasperated, TJ discovered, had made him hungry again, so he filled his tin plate and gobbled a second supper. He sat next to Samantha munching away. As they ate, they both listened, fascinated, while the professor described in stirring detail all of the troop movements and engagements and plans between the opposing armies of tomorrow's conflict. TJ was always amazed at the intricate knowledge his dad had even of trivial battle events and minor tactics. Mr. Cockrell was a skilled historian, leaving no stone unturned or fact unchecked.

TJ was proud of his father.

Vern kept his voice low so just TJ and Sam could hear. It wouldn't be wise to let passersby or eavesdroppers overhear things that couldn't possibly be known in advance of the events happening. But the professor knew, of course. He was from the future. And he'd studied the

Battle of New Orleans along with other the conflicts of the War of 1812 in scholarly fashion.

In more or less chronological sequence, he told them how the fight tomorrow will unfold and how the Americans will be able to win. Here's the tale TJ and Sam heard as the professor recounted the facts of the great battle.

"Basically, the British strategy is twofold. Redcoat General Pakenham will send Colonel William Thornton, one of his best officers and an aggressive chap, with a boat brigade to attack our militia on the west bank. His goal is to overrun us, seize Commodore Patterson's guns and turn them on our breastwork otherwise known as the Jackson Line. Upon that, General Keane will attack us along the river front while Major General Gibbs will attack along the swamp line. Major General Lambert's brigade will be held in reserve, ready to strike wherever we seem most vulnerable. Keep in mind all these attacks will begin in the pre-dawn hours when it's still dark. There'll be no moon out. And tomorrow morning will break very hazy. Thus, making it harder for the British to execute their strategy.

"On paper, at least, it's a decent plan. But thankfully for our side, things will go wrong for the British right from the start. Thornton's boats will get stuck in the thick river mud. So he'll only get some of his men across and they'll be woefully delayed. Gibbs' men will forget to bring fascines—that's long bundles of wood—to fill in the Canal, making a type of platform to cross over. And they'll also forget ladders to scale our breastworks. He'll have to send a regiment back to fetch these items. Until then he'll be stalled.

"Meanwhile, Pakenham will be waiting, and waiting, for gunfire, alerting him Thornton's attack has begun. As he waits, the night darkness will be fading into morning light. The fog will start lifting, too. He should postpone his attack for another time. It would be the prudent course of action. But British pride and stubbornness will get the best of him. He'll order a general advance anyway. Gibbs will have to go forward without fascines or scaling ladders. On the opposite shore, Thornton and those of his men able to make it across will be far downstream from their target because of the strong Mississippi current.

"We'll hear the British coming before we see them, by the sound of their beating drums. Fate will continue to shine upon us. The heavy morning mist will lift as they approach within three-four hundred yards of our front line. Our cannons and our sharpshooters will tear huge holes in their ranks long before they get close enough to do us damage.

"Before the battle is over, our marksmen will wound or kill almost all of the commanding British officers including Generals Gibbs, Keane, and Pakenham. Many senior field officers will also be incapacitated. Over half of the attacking army will be lost to death or injury. On all fronts, the British will be defeated. Except for Thornton.

Even with his limited force, he'll chase away our boys—untrained Creole and Kentucky militia—and capture the American canon left undamaged by our retreating troops. But it will not be enough.

"At battle's end, we'll suffer eight men killed and fourteen wounded…an astounding measure of victory by any stretch. But the British losses? That's several orders of magnitude difference."

He smiled grimly at Samantha. "That's the bloodshed TJ was trying to spare your eyes. I've seen war before, firsthand. So has he. And trust us, it's not pretty. It's not glamorous."

She sat silent for several seconds staring into the crackling flame tips before saying anything. "No. No, of course it isn't. I'll try not to be squeamish. But…I'd still rather be here with TJ and you, Mr. Cockrell, seeing that awful sight…versus being by myself, back in the city alone, not seeing it."

"Fair enough." Vern slapped his hands on his knees and stood up from the big log he'd been sitting on. He stretched and yawned.

"Well, kiddos. If we're going to rise and shine before dawn, we should be getting some sleep. I have an extra blanket and a nice heavy jacket you can use to cover up, Samantha. It's old and worn but it's thick enough to help cut the chill in the air. TJ has a bedroll and borrowed blanket he can use. I share a tent with two other soldiers in my unit so I'm stuck where I am. You two can lay your pallets close to the fire for warmth. One of the sentries on patrol duty will put more wood on it to keep it going through the night."

They said their goodnights. Each got ready for bed. TJ fell asleep within seconds of lying down, but Sam lay gazing into the fire for hours, restless, her mind filled with thoughts of the horror and carnage that Mr. Cockrell had described.

It seemed like mere minutes had passed before Vern was calling their names and nudging their shoulders to wake them up.

TJ woke refreshed and ready for the day. Sam, who'd slept fitfully on the hard ground, was groggy and a little jumpy. Despite her bravado of the evening before, she was more than a little nervous about the sights and sounds to come.

After a hasty breakfast, all troops were mustered and set in rank formation behind the curving ramparts of the Jackson Line. Sam, who was still disguised as a man, was handed a rifle. She and TJ were instructed to go further down, closer to the center of the front battle line where a handful of Lafitte's men joined them. Most of the pirates assisted artillery units such as Vern's, but a few choose to fight with rifles.

She and TJ were placed along the very top platform of the rampart, crammed elbow to elbow with other pirates. Where their section of rampart was located, it had a flat shelf of earth perhaps two feet wide upon which they stood. In front of them was the rampart's inner facing wall, also made of hardened earth, which rose up to a height of three to four feet above the standing ledge, leaving the defenders' upper torsos and heads exposed to enemy fire if they straightened up. On the outside of the rampart facing the enemy, the outer wall surface rose twelve to fourteen feet straight up above the land, giving defenders protection against both hostile cannon and rifle shot. Beyond the leveled shelf inside, the earthen slope fell with a modest slant some twelve or thirteen feet down to the natural ground. A row of armed pirates stood waiting behind the firing group, ready to take a place if someone in the first group was wounded or killed or tired. They held loaded guns to be handed up to the first group, taking the spent guns in return and reloading them for further action. At the bottom of the slope, another row of soldiers helped pass up new guns or reload the used guns, thereby maintaining a fresh supply of ready-to-fire weapons. And behind them stood others, perhaps not in strict formation but available nonetheless, to take their comrades' place or assist as needed.

This is like a human machine gun, thought Samantha, glancing around and behind, seeing the well-oiled organization of shooters and re-loaders rend helpers.

Although she'd been deer hunting twice with her father and uncle, had basic training in gun safety, and felt she knew how to handle a rifle, she recoiled at the idea of aiming a loaded weapon at another *human being*. TJ saw the look on her face and leaned over and whispered.

"Don't worry. You can't shoot anyone. Neither can I. The rifle makes the sound but it doesn't harm your intended target. I shot pointblank at that bandit, remember, and nothing happened except the noise."

He nodded. "It's the little green book. Trust me. You're safe. *They're* safe."

She swallowed hard but acknowledged his words with a shaky nod back. She tried not to let the helpless feeling of panic grow in her stomach. Waiting for the enemy to appear became a dull torment, magnifying her sense of fear.

Ten, maybe fifteen more minutes passed. She shivered in the morning chill. All of a sudden, in the distance Sam heard the faint synchronized beat of a chorus of wooden sticks on drumheads. Marching closer. Closer. Ever closer. She peered out over the top of the rampart into the swirling mist. She felt like she was staring into a cloud of death, a surreal landscape of gray lifelessness that mocked the approaching slaughter to come.

Even as Samantha continued to stare into the fog, it began dissipating. Then she saw them emerging out of the mist; a sea of blood red four hundred yards away or more, creeping over the earth toward them like a slow moving flood. Another minute passed. Crack! The loud obnoxious sound made her jump out of her skin. Soon the air was filled with the sounds of hundreds of rifles discharging. She flinched at the hellish noise. Sam glanced to her right and saw TJ was firing his rifle, then handing it back to the person behind to take a fresh gun.

Realizing she could no longer hold her rifle unused while others around her were firing away, Sam bit her lip, drew a deep breath, and raised her rifle to sight and shoot. She aimed at a specific group of marching soldiers in the distance, knowing if it weren't for the little green book that it would be unlikely she would miss, even at such long range, because the oncoming redcoats were packed so close together. Sam had been to a rifle range once with her dad. She squeezed the trigger slow but firm. She heard her own rifle crack but could not tell if a body that went down was due to her bullet or someone else. Did she do it?

I can't worry about that! Tege just has to be right! I don't want to be killing anyone. And I don't want to think about it anymore either. Little green book, please. Do your thing.

She gave her rifle to the person behind and reached for the loaded gun. She aimed and shot again. One frightful minute passed, then another.

Sooner than she hoped, the macabre target shooting was over.

It was after seven o'clock in the morning. Sam's arms were weary from the rapid rotation of rifle handling, lifting, aiming, and firing. Nearly sixty times she did it, with half a minute in between each shot. Samantha fired, only to turn and hand the spent gun behind her, and grab another fresh one. The soldiers on either side of her were spelled by the people behind them, but she refused rest. Having to hold up her gun and sight it at a specific individual each time—a tiny figure out of the massive wave of approaching soldiers—was exhausting both psychologically and physically. Sam's mind was numb from the trauma of witnessing tens of hundreds of men slaughtered on the bloodied field of battle right before her eyes. Her left forearm shook from fatigue. Her left bicep were starting to cramp up; it throbbed and hurt. Her right shoulder muscle felt knotted and sore. Worse of all, her left eye was now twitching from having closed it so many times to sight down the barrel with her right eye.

The nearest bodies of the dead and wounded redcoats were a mere fifty yards away. Too close. Close enough for her to hear the gut wrenching cries and moans of men still alive but in excruciating pain. Close enough to see bodies twisted still in death agonies that would never move again. The sad sight was something the little green book could not block from her memory.

Tege and Mr. Cockrell had been right. War was horrible no matter who the victor was.

It took twenty minutes for TJ and Sam to fight their way through the hordes of cheering, celebrating, crowding soldiers. They found Mr. Cockrell standing, watching, near his battery of artillery. His face and neck were blackened from the drifting residue of blasting power and curling smoke left by the belching of the big cannons. Narrow lines of sweat cut paths through the grime caked on his forehead and cheeks.

Although General Jackson himself remained wary of the British intentions and didn't quite yet believe the conflict was fully over, the professor, Tege, and Sam knew different: The great battle, mercifully, was won.

There was nothing else for them to do at the front lines. Angel happened to see his friend Thomas among the milling crowds, and called out to him. Tege waved acknowledgement but didn't walk over. Instead, together the three adventurers from the future began to wind their way back through the village of camps and on toward the city, ignoring all greetings and shouts from other friends and comrades they passed. Once beyond the last row of now vacant campsites, they saw no one else. There were birds aplenty flying overhead in the overcast sky or alight in neighboring trees all making noises and fussing at the passing intruders, and some wild animals lurking here and there. But no humans.

They trudged on. The miles in between the outskirts of New Orleans and General Jackson's jubilant army were devoid of people, it seemed. The entire city waited, cloistered, anxious to know but afraid to ask, to send out emissaries to inquire which side won.

It was not until horsemen galloped to New Orleans an hour or so later with the stunning unexpected news of complete victory that most of the city inhabitants breathed a collective sigh of relief and erupted in wild celebrations.

Chapter 24
GOOD DEEDS AND GOODBYES

Mr. Cockrell, TJ, and Samantha walked on in silence amidst the total absence of other people, lost in their own thoughts. Mile after mile passed as they tramped across the sparsely wooded terrain, and not a word was said. The land was marshy in spots and so they had to watch their step.

Breaking the quiet, Sam spoke first. "Tege, did you say you felt tingling sensations when the robber shot at you on your first adventure?"

"Yeah. I did say that."

She got a weird look on her face. "I think…I think I may have been shot by a British bullet. I had a tingling feeling at the base of my throat. And then…and then… the feeling went away."

"Very possible. Actually very likely," said TJ glancing at her.

"So that means I couldn't have killed anyone, doesn't it?" She sighed. "I'm so glad that's all over," said Sam in a subdued voice. "Of course, I'm glad we won.

We had to win. For the future of the country and future generations. For our future, even. But you both were right. I wish now I'd stayed at the hotel."

"Forget the hotel, Sam. Myself, I'm ready to return to our real home, our past present, if you know what I mean," TJ said. "This has been, well, it's been a strange adventure. Far stranger than my first time out. But also, it's been a satisfying one in a way. Wouldn't you say so, dad?"

"Yes, I agree, son. I'm ready for this trip to end, too." He pulled out a handkerchief from his army coat pocket as he walked, and attempted to scrub the film and dirt off his face and neck.

They made it back to the city downtown in less than fifty minutes, striding along with ample purpose and little talk. They were all tired, not so much from the long stroll itself but from the strain of battle.

"I'd like to go to the hotel and freshen up before we do anything else," said Samantha. "Mr. Cockrell, there's a wash basin and soap in my room. They refill it every day, I think, so the water should be clean. You can get that gunk off your face. As soon as I come out, you and TJ can go in to do what you need to do."

TJ and his dad waited outside until Sam was through. Tege and Sam then waited in turn for Mr. Cockrell to step in and wash his face.

"Better?" asked TJ when Mr. Cockrell came out.

"Much. I feel like a new man. Almost." He smiled

at them. "And do I hear the rumblings of three empty stomachs?"

"Oh, yes! I'm starving," answered Sam. The only breakfast they'd had was a few bites of burnt bacon each and that was at four o'clock that morning.

They went to the big dining room and ordered a second breakfast. *Gosh, it seems like we live in this cafe*, thought TJ. When the food came, though, they all dug in with hearty appetites.

Tege pushed away his plate and let out a huge burp when he was done.

"You're disgusting, boyfriend. No wonder I'm ashamed to be seen in public with you," kidded Samantha, although she had to swallow back a petite belch herself moments after chiding him.

"Well, everyone. The battle's won. The war's over. Yet we're still stuck here at this same place," said TJ, tapping on the table. "I wonder when the little green book will get busy again."

"Be patient, guys. It'll happen when it happens. It always has, before."

They sat and watched Mr. Cockrell finish his meal. He was as unflappable as could be. He acted as if making it back to the future was a non-issue. Like he'd didn't have a prestigious, demanding, famous professorship…classes of upper level and graduate students depending upon him to teach them…and many other urgent responsibilities.

Sam again pictured in her mind her parents

frantic, her friends distraught, a missing person bulletin issued with no clues and no hope of ever discovering the truth behind her sudden and complete disappearance. No matter what Tege and Mr. Cockrell told her, until the little green book returned *her* to her real life and she knew from personal experience she could trust it—well, until then, she didn't one hundred percent trust it.

It was a scary image, but she made herself stay calm.

While the professor drained the last of his coffee, Sam paid the waiter, and they were free to go. They decided to head outside and see how the fair citizens of the city were reacting to the good news. As they entered the front lobby from the dining room, they noticed the Spanish girl Juanita. She was crouching, utterly terrified, hiding behind the motionless statue that was her forbidden boyfriend. Confronting him was Juanita's enraged older brother. He was shouting loudly and threatening the boyfriend with a long sharp blade.

That's a wicked looking knife. TJ had seen a knife just like that one during his fight with the Indians on his first adventure.

Before he or his dad could react, they saw Sam racing toward the three figures. Her face was set and her eyes were blazing. Amazed, Vern Cockrell and TJ watched her hurl her body forward into a lightning fast side somersault. In a blur of motion, she continued with a second then a third somersault, the last of which swung both her heels hard into the thigh and chest of the big brother, who was so surprised he didn't have time to slash at her with the knife in his other hand. The blow pitched him crossways, slamming his head into the floor and stunning him. The big blade spun out of his hand, skidding several feet across the smooth marble surface. Samantha, who'd landed on her feet after the hit, coolly walked over and picked up the knife and gave it to the crouching Juanita who seemed more fearful of holding the knife in her hand than of her brother wielding it.

"If he tries to attack again, give this to your boyfriend for self-defense." The girl tried to give it back to Sam.

"No!" snapped Samantha. Juanita jerked the knife back. "Keep it. And if your brother comes at your boyfriend again then you give it to him to protect himself. And not before. Understand? I'm trying to prevent either one of them getting stabbed or killed here. Comprendes?"

The girl nodded like a small frightened animal.

"Fine. I hope this is the last time your family gives you any trouble about your boyfriend." Seeing the girl's timid uncertain face, Samantha softened a bit. She reached out and squeezed Juanita's shoulder. "Goodbye now. Take care."

"Si." The girl smiled sweetly at her protector, both gratitude and amazement etched in her expression.

Sam glanced over her shoulder at the open-mouthed Mr. Cockrell and TJ, and strolled ahead, letting them catch up with her at the front door.

"To quote Harry Potter that was brilliant!" Tege gushed, astounded once again at his wonderful resourceful unpredictable girlfriend.

"Yes it was. TJ, you've got a tigress by the tail, my young man."

"Indeed!" he grinned, holding the heavy door open for her like a gentleman should, and slipping his arm around her slim waist as they spilled into the open air.

"Since we're on borrowed time, not knowing when the little green book will act, what direction do you want to go now?" he asked them. "Let's see if there're any more scamps Sam can finish off."

"Oh, why not head toward the jail house for grins," said Samantha. "And you better behave, sir, before I take *you* out." He only held her waist tighter at her jesting.

They hadn't gone but three blocks down street when they saw a young black child, maybe six or seven, attempting to help a very old crippled man—maybe the boy's great grandfather or great granduncle, assumed TJ. They were struggling to cross a crowded street filled with drunks, partiers, ruffians, as well as average citizens celebrating the victory a little too much. Letting go of Sam's waist, Tege rushed over to the side of the old man opposite the little boy. He held the man up and had him sling an arm around his own neck. Walking together the child and TJ guided the old man through the twirling crush of bodies. As they made it to the other sidewalk, TJ heard a harsh deep voice.

"What the blazes do you think you're doing?"

TJ looked up. There was a heavy set scowling bearded man standing in front of them, blocking the last few steps. He was grimacing at Tege something fierce.

"I'm helping this black gentleman cross the street."

"Say again?" the man spat on the sidewalk.

"I'm helping this black gentleman."

"Come again, boy?" The man stared daggers at TJ.

Tege was a little confused by the repeated question. Perhaps the man didn't understand his choice of words. He tried again, thinking use of a different adjective would make it more clear or acceptable to the man. "I said I'm helping this elderly African-American man and this young man here cross the street."

"African-Am—!" The stranger swore. "Tell me one more time what you think you're doing, boy?"

TJ let go of the old man. He tensed his muscles under his clothing, angling into position. Now he knew what the man's problem was, and he didn't like it or the man one bit. One more word, just one more. He enunciated his reply very deliberately, keeping his eyes focused on the angry face in front of him. "I'm…helping…this old man…and this young boy…cross the street…safely."

"You pile of trash. You must be one of them northern

idiots! You mean you're going to stand right there and tell me to my face that you're helping a worthless n—"

The man never finished his sentence. TJ took one step forward and swung into the fastest hardest tightest roundhouse kick he'd ever done. It caught the man full jaw—TJ heard the bone pop—and dropped him to the sidewalk. The man lay there, dazed, moaning inarticulate curses but not loud enough for TJ to hear the words. He resumed his gentle arm around the old man and led him the remaining steps to the sidewalk.

The old man mumbled, "I be a' thankin' you kindly, sir. I thanks you, sir," but TJ shook his head. "Please don't call me, sir. I call *you* sir. I respect my elders. I respect you. I'm not your better. I'm probably not your equal either, tell the truth." He gripped the old man's forearm with meaning. He knelt down to speak to the little boy. "You take care of him now—is he your great grandfather?" The young child's head moved up and down once, shy, almost unperceptive.

"Here," he reached in his pocket and pulled out a chuck of money and handed it to the old man to stuff in his pocket. Tege patted him on his frail back and said, "I'll keep watching him to make sure he doesn't try anything else, okay?"

The old man's eyes filled with tears and he gave TJ a smile of wonderment. "I thanks you, young man," he said, before heading down the sidewalk in halting steps away from the prone figure of the bearded bigot.

"So you're at it again, I see, boy," but the voice was friendly. "Fighting more riff-raff for me? I suppose I ought to give you a raise."

TJ turned to see Constable O'Grady approaching him with a smile on his chunky face.

"And I see you made it in one piece from the front line. I'm glad." He held out his big paw to shake hands. "By now, everyone's heard the good news." He looked down at TJ with a touch of fondness. "So I guess that means you'll be coming back to work full time now, right, boy?"

"Probably, but not today, for sure. Say, do you know that guy over there?"

O'Grady glanced with a disparaging eye at the man who was only now beginning to struggle to his feet, still moaning in pain, and woozily shuffle down the street. "Ah, that's Ham Strickland, that is. He's a nasty piece o' work, he is. Twisted mother. Hates all blacks with a passion. Judas Priest but his heart's blacker than any skin could be. He's evil even by the foulest plantation standards."

The constable scratched his chin watching the man disappear around the corner. "Why, he worked on a slave ship when he was younger. Brought them here from Africa. Word was he did horrible things to those poor devils, male and female, young and old. Then he became an overseer at the Oak Meade plantation. That is until he got fired for holding back most of the food and clothes intended for the slaves, poor enough quality as it was, and selling it under the table for whatever he could get to some of the smaller plantation owners. Stealing stuff meant for slaves is about as dishonest and low as a business man can get. Tell the truth, I'm delighted to see you settle him, lad.

"You know my father came from Ireland when I was four and my older brother was seven. Back in the old country, to hear daddy talk, we were poorer than any slaves here. Just starving. Crops failing every year. We lost my baby brother and older sister due to famine. Family unable to rub two pence together. Daddy, Sean and I see eye to eye on most things. None of us have ever cottoned much to the idea of owing people like a plow mule. Ham there is one of the meanest slavers I've seen."

O'Grady hitched his belt up. "Well, I guess I best be making my rounds, with all the extra drunks and deadbeats out today. We'll see you in the morning then?"

"Yes, sir. Unless something happens unforeseen I should be able to make it." TJ said. Secretly he wished the little green book would make that something happen before tomorrow morning.

"Goodbye, constable."

"Goodbye? You'll be seeing me tomorrow I reckon."

TJ waved at him. He turned and walked back to his dad and Sam, who'd been watching the whole episode from across the street. Although they could figure out most of the tale by observing the action, he filled them in on Ham Strickland's unsavory background.

"That makes two good deeds in one morning. I'm very proud of both of you for standing up for good causes, good principles, helping the weaker against wrongful attack." Vern said it and meant it.

They watched the throngs of revelers, which had begun to shrink in the past half hour. Word of the victory was fast becoming old news with each passing minute, and fewer people were celebrating. TJ wasn't sure where they should go. Not to the jail house, now that he'd talked to O'Grady. They stood on the sidewalk discussing their options.

It struck all three of them at once: A dream-like mist swirling, surrounding, seizing their minds, clouding their vision. They were falling. Falling. Falling. To an unseen ground, an unknown destination. The surrounding images of colorful buildings, swirling crowds, and even each other's surprised faces begin dissipating into an all-encompassing blinding white fog.

Chapter 25
HOME AGAIN AND THINGS LEARNED

TJ, his dad, and Samantha awoke to find themselves prone on the floor in Mr. Cockrell's master bedroom, all three crowded into the open space between the big king-sized bed and the little desk in the nook corner. It took several seconds for their brains to process the new reality, their minds still focused on their last conscious thoughts, sights, and snatches of conversation right before the overwhelming mist set in.

"Whoa," TJ said, his mind still reeling. His dad got up while Tege rolled off Samantha's figure.

"Sorry, Sam." TJ sat upright for a few seconds, letting his senses catch up, before attempting to stand up. He nearly toppled and grabbed his dad's nearby arm to steady himself.

"Wow. That was…unexpected," said Sam, standing now, her lovely face still bathed in shock.

Only Mr. Cockrell stayed cool, calm, and unaffected by their sudden return. He'd had enough experience with the little green book to know it happened when it happened. All you could do was be ready at any time to return. Or be transported as happened on this mutual adventure to a different time and location. After all, both the going and the coming back were never within their power or discretion. The green book did what it did, and you went along for the ride, so to speak.

"Oh gosh, what *time* is it? And I'm afraid to even ask what *day* is it?" Samantha moaned. She searched the bedroom for a wall or nightstand clock, slight panic filling her voice.

Vern patted his suit coat and felt his iPhone still in the left pocket. It was one of the strangest but useful phenomena of the little green book that whatever clothes and modern devices you had on your person at the time your adventure began were on you when you returned. He hit the bottom button then the clock face to see the date and time displayed on the screen.

"It's eleven forty-seven. It's Thursday night. And yes, it's the same Thursday night that our little adventure began." He smiled at Sam. "I believe you'll find your phone wherever it was when you left the house."

"That's just freaky…totally unbelievable. But awesomely okay!" Seeing Mr. Cockrell in his suit, she looked down at her own clothes to check, too. Sure enough, she had on what she wore that afternoon when she'd picked up the little green book in a sudden urge of curiosity.

So everything was back to normal. Well, almost!

She breathed a huge sigh of relief. "I told Mom we might be as late as eleven, so I bet I have a message from her. I just remembered I put my phone down on the kitchen table." She rushed out of the room to go downstairs and check her phone. TJ followed her.

He called out after her departing figure as she hurried down the stairs, "You know we have to finish studying for the rest of the history test."

TJ heard her voice from the kitchen, "Didn't we just witness the Battle of New Orleans for real, and experience the lives of real people affected by the war?"

"That's true, very true," admitted TJ, trailing her to the kitchen table. "That should give you a leg up on the Battle of New Orleans. But we need to bone up on the causes of the War, and the big picture. Well, you still do, Sam. You know I've got it down already." He said it matter-of-fact without any trace of smugness.

"I can review my notes before I go to sleep, on the ride to school, before first period, and in between classes. That should be enough. Hold a sec," She waved in his face to quiet him up so she could listen to the two voice messages on her iPhone.

"It's just what I thought. Mom called. She's wondering how much longer I'll be." Sam dialed her mother's cell. "Hey. We're just finishing up. Running a little late."

TJ couldn't hear what Mrs. Robertson was saying, but could guess.

"I know, mom. Sorry. I was, uh, I was out of the room and didn't hear my phone," she answered, mostly truthful. Samantha listened as her mother continued to fuss at her. "All right already! I know it's late. I'm on my way. In just a little bit, okay?" She clicked her iPhone off and wrinkled her nose with a trace of annoyance.

"Dad can take you home and I'll ride along. We can see each other in the morning before the first class. Let's meet in the library. Say forty-five minutes before? That should give you enough time to do a final brush up on history."

"Okay, sounds good, Tege." She shouted for the professor to come down. "Mr. Cockrell! Mr. Co—! Oh, there you are," she said, seeing the professor enter the kitchen from the other side.

"Yes, I'll be happy to take you home, Samantha. Call your parents again to let them know you're on your way. I'll drive extra slow…and I'll go over the main causes of the War as I drive. How about that?"

"Oh, you're a real life-savior, Professor Cockrell." She beamed . "Tege, find me a pad of paper and a working pen, so I can take notes." From TJ, of course, she'd learned of his dad's stellar academic reputation and knew his knowledge of the time period had to be far superior to that of Mr. Smith, their Highland Hill history teacher.

TJ was in high spirits. Not just because they were back, but also because they were back on time.

"You betcha, you pur-ty thang." TJ drawled,

grinning at her. He left the kitchen in search of the items. "Got it," he announced, returning minutes later, holding a full-sized yellow writing tablet in one hand and two pens in the other.

Sam discovered the professor was indeed a fountain of useful facts, and of the sort that would surely be on the test tomorrow. She took careful notes, and believed she had more than enough specific information to earn a good exam grade just by learning and memorizing his helpful overview.

As Vern pulled up in front of her house, Sam hesitated with her hand on the door handle. "Look, I know you two have already explained some of it to me. I mean, about the little green book and all. But…there are some things that seem… impossible. There are other things that are still confusing to me. I know you can't give me answers right now. We don't have the time to discuss it further, I've got to get inside and get to bed. But—I need to know…some things. There're a lot here I don't understand."

She looked at TJ, an earnest plea on her countenance. "For example, do all the people we met remember us now that we're gone? How can they not? I remember *them*. And doesn't going back in time like that alter history. How can it not? You know, the pattern of things that happened, a ripple effect, rearranging what might have been?

"My clothes kept changing depending where I was

and who I was with in the past. But once I returned to the present, I had my real clothes on. Now how exactly does that work? Yet another thing: I got shot! Mind you, shot! Not shot at, but shot. Hit. As in struck by a bullet. I've gone hunting before. I know what a bullet does when it tears into flesh. By any law of reality or physics or… or nature, there should have been a bullet. There should have been a wound. Pain. Blood. But there was…nothing. There was no effect on my body. Like I was a ghost or a shadow. But if I was a ghost, shouldn't the bullet have traveled through me and struck the real person behind me? Don't you think? But it didn't do that. It's like the bullet was vaporized or simply disappeared upon contact.

"But I *know that I know* I wasn't a ghost. I was flesh and blood. I was real. People could see me. People could talk to me. They could interact with me, and I with them. Some of them touched me, and I was able to touch them."

She paused, uncertainty clouding her face. "I can't wrap my brain around some of this stuff. Almost nothing about what happened today, almost nothing about this experience makes sense. There's so much more I want to ask you about the little green book…"

She looked hopefully at TJ.

"I understand, Sam. The first time is always the most confusing. Look, why don't you come over tomorrow after school if you can. Better still, tell your parents you'd been invited to another dinner with the Cockrells to celebrate acing all your tests." TJ said.

"*Acing* all my tests? Yeah, I wish," she snorted.

"You'll think of something to tell them. If you can come, once you're here, Dad and I will give you the full story. We'll answer all your questions to the best of our ability."

"Keep in mind that there many things about the little green book we still don't understand ourselves," smiled Mr. Cockrell.

"Okay. I'll sweet talk them into it. I'm sure they'll let me come over again." She glanced up at the professor's reflection in the rear view mirror in the front seat then back at TJ sitting beside her. "Will you excuse us for a second, Mr. Cockrell?" Samantha leaned over and kissed TJ on the lips. He kissed her back, pressing hard enough to make her start laughing instead. "You're crazy, boy." After the kiss, she leaned away but kept her lips pursed and blew out, vibrating her mouth in a show of mixed perplexity and humor over her bodacious adventure.

It was all so confusing and amazing at the same time!

"Well, good night, Tege. Good night Mr. Cockrell." She pushed down on the door handle.

"Good night, Sam," said TJ. "See you tomorrow."

"Bye," Mr. Cockrell added.

They watched her make it to the door, then drove home, father and son revisiting and discussing what had been their first green book adventure *together*.

The next morning Mr. Cockrell dropped TJ off

early at Highland Hill High School. Tege met up with Samantha at the school library to help her review for the history test. There they saw David Beam. His head was buried in a textbook and he had a stack of other books and notepads spread out on the table in front of him. Next to him was his girlfriend, Renata Wellesley, studying hard. Across from her was her good friend, Candice Harper. At yet another table nearby sat a larger group of students doing last minute cramming, including Robert Whitlock.

"Pssst. David. How's it going?" whispered TJ across the tables.

The boy looked up. "Uh, all right, I guess. I just wish I had more time to bone up on Math and Science. Not my best subjects," grunted David, who seemed a bit rattled.

"S'up, Robert?" TJ called out as loud as he dared. Robert's table was further away.

"Hi, Tege," Robert responded but returned to his books without further comment.

TJ, David, and Robert were best buddies. Renata and Candice were on the cheerleading squad together.

As he promised, TJ helped Sam throughout the school day, going over study notes and reviewing important questions with her whenever they found a few minutes together. They bumped into Brad Simmons between the Math and Science exams in the crowded hallway.

"Hey, man, that was a tough loss," said Tege. "You

played great, though. You had those two steals back-to-back. Then you made an unbelievable pass. From the back left wing to Brent at the other end five feet from the bucket. Plus, you scored three tough baskets and a free throw. Nice."

Brad was a very likable jock with a normal-sized ago. He'd been demoted to second string quarterback on the football last fall, and had gone out for the basketball team in the winter. He surprised almost everyone except his girlfriend and his dad by making the squad. Although Brad had never played basketball much before, even pickup games, he was a fine overall athlete and proved to be a scrappy defender as well as a decent shooter and ball handler. As the season wore on, he'd become a valuable bench player, putting in quality minutes whenever the coach needed more defensive stops on the court. The team had won the first round in the playoffs only to lose a real heartbreaker in the final ten seconds against Richards High School in the second round.

"Doesn't matter how good I played. We still lost," Brad grumbled. He was a fierce competitor and hated losing no matter what the game.

"I know. Losing always sucks. Well…gotta go. I'm helping Sam here get a little more studying in for the history test. See you round."

"Yeah. Bye, Samantha."

"Bye."

The succession of homeroom, morning classes,

lunch, and afternoon classes passed in a blur for everyone. Exam days were always busy and stressful for most high-schoolers. A year ago, TJ had been barely passing in most of his classes. But since his first adventure, TJ had become a serious student and a top achiever. Now he made high A's in every subject. He earned the praise of all of his teachers and the admiration of his friends.

Because it was mid-terms, there were no lacrosse practices after school for either the boys' or girls' teams. It left TJ and Sam free for the afternoon. After pleading with her mom that morning, at lunch, and again right after the last bell rang, Sam had gotten Mrs. Robertson to cave. Her mom agreed to let her go to the Cockrells after school and stay for dinner. But, Mrs. Robertson added, "You have to be home by eleven-thirty—without fail, Samantha—or you're grounded for the weekend."

TJ caught a ride after school with David's mom, Mrs. Beam, who also dropped off Robert at the Whitlock home. Sam rode along with Tege to his house.

No sooner had TJ gotten his seat belt fastened than his dad called him from the university. "Tege, I'll be home a little after five, as we discussed this morning. And I'll pick up a takeout order from Royal Beijing for the three of us. Samantha likes sweet and sour pork, if I remember right."

"Oh, great!" TJ loved Chinese food. "I think so, but let me check." He turned to Sam, "Dad's bringing Chinese. You like sweet and sour pork best, don't you?"

She nodded.

"Yeah. Get that for her." He hung up the call. "So how'd you do on the history?"

"I'm pretty confident I did okay. Maybe better than okay. I appreciate you and your dad going over everything. It made a difference, for sure."

"I exist only for your pleasure, my fair maiden," TJ grinned.

"And don't you be forgetting it," replied Sam, poking him in the ribs.

Once they got home, Tege decided to spend the hour and fifteen minutes or so before his dad got there by telling Samantha again the basic facts of his own first adventure, and of his dad's first two trips back into the past. He'd let his father handle the philosophical and theoretical questions from Sam about the little green book. He poured tall glasses of iced sweet tea for Sam and himself, and they sat together on the big comfy couch in the living room; him talking, her listening, and both taking sips of their drinks now and then.

A little over an hour later, they heard the garage door open and close, and then the back hallway door closed shut. Mr. Cockrell came into the room carrying a huge plastic bag of carryout food in one hand and his Tumi leather briefcase in the other.

"Hungry?" He asked, walking through the living room past them into the kitchen.

"I'm starved," said TJ, sniffing the air. The Chinese

takeout smelled wonderful. After getting up early to make it to school well before the first bell and also eating a rather hasty lunch, both to spend more time helping Sam study, his appetite was tremendous.

They brought their iced teas to the kitchen, refilled their glasses, and joined Mr. Cockrell around the dinette table to dig in. They ate with gusto for twenty minutes, no one talking, just chewing and looking at their plates of disappearing food and glancing up at each other.

They finished the meal and went back to the comfort of the living room to talk.

"Need a refill?" Tege asked Sam. She shook her head. He helped himself to a third glassful.

"However, excuse me for a few minutes." She walked down the hall.

They waited until she returned to begin. TJ and Sam sat close together on the sofa and Mr. Cockrell on the plush loveseat that faced them.

"So. Here we are. The three intrepid adventurers. Ask me anything you want, Samantha. I'll do my best to satisfy your, uh, curiosity and thirst for knowledge about the little green book." Mr. Cockrell looked at her expectantly.

She knit her slim eyebrows together, running through her mind all the many things that puzzled her about both her strange experience and the green book itself. Some of her questions they'd already answered or touched upon—but she still wanted to ask them fresh.

"Well, for starters, how does the little green book know where to put us? It seems each one of us landed in a different place and situation, yet somehow before the end of the adventure we wound up together, as if it were planned. Or fate."

"This is a brand new scenario for Tege and myself. As you recall, we went alone on our previous trips. No one else was involved. I suppose that, in the same way the book knows where to put an individual where his or her journey results in the intended circumstances, it also somehow knows where to put multiple people where they should be. All I can tell you is that I knew, beyond a shadow of a doubt, that I would be reunited with both of you before the end of the journey."

"And as I landed, I had the same unshakeable feeling that I, too, would hook up with you, sooner or later," added TJ. "A hundred percent certainty."

"What about the changing clothes? Every time I landed in a new situation, my attire seemed to fit the surroundings."

"Yes, I can tell you that wherever you go while under the power of the little green book, you will be clothed accordingly. There are other related things I don't yet know. For example, I can't tell you what happens if you land in another country where English isn't spoken. Whether the modern English words out of your mouth become the other language without effort on your part. Whether your natural speech is heard in their native language by the listeners. But I do know Professors Manchester and McCarty traveled to historical Europe and not all of their adventures took place in England."

"Okay. That makes sense. Hard to believe on one level, but logically, it makes sense. What about the fact I can't hurt anyone and they can't hurt me?"

"I believe the little green book's mission, as it were, is to place the user—or in our case, users—in what I would term a safe learning environment. Just like we can't materially affect or alter the course of history or even, narrowly speaking, of individual's lives, we can't materially hurt them either. Any action we take produces a far more limited, gentler, short-term reaction. For example, all of the kicks and punches and knockdowns that you two did *there*, would have had severe lasting effects on people *here*. Cracked teeth, broken jaws, black eyes, bloody noses, battered faces, lengthy unconsciousness, etc. The roundhouse kick you struck the bigot with might have killed him in real life. You hit him hard. You twisted his head violently enough to snap the spinal cord at the base of the neck. And you'll remember he hit the sidewalk with sufficient force to crack his skull open. However, he was just dazed a little, not hurt much at all. If you think back, the only time harm was done was when the Spanish brother and father ran into each other. People in the past can hurt one another. But we can't."

"That's why the British bullet had no effect on you. And why your own shots, even if you aimed perfect each time, had no effect on your intended targets," said TJ.

"But where do the bullets go? Do they disappear? Became vaporized?"

"We don't know the answer to that," said the professor. "We just know there is no effect, from us to them, or from them to us."

"Yet when that ape Armand groped me, I kneed him hard in his…you know, privates…and I punched his nose out. He went down in pain and his nose bled a lot, too."

"Yes, but I think I can assure you one hundred percent that your kick to his privates didn't damage him down below and that his nose wasn't broken, just bloody. The little green book allows for, let's say, temporary minor effects."

Sam sat pondering that for a second. "You may be right, because the jerk did seem to get back up awfully quick. Drat! I would've liked for him to feel some serious pain, as a lesson. Fine, then. Last question. Do people we meet and interact with in the past ever remember us? After all, we remember every detail of them?"

"The answer to that is a resounding negative. They retain no knowledge or remembrance of us. To them, afterwards, in their minds it's as if we never visited and never existed. That's one of the safeguards the little green book has to ensure the course of history is never changed."

This was heavy stuff indeed. Deeply metaphysical. It was fully abstract on one level, yet fully real life, flesh and blood on another. After an exhausting day of exams and pressure, it was somewhat difficult to wrap her brain around all the different implications of Mr. Cockrell's answers about the mystery that was the little green book. Samantha leaned back into the softness of the sofa cushion, mulling over everything her fingertips tracing over the top of TJ's arm resting on her leg.

She was involved now whether she wanted to be or not. It's as if the little green book had selected her without her advance permission. She was a member of a very select club. A time-adventurer of proportions that only science fiction could dream up.

They continued talking for another hour or so. Both the questions and possibilities seemed endless.

Finally, Sam leaned over and gave TJ a gentle peck on the cheek. "Thank you for coming after me. You too, Mr. Cockrell." She looked at both of them with wide eyes. "So much to think about. But…this is probably enough for one night. I'm beat. Ready to sleep in my own twenty-first century bed. Tomorrow's Saturday. I definitely will be sleeping in late, so don't call me and wake me up, boy toy." She pinched TJ's arm.

They called it an evening and took Samantha home.

"You're home early!" Her mom was surprised.

"Yup. Good night, mom. Night, dad." She walked straight through the living room without stopping.

They heard her say from the hallway, "Love you both. I'm going to bed."

Mr. Robertson glanced up at the small yellow clock mounted on the far wall. "What was that about? It's just a little after nine o'clock. And on a Friday night?" He turned to his wife, a puzzled look on his face. "Are you sick or something, honey?" he called out to Samantha.

"I'm fine, Dad. Really. Just sleepy, is all," they heard her mumbled reply.

Chapter 26
SECRET SOCIETY OF ADVENTURERS

Natalie, TJ's beloved little sister, had been allowed to join him and Dad for last year's fun-filled spring break at Disney World. This was following a deadly robbery attempt that TJ had foiled by returning home just in the nick of time from his first history adventure. Now that Mom and Dad were each dating and serious about another person, Tege hoped his mom's feelings of anger, frustration, and blaming Dad for the divorce would begin to subside a bit.

He loved his parents. But tensions and disagreements still arose on joint issues even after the divorce and mom's move to Atlanta; it pained TJ to still see them fighting and bickering over things he thought were of little consequence. "I just want them to get along better," he'd sighed and told himself many times over the past year and a half.

Last spring break, Anne Cockrell had given in to Natalie's pleadings to be with TJ only because she knew her son could have lost his life in the fight with the robbers.

The shock of hearing the news of her son's perilous ordeal had made her agreeable for the moment. However, in another surprising show of largesse, Ms. Cockrell had taken them all aback by permitting Natalie to again be with her father over the upcoming school break.

Hearing the good news, Mr. Cockrell had begun making plans for a vacation over the break including Tege, Samantha, Nat, and himself.

"Mom said I could come," Natalie had announced to TJ.

"Wow! That's tremendous, Nat. I'm psyched about this trip. It's going be a blast with you and Sam there."

The getaway had been in the works for over a month. The four of them were going to stay at a nice cabin at the Pickwick Dam State Park. "Hey, it's got a full kitchen setup, cable TV, and a big fireplace," TJ had enthused to Sam when they first started planning it in late January. The Park itself offered abundant hiking, fishing, boating, plus good Southern food at the grounds restaurant if they didn't feel like cooking in. Although the cabins were popular and booked as much as a year in advance for in season dates, the fact that they were going out of season and a group had just cancelled their reservation made it possible to snag one.

Sam and Natalie were tomboys at heart. Even Mr. Cockrell and TJ conceded they just might be better than they at catching fish that were keepers. In any event, the girls were looking forward to the outdoor activities as much as the boys. Best of all, agreed Tege and his dad, the Park was only ten miles from the Shiloh National Military Park, commemorating where the bloody battle of Shiloh had been fought during the Civil War. Two days of the group's stay would be allocated to hiking and investigating all that a walking tour of the great battlefield could reveal. Sam pretended curiosity while Natalie was genuinely interested because her dad and brother loved history. But both girls loved to hike and experience new things, even if their enthusiasm for seeing the battlefield was not quite as great as the guys.

A professional tour guide would be leading them on their first day at Shiloh, navigating the more famous places around the battlefield. The second day they'd hike on their own, sightseeing and visiting lesser known spots on the Park grounds.

With average temperatures predicted to be between the upper thirties and the mid-sixties, and the forecast calling for dry weather during the week, everyone felt it would be perfect weather for walking, hiking, and fishing.

So Sunday after church and a hurried meal at the house, they packed Mr. Cockrell's new Lexus SUV and headed out.

Seconds after the car left the entrance ramp and maneuvered through upcoming traffic into the center lane on the crowded Sunday afternoon freeway, Sam in the back seat and Nat in the front seat chimed in together, "Are we there yet?" They broke out giggling. "Are we there yet? Are we there yet? How much further? Are we there yet?"

"Very funny. So funny, I forgot to laugh." TJ made a grimace. When he was a small boy, Tege had badgered his parents whenever they traveled by car or plane. It had become an old family joke he thought wasn't humorous at all. "It's six hours there, isn't it, dad?" he asked in a serious tone.

"If we make good time, it should be about five hours and fifteen minutes." He looked up at the rearview mirror to see their reflections. "I put some steaks, chicken breasts, and a nice assortment of frozen veggies in the ice chest. We men can't count on you girls' fish catching prowess for all our meals."

"We'll show you," retorted Natalie.

"I also brought eggs, bacon, deli turkey and ham, potatoes, rice, beans, apples, oranges, bananas, three loaves of bread, peanut butter, butter, condiments, and such. And there're two huge cartons of Haagen-Dazs strawberry ice cream just for you two."

"Oh goody!" Sam's eyes twinkled at the announcement. Like TJ, she loved strawberry ice cream any time.

"For drinks, we have another big ice chest filled with Dr. Pepper, Sprite, Coke, and bottled water. I thought we could have steaks with all the fixings for our first night."

"Did you remember to bring some half and half?"

asked TJ, who had to have lots of cream in his coffee, whether brewed or latte.

"Yes, and I also brought a gallon of milk, too."

"Well, that's enough food for about three days for this bunch," deadpanned TJ. "Six days if we scrimp and hide the food from the girls."

"You just try," said Nat, "and Sam and I won't share any of the fish we catch with you."

"In your dreams."

"For real. Wait and see who gets the biggest and most fish," said Natalie, matter-of-fact. She stretched out her arms in front of her—locking the fingers of her hands and cracking her knuckles together—and gave a loud sympathetic sigh. "I'll hate seeing my big brother begging for some of my huge, record-setting, delicious bass."

The banter and jabs continued back and forth for an hour. It kept everyone entertained until the girls became drowsy. Neither had gotten their normal hours of sleep last night due to their excitement about the trip. They each loosened their seat belt around their waist as much as they could and slipped out of the shoulder harness. Nat lay down on her side of the big back seat with her feet scrunched up against the door, her body in a tight curl, arms folded, and her head against the seat back. Sam lay down on the seat in the opposite direction with the back of her head positioned right in front of Natalie's face.

"Scoot forward a little bit. Your hair's tickling my nose."

"Sorry." Sam moved her head an inch closer to the very edge of the seat.

TJ glanced over at them. He chuckled seeing their respective cramped fetal positions. "You know one of you *could* climb into the far back seat and have your own bed."

"Z'okay," mumbled Sam, already half asleep.

"I'm fine," replied Nat, whose form reminded TJ of Samantha's chocolate dapple mini-dachshund, Snickers. Snickers loved to sleep in a near-perfect ball on the Robertson's main sofa while the family watched TV. Natalie had her bent knees and folded arms and down-turned face curled close together, knees touching elbows and chin touching arms.

TJ watched them for another minute or two, amused that they were too lazy for either one to get up and take the far back seat.

"They don't look very comfortable to me. You'd better not make any sudden stops, dad, or Natalie will slam into Samantha and both of them will wake up to find themselves on the floor."

He laughed again at the funny thought. He was tempted to reach out and play with the stub of Sam's nose, but decided better of it.

Let the sleeping dogs lie.

He turned back around. He and Mr. Cockrell spent the next few hours watching the scenery and miles parade by them. He was thankful the view wasn't boring. Along the way, they passed through some interesting looking places and by wooded areas and small lakes and streams and pastures and farms off in the distance.

They pulled up in front of their cabin before nine that night. The breeze off the big lake was pleasant and not too cold. The evening air felt and smelled good. They heard the pleasing melodic sounds of the forest creatures and birds and insects around them. It was nice to be in the great outdoors, away from the hassle and stress of school or office. They unloaded the van, the girls still drowsy and fumbling a bit, and took everything inside.

TJ and the girls got the fireplace going while Mr. Cockrell began preparing the steaks which he was going to cook on the stovetop. Although the cabin provided basic eating utensils, he'd taken the precaution of bringing along a carton full of necessary pots, pans, an old cast-iron skillet, storing bowls, plastic containers, carving knives, spoons, folks, table knives, and other items from his own kitchen. He washed and peeled four big potatoes and cut them up into thick French fry sticks ready to be added to a pan of vegetable oil he was heating up. In a pot, he dumped the contents of a big can of baked beans to warm the food up.

Since his divorce, Mr. Cockrell had learned to become a chef of sorts. He cooked at home often after work and on the weekends. It was relaxing to him, and at home meals gave him and TJ a chance to communicate and catch up. He soon had the cabin filled with the delicious smells of sizzling steaks, fresh French fries, and tasty beans. In thirty-five minutes time, they all sat down to a fine first meal.

The girls had insisted on bringing board games, of which Scrabble, Trivial Pursuit, and Clue were their favorites. They also brought dominoes and two decks of cards. That evening before bed, the four of them played Scrabble. To make the competition more even, they agreed beforehand the professor would have one hundred points shaved off his total score, and Natalie would have fifty points added to her score. It was a tough contest, but TJ beat out his dad and Sam at the end with Nat not too far behind.

Sunday night they all slept like logs, everyone thinking of the weeks' fun activities ahead before drifting off to sleep.

The next day after a hearty late breakfast—everyone slept in—they grabbed their fishing gear and rented an outboard pontoon boat to try their luck. The professor, Tege, and Sam had their own equipment, and TJ brought extra gear for Nat to use. Mr. Cockrell asked the person at the rental counter about the recent hot spots and general directions how to get there.

They tried three different locations over the course of the lazy afternoon. Much to TJ's consternation, the girls beat out the menfolk no matter where they went.

"Tege, help?"

Nat, who hated to touch fish but loved to watch them being cleaned, had TJ remove her catch off her line each time. She reeled in the day's best effort, though, a heavy largemouth bass that fought and jerked her rod before she got it inside the boat.

"I bet that weighs over seven pounds, Natalie," beamed her dad, looking at the great catch with a look of pride. Sam also had a nice sized bass, and caught nine fish in all, including three catfish keepers and one large brim. Unlike Natalie, she had no problem taking her fish off her line. At afternoon's end as they were heading back to shore, Samantha couldn't help but give TJ a sassy smug look that said *I told you so.*

But between the four of them, they had enough catch in one day to satisfy their craving for fish meals for the rest of the trip. That evening they made pigs of themselves, eating fresh fish, baked potatoes with all the fixings, beans with special Cajun zesty seasonings, and hot buttered cornbread—the one item Sam excelled at cooking. She'd learned how to make the soft cake-like cornpone from her grandmother on her daddy's side.

"Sam, this is *so* good," Tege said, biting into another piece of the wonderful cornbread. It was TJ's favorite.

"Gross! Don't chew with your mouth open. And don't speak with your mouth full of food, either," chided Samantha. "But thanks for the complement."

"Yes, ma'am," he laughed and took another bite.

Even with a bursting belly after the meal was over, TJ kept slicing small squares of the delicious cornbread, lavishing butter on it, and wolfing it down while the four of them played the card game Oh Hell. It was after eleven when the professor won the game. Tege was so stuffed with food he didn't fall asleep until the wee hours of the morning. He woke up tired and a bit groggy, while the girls were refreshed and ready for the day.

They took the boat out again Tuesday. "Everyone, I thought we'd go fishing with cane poles and just take it easy. See a lot of the lake and do a little fishing along the way." The professor rented four elongated bamboo poles equipped with old-fashioned red and white bobbers from the boat shop. Natalie loved watching the big ball jerk below the surface when a fish struck.

The day was indeed lazy but satisfying. They visited nearly twenty spots, often venturing up riverlets and side streams where the limbs of the trees large and small along the banks sagged and overhung the gentle rippling surface. The water was translucent green with traces of brown. There were patches of the river water here and there that seemed a darker color to TJ. The lower trunks and branches of other trees and entire thickets of entangled brush were covered by the river, their moss-covered roots and limbs providing ample feeding and hiding places for fish and other things.

"Oh, wow!" exclaimed Samantha at one place. "Hey, Nat. Tege. Those two trees." She pointed. "Look. Over there." The afternoon sun filtered through the uneven forest canopy above them hitting the river at just the right angle, making it possible to see well below the surface of the undulating water. Staring into the emerald green depths, they all saw the two trees' roots protruding above the shallow river bottom and intertwining to form a huge shaped heart.

"That's cool, Sam," said Nat.

They didn't stay at each location long, taking care not to disturb serious anglers, and spending more time enjoying the beautiful scenery, sunshine, and fresh breezes than worrying about the amount of fish brought into the boat. The girls had packed a tasty lunch, some snacks, and beverages. They spend six relaxing hours on the water. They came back tired but happy.

"Well, tomorrow's the big day," TJ remarked to Sam after the four of them played their third and last game of Clue before heading to bed. "You know my dad was there during the actual battle. Returning there over a hundred and fifty years later will be pretty special to him."

"I should think so," answered Sam.

Wednesday dawned much colder than the previous two days with intermittent light showers and some gusting winds. Mr. Cockrell and Tege wore a t-shirt underneath a camping shirt that was long-sleeved. The girls each sported a durable heavy sweater. And they all donned their favorite rain slicker with hoodie.

By ten thirty that morning, they were at the starting point of the Shiloh battlefield tour with their guide, Mr. Henry Dunbar. Henry's ancestors had lived in the area going back to before the Civil War and he'd studied the great battle and walked the hallowed grounds since he was a teenager and he was now in his forties.

"Hi, Professor Robertson. It's a real honor to meet you, sir." He shook Vern hand with enthusiasm.

"Hello, nice to meet you, Henry."

"I want you to know, professor, that I've read your book on Shiloh. Several times, in fact. It's very well done, sir." He gave a thumb up. "Much, much better than anything else I've seen by other, quote, professional historians. They're too dry. Boring. Opinionated. Know it all's. Not only did you nail down all the facts, big and little. And the people involved. And the troop movements. And the different scenarios. But you did an exceptional job in my opinion capturing what the soldiers were feeling… while they were waiting to go into battle…during the actual fighting…and such." He nodded his appreciation and rubbed his hands together in anticipation. For him, each guided tour he did was pure excitement. After twenty years of doing it, Henry Dunbar still looked forward to each new group of visitors, regaling them with his in-depth knowledge of the movement of armies and soldiers, answering their questions, sharing tidbits of interest, and exploring the pivot points of the battle, the what if's and the lingering mysteries of the conflict.

During the course of the day, they visited the *Shiloh Log Church, the Hornet's Nest, Sunken Road, the Peach Orchard, Pittsburgh Landing, Grant's Last Line*, and other places. At the Hornet's Nest, Vern took the girls and Tege aside. His eyes sparkled with moisture, and Nat thought she saw a tear streak down his cheek. He stared out at the grassy field with the green blades blowing in the wind beyond the Sunken Road.

"Excuse us, Henry, for a moment. I'd like to, umm, take everyone out into the field. We'll be back in a little bit."

"Oh, sure, professor. Take your time, sir. No hurry at all. I expect you want to see things from the Confederate point of view."

"Yes. Yes, I do, thank you." He waved at Henry. Mr. Cockrell led the group through the waving grass. He walked slow, purposeful, striding silently a hundred yards out before turning to look at the winding dusty country lane they called the Sunken Road. He stared at the road for several minutes, the wind gusts drying his eyes.

He was solemn, almost brooding.

"Back then, this was all wooded area, not the treeless bush hogged field you see around you. I was standing right about here." He pulled in a deep breath and held it a long while before letting it out, his thoughts disappearing into the past. "I was aiming and firing my rifle with the rest of the regiment when James Wyatt, who I'd become friends with—if you can become friends in the span of twenty-four hours—was shot in the head…" he sighed, "shot in the right temple—I was on his left side. His skull fragments and blood and brains splattered the two soldiers next to him on his right. I saw his head jerk back, saw him topple backwards, saw the huge gaping hole and knew there was not a thing I or anyone else could do. James was the first of many, many men I saw killed on the field of action that day. He'd spoken to me of his wife and little boy back in Mississippi. He hadn't seen them in nearly nine months. He was just a boy himself, just turned eighteen."

The girls and Tege said nothing but looked back at the winding brown stripe off in the distance, trying to visualize what it was like being in the heat of battle that day.

That evening everyone was unusually quiet. TJ, Mr. Cockrell, even Samantha, had all been in battle because of their green book experiences. But somehow the professor's sadness at revisiting the Hornet's Nest resonated with the others. The intermittent rainfalls of the morning had stopped by mid-afternoon and the ground began to dry up. That night instead of playing a board game, they each grabbed a wooden chair from the little dining table and went out on the sparse grass in front of the cabin and just sat, listening to the forest sounds and creatures and feeling the soft swirling breezes and thinking.

In the stillness, the noise of the crickets in the woods and the wind among the treetops and the waves of the nearby lake against the shore became a rich soothing symphony. An owl hooted several times. Minutes later they heard another bird answer with a series of plaintive cooing sounds.

"That's a mourning dove," said TJ.

"Yes, it is."

"I thought so," Sam replied, listening for more woodland sounds to identify.

They went to bed earlier than usual and all slept soundly. Everyone woke refreshed with huge appetites. Mr. Cockrell scrambled up a big batch of eggs with milk and cheese and lots of torn pieces of tasty deli turkey cooked in. He also made a platter of French toast, keeping the stack hot until ready to eat with a shot of microwave. There was plenty of butter and maple syrup on the table for the toast. They'd purchased a gallon of orange juice from the local camp store, so there was fresh OJ for all and hot coffee for Mr. Cockrell and TJ.

"Okay, everyone. It's ready," said Vern. "Tege, you do the honors this time."

TJ prayed a quick grace over the breakfast meal before everyone dug in.

Once again, TJ felt he ate too much.

It was Thursday. That meant a second tour of Shiloh, but without a guide, spending a little more time at previous stops or seeing new sights. In all, they visited Rhea Springs, Fraley Field, Duncan Field, the place where confederate General Albert Johnston died, the Bloody Pond, Shiloh Indian Mounds, Shiloh National Cemetery, confederate Burial Trenches, and the Confederate

Monument. It was a long jaunt. They walked at a fast pace between stops, drinking beverage of choice from their individual bottles or canteens, and making a quick lunch around noon.

In the forest thicket near the edge of the confederate Burial Trenches, Natalie tripped on a low hanging tree root that was hidden by thick foliage. She landed on her knees; her hands pitched forward catching her weight. In doing so, she pushed aside a small section of the heavy ground cover with her hands, her nose inches from the separated undergrowth. She saw a dullish white spot, almost like a pearl or marble except not as smooth or pretty, right in front of her. Curious, she began digging around the white dot.

"Dad?" Her voice sounded a little scared. She kept digging, but more slower now. "Dad, come here."

The others halted. They came and stood around her watching as she finished her task.

"Oh, Nat," exclaimed Sam at what Natalie held up. She had soil crud and mud residue under her nails and her hands were dirty from the digging but it was what was in her hand that made Tege and Samantha gasp.

She'd dug up…some finger bones. From a human hand. They'd been buried in the earth with the barest tip of the longest bone peering above the soil top. The thick cover of leaves and twigs and rocks had hidden the little white knob until her fall.

It was a grisly discovery.

The professor inspected the small bone fragments. "I suspect some wild beast dug into one of the shallower graves soon after the bodies were buried, carried off some part of the corpse to devour and left this here after its feast. These have probably been lying here for the past century and a half waiting for some passerby to find." He gently handed the bone pieces back to Nat to hold. She shivered when she felt the brittle twig-like remnants touch her palm again.

"You all right, sweetie?" he asked her.

"Yeah, I'm okay."

"Well, we didn't expect to unearth something like that, did we?" but his voice had no mirth in it. They all had fantasized about finding a rifle bullet or belt or piece of clothing intact or bugle or sword or something else of pleasant surprise.

"No."

He searched around until he found a big rock that had a sharp protruding ridge on one side. He picked it up and walked out into the middle of the trenches without speaking. The others followed. Mr. Cockrell patted the ground all around with his fingers, looking for a level spot he assumed was unused because the surface was flat and undisturbed. Finally, he selected a place. He dug a hole six inches deep and six inches wide and reverently laid the finger fragments into the little pit, covering the dirt back up and packing it as hard as his hands then feet could make it.

They finished their tour and made it back to the cabin after dark. They had dinner and played a game that night. Scrabble again. But everyone was extra solemn before going to bed.

Friday dawned.

Our last day, thought TJ.

They breakfasted quickly and got a much earlier start than usual. They had a lot of territory to cover. Today they planned to walk the lake grounds next to their cabin, sampling the hiking trails, viewing more of the surrounding woodlands and nature, and seeing what they could of other camping and fishing locations. They stayed in the thick of the forests, emerging close to the lake only when there was an interesting looking camping area or shoreline to explore. By early afternoon, Mr. Cockrell estimated they'd covered maybe fifteen wooded miles around much of the lake's circumference. He decided they'd better head back the way they came, sticking this time to the main roads and trails to make better time. They'd spotted some people out and about that day, most of them stirring around in camping sites and a few others seen as tiny figures in tiny boats already on the lake. But when they saw the man crouching in the woods on the left, something didn't seem right. He was kneeling down next to an old pine long since dead. It was surrounded by broken limbs and tree trash. The man seemed intent on whatever he was doing. A few moments later, he stood up and left, but not before glancing furtively around. He didn't twist his head far enough to glimpse them watching him. They kept both him and the pine tree in their sight. Shocked, they spied a trail of smoke and a quickening small blaze at the base of the old tree. Mr. Cockrell and TJ rushed over and stomped the fire out.

"What does he think he's doing?" said Sam, hands on hips, with an exasperated look and tone.

"I don't know, but I have a pretty good idea," said Mr. Cockrell. "Let's follow him."

They trailed the man to another location, lurking far enough behind him to stay out of his sight. And sure enough, he was kneeling down again and starting another blaze. The smoke had already begun to drift up in the breeze.

"This dude's crazy. We've got to stop him before he causes a real catastrophe." TJ exclaimed under his breath.

"I'll get him," Mr. Cockrell replied.

"Dad, we'll nab him. Come on Sam." Tege tried to put his feet down softly but he couldn't help the crunch of groundcover beneath his stride. At twenty yards away, the man turned to see what the approaching noise was. The four of them sprinted the remaining distance to surround the individual before he could dodge away. Mr. Cockrell put out the fire then joined the ring around the man.

Now that they were close to him, they could tell the individual was a teenager; older than TJ and Samantha, perhaps out of high school, college age.

"What the heck do you think you're doing," Tege

confronted the young man. He was already in a fighting stance, his jawline and his body muscles tight now, anticipating action. On his right, Samantha was posed as well. Mr. Cockrell stood on TJ's left, leaving Natalie behind the man where he couldn't see her.

"Bug off, kid," snarled the young man. "It's none of your business what I'm doing. It's a free country, ain't it?" He stared warily at the three unexpected figures confronting him, his face taut and his mind calculating the odds of beating them and escaping.

"Wrong answer, jerk face," said TJ. His voice was calm but his body was tense.

The young man didn't reply. Without warning he lunged at Samantha, thinking the girl was the weakest link in the human fence hedging him in. Dodging under his outstretched fists, she leaned hard right and struck him in his privates with her left kneecap as their bodies collided. At the same time, TJ lashed out with a high sidekick that hammered the back and side of the young man's head with a brutal blow. He fell to the ground, moaning, holding first his crouch then the side of his head, twisting in pain. Sam scrambled to her feet.

"Nat, you said you didn't like the green scarf you have on, right?" said TJ.

"Nah. Hate it. Take it." She already knew what he meant.

Tege rolled the young man on his stomach and grabbed his arms, crossing one hand over the other behind the man's back and tying them tight using Nat's scarf. He waited until the young man stopped retching and groaning before helping him to his feet.

"Who the blank are you?" the young man whined, glancing at TJ then at Sam.

"Just concerned junior citizens."

"Actually, we work for Smoky the Bear. His deputies, you might say," said Sam.

The young man muttered a vile retort at her.

"Shut it," growled TJ, angry now for the first time, "or I'll let her work you over instead of love taps."

The young man clammed up.

Their trip back in to the main office and check-in area was far less enjoyable than their outgoing trip that morning. Guarding the prisoner was no fun; he alternated between sullen silence and mumbling curses under his breath. They reached the park headquarters right before dusk. After filling out and signing a joint letter of testimony, they left the miserable young man with the senior park ranger on duty.

"I'm heading in that direction. Would you like a ride back to your cabin?" asked the other ranger.

"Yes, that would be nice. I think this crew is beat. We've had enough hiking and excitement," said Mr. Cockrell.

Around dinner that night, the four of them were contemplative.

"You know, only our group could find part of a

Civil War skeleton and catch an arsonist…all in the same day," observed Nat.

"Yeah. Only the keepers of the little green book," said TJ. "That's us."

"But I'm not a keeper. I haven't been on an adventure yet," Natalie said, frowning a little.

"But you know all about the book and you've kept the secret in strictest confidence. That makes you a member of the little green book society in full," TJ told her.

"We're the society of adventurers of the little green book," said Samantha. "In the whole entire world, there's just the four of us. Only *we* know."

"Yes, we're the secret society of adventurers," added Mr. Cockrell.

"But I still want to go on an adventure, too," pouted Nat.

"I have a feeling your time will be coming soon, honeybun," smiled Mr. Cockrell. It was Natalie's favorite nickname from daddy when she was a very little girl.

"I sure hope so."

Chapter 27
LAST ACT AND FINAL STRAW

Their van pulled out of the wooded parking space at the Pickwick camp before ten Saturday morning. Mr. Cockrell wanted to make sure he got everyone back for the big youth concert at the church that evening. TJ, Samantha, and Natalie chatted and sang songs and played cards and guessing games. Nobody was sleepy much after such an unusual vacation.

They talked about discovering the remains of the human hand and the girls beating the boys in fishing competition. Tege and Sam answered many questions from a curious Natalie about details of their little green book adventure.

"Tell me how you felt when you landed in Washington D.C. and what it was like two hundred years ago," asked Natalie.

"Well, Nat, I wasn't scared as much as I was… confused. Weirded out. You can imagine my shock. When I first got there, it was mind bending. I'm sure TJ felt the same way when he landed in the past in his first adventure, you know, without any advance warning or instruction from his dad about the little green book. All I saw were hordes of people running down the street. All in a panic. Like something terrible was coming. Or happening. When I was told it was the *White House* I was seeing across the way, a shell of what it looks like today…that freaked me out. And when the girl told me it was President *Madison* who lived there, not you-know-who—well, than I was frightened out of my wits for at least a minute or two."

Natalie was fascinated about the time jumps in between each new situation. This hadn't happened to her father or brother during their previous time-travel trips. Their stays in the past had been continuous and unbroken timelines. Nor had the little green book pulled more than one person into an adventure before now.

TJ and Sam went through each of their escapades in chronological order, describing the circumstances, the people they met, and where they landed geographically— or thought they'd landed—in each mini-adventure. They took pains to try to figure out the exact days of the week and the month for each new circumstance, and how they thought each scenario somehow connected or brought them closer to the little green book's ultimate destination of the Battle of New Orleans. They discovered that some of the events overlapped or occurred close in time to each other.

"So you were at the British fort…what was it called, Mr. Cockrell?"

"Prospect Bluff."

"Thank you. So Tege, you were being held a prisoner at the British fort Prospect Bluff at the same period I was in Washington D.C. before the British marched in," said Sam.

"From what you told us, it sounds that way, yeah."

"And then…you were forced to go along by the British when they and their Indian allies attached that other fort called whatever—"

"Fort Bowyer," added Professor Cockrell.

"Right. That means the attack on Fort Bowyer happened just about the same time the British attacked the city of Baltimore."

TJ, Sam, and Mr. Cockrell continued analyzing the times and places of their respective stops, filling in the gaps, correcting and assisting each other in putting the pieces of their mutual adventure together into a coherently solved puzzle. It was illuminating to connect all the dots. It was obvious the little green book had a master plan in mind from the beginning.

Satisfying all Nat's questions took several hours. Each answer seemed to lead to another question. And another. And another. Upon hearing all the wonderful things that had happened to the others, more than ever Natalie wished to go on a journey herself.

The others reassured Nat that it would occur for her, too, some day.

"I hope so," she pouted. "You three have all the fun."

In that fashion, they kept themselves occupied for much of the trip. The hours sped by. Traffic was light and they made excellent time getting home. This allowed Tege and Sam and Nat to each take showers at the house and grab a quick bite before heading out to Northmark Bible Fellowship. When Mr. Cockrell dropped them off at the church, the huge sanctuary was already three quarters full. General youth activities were held in the small auditorium added a year and half ago next to the gymnasium for middle school and high school functions. But the popular annual concert pulled in youth groups from many churches and different denominations all over the city, and the main sanctuary floor with the large balcony was the only space large enough to hold the crowds.

"Wow. Look at this place. Even with spring break going on, it's still packed," Tege said to Sam, a bit incredulous.

They looked around the big sanctuary seeing who they could recognize in the throng.

"TJ! Samantha!" Benny Cuevas called out as he saw them enter the back of the big room.

Benny was with his younger brother Bobby and his best friend Henson McHenry that everyone called Mac. "Hey and there's Natalie, Bobby," Benny nudged his brother. Bobby had liked Nat since fifth grade and had been very disappointed when she moved to Atlanta with her mother after the Cockrell's divorce.

TJ and the girls walked over to them. "Hi guys." Tege looked around. "Boy, this place is filling up fast. We better grab our seats. Jessica and Brad said they would hold some spots for us near the front." Jessica Smith had been one of the original Highland Hill Angels, a clique of popular cheerleaders with wild reputations who'd gone out of their way to humiliate TJ last school year before his first adventure. But Jessica's family had started going to the church since then, and she'd made a decision for Christ and become a much nicer person. She and Brad were dating, having grown close to each other during youth meetings and outings. Brad's dad, who was divorced, went to a Methodist church but he let his son attend the youth group at NBF.

"Hi, Natalie," said Bobby. He smiled big. "How are you doing?"

"Fine."

Being too young to date at the time, Nat had never encouraged Bobby. She was never mean to him, just not interested in his company. Until recently, her brother TJ had been her only close guy pal. But now she had her first boyfriend at her own church back in Atlanta and she couldn't be too cordial with Bobby.

"We better go find Brad. See you guys later." TJ jerked his chin up in goodbye. The three of them eased their way through the milling bodies in the long aisle, greeting people they knew, and saying quick hellos as they continued to press through to the front rows.

"There they are!" exclaimed Sam, pulling on TJ's sleeve to get him to look toward the right. Brad and Jess were sitting near the middle in the next aisle over, waving at them and shooing away people seeking to take the reserved spots.

TJ and Samantha also saw Jasmine Williams, Jason's big sister, sitting with her boyfriend, Ed Freeze and some other friends, across the aisle. They all waved to each other.

"We're almost family now, Sam," TJ smiled. "You know my dad is going to propose to their mom next Saturday night at Le Parigo, right?"

"Yeah, I know. You told me after Jason called you. The same evening right before our adventures began. Remember?"

TJ grunted. He'd forgotten he told her but didn't want to admit that. She badgered him enough about his short term memory!

"Anyway, that's really cool."

Tege, Sam and Nat took their seats with Brad and Jessica, making small talk and waiting until the lights dimmed and the musicians and singers strode on stage from the back wings to take their places. The NBF high school and middle school pastors walked to the center microphones. They were joined by youth pastors from the other participating churches. The leaders formed a line across the front. They all held hands and bowed their heads as Steve Farley, the Northmark senior youth minister, prayed to start the concert.

The prayer done, the leaders walked off the stage to take their front center seats. Murmurs of excitement began building among the audience as the guitarists and bass players made last second tuning adjustments, the organist and pianist played a few soft notes, and the drummer and the singers checked their sound microphones.

Then the concert began. There were four different groups of musicians and singers, each selected to perform a different style of music than the other bands. One band brought a hard-edged rock flavor. Another combined jazz, rhythm and blues in their approach. One did hip-hop and rap. One was country-swing. But whatever the genre of music, the messages and lyrics of all the songs were more or less consistent in presenting the gospel and encouraging teen believers to live all out for the Lord. In between concert sets, there were awesome video productions, scintillating and motivational, each designed to energize the youth audience in specific areas of outreach, life walk, and daily commitment.

TJ and Sam clapped hardest and longest for Jason's group. They were the country-swing band. In Knoxville, good country was every bit as popular as rock and hip-hop even among teenagers, and Jason's hand-picked collection of musicians and singers were talented and outstanding performers.

They're better than most adults who make a living as musicians. Jason's a fantastic drummer for sure, Tege thought, watching his friend and band mates exit the stage after their set for the next group.

The concert lasted over two hours. Pastor Steve gave a short but hard-hitting concluding talk calling Christians to discipleship and action. He also extended an invitation to those listeners who had yet to make a spiritual decision. The front of the sanctuary filled with two hundred and fifty teenagers who came forward to commit or recommit their lives.

"I told you this would be awesome," TJ grinned at Nat as they joined the huge throngs leaving the building for the parking lot after the concert.

"Pretty fair, big bro. It's almost as good as our Youth Quake at my church," Natalie fake sniffed.

He laughed. "You wish."

TJ, Sam, and Nat caught a ride with Jake Rollins who had a car. They rode with Jake and his and girlfriend, Carol Hopkins, to IHOP where a number of their friends from the youth group were headed.

They all had a blast. It was eleven thirty when Sam was dropped off and Tege and Nat got home. The next day after church, Mr. Cockrell and TJ took Natalie to the airport to return to Atlanta. Their spring break together had been so much fun and it was harder than ever to say goodbye.

"Well, bye-bye, sweetheart," Mr. Cockrell said, halting at the entry to the snaking passenger lanes for security check-in and setting her carry-on luggage down. "Tell the dragon lady we appreciate her releasing our most beautiful daughter from her evil clutches for a spell."

"Oh, dad, stop it," Natalie slapped his arm and screwed up her face at her father's lame attempt at post-divorce humor. If she'd had her way, she would have chosen to stay with her father and brother. Living with her mother and being separated from the two most important men in her young life had been an extra burden she'd had to bear. Dad had always been much the kinder and more supportive of the two parents.

"I love you so much, dad." Nat rarely cried but she now fought back tears as she embraced him tightly. "You, too, Tege." She wiped her eyes before she gave her brother a big hug, too.

"I love you, too, Sis." He squeezed her hand. "It's not all bad. Remember you get to spend Christmas with us this year."

"Yeah, I know. That's one good thing I've got to look forward to, I guess." Wistful, she looked at the two of them, her eyes glistening, before picking up her luggage and getting behind a boisterous group of teenage boys returning home after a wild spring break themselves. Several men followed after her in queue. They were dressed in gray dress pants and white or blue shirts and looked to be businessmen heading to Atlanta for Monday meetings and appointments. Mr. Cockrell and TJ stood there watching Nat progress all the way though the long line before turning to go. She smiled one last time and waved as she saw them getting ready to leave.

With spring break over and the final months of the semester fast approaching, Sam and Tege found they had to be more disciplined than ever. "We've got to be kamikaze," said TJ.

April and May became their busiest time of the year to date. They both had the all-important end-of-school play for theatre/drama, as well as upcoming district games and playoffs for lacrosse, in addition to school studies and finals.

Their schedules were hectic. It seemed now the only free time they had together was their planned Saturday dates and youth church activities.

"Gosh, I'm flat out exhausted today," said TJ, catching up to Sam in the parking lot outside the lacrosse fields after a hard practice. "I don't know why, either. I got a decent night's sleep. But my energy level is lower than usual."

"Me, too," said Samantha. "Must be the stress of a major production. Bane of all us actors."

"Could be. Yeah, I think you're right. It does seem like there's even more pressure on us for our show to go well than to win ball games."

Mr. Mackey their drama teacher was an incredibly positive, encouraging person. But in his own nice way he was more demanding than any sports coach TJ had ever had or seen. Like a super polite but equally tough version of Vince Lombardi. A master motivator who used sugar rather than vinegar and somehow got stellar results. Everyone in theater liked him.

"I know. It's like the band practices are harder than that of sports. At least that's what all our friends in band tell us. Hey," she nudged his arm, "that *was* a great rehearsal we had in theater this afternoon. No flubbed lines. Everyone on cue. Perfect timing. Solid voice projection. Even Ben Crossley did a lot better."

"I could tell Mr. Mackey was pleased. More than normal, I mean."

"Yeah."

They talked for another minute or two before TJ had to jog over to the other side of the parking lot. TJ always got a ride home with David Beam, one of his best friends. David's mom picked them up outside the track stadium. David was running the four-forty this season. He was already one of the best in the state as a sophomore.

So both theater and lacrosse had intense practices. Fortunately for TJ and Samantha, drama was considered a credit class and they had most of those practices during the regular school hour. Lacrosse was every afternoon after the last bell, leaving them tired. After dinner and studying hard and chores, there was little spare time left on their over busy week nights.

Both Tege and Sam were gifted actors. They loved everything about theatre; the sets, the scripts, the rehearsals, the interaction and fun times with other actors, the rush of adrenalin on opening night, the thrill of a well-executed play, and the thunder of applause from an appreciative audience.

TJ was a poor dancer but decent singer. On the other hand, Sam was a far better dancer than he and she had a good singing voice. But they both much preferred dramas, or better still comedies, rather than musicals. They were quite excited the play selected by drama team vote last fall for this year's spring performance was *Little Shop of Horrors*. TJ and Sam had beaten out very stiff competition from juniors and seniors for the starring comedic roles of the hapless Seymour Krelborn and his sweet pretty coworker Audrey that Seymour secretly loves for most of the plot.

The busy weeks passed in a blur. The date of the opening performance loomed closer. Finally the big night arrived. A hush settled over the packed waiting crowd in the big school auditorium as the lights dimmed out and the ceiling-length dark green curtain began to rise, revealing the scenery and players of the first act of the play.

As the play progressed, the jam-packed audience of parents, siblings, relatives, school chums, other pals, friends from church or synagogue or temple or mosque, teachers, and casual observers all responded with appropriate titters, chuckles, and outright laughter in all the right spots. The performances of all actors were flawless and the mechanics of sets and sequences were error free. When the curtain arose for the last and final act and TJ reappeared, a group of teenagers in the third row abruptly stood to their feet. They held up a huge sign that was composed of four big poster boards reinforced together. On the gigantic sign they had drawn a picture of a big green plant with the buttocks and legs of someone kicking in the air as the plant was swallowing the upper body. Below the dangling legs and the over-sized exaggerated backside was written in large green type the words: 'Seymour Butts'. The two teens holding the sign at either end motioned at it with their free hands, while the others beside them waved to get TJ's attention. All were hollering and hooting under their breath at Tege, making sure he saw them and read the sign.

"Will you kids please sit down? Right now!" Ms. Primm, the stodgy cranky ninth and tenth grade English teacher, turned in her second row seat, snapping in a loud stage whisper at the miscreants.

They sat down but not before their leader, Robert Whitlock, one of TJ's best friends, mouthed the words 'Seymour Butts' one last time, nodding and pointing at Tege then back at the sign. He and the others were grinning like Cheshire cats. Among them were Robert's girlfriend and three of TJ's teammates from the lacrosse team.

TJ smiled at the amusing sight; yet he kept to his script and pacing without missing a beat. When the 'mean, green mother from outer space' did gobble up TJ *for real* at the end of the play, the entire audience erupted in sustained applause with loud whistles and catcalling from school and church friends. The clapping continued as the curtain came down and the players came out in front a minute later to take their bows and acknowledge the appreciative crowd.

The clapping and cheering continued for several satisfying minutes. In conclusion the lights turned back on and the audience began dispersing. Mr. Mackey gathered everyone involved with the play around him behind the stage before releasing them.

"An outstanding job! Kudos to all. Macey, you did a wonderful thing handling that prop malfunction like you did, fixing it on the spot and right before the curtain opened back up. Very creative. Highly resourceful. Thank you! TJ and Samantha, you both were wonderful. I want to tell everyone that this is the best performance Highland Hill drama has done in the past five years. Magnificent! I salute you." He began applauding vigorously, leading all in a rousing group ovation.

It indeed had been a great performance. The rest of the evening was just as gratifying. Sam and TJ were exhilarated but exhausted when they got home after a raucous post-performance dinner party celebrating with the rest of the cast, stage crew, and Mr. Mackey.

"Well, night, Tege. I'll be in the stands cheering you on at the game." Sam kissed TJ on the cheek before heading out with her ride home from the restaurant.

"Good night, sweetness. You did wonderful." He squeezed her hand.

"I know. I *am* a fantastic, talented, and gorgeous actress, aren't I?"

"Well, I never can tell when you're acting and when you're being real, you're so good." He laughed. "You fake me out all the time, girlfriend."

"Oh, you," she laughed and gigged him in the side. "Bye."

The drama play happened Friday night. TJ had the first round of district playoffs for lacrosse the next afternoon, Saturday, at six. The game was being held at a neutral high school location across town. Coach Loggins wanted everyone at the Highland Hill field at three-thirty for a final quick run through of his new offensive winkles before they boarded the bus at four-thirty to leave for the game. Tege slept in until eleven that morning.

"Ready for your big game," asked his dad when he ambled down the stairs, sleepy-eyed, for a late breakfast. Mr. Cockrell offered to scramble some eggs and fry some bacon and make toast, but all TJ wanted was a big bowl of his favorite cereal Shredded Wheat with fresh blueberries and cut up banana added.

"You came in late last night so I let you sleep an extra hour or so," said Mr. Cockrell.

"Thanks, I needed it," replied TJ before shoveling in a big spoonful of cereal and berries. Dad was right; the day ahead promised to be busy. He wondered aloud what he should do if 'Pelvis' tried anything sneaky during the game.

At three twenty-five, Mr. Cockrell dropped Tege off at the lacrosse field. The professor planned to drive to the playoff game and arrive around five fifteen to get a good seat.

Before practice started, the coach gathered the players around him for final instructions. "Remember, men, we're going to switch from our usual three offensive plays off the 2-3-1 to the new two 1-4-1 plays in the third quarter. Then in the fourth quarter, as we discussed, I want you to switch from the 2-3-1 to the 1-4-1 on alternative plays. It should confuse them."

He looked at the players crowded around him, studying their faces. He lingered longest at TJ and Wilson. They were his two best offensive players. Wilson was technically still the better player. But TJ was very reliable. He always listened and executed well. He acted as a quarterback directing his teammates whenever they were unsure or went the wrong way or got out of position in the team's intricate motion offensive sets.

"I know this may seem a bit complicated, but it's not all that difficult. I want you to concentrate as never before when we run through our final practice today. Focus! It's all about keeping the defense confused and out of position, finding the most open man with the best angle for punching it in. Take what the defense gives you and just…flow with the game."

Coach Loggins' squad was known throughout the district competition for the intricacy of their offensive schemes. In that regard, their offense—if not their execution—was closer to a college team than most high school teams.

Time sped by. They only got a few reps in on the new offensive wrinkle before practice was over, it seemed to TJ. Then the team boarded the bus for the game.

The game itself was exciting, fast-paced, and close. Their opponent, Andrew Jackson High, was tenacious on defense and methodical if not brilliant on offense. The score was tied 7-7 at halftime, thanks to two goals each by TJ and Wilson. The third quarter started. The switch to the 1-4-1 confused the other team, as Coach Loggins had hoped, for the first four minutes before they adjusted, allowing Highland Hill High to score two easy goals, making the new score 9-7. Jackson High scored once more to end the quarter 9-8.

The fourth quarter begun ragged, as Tege had to yell out instructions to teammates to get them switching every play between the 2-3-1 and the 1-4-1. Once they settled in and executed better, however, it did keep the other team off balance, allowing Wilson to score twice more and Tom Brody once, giving Highland Hill a 12-8 advantage, with three minutes to go.

It was with time winding down that Wilson did his nasty again. An inadvertent loose ball led to the closest players scrambling for it. There were numerous hard but legal body checks and cross checks as well as pokes and slaps by both teams. The ball on the ground squirted away several times when multiple sticks darting for it at the same time clashed together and the tops of the battling stick heads struck the ball. Tege had just cross checked his nearest opponent, spying the ball at the person's feet. That player tripped over a teammate's foot, stumbling to the ground. Just as Tege was reaching for the ball with his stick pocket someone behind kicked *him* on the back of his left knee, causing first his left leg then his right leg to buckle, and he fell backwards onto the ground on his rump. He saw Wilson flashing forward to retrieve the ball instead of himself and dart forward and score.

Furious, he got to his feet, staring at Wilson's figure ahead of him jumping up and down in celebration and high-fiving the other teammates.

That's the last time you ever do that to me, you jerk. I swear. That's the straw that broke this camel's back. And this camel bites and kicks hard, bro.

The final score was 13-9. Viewing the fray of players from the sidelines, Coach Loggins didn't catch Red Wilson's treachery in his overall excitement for the last added goal. Coach, of course, was happy with the win and the fact they now advanced to quarterfinals. He gave everyone a quick rousing victory talk in the locker room afterwards, lavishing praise on both TJ and Wilson, but Wilson most of all. TJ ground his teeth as coach spoke, keeping silent.

Most players had rides with parents or older school friends. The rest rode the bus back. Mr. Cockrell was waiting for TJ outside the locker room.

"He did it again, dad. Did you see it?" Tege mumbled in a low voice only his father could hear. They both glanced up just then. Wilson was strolling by with his mom and dad beaming and full of pride for their star athlete son.

TJ and Mr. Cockrell waited until the three Presley's walked out of room to continue speaking.

"I saw you go down and I noticed he was behind you at the time. What did he do, son?"

"He kicked me back of the knee, making me fall so he could get the ball and score instead of me." TJ just shook his head in disgust.

"I'm sorry, Tege. Sorry. You're not hurt, are you?"

"Nah. Just pissed off."

"Well, I'm very glad you're not like that; do anything to become number one or to win."

"Yeah. Me, too. You don't have to cheat or be a jerk to be a good ball player."

Tege seethed all the way home. His dad's empathetic statements didn't help much. He was unable to take full pleasure in a great win because of Wilson's dirty actions.

Next time I'll be alert and ready, he swore.

Chapter 28
EXPOSÉ AND CHAMPIONSHIP

Mr. Cockrell's planned special evening went so smooth, his head was spinning and his heart soaring, afterwards. He knew Helen's favorite desert after dinner was dark fudge chocolate cheesecake with fresh strawberries and whipped cream. So he arranged and paid beforehand for the chef to make and place several miniature hollow chocolate balls beside the cheesecake as added tasty decorations. But one of the balls had the engagement ring hidden inside with a tip of the ring showing. (He didn't want her to bite into that chocolate sphere and break a tooth!)

"M-m-m-m, this is *so* good!"

She ate several forkfuls of the delicious cake, taking care to balance the whipping cream on top of each bite and stabbing a succulent strawberry on the way in. With most of the cheesecake gone, she turned her attention to the tempting dark brown spheres beside it.

"What's this?" she had asked, picking it up and examining the second little ball. She ran her fingertip over the surface where the odd little protrusion was. She saw a tiny spec of *something* that reflected the soft overhead lighting when she rotated the ball in her hand, examining it up close. She frowned at first, and then she gasped.

"Oh…I…" she smiled than bit into the soft side of the little ball, tearing its wall open and taking a small piece into her mouth. As the wonderful dark chocolate flavor melted upon her tongue, she drew a sharp breath in and held it—for an eternity, it seemed to her—frozen at the fantastic sight inside the broken ball.

"Vern," fresh tears sparkled on her cheeks.

"Will you marry me?" he blurted before his courage failed and he said something stupid or inane.

Her radiant beautiful smile said it all. "Yes. The answer is yes! You wonderful, sweet, darling man!"

She stood up and walked to his side and with God and everyone in the crowded restaurant watching, she leaned over, put her fingers on his chin tilting his head back, and planted a long passionate kiss on his surprised open mouth.

Applause broke out, first among those patrons closest and then even among those further out and against the far walls. For fifteen full seconds the entire restaurant was filled with clapping and yells of encouragement.

Vern's face was flushed with embarrassment at the attention but he was pleased, too.

"Way to go, dad!" TJ had enthused when Mr. Cockrell came home well past midnight, pounding him on the back as his dad recounted the details of the dinner surprise. Tege had stayed up waiting for him to hear how things had gone. Vern and Helen had spent two hours in Mr. Cockrell's car after dinner just talking, sharing about everything. Planning. About their future, their families together, about vacation destinations, bringing two households full of pets into one dwelling, handling the demand of Helen's constant travel as flight attendant, about their recent commitment to put God first in their lives, about how blessed each was to find the other person.

"So Jason is my step bro now. Or soon will be. Boy, how am I *ever* going to put up with more of him?" Tege joked. "Yikes. I guess I'll have to 'step' all over him to keep him in line. Jasmine's not too bad, though. She's pretty cool." He grinned from ear to ear. He couldn't be happier for Dad, for Helen, for both families.

The wedding was planned for September fifteen to be held at the general chapel at the church. From that moment on, TJ, Jason, and Jasmine began to spend more time together as real brothers and sisters who love one another would do. Two weeks later, they all went to see the spring performance of Jasmine's ballet company at the fine arts building on the campus of University of the South. The production was Coppelia. Ballet was not TJ's cup of tea or Jason's, but they went anyway to support their big sis.

Jason, who didn't have a real girlfriend yet, just lots of female friends and admirers of his drumming fame, flirted with a very pretty member of the junior ballet company. The juniors all had minor supporting roles in the performance or helped in off stage duties. Her name was Carissa and her long blond hair and gorgeous smile intrigued him. She returned the attention. He found out she went to Malvern High.

"What's your twitter?" he asked. He typed and saved it on his phone. "And how about your digits?"

She flashed a provocative smile and answered, "You give me yours and if I decide to call or text you, I will."

"Fair enough," he grinned back at her and gave her his cell number.

"Okay, Romero. Time to go to the post-performance reception," teased TJ.

"Hitting on the babies already, are we?" added Jasmine, coming up to join them from the backstage. She was still in costume. "Better watch him. You're Cari, right?"

"Ye-e-e-s." Carissa became deferential. "You were *very* good tonight," she mumbled. Most of the company senior dancers didn't talk much to juniors. The ballet pecking order was quite structured and brutally competitive.

"Thank you. Anyway, I just want to warn you my little brother can be a real hound dog sometimes." She poked Jason in the side.

Jasmine was so nice and friendly that Carissa found her tongue. "That's okay. I'm more of a dog than a cat person anyway." She smiled big again at Jason and waved bye as she walked off with her parents to the reception area.

Jason just laughed and they joined their own two grown-ups for the big gala in the main room.

Yes, TJ thought it was a real sweet deal having Jas and Jaz as family. He was looking forward to his dad's wedding, too. Meanwhile, he shared with Jason his troubles with his lacrosse teammate. Jason was a creative thinker, often coming up with out-of-the-box ideas on various problems and other things. Together they brainstormed ways Tege might best protect himself from further humiliation and help coach see what a snake Wilson was.

Over the coming weeks, the boys' lacrosse team won close, contested battles by one point each to advance in the quarters and semifinals to reach the state championship matchup against top-ranked Emerson High. Wilson behaved himself; he didn't do anything untoward to TJ in those games. Tege cut him no slack, whatsoever. He knew snakes didn't change their skin or sneaky slitherings overnight.

Probably because the score was so close in the two games, Pelvis boy just didn't have time to focus on anything else but helping the team win. Rah rah him. He's still a big jerk and I don't trust him for one second.

When the Saturday morning of the championship game arrived, TJ had a plan. It was suggested by Jason based on TJ's description of some of his martial arts moves. It required he keep Wilson in his peripheral sight at all times which might be difficult to do. But he had no choice. And he had to do it in such a way that Wilson couldn't tell he was keeping him in his field of vision.

The bus ride over was a brief twenty minutes from school parking lot. The team arrived, as usual, an hour before the game to suit up and check equipment. They listened intently as Coach Loggins reviewed the game's offensive and defensive strategies on the locker room white board. They knelt together for their normal team prayer. The two team captains—both seniors—each gave a quick pep talk. Then coach said his final speech, offering stirring words of admonition and encouragement, pumping them up to the sky. They blasted out of the locker room, yelling and cheering, sprinting down the long corridor and racing out on the field for pregame stretching and sideline drills. Adrenaline and emotions were high.

The stadium was already filling to capacity. The buzz of conversation and excitement from the swelling stands was palpable. Eight more minutes until faceoff to start the game. Seven minutes. Six…five…four…three… two…one. The crowd stood for the national anthem. The players for both teams stood at attention, their hands over their hearts but their minds galloping ahead to the game—each going over nuances, things to remember, keys to the game, plays, strategies, mental replays of films of opponents they would be facing. Some had butterflies or knots in their stomach or chest. Some were close to throwing up on the sidelines before they even begun the competition. Some chewed their wads of gum so fast it seemed certain their jaws would lock up or the wads would disintegrate in smoke against their tongues.

Senior Tom Brody stepped to center field to do the faceoff for Highland Hill High as his teammates took their respective positions.

The game begun. The crowd roared. Emerson High got first possession. And the night's mighty battle got underway.

Emerson was noted for having a methodical, well coached team with superior athletes. Except for two players, everyone else on their team was fast; like a squad full of Wilsons. They weren't flashy but wore opponents down by solid executed fundamentals and wave after wave of attack. On defense, they were tenacious and unrelenting in coverage.

They got the Highland Hill long-sticks out of position with their quick passing and speed and scored the first goal less than four minutes into the game.

Coach Loggins called a time-out. He didn't like what he was seeing. "Everyone, you've got to keep your stick on your man at all times. Ben, you almost tripped and took yourself out of the play when your man changed direction. That one small letdown gave them the opening they needed to score. Ben, you know better than that. This is the state championship, not our first game of the season. Basics! Foot placement! Shuffle instead of crossing your feet. Don't get lazy and don't be careless." Coach spat on the ground in annoyance, but he shot Ben a look of reassurance, nevertheless.

"Sorry." Ben mumbled; his mouth and eyes wide open in repentance. TJ, standing behind him, gave Ben a meaningful punch on the shoulder and nodded encouragement to him when Ben turned around.

"Everyone, call out to your teammates what's happening behind them; they don't have eyes in the back of their head. You've got to communicate! And study the opponent; watch what he likes to do most—roll or split— how he moves. But all of you know that already. Just… stay proactive. Anticipate the dodge. Always, always, always"—he pounded his right fist into his left palm— "try to force the man you're guarding to his weaker hand and toward defensive help."

Coach took a deep breath of determination, his steel-gray eyes boring into each player to emphasize his words.

"Okay, offense. You men know what to do. Alternate between 2-3-1 and 1-4-1 *every other play* just as we practiced. Defense, basics. Now get out there and make something good happen!"

The defenders responded with a smothering coverage that held Emerson scoreless for the rest of the quarter. When Highland Hill had the ball, their attackers found a chink in Emerson's armor and scored the team's first goal just before the first period ended, tying the game 1-1.

From the second quarter on, it became a furious cat-and-mouse contest of wills, a high stakes chess match between the two coaches trying to outthink and outsmart the other. Highland Hill High continued to make adjustments in defensive strategy to try to negate Emerson's speed advantage, and Emerson High sought to master the changing, confusing offense sets used by Highland. At the end of the third quarter, it was 4-3 in favor of Highland Hill.

The fourth period began. It took over three minutes before they got the ball back, but once they did, Coach Loggins had the offense execute a special trick play they'd been practicing for weeks. It was a one-time thing. If the play didn't work, they wouldn't try it again.

Highland Hill's unusual and unexpected motion shift caused two Emerson defenders to bump into each other, producing a momentary open lane and clear shot at the net for the far left attack man. Highland scored, making it 5-3.

Now, TJ went on highest alert, keeping 'Pelvis' in his vision at all times. It was difficult to do because he had to pay attention and stay in the offensive flow, yet he also had to maintain peripheral sight of where Wilson was, particularly if the offensive movement caused Wilson to flow nearby. He knew if Wilson was going to attempt something devious, it'd be when their two positions were close together. Wilson would love nothing better than to trip TJ up and come in to make the goal. They were tied two each in goals, and Wilson hated for anyone else to get the glory. His past modus operandi had been to take out TJ if Highland Hill was up by more than two or three points late in the game.

Sure enough, the special trick play not only caused confusion among Emerson defenders, it caused them to align their defense thinking Highland High would attempt the same play again but on the other side when Highland got the ball again. Their nervousness allowed Wilson to move right behind TJ just as he was receiving a pass from Tom for the score attempt.

Wilson launched a kick at the back of TJ's right knee. TJ anticipated this exact ploy. With lightning speed, he turned his body sideways to his opponent, using his left foot as a pivot and causing the attempted strike to miss. This resulted in Wilson's launched right leg hanging in thin air where TJ's knee had been, his body weight swaying on his left leg. In a blur, TJ spun left three quarters on his pivot foot, a back round kick bumping Wilson's rump in the process. Wilson lost his balance and pitched forward on his face into the turf. In one fluid motion, TJ stepped forward, planting his right foot in between Wilson's splayed legs, keeping sideways to the goal and hurling a sizzling shot into bottom of the net just out of reach of the lunging stick head of the desperate Emerson goalie.

All the action happened on the same side as the Highland Hill bench where Coach Loggins raced to the far end of the bench area to better see the outcome. For once, coach witnessed what Wilson had tried to do. And he was livid! Wilson raised himself off the ground, his nose bleeding from the fall and his face a scowl of vengeance as he turned to find TJ. But just then Coach called time out. He made an immediate substitution. Henry Cooks, a little used senior, was in for Wilson to finish the game.

"What the heck were you doing out there?" Coach's beet-red face was inches away from Wilson's shocked countenance. He looked white as a sheet.

"I was…I was only—" he sputtered.

"You were attacking a teammate. I saw you. Don't try to deny it. One of your own teammates!" Coach was shouting now. He furrowed his bushy eyebrows and glared at Wilson. "How many times have you done that to a teammate? How many other times?"

Coach turned on the spot and began questioning the players on the bench. One by one several of the underclassmen told tales of Wilson's shenanigans and his actions toward TJ Cockrell throughout the entire season.

Coach's frown grew longer and longer as he listened to them. When he heard how it wasn't an accident or carelessness on TJ's part in the first playoff game that he stumbled and Wilson scored instead, he swore under his breath.

Wilson Presley stood stiff as a board, his eyes afraid to meet Coach Loggins.

"We'll talk about this some more after the game,

young man. I also intend to talk to your parents, too, before the night is out. They came to the game, right?" He glared at Presley before turning his attention back to the game.

"No sir, I do *not* like bullies and deceivers and cheaters of any kind," he muttered. "I don't care how gifted an athlete you are. I don't know what I should do yet to rectify the situation and what the punishment should be. But there will be *severe* consequences, Wilson!"

He turned and stared at the boy one last time. "Maybe I'll just let your teammates take a vote on what to do about you. How about that?" He said this loud enough for all the players present to hear it.

Coach's last comment scared Wilson to death. He knew he was disliked by almost all the other players, especially the forwards and middies. His friends on the team were the starting and backup goalies. Even the other defenders didn't much care for him.

The atmosphere on the sidelines grew frosty. Ignoring Wilson's agitated pacing form, the players on the bench and coach began focusing on the game instead.

They all watched, nervous, as Emerson scored again. There was too much time left and Emerson was too talented for the team to let their guard down now. But then the Highland Hill defense rose to the challenge, shutting the opponent out. The game's final minutes, then seconds ticked off, in slow motion it seemed to Coach Loggins and the players watching from the sidelines. Yet

Emerson's increasingly frantic attackers tallied no more. When the game ended, the blue and gray of Highland had prevailed 6-4.

Hurray! Highland Hill High was the state lacrosse 5-A champions! The players on the bench sprinted onto the field joining their teammates in the middle of the arena, forming a writhing whooping leaping mass of revelers. In the middle of the happy scrum TJ's back was pounded so hard and so many times, he found it difficult to breathe but he didn't mind one bit! Wilson was left by the bare bench, forlorn, looking on at his celebrating teammates. After coach's angry confrontation in front of the other boys, he didn't have the guts to join the circle.

Best of all, making the end of their fairy tale season perfect in Tege's mind, Wilson the 'Pelvis' Presley had been revealed as the snake he was.

Chapter 29
LOOKING FORWARD TO THE PAST

The weeks sped by. Spring semester was winding down. Except for Wilson's shady tactics, it'd turned out to be a superlative school year for Tege overall. His grades, as usual, were outstanding. He would finish the year earning high A's in all his subjects. He carried a four plus GPA, due to his AP honors classes, special projects, extra credits, and other adders.

His history teacher, Mr. Smith, was particularly pleased with his continued progress. Over the last year and a half, TJ had transformed from a struggling student to an honors scholar not only at the top of his sophomore class, but performing better on his papers and AP tests than the leading juniors and seniors in history. He ranked number one in the AP sessions. His papers were advanced college quality. In fact, Mr. Smith had seen a fellow graduate student or two during his own Masters' program who didn't write as well as TJ could.

"Young man," Mr. Smith came up behind Tege in the hallway and clapping him on the back, surprising him, "I want to tell you your last essay on the origins of the War of 1812 blew…me…away. I don't believe I've *ever* seen a better written, more cogent paper in my ten years here. Good work! Very good stuff, indeed, Mr. Cockrell. I'll be telling your father, too. I'm sure he'll be delighted to hear it."

He beamed. "You're becoming a real chip off the old block, I must say."

"Thank you, Mr. Smith. Thank you very much," said TJ, a touch of red on his cheeks from embarrassment. Like his dad, he wasn't comfortable with high praise. They shook hands and Mr. Smith smiled again and dashed away to the teacher's lounge.

Yes, he had made tremendous strides and it was all due to the little green book, he knew. His transformation had jumpstarted with his Tennessee frontier experience.

As he walked to his next class, he mused. He would turn sixteen near year, have a car, and be a junior next year…but there was still so much to enjoy before the fall started.

He was well liked at school with many friends. Having been the favorite target of a certain in-group of arrogant cheerleaders and bullies the first half of his freshman year, he went out of his way to be nice to everyone, including kids who weren't popular. He loved his church and youth group. In his martial arts classes he had recently earned a second degree black belt. He had a great relationship with his dad. Samantha was as perfect a casual girlfriend as he could wish. And his most recent time-travel adventure had been an absolute blast!

As tremendous as it was, winning the lacrosse championship was icing on the cake.

He and Samantha looked forward to a jam-packed fun-filled summertime, most of it together. However, in late July and early August, Sam's family would be leaving the city and vacationing near the Blue Ridge Appalachian Mountains. While everyone else was baking in the sizzling heat of the summer back in Knoxville, they'd be enjoying the cooler air and refreshing breezes of the wooded foothills and fabled smoky peaks of the ancient mountain range. They'd be staying at her uncle's spacious rustic log-hewed home where she had three cousins near her age, two of them girls. Uncle Mike was her dad's older brother. They were the seventh generation of the Robertson clan to stay and live in that same area.

Upon first meeting Samantha last year and learning her last name and hometown, he'd done an ancestry search on the internet out of idle curiosity. What he'd found shocked and then delighted him. He'd discovered that Sam's father was a direct descendant in the bloodline of a Thomas Henry Robertson born March 17, 1789 in North Carolina to a Samuel P. Robertson. At first, TJ couldn't believe what he was seeing on the computer screen. Big Sam had been his protector and surrogate father and his youngest son Thomas had become TJ's best friend during his first time-travel adventure back into the wild frontier days of early Tennessee. One of Thomas' sisters, Sarah, had become Tege's first young love and first real girlfriend.

His second adventure had been much in his thoughts of late. He remembered the young pirate Angel and the burly constable and his awe-inspiring quick glimpse of the great General Jackson.

Whenever they got the chance, out and about by themselves or at Tege's house, he and Samantha reminisced about their respective escapades, comparing notes, recalling details, and wondering what their next journey might be. Knowing just how thrilling such an experience could be, they both hoped his little sister Natalie would get the chance soon to go on a time-travel trek herself. She was a member of their secret society of the little green book, but as yet had not gone on a trip.

"I'd like to travel back to the age of Queen Elizabeth the first and visit merry old England," said Sam, her pretty eyes dreamy and her mind already imagining the sights and sounds of such a romantic era. They were sitting close, holding hands, on the big sofa in the Cockrell's living room after school. Dora, the maid, had just left.

"Well, I'd like to ride horseback, and canoe and backpack and go exploring with Jim Bridger, and see the plains and the Rockies and the untamed Indian tribes and the unsoiled old west before the arrival of the other buffalo hunters and trappers and white settlers," TJ said.

"Hmmm! You can just keep your stinky hairy mountain men. I'll take the gallantry and culture and pageantry of Elizabeth's age anytime," she replied with some sass.

"So where would you like to go together again, then, girlfriend?" he asked, curious.

"What, with you?" But she smiled big. "Oh, I don't know. How about visiting Venice or Rome during the Renaissance Period?"

"Too high-brow for me. I like plenty of action and danger, if you please."

"Okay. How about Athens, ancient Greece? You're plenty greasy, snookums, so you should fit right it," she teased.

"Fun-n-n-y. So hi-larious. Don't quit your day job yet. First, I'm one clean machine. I keep my chassis spotless; spotless and gleaming, gal. No mud on this bud. No dirt on this squirt."

"Ha, you say!"

"And second, I hate that name, girlfriend. You know that."

"Too bad. You look, walk, and talk like a snookums, s-o-o-o..."

"Ha, ha, yourself. How about a steamship race from England to Australia or China, say, in the eighteen eighties? Or visiting India at the height of English rule during the same period? Or taking the Orient Express in the eighteen nineties from Paris to Istanbul?"

"Interesting. That's a little more exotic and romantic. Perhaps. Of course, you make it sound as if the little green book is a travel agency to the past at our beck and call…when we both know it's the one in control and there's pretty serious business going on where it lands you."

"Yup, you're right. That's why I call it adventure."

They leaned back, not talking for a while and letting their thoughts wander, each picturing their own ideal time-travel venture…replete with heavy doses of action, fighting, and heroics in TJ's version and heavy doses of drama, fine culture, and romance in Samantha's version.

TJ thought back to his great adventure in the Tennessee wilderness. He'd found his first real girlfriend there. Beautiful sweet Sarah Robertson. Samantha looked the spitting image of Sarah in so many ways. Even her hair and voice inflections and mannerisms. It was one reason he was attracted to her the moment he met her.

He thought, too, of big Sam Robertson, Sarah's father, who was bold and brave and strong and kind-hearted. Everything TJ aspired to be. He recalled his late morning hunting excursion with Thomas, a full year younger than he but already as deadly a sharp-shooter as most grown men of his day. Tege remembered the notorious Hansen Gang, though not with affection. It seemed one or more of them kept trying to kill him or other members of the Robertson household his whole time there.

TJ's most recent time-travel escapade, where he'd been hurled backwards into the waning months of the pivotal War of 1812, brought even new surprises and unexpected occurrences. He, Sam, and his dad had each followed their own trail of events and twists and turns and assortment of unusual characters before meeting up in a climatic fashion—just before the British launched their fateful invasion of the city of New Orleans.

Yes, he'd experienced many incredible things because of the little green book. Tege had also become a better person through his time-travel treks, he acknowledged. The experiences had been life changing for him. He'd never have had the courage, resourcefulness, and determination to handle the bullies and robbers and mean teachers and meaner girls afterwards…had his curiosity not gotten the better of him some fifteen months ago when he found the forbidden desk drawer open in Mr. Cockrell's little bay office.

He wondered when and where his next journey into the distant past would be. One thing was certain. Wherever he went, danger and thrills and action were sure to follow!

Green book, I'm ready to go again whenever you're ready.

He grinned at the happy prospect and squeezed Sam's hand.

"Yes?" Her own train of thought derailed, she glanced over at him. "Did…did you want something, Tege?'

"You betcha, sweetness!"

And TJ smiled bigger than ever in anticipation.

ABOUT THE AUTHOR

 **B**orn in Tennessee to a military family, Jack King crisscrossed the country multiple times growing up. After obtaining graduate degrees in both business and history, he began a successful career in sales and marketing working for Fortune 500, mid-sized, and start-up firms along the way. *Time Rider - Red Attack* is his third novel. Mr. King is currently at work on the next book in the *Game for the Middle Kingdom* saga: "The War Years".

www.ingramcontent.com/pod-product-compliance
Lightning Source LLC
Chambersburg PA
CBHW030650120726
47905CB00001B/151